KT-217-156

BRAVO TWO ZERO

In January 1991, eight members of the SAS regiment, under the command of Sergeant Andy McNab, embarked upon a top secret mission in Iraq to infiltrate them deep behind enemy lines. Their call sign: 'Bravo Two Zero'.

IMMEDIATE ACTION

The no-holds-barred account of an extraordinary life, from the day McNab as a baby was found in a carrier bag on the steps of Guy's Hospital to the day he went to fight in the Gulf War. As a delinquent youth he kicked against society. As a young soldier he waged war against the IRA in the streets and fields of South Armagh.

SEVEN TROOP

Andy McNab's gripping story of the time he served in the company of a remarkable band of brothers. The things they saw and did during that time would take them all to breaking point – and some beyond – in the years that followed. He who dares doesn't always win . . .

Nick Stone titles

Nick Stone, ex-SAS trooper, now gun-for-hire working on deniable ops for the British government, is the perfect man for the dirtiest of jobs, doing whatever it takes by whatever means necessary...

REMOTE CONTROL
⊕ Dateline: Washington DC, USA

Stone is drawn into the bloody killing of an ex-SAS officer and his family and soon finds himself on the run with the one survivor who can identify the killer – a seven-year-old girl.

'Proceeds with a testosterone surge' *Daily Telegraph*

CRISIS FOUR
⊕ Dateline: North Carolina, USA

In the backwoods of the American South, Stone has to keep alive the beautiful young woman who holds the key to unlock a chilling conspiracy that will threaten world peace.

'When it comes to thrills, he's Forsyth class' *Mail on Sunday*

FIREWALL
⊕ Dateline: Finland

The kidnapping of a Russian Mafia warlord takes Stone into the heart of the global espionage world and into conflict with some of the most dangerous killers around.

'Other thriller writers do their research, but McNab has actually been there' *Sunday Times*

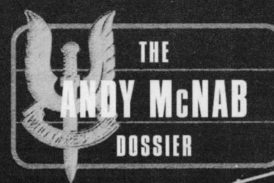

THE ANDY McNAB DOSSIER

CONFIDENTIAL

www.andymcnab.co.uk

ANDY McNAB

➲ In 1984 he was 'badged' as a member of 22 SAS Regiment.

➲ Over the course of the next nine years he was at the centre of covert operations on five continents.

➲ During the first Gulf War he commanded Bravo Two Zero, a patrol that, in the words of his commanding officer, 'will remain in regimental history for ever'.

➲ Awarded both the Distinguished Conduct Medal (DCM) and Military Medal (MM) during his military career.

➲ McNab was the British Army's most highly decorated serving soldier when he finally left the SAS in February 1993.

➲ He is a patron of the *Help for Heroes* campaign.

➲ He is now the author of seventeen bestselling thrillers, as well as three Quick Read novels, *The Grey Man*, *Last Night Another Soldier* and *Today Everything Changes*. He has also edited *Spoken from the Front*, an oral history of the conflict in Afghanistan.

LAST LIGHT
⊕ Dateline: Panama

Stone finds himself at the centre of a lethal conspiracy involving ruthless Colombian mercenaries, the US government and Chinese big business. It's an uncomfortable place to be . . .

'A heart thumping read' *Mail on Sunday*

LIBERATION DAY
⊕ Dateline: Cannes, France

Behind its glamorous exterior, the city's seething underworld is the battleground for a very dirty drugs war and Stone must reach deep within himself to fight it on their terms.

'McNab's great asset is that the heart of his fiction is non-fiction' *Sunday Times*

DARK WINTER
⊕ Dateline: Malaysia

A straightforward action on behalf of the War on Terror turns into a race to escape his past for Stone if he is to save himself and those closest to him.

'Addictive . . . Packed with wild action and revealing tradecraft' *Daily Telegraph*

DEEP BLACK
⊕ Dateline: Bosnia

All too late Stone realizes that he is being used as bait to lure into the open a man whom the darker forces of the West will stop at nothing to destroy.

'One of the UK's top thriller writers' *Daily Express*

AGGRESSOR
✛ Dateline: Georgia, former Soviet Union

A longstanding debt of friendship to an SAS comrade takes Stone on a journey where he will have to risk everything to repay what he owes, even his life . . .

'A terrific novelist' *Mail on Sunday*

RECOIL
✛ Dateline: The Congo, Africa

What starts out as a personal quest for a missing woman quickly becomes a headlong rush from his own past for Stone.

'Stunning . . . A first class action thriller' *Sun*

CROSSFIRE
✛ Dateline: Kabul

Nick Stone enters the modern day wild west that is Afghanistan in search of a kidnapped reporter.

'Authentic to the core . . . McNab at his electrifying best' *Daily Express*

BRUTE FORCE
✛ Dateline: Tripoli

An undercover operation is about to have deadly long term consequences . . .

'Violent and gripping, this is classic McNab' *News of the World*

EXIT WOUND
⊕ Dateline: Dubai

Nick Stone embarks on a quest to track down the killer of two ex-SAS comrades.

'Could hardly be more topical . . . all the elements of a McNab novel are here'
Mail on Sunday

ZERO HOUR
⊕ Dateline: Amsterdam

A code that will jam every item of military hardware from Kabul to Washington. A terrorist group who nearly have it in their hands. And a soldier who wants to go down fighting . . .

'Like his creator, the ex-SAS soldier turned uber-agent is unstoppable'
Daily Mirror

DEAD CENTRE
⊕ Dateline: Somalia

A Russian oligarch's young son is the Somalian pirates' latest kidnap victim. His desperate father contacts the only man with the know-how, the means and the guts to get his boy back. At any cost . . .

'Sometimes only the rollercoaster ride of an action-packed thriller hits the spot. No one delivers them as professionally or as plentifully as SAS soldier turned author McNab' *Guardian*

SILENCER
⊕ Dateline: Hong Kong

To protect his family, Nick Stone must journey to the Triad controlled metropolis and a brutal world he thought he'd left behind.

'Nick Stone is emerging as one of the great all-action characters of recent times' *Daily Mirror*

FOR VALOUR
⊕ Dateline: Hereford

When a young trooper is shot in the head at the Regiment's renowned Killing House at the SAS's base in Hereford, Nick Stone is perfectly qualified to investigate. But then a second death catapults Stone himself into the telescopic sights of an unknown assassin bent on protecting a secret that could strike at the heart of the establishment.

Meet Andy McNab's explosive new creation, Sergeant Tom Buckingham

RED NOTICE

Deep beneath the English Channel, a small army of Russian terrorists has seized control of the Eurostar to Paris, taken four hundred hostages at gunpoint – and declared war on a government that has more than its own fair share of secrets to keep. One man stands in their way. An off-duty SAS soldier is hiding somewhere inside the train. Alone and injured, he's the only chance the passengers and crew have of getting out alive.

Andy McNab and Kym Jordan's new series of novels traces the interwoven stories of one platoon's experience of warfare in the twenty-first century. Packed with the searing danger and high-octane excitement of modern combat, it also explores the impact of its aftershocks upon the soldiers themselves, and upon those who love them. It will take you straight into the heat of battle and the hearts of those who are burned by it.

WAR TORN

Two tours of Iraq under his belt, Sergeant Dave Henley has seen something of how modern battles are fought. But nothing can prepare him for the posting to Forward Operating Base Senzhiri, Helmand Province, Afghanistan. This is a warzone like even he's never seen before.

'Andy McNab's books get better and better. *War Torn* brilliantly portrays the lives of a platoon embarking on a tour of duty in Helmand province'
Daily Express

BATTLE LINES

Coming back from war is never easy, as Sergeant Dave Henley's platoon discovers all too quickly when they return from Afghanistan – to find that home can be an equally searing battlefield. When they are summoned to Helmand once more, to protect the US team assigned to destroy the opium crop, it is almost a relief to the soldiers. But now Dave's team must learn new skills to survive, while their loved ones in England find their lives can be ripped apart by prejudice, corrosive anger, harsh misunderstanding and ugly rumour.

ANDY McNAB

SILENCER

CORGI BOOKS

TRANSWORLD PUBLISHERS
61–63 Uxbridge Road, London W5 5SA
A Random House Group Company
www.transworldbooks.co.uk

SILENCER
A CORGI BOOK: 9780552161428 (B format)
9780552170413 (A format)

First published in Great Britain
in 2013 by Bantam Press
an imprint of Transworld Publishers
Corgi edition published 2014

A CIP catalogue record for this book
is available from the British Library.

Addresses for Random House Group Ltd companies outside the UK
can be found at: www.randomhouse.co.uk
The Random House Group Ltd Reg. No. 954009

The Random House Group Limited supports the Forest Stewardship
Council® (FSC®), the leading international forest-certification
organisation. Our books carrying the FSC label are printed on
FSC®-certified paper. FSC is the only forest-certification scheme
supported by the leading environmental organisations, including
Greenpeace. Our paper procurement policy can be found at
www.randomhouse.co.uk/environment

Typeset in 10.75/13pt Palatino by Falcon Oast Graphic Art Ltd.
Printed and bound by CPI Group (UK) Ltd, Croydon, CR0 4YY.

2 4 6 8 10 9 7 5 3 1

SILENCER

PART ONE

1

Jaco, Costa Rica

29 November 1993
07.37 hrs

The Nazi eagle and swastika were still stamped under the Mauser bolt housing. Its sniper sight looked like a pointy fence post. Most novices aimed where a thin horizontal line crossed it, about two-thirds of the way up, but that was only there so you could check for canting – weapon tilting. The correct aim was right at the pinnacle.

I squinted into the very basic x4 magnification Second World War Zeiss optic. The target building in the valley below us was a blur. Torrential rain stung my face and battered the lens; the wipe I gave it with my thumb only made things worse.

'One shot, one kill – still sure you can do it, *hombre*?'

I nodded a yes to the black-and-white western piss-take he'd been dishing out since we'd first met, but in fact, you know what, I wasn't sure. I was soaked to the skin, covered with mud and leaf litter, and bitten to fuck by every insect in Central America that could fly, crawl, or sit and wait for you to put your arse down alongside it.

Worse still, I felt jumpy. This was my first job for the Secret Intelligence Service. It might have been same shit, different boss, but my whole future with them could hang on this one shot, and the dickhead I'd had to drag along with me was a millstone round my neck.

I eased my head away from the weapon. Dino was partially submerged in mud; the rest of him was covered with big lumps of rainforest. His eyes were pressed against what looked like a pair of binos on steroids. For the hundredth time since we'd got there he pressed a button on the casing and fired off a beam of invisible infrared light, in case the shack might have legged it further down the valley in the last few minutes.

'Four hundred and forty-seven metres.'

'I know, Dino. I know.'

The range was adjusted via a dial on top of the casing. I had it at 450.

Dino had shaved his head to a number-one for this job, and dyed what was left blond. To look at him, you'd think that the Mauser had belonged to his granddad. Maybe it had. 'Need-to-know' didn't seem to be high on the DEA's standard operational procedure: Agent Zavagno had already told me way more about his background than I needed to know.

His Mexican grandparents had swum the Rio Grande with their kids after watching too much *Dallas* and *Dynasty*. Dinner with JR and Joan Collins never materialized, but little Dino had begun to live the American Dream in the shack next door to them in some shit-kicking town just inside the border.

I was no linguist, but he sounded more Italian to me than Mexican, and there was definitely a touch of European in Dino's DNA. Hundreds of Mussolini's old mates had joined the flood of Nazis to Central and South America immediately after the Second World War – which probably went some way towards explaining his *Boys from Brazil* hairdo.

Dino might have been in his mid-twenties with a wing forward's physique, but I felt like I'd had to drag him every centimetre of the twelve Ks from town. It wasn't that he didn't want to be there; I was sure his passion and enthusiasm ticked all the boxes at the DEA's Washington HR department. But he operated out of New Mexico, the land of tacos and dustbowls. He'd never spent time in the rainforest. He'd had no operational experience in the field, come to that, and didn't know how to pace himself.

That wasn't his only problem. He'd got it into his head that Brits liked a brew, and insisted on Lipton's – the bags in the little yellow packets.

To make things worse, the one-horse town we'd hung out in was crawling with hippies, who'd gone there for the Summer of Love, and swathes of young surfer dudes, who'd come to catch a wave or two in recent years and also forgotten to leave. The girls looked tanned, fit and up for a party. Dino wore his cock on his dyed-blond head and had been reluctant to up sticks before he'd even received an invitation.

It had taken us ten long, sweat-soaked, mosquito-bitten hours to locate Jesús Orjuela's latest hideaway. It had then taken us three more to crawl undetected into our fire position on the high ground to its south. We'd been lying there ever since in a tropical downpour while the Wolf – as he liked to be called, these days – sat and drank coffee in the dry. The thing about wolves is that they're bold in packs but super-cautious on their own. This one knew that concealment was his best weapon.

The hardwood bungalow I could see through the Mauser sight was a far cry from the Mayfair apartments, Swiss ski chalets and Malibu beach houses that comprised the rest of his property portfolio. It stood on tree-trunk stilts, with a wiggly tin roof that also stretched across a veranda. There was a shuttered window on each gable end and a badly fitting door at the front, between two more windows with shutters, but at least everyone inside was sheltered.

And anonymous.

The only giveaway was the chunky, all-American Ford F150 pick-up parked outside. It would have been up to its axles in mud, had it not boasted the kind of lifted suspension that any redneck would have been proud to show off at the local monster-truck fest.

A rusty barbed-wire fence encircled about half an acre of long grass that drifted to the edge of the canopy. A swollen stream the width of a road snaked along the valley a hundred metres or so beyond it; I could see several other shacks spread out on its bank, each with its own patch of mud for the pigs to have fun in. Half a dozen crocodiles lazed nearby, jaws propped open as if they were playing raindrop catch or waiting for some fresh pork to wander in. They looked as laid-back as the country they called home.

Big government had protected this place from the nightmare civil wars and American-backed insurgency that had contaminated most of Central America in the 1970s and 1980s. Costa Rica didn't even have an army. All it cared about was developing tourism and protecting the rainforest. Hardwoods towered forty metres above us, man-made buttresses a couple of metres high supporting them like stabilizers on a Christmas-tree stand.

I felt a little sorry that some of the shit spreading from the south was about to stick to this garden paradise.

I focused once more on the view through the blurred optic. I had the door and windows covered. Wherever the Wolf emerged, I'd have him. One good shot and he'd be flat on the veranda floor, victim of an old-fashioned assassination by a rival drugs cartel based beyond the horizon.

2

The Wolf was Colombian to his lizard-skin loafers. I couldn't help smiling when I was shown photographs of him at the briefing in MI6's Vauxhall HQ. I'd always associated wolves with lean and hungry; this boy could have fitted a whole pack into the waistband of his jeans. But there was no mistaking the sharpness of his teeth – or those of the cartel he ran in conjunction with his old schoolmate, Pablo Escobar.

Both born in 1949, they had grown up together in the hills around Medellín; right place, right time – if your career of choice happened to be drugs baron. Colombia has direct sea access to both the west and east coasts of the United States, and that puts you in the box seat when you're shipping illegal gear on an industrial scale.

Jesús and Pablo had started out as debt collectors and gang enforcers in their early teens. They soon developed a reputation for casual and lethal violence. Kidnap for ransom was one of their favourite tricks. If the family refused to pay or couldn't come up with the cash, the dynamic duo would torture their captive, then kill them. Sometimes they'd do it anyway, just to make a point. '*Pour encourager les autres,*' Jesús liked to say. 'That means to encourage the others.' According to an associate turned DEA informer, he was never without a book, and had a particular weakness for Voltaire, another great defender of civil liberties.

He knew that guns and torture would not be enough to protect their growing fortune. The pool around Medellín teemed with sharks, ever circling, always looking for the kill. They had to show they were capable of defending what was theirs. And, as the military memoirs he devoured had taught him, the best form of defence was attack.

Jesús and Pablo took terror to new levels. Women were raped as punishment for a crime by a family member – and every relative, children included, was rounded up to witness it. They made their victims beg and scream in front of their loved ones, and left their mutilated corpses on display. Sometimes he and Pablo put their heads on stakes and hung their intestines from trees. Male victims had their cocks chopped off and stuffed into their mouths. Women had their breasts sliced off with machetes, their stomachs cut open and their wombs stretched over their heads.

The Wolf soon perfected the signature dish that earned him his nickname: he'd rip open the throat of a victim and pull his tongue through the gash like some grotesque necktie – which went to show that your worst enemy was the psychopath with a library card.

The Wolf and Escobar wielded the raw power that only terror can bring. In its wake came so much wealth they offered to pay off Colombia's national debt. Escobar even became a congressman, a respectable citizen, a representative of the people. His new status gave him judicial immunity, which meant he could no longer be prosecuted for crimes under Colombian law – and he made sure the Wolf couldn't either.

Escobar also had a shiny new passport that gave him international diplomatic immunity. He took his family north of the border for their holidays, even posed for happy snaps in front of the White House. The DEA were pulling their hair out – not just because he could mince around his Miami mansions with impunity, but because they knew he planned to become president of Colombia and there was nothing they could do to stop him.

Ironically, it only went tits up for the congressman and his mate when some bright spark in the US discovered that everyday baking soda provided a simple, low-cost alternative for the highly flammable diethyl ether used in the manufacture of freebase cocaine – and the new cocktail was also much more addictive. Crack spread like wildfire through the USA's inner-city streets and was soon a social epidemic. Almost overnight, the white stuff lost its chic. It was no longer the recreational substance of choice for the well-heeled trendsetter. Washington had no choice but to grip the situation – and that meant gripping the cartels.

What had started as a profit bonanza was the beginning of the end for the dynamic duo. Their political platform disintegrated beneath them; they'd become plague-carrying rats, enemies of the state. Which was when the SAS was called in to help.

Me, Pablo and Jesús went way back.

3

Dino fired the infrared beam for the hundred and first time. 'Four hundred and forty-seven, *hombre*. Don't screw up, will you?'

His voice was too high-pitched for someone his size. It had been funny to start with, but now it was starting to get on my nerves even more than the fucking rain. The finger I invited him to swivel on was white and wrinkled, like I'd been in a bath all day.

Margaret Thatcher had been in Number Ten when crack cocaine appeared on UK streets, and she took it very personally indeed. I was a corporal in the Regiment at the time she offered us to Reagan as part of the First Strike Policy to stop the drugs at source. But it was easier said than done. With twenty thousand drug-related murders a year, Colombia, a country the size of Spain, Portugal and France combined, had become the most dangerous place on earth. A Colombian male between the ages of eighteen and sixty was more likely to die of gunshot wounds than any other cause.

We had flown down in 1988 to train the anti-narcotics

police, first to penetrate the rainforest, then to find and destroy the manufacturing plants. The problem was, these guys were only on about a hundred US a month. For that, they risked getting killed – their families raped and murdered – by Pablo and the Wolf. So they didn't give a shit if rich, overfed North American gringos were off their heads on coke.

Colombia, I soon learned, was all about self-interest. An airliner went down in the jungle while I was there. When the police arrived on the scene they found the local villagers scavenging through the wreckage. Quite a few passengers had survived, but were badly injured. The villagers didn't give them a second glance in their rush to rip the watches, rings and wallets off the nearby corpses.

Life was cheap in this neck of the woods. And everyone had a price.

4

The village was dead – not surprisingly, beneath this weight of rainfall. Ahead of me was a solid wall of water, thumping into the ground with such force it created mini mud-craters. Even the scabby chickens and the pot-bellied pigs had got their heads down. Raindrops stitched the mud all around them like machine-gun fire. At least it washed the leaf litter off our faces.

I had the continuous fuck-ups by the Blocada de Búsqueda (Search Bloc) to thank for this. The Colombian Police unit's sole purpose was to hunt down Orjuela and his mates, and if they'd done a proper job I wouldn't have been turning into a human prune.

The US Army's secret electronic surveillance unit, codenamed Centra Spike, crammed the small Beechcraft turboprop with high-tech gear that tracked mobile-phone and radio transmissions. The theory: pinpoint Escobar and the Wolf by finding their voices. It hadn't taken them long – Jesús was always gobbing off about something – but high-level corruption and incompetence in Search Bloc meant they were too slow reacting. Its commanders didn't know which of their two hundred officers they could trust not to alert the Wolf in time for him to do a runner.

I couldn't blame them: there were life-changing amounts of money on offer. The bad guys had bags of the stuff stashed along every escape route so they could instantly pay their way out of any drama. Even the low-tech drug-manufacturing plants in the rainforests had cash close to hand for the runners. They'd already cut tracks or tunnels to the riverbank where fast boats were hidden. The key was always to keep things simple – as they need to be when you're under pressure.

But that didn't mean I enjoyed being at the shitty end of the stick, getting pounded by the rain, while a bunch of Centra Spike geeks sat in cosy ground-listening stations all around Medellín or aboard Beechcraft at 30,000 feet as the USAF U2 spy planes buzzed about at twice that height in search of the other fat man, Pablo.

The Americans wanted Escobar's head on their wall more than that of any other member of the cartel – which left me aiming for second prize, alongside a DEA newbie whose mind was perpetually elsewhere, with a strong chance of getting banged up for murder.

As I lay there with the rain drumming through my hair, I thought, Why the fuck did I leave the Regiment? I was a K, a deniable operator, working for the SIS. I didn't pay tax, everything was cash in hand, but even that wasn't a perk – if I got caught, it meant they could deny I existed.

I kept my eyes on the Mauser's back lens, hoping the Wolf was just waiting for the rain to stop. I wanted to get this thing over and done with. As Dino kept

28

reminding me, the time it would take him to get the three or four metres from the veranda to his wagon would allow me one shot.

If I didn't drop him with the first round, that was it, game over. He could have an M60 machine-gun in that shack for all I knew. And if he disappeared beneath the canopy instead, he'd be gone for good. We couldn't chase him: we couldn't risk our faces being seen. This was supposed to be a revenge killing by a rival cartel, not an assassination by a government-sponsored gringo and the grandson of a couple of Mexican wetbacks.

5

We'd pinged the target two days ago outside the grocery store in Jaco, loading bottled water and provisions into the back of the pick-up. And once I found the shack I knew why. He wasn't in Costa Rica alone. I recognized them all – the three small children, two girls and a boy, and the much younger wife – from the Vauxhall photos. She had shoulder-length jet-black hair, high cheekbones and dark-brown eyes, the classic South American beauty queen. I reckoned Jesús would die a happy man.

If you take the knock-on-the-door option, there's a decision to be made: do you wait until it's fully open so you can ID the target before firing? That's high risk. You'll be in the killing area longer than is healthy, and whoever answers the door may take the trouble to check who's delivering the good news.

So why not start blasting as soon as you hear someone approaching, then barge inside to check who you've hit? I didn't want any of that. The Wolf was a player; he practically invented the game. But drop the family as well? That was the Wolf's favourite trick, not mine.

Another option had been to wait until he went back into town for food and water. But drop him on the move or close up and in an urban environment? There's always a third party with eyes-on. At least we had a concealed fire position in the jungle, a clear arc of fire, and the capacity to exfiltrate unnoticed.

I'd opted for a distance shoot and picked up the Mauser from an embassy-sponsored dead letterbox. The weapon was used by hundreds of thousands of hunters around the world. The German Army still used them for ceremonial duties. Best of all, it wasn't only quick for the spooks to acquire covertly when the Wolf was in-country, it was untraceable. And that's harder to manage than you might think.

6

'Still four hundred and forty-seven metres, is it, Dino? It hasn't been scared off by that fucking haircut of yours and legged it down the valley?'

Dino turned to me and grinned. Flecks of the Spam he'd been munching speckled his teeth and its unmistakable aroma wafted towards me.

We were on hard routine. On the way in and all the time we were in the fire position, there was no cooking, no flames, no smoking – not that either of us did. Even our shit travelled with us in plastic bags. If the target didn't show because we'd fucked up and missed him, or if for any reason I couldn't take the shot, we might have to come back again. Nothing could be left to give away our presence, even after he'd been dropped.

Which was a pity, because right now I was quite tempted to stake Dino out on the ground and leave him to the insects that still hadn't finished with me.

'Mate, do you always dye your hair?'

'Of course.'

'Why?'

'The chicks love it, *hombre*.'

'Platinum blond? They obviously can't see that what's inside your nut is dark brown.'

He looked puzzled for a moment. Then his face collapsed into an enormous grin. His chin headed east and his nose headed west.

He'd been in a lot of fights, he said, and most of them were over women. He loved them all: any shape, age or vocabulary. His basic philosophy was that everything in life boils down to getting laid. And why not? He was in his late twenties with a cock instead of a brain: how else was he to think? Certainly not about this job. He didn't seem to give a fuck if it was a success. He was wasting time here in the jungle, without an eligible woman in sight. 'You take the shot, *hombre*. Then we bug out to Miami, right, and I show you some things.'

I knew what was going through his head as he got busy with the range finder again, and it had nothing to do with the target.

'Not Toronto?'

He'd met a couple of Canadian tour-company reps in one of the Gulf-coast bars a couple of months back, taken them both to dinner, then back to his king-size bed. Or so he claimed.

'My head might be full of shit, man, but those babes will be full of me as soon as you finish this job, you know what I'm saying?' His shoulders shook with laughter. 'Four-four-seven, man. No pressure.'

I wasn't going to bite. 'No, mate. No pressure.'

7

Your bones are your weapon platform. Your muscles are the cushioning. I made a tripod of my elbows and the left side of my ribcage. The Mauser didn't have a stand so I had to use the conventional method of support: left hand forward on the wooden stock with my forearm resting on a log. A bipod would have allowed me to bring it across my body and into the butt, but you have to work with what you've got.

I peered through the sight, making sure there was no shadowing around the edges of the optic. I took aim at the centre of the door, emptied my lungs, stopped breathing, and closed my eyes. I relaxed my muscles slightly, started to breathe normally, and looked through the sight again. My point of aim had shifted to the left-hand edge of the door.

While Dino delved deeper into his can of luncheon meat and store of fantasies, I swivelled to the right to correct, then repeated the whole procedure until I was comfortably aligned to the target. It's pointless trying to force your body into a position that it doesn't want to adopt. The weapon has to point naturally towards the target.

Dino hadn't given up trying to get a rise out of me. 'That wife of his, *hombre*, she's . . . *hot* . . . Hot – and *loaded*. She'll be a vulnerable widow soon . . .'

My eye never left the optic. 'Any wind out there?'

The spotter is like the co-driver in a rally car. All the heroic stuff is done by the guy behind the wheel – changing gears and sliding round corners, waving to the girls; all that shit. But without the co-driver telling him what's ahead, when to turn into the next bend, what sort of bend it is, they'd both be history. Under the canopy, there was no wind. But out there, on the edge of the village, there might be. And that would affect my round at this distance. I needed my co-driver. Even if he was the world's biggest dickhead.

'None out there, *hombre*. Only what's leaving your ass.'

I glanced up as a shiny black thing with far too many legs for its size made its way along a leaf just above my arm in search of breakfast. It could smell me and was getting very excited. A raindrop knocked it onto my hand. It was probably still feeling pretty pleased with itself – right up to the point when I squeezed tight around its middle and broke it in two.

'Hey, *hombre* . . . We got movement.'

8

My eye shot back to the optic as Dino began his running commentary. 'I've got the door open – you copy? It's on, *hombre*, it's fucking *on*.'

The lens steamed up. I rubbed it with my thumb. 'Yep.'

'I've still got no wind. And I've got movement inside.'

I watched through the curtain of rain as the Wolf's two little girls tumbled out onto the veranda. They had their hair in pigtails. Both wore shorts and Disneyland T-shirts and were barefoot. They ran straight to the rail and stuck their hands out into the torrent cascading from the roof, playfully flicking water at each other.

'Nick, I got the target. It's fucking on . . .'

A pair of adult sandals appeared at the threshold. The Wolf had rolled up his baggy jeans above the knee. A very hairy gut hanging out between his waistband and a blue T-shirt completed the look.

'Yep.'

I eased the aiming post up to where his collarbones

met, a centimetre or so higher in my sight picture than the two little heads bobbing up and down in front of him. The Wolf took a cigarette from his mouth and flicked it past them into the mud.

My finger took first pressure.

Holding the post level on the centre of his chest I let out my breath and held it. Then his wife entered my sight picture. The Wolf scooped her up in his arms and they kissed. Her loosely tied hair brushed her shoulders, and the hem of her plain blue dress rode up her thigh. I began to see what Dino was so excited about.

Arms still full, the Wolf turned back towards the door. I took a gentle breath and kept first pressure – but knew that if I put a round into the target there was a good chance it would also drop her. That wouldn't be good: someone would have to look after those father-less kids.

The couple disappeared back into the shack with the two girls in tow, but the door stayed open. At least the kids were out of the killing area. To hear a gunshot and then discover that your dad is dead is bad enough; to be standing next to him as he goes down would not be the best day out.

I knew Dino was pissed off. Maybe he thought taking a shot at this range was as easy as Arnie made it look. 'Fuck, *hombre*, maybe a change of angle . . . ?'

'No.' I gripped his arm. 'The rain's easing. He could be out again any minute. We stay where we are.'

He slumped back into the mud, muttering to himself like a down-and-out.

We were well concealed, with a great arc of fire. No one was going anywhere. I breathed slowly and deeply, keeping a nice, easy rhythm so I could control the weapon at any moment.

Dino shook his head to clear his ears and wiped them with the back of a muddy hand.

'Dino, we got movement.'

The Wolf and his wife appeared on the veranda again. He was now carrying a furled red-and-white golfing umbrella.

Dino resumed his commentary. 'Still no wind . . .'

I had him at the same point of aim as he called back into the shack, probably yelling goodbye to the kids. Only one problem: Mrs Orjuela's very attractive head was at the centre of my target. All I could see of the Wolf was his gut ballooning either side of her small frame, like the human version of a solar eclipse. I waited for her to move. I wasn't sure if Dino was waffling or not. My brain had shrunk and pushed itself into the optic.

I breathed out; held it; took first pressure. All she had to do was move one step left or right and I'd take second pressure.

'Stop, stop!' Dino's hand fell onto my right shoulder.

I couldn't see what was wrong. The couple were still on the veranda. She was still obstructing the shot.

'Fuck . . . They—'

I didn't need to know the reason. 'Shut up. Just tell me when.'

I waited on the target, top of the aiming post still where it needed to be, rising up gently as I breathed in. I'd also have him if he moved towards the pick-up, as long as she got the fuck out of the way.

Still nothing existed in my head but the sight picture, the water pounding on my back, and the wait for Dino's OK.

I held the weapon firmly but gently, not wanting to grip it so tightly that my muscles started to shake. I just wanted to keep the weapon as it should be: a natural extension to my body. I took slow, deep breaths to keep myself oxygenated, ready for when I stopped breathing and squeezed the trigger.

9

It didn't take long to see what the closedown was about. Just beyond the target, inside the shack, the kids were criss-crossing the doorway in some sort of game. There were three of them now. The boy was a lot bigger than his sisters.

'Here we go.'

'What?'

I realized I'd spoken aloud.

I wiped as much rain as I could off the optic without shifting my elbows from their anchor points and returned to the firing position. The Wolf took his wife's arm.

'Nick, she's going with him. She's in the fucking way . . . The shot, she's in the way . . .'

The target held the umbrella at an angle to protect them as they emerged from cover. They moved down the steps together. The pick-up was only three or four paces. It was parked nose-out from the shack, which meant if I couldn't take the shot before he reached the cab, she'd still be in the way.

I crawled out of my position.

'Nick . . . What you doing, man?'

There was no time to explain. I started legging it to the right, but the mud tugged heavily at my Rohan tourist-on-safari shirt and trousers. Maybe I could put a round through the windscreen. Hugging the high ground, I tried to protect the weapon as I tore through the foliage. I didn't want to damage the optic or dislodge it and fuck up the zero.

I was starting to breathe heavily, and that could jeopardize the shoot as badly. But I didn't have a choice. I had to keep running to get ahead of the target.

I reached the treeline again, overlooking the valley. With luck, I'd be in front of them, or at least at a better angle to take the shot. My lungs burned; my throat was dry.

I was in time to see them dodging puddles beside the pick-up. She had the umbrella now. The Wolf was between her and the driver's door. The height of the vehicle meant that he was completely obscured, but I had an angle on the windscreen.

I fell into the mud, trying to slow my heart rate, trying to stop my chest heaving, then realized I didn't have enough muzzle clearance. The slope wasn't steep enough. All I could see through the optic was a haze of green.

I got to my feet again as the driver's door opened. I couldn't see the Wolf. The umbrella was still up and static.

I ran to the nearest tree, jammed myself between two of its buttresses, arse in the mud, back firmly against the trunk. Heels dug in, elbows inside my knees, I tried to make a quick but stable platform for the weapon.

Dino crashed down the other side of the buttress, his breathing noisier than the water still pouring from the canopy. He pressed the range-finder button. 'I got four—'

'Dino, shut *up*.'

Eighteen years in the military gave me enough experience to know that this was a bit further than 447, but no way was it 500. I'd still aim a fraction higher. There was no time to mince about, bring the weapon out of the aim and adjust the sights. I kept the aiming post slightly above the steering wheel as the Wolf fell into his seat.

I waited. My chest heaves slowed as I took control of my breathing. The wife closed her door.

'Nick, take the shot! He'll be gone . . .'

I waited. Two seconds later, the massive V8 engine roared into life. Smoke belched from the exhaust.

'Nick – fuck . . .'

I breathed out, moved the centre of the top pad of my right index finger gently against the trigger. The wind-screen wipers began their sweep and cleared my sight picture for me. The post was slightly lower than it needed to be. I adjusted up a millimetre so it rested dead centre of his collar.

I took three deep breaths. If you're not oxygenated you can't see correctly and your muscles start to tremble. I squeezed until I felt resistance; second pressure. I emptied my lungs and stopped breathing in order to steady the weapon.

And then I took the shot.

10

I didn't even hear the crack. I was too busy maintaining concentration while the firing pin struck the round and the expanding gases forced the bullet up the barrel and out towards the target. But the parakeets heard it. They screeched and catapulted from their perches high in the canopy as the weapon jumped up and back into my shoulder.

The aiming post fell back to the neat hole at the centre of the spider-webbed screen. The parakeets regrouped and flew in bomber formation, metres above the F150, as they escaped down the valley.

No one emerged from the cab.

I'd kept my right eye open throughout, followed through the shot, watched as the point of aim settled once more on the centre of the target.

Dino mumbled unintelligibly. I couldn't work out if he was excited or terrified. Then he blurted, 'Did you get him, Nick? Is he dead?'

He probably thought the shot had been loud enough to get the whole village pouring out of their shacks. But it was nothing compared to Mrs Orjuela shrieking at her children to stay inside the shack. She slipped over in the mud, dropped the umbrella, then struggled to her feet.

'Nick, she's running, man. You got him!'

She slithered and slid towards the shack.

'Let's go, man! We've gotta go!'

I kept my eye glued to the optic as she reached the steps.

One of the little girls ran out onto the veranda, looking confused. Her mother continued screaming at her to go back, took the three steps in one bound and shepherded the child into the safety of the house.

'I don't get it, man. What the fuck we doing?'

I stayed in the fire position and watched the shadowy blob behind the wheel as the windscreen wipers bumped over the spider-webbed glass.

Dino was behind me now, maybe thinking that if he got the hell out of there, so would I.

'He's still moving.'

I braced my elbows to maintain the fire position and used my right forefinger and thumb to push the bolt handle up and back to eject the round.

'Grab it.'

Even empty cases left with us.

I pushed home the bolt to pick up another 7.92 round from the five-round mag. As the round found the chamber the driver's door opened. With agonizing slowness, the Wolf slumped sideways. I pulled the bolt handle down to close the action and got treated to a running commentary on the fucking obvious.

'He's under the truck, Nick. He's fucking crawled under the truck. What we going to do? *Fuck . . .*'

I watched the rain-stitched mud, hoping to see

Orjuela try to crawl, walrus-like, towards the shack. But he wasn't that stupid.

I sprang up, keeping eyes on the truck, scanning for movement. So far there hadn't been any sign of it from any of the other shacks along the river. They probably did enough hunting around there not to worry about a gunshot. 'Dino!'

No answer.

'*Dino!*' I didn't look round, just thumbed back the way we'd come. 'Go to the RV. Remember the road j unction? Go there and we'll meet up. Go there now.'

He swam into my peripheral vision. 'Why, Nick? What you doing?'

'Making sure he's dead. And that doesn't need two of us. Go, fuck off.'

He was more than willing to take that order and I was more than happy to see the back of him.

I scrambled faster and faster down the hill, then slid on my arse across the wet grass, all the way to the valley floor. The rain was still hammering down. I could hear cocks crowing and, further along the valley, could see smoke belching from the stone chimneys and settling across wiggly tin rooftops like a pall. There was still no breeze to pick it up and take it away.

Less than fifty metres now to the F150 . . . I stooped as I ran towards it, weapon in the shoulder, always checking the gable end shutter, expecting it to open any minute, or the wife to storm back out onto the veranda and start shooting.

The Wolf was still under the vehicle. I could see no movement, but that meant nothing. I could hear the kids howling inside the shack, which was good. I preferred sobbing to shooting.

I dropped down next to the wheel arch. The Wolf was wedged by the driveshaft, his eyes glazed as he bled out into the mud. His retinas looked as dead as fish on a slab. I couldn't see any chest movement, any twitching. But I'd long since stopped taking anything like that on trust.

I crawled in next to him and pressed my middle and forefinger into the fatty folds of his neck to feel for a carotid pulse. There wasn't one. The round had entered high in his right shoulder and blown a king-size exit wound through his lower back.

I reversed out into the daylight and turned back towards the high ground, aiming for the cover of the canopy. As I started to move, something caught my eye at the gable end of the shack. The shutter was open. I swung up the weapon, using the crown of the optic as a battle sight.

The Wolf's son stood there, framed by the window. He had clear olive skin, short dark hair and eyes like saucers. He stared at me, unblinking. He wasn't scared. I could still hear his sisters wailing, but he looked like stone. His eyes bored into mine. They told me that while I might feature in his three a.m. nightmares, he would take his place in mine.

Then his mother appeared, her mud-covered arm reaching across the boy's shoulders – not to move him away from the threat of my raised Mauser but to bind them together. Her gaze was as dark, unblinking and devoid of emotion as her son's.

I lowered the weapon and broke into a run.

PART TWO

1

Moscow

26 August 2011
11.27 hrs

Life as I knew it was about to end.

I stared at my reflection in the triple-glazed, floor-to-ceiling balcony doors overlooking the Moskva River and Borodinsky Bridge, but my eyes kept being tugged back to the one of the swollen belly on the sofa behind me. Four weeks to go, and Anna was so heavy with our unborn baby she found it hard to stand, let alone walk. It was like she was on the sea-bed in an old diver's suit and lead boots, hardly able to put one foot in front of the other.

I'd come to like this city in my year here. You knew where you stood with Muscovites. They didn't open doors for each other. When you wanted something, you said, 'Give me.' And as long as you had the roubles, you got.

The main reason I liked it, of course, was that Anna was here. In between living with me, investigative reporting for *Russia Today* and flying around saving the world, this amazing woman had opened doors for me. She'd introduced me to ballet and art, music without bass guitars and synthesizers, and books without pictures.

Thanks to her, my brain had been getting a serious workout. She'd introduced me to Tolstoy's *War and Peace*, and two years on I was still at it. The fucking thing had over twelve hundred pages. It had taken me longer to get a third of the way through than it took Napoleon to reach Moscow, be defeated and sent into exile. Twice.

I read in English. I'd only gathered a phrase or two of Russian in the time I'd been there. Moscow was a big tourist destination, these days, and most people knew enough English for me to get away with that. If they didn't understand me I'd do the British thing of pointing and shouting. It seemed to do the trick.

As the days got longer and warmer, Anna and I headed for Serebryany Bor. The island was a trolleybus ride away. It could be walked at any time of day, but it was especially great in the evening when the late-setting sun bathed the *dacha*s, the woods and the river. She pointed out the spring buds and flowers, the families with babies in buggies and kids on bikes with stabilizers.

The more I'd got to know her, the more I realized how alike we were. We gave each other loads of space and got on with our own lives. I knew that her job was about doing the right thing, and that it made her happy. And

I knew we'd probably get on each other's tits if we lived a more conventional lifestyle. Maybe having gaps, then coming back together was the only way that a relationship would work for me.

Just when I thought we'd got the balance right, we discovered she was three months pregnant. Our lives changed almost overnight; it was like a switch had been thrown inside her.

'You ready, Nicholas?'

Anna's reflection was slumped in the leather sofa. Dressed in one of her smart pregnancy outfits, she was working her way through a plate of cupcakes, her latest craving.

I turned. 'Ready if you are.'

Hmm, was I? I was far from ready to leave what we had there – the apartment, the view and, most importantly, our old life.

I loved everything about the penthouse. I loved the basement gym. For me, the gym had always been famine or feast. When I was working or injured I did nothing for months on end, but when I had the time, I was in there every day.

I loved the dual-aspect reception room, which opened onto the roof terrace and gave me a near 360-degree view of the high ground. I loved the secure underground parking space; the private balcony, overlooked by no one; the walk-in wardrobe that hadn't yet been filled on my side with more than a couple of pairs of jeans and some shirts.

The only thing we lacked was a decent-sized second bedroom. But even if it had had one, an apartment wasn't the right place to bring up a child. Anna was right about that, as she was about most things. We had to do what city-based parents did all over the planet – move out to the suburbs.

I helped her to her feet. Strange to think it was only two years since I'd first gripped her hand. Even then – standing among the wreckage of an aircraft full of dead men and drug dollars I'd shot down – I'd felt I'd known her all my life.

I'd been working undercover for the Firm; she'd been investigating a corrupt Russian industrialist's links with the Iranian ayatollahs. She said she wouldn't have touched me with a ten-foot pole if she could have sorted it on her own. Then she gave me the kind of smile that makes your knees go funny.

She was a dead ringer for the girl from Abba with blonde hair and high cheekbones. I fancied her big-time. As a sixteen-year-old boy soldier I'd sat in the NAAFI with my pint of Vimto and steak-and-kidney pie, waiting for *Top of the Pops*. 'Dancing Queen' had already been number one for about five years, and I took my seat in front of the TV every week hoping her reign would be extended.

I smiled as I draped her black raincoat around her shoulders. 'OK, let's get this little soldier on the road.'

She didn't smile back.

2

We drove out towards the ring road to the east of the city, scanning the various neighbourhoods that had spawned since the collapse of Communism.

Suburbia was beginning to take shape on the Moscow margins. The media were full of it – all the usual moaning about forests having huge holes ripped out of them to make way for gated communities with names like 'Navaho' and 'Chelsea'.

At first glance, the area she wanted us to concentrate on – wide boulevards, criss-crossed with electricity and phone cables and jammed with four-wheel-drives and people-carriers – reminded me of an American Midwestern sprawl. But the planning department must have been sick the day they'd dreamed this place up, or at a resort on the Black Sea spending the contents of the brown envelopes the developers had slipped them. Huge apartment blocks reared haphazardly between small houses with a bit of yard and big ones with gardens.

Alongside the biggest collection of billionaires on

earth, the massive migrant population, as well as the poor, old, dying, drunk and drugged, scraped a living in these old Soviet concrete blocks. They were all fucked big-time. In winter, portable paraffin heaters provided their only warmth, but gave off so much moisture that their windows still froze solid on the inside – unless they'd already sold the glass and shoved up plywood in its place. In Putin's Russia, everyone was an entrepreneur.

Anna was determined to find somewhere our baby could grow up safe from predators – somewhere with gates; big ones. Gates to her were things that kept people out. She was right, of course, but to me they had always been things that locked people in.

We had no idea of the kid's sex – Anna didn't want to know, and I wasn't bothered as long as all its arms and legs were in the right places. We hadn't even talked about names. But she wasn't the only one whose switch had been thrown. I felt stuff the moment I saw the first scan, even though it looked like nothing more than a grey peanut, and those feelings got a whole lot stronger when I felt the first kick.

I hadn't expected ever to have kids of my own; I could only just look after myself. And I certainly hadn't expected to feel this way if I did. I already knew I'd go to the ends of the earth to protect it.

The rest of the package I still wasn't sure about: the nuclear family. I'd seen it, at least from a distance, but never *needed* it. I'd been a best man once; that was as close as I ever wanted to get to a wedding.

'Nicholas?'

'Hey, I've been thinking, maybe we could keep two places. Live in the apartment and have a *dacha* for weekends?'

It wasn't like we were short of money. If Anna had taught me one thing, it was that money isn't everything. But I'd scooped enough drug dollars from the industrialist's aircraft to last us a while, and it was a fuck of a lot better than having to nick your own trainers.

'Nicholas – look.'

I glanced towards her. 'Seen a place?'

'No.' She pointed at her lap. 'I'm bleeding.'

3

I brought the Touran to a screeching halt in what turned out to be a McDonald's car park.

'You want the clinic?'

She shook her head. 'I'll go inside and check. You phone Katya.'

Anna didn't go anywhere without her 'hospital bag', these days. In the Regiment we used to keep a grab bag close by: a Bergen with all the 'one hour's notice' gear – from trauma care to demolitions kit – that we might need on a call-out. Anna's contained knickers and slippers, a change of clothes, the baby's first outfit, nappies and hundreds of muslin squares – I still hadn't worked out what they were for. In my little compartment there was a change of clothes, a camera, a tube of Pringles and some bags of Haribo. I fished out a pair of her trousers with a big, elasticated waist, some knickers and packs of wet wipes just in case.

She set off for the toilet and I pulled out my phone. I wasn't unduly worried. Anna was thirty-six weeks into her pregnancy with no complications. Katya had taken care of her throughout and assured us the baby was in launch mode, upside down and ready to get tabbing.

We hadn't even bothered signing the birthing contract; they're a Russian thing – you pay about a month before the due date, according to the level of care you think you'll need. We were going to do so at Katya's clinic the week after next.

I punched the speed-dial key for her mobile and got voicemail. Not a complete surprise: she hardly ever picked up even when she wasn't working, and today was a Friday – she'd be busy. I'd have to wait for Anna to come back with the clinic number, unless Googleski found it for me first.

I was glad the waiting was nearly over. Anna had become increasingly impatient with me, the more uncomfortable she got. The epic heat of the Moscow summer and a fair amount of pelvic pain had made the last few weeks a real struggle – and I was increasingly on the receiving end. I wasn't cut out for family life, she reckoned. I told her that, whatever family life was, I was up for it. That went down like a wagon load of shit. She said she wasn't sure if she still wanted me in this new life, or just her and the baby.

'Things are changing in me – and not just down here, Nicholas.' She'd pointed at her bump. 'In here as well.' Then she'd tapped the side of her head. 'We don't only have to change our lifestyle, we have to change our way of thinking. I'm not sure you can.'

I'd waved my arms at the mountains of baby kit around us. 'I'm already in baby mode. I'm prepared for whatever that means in the future.'

I wasn't convincing her. She was obsessed. I wasn't ready to change; I wasn't ready to settle and to do the right thing for our child. She needed someone who was going to be there not because they had to but because they wanted to. And this 'wanting to' feeling – well, she wasn't getting it from me.

One day she was worried about my lack of excitement, the next my lack of commitment. I couldn't keep track of what she wanted from me. I wasn't going to win *Mr & Mrs* anytime soon, but I didn't drink, didn't smoke, didn't gamble, didn't do drugs, didn't spend nights out with the lads. I told her I'd get plenty excited and committed once the baby was there. Then I really fucked up. I wondered aloud if the problem had more to do with her hormones than me not being connected to the idea of fatherhood.

It took a couple of days for the volcano to stop erupting and a whole lot more for the ash cloud to settle. Hormones or not, she worried that our child wasn't going to have a proper relationship with me because of what I was, and what that brought into our new family. 'I don't want our baby to become like us, Nicholas. That's why I'm changing. This child is the only thing I'm concerned about. I have to be. I've got to make sure it grows up in the best environment possible. Surely we both owe it that.'

I tried to understand. I'd have hated lugging round the equivalent of a Bergen strapped to my stomach 24/7. For the last couple of weeks she'd looked more and more like the big purple Pilates ball she was always sitting on, and when the baby moved it was no longer the vague flurry or two of the second trimester, it was the Klitschko brothers having a full-on spar.

I checked my mobile. Googleski wasn't co-operating. I kept getting pages in Cyrillic.

If she didn't come back in a minute I'd go and find her. What did the blood mean? I'd learned enough obstetrics as a patrol medic to win the soft-power war with indigenous populations, but not much more. I could handle an uncomplicated delivery, but for anything else she was going to need expert help.

Anna came out of McDonald's clutching one of their brown-paper carrier bags, and I was sure it didn't contain a couple of Happy Meals.

It seemed to take her for ever to cover the few metres to the wagon but I knew that if I got out and offered to help she'd go ballistic again. She finally made it and climbed back in.

'I think it's stopped. Let's carry on a bit and see what happens.'

I touched her shoulder. 'OK, but give me a bit of warning – the clinic's an hour away . . .'

We hadn't got further than the end of the road when I saw Anna's hand dip down to her lap. When she brought it back up her fingers were red.

'No messing. We're going right now.' I handed her my mobile. 'Tell them we're coming.'

She fumbled with the buttons and slumped in her seat. 'I don't feel too good, Nicholas. I feel . . . dizzy . . . This baby is beating me up from the inside . . .'

I grabbed the phone back and pulled over to the kerb. My call was answered after three rings. It was the twenty-something from Ukraine I'd met when I'd gone in to sort out the first round of paperwork. 'Sasha, it's Nick Stone. Is Dr Fuentes there?'

When it came to phone etiquette, she'd been really well trained in the art of pissing everyone off. 'Hello, Mr Stone. How are you today?'

'Sasha, stop. There's no time. Is she there?'

'Dr Fuentes has gone for the day. Can I take a—'

I cut in again, told her what had happened.

'She is losing bloods?'

'Yes.'

'One moment.'

A few seconds later a new voice. Sasha must have transferred me to a doctor. She kicked off in Russian, caught herself, and switched to garbled English, but I got the gist. 'You must to go to the nearest public hospital, Mr Stone. Where is your position?'

I gave her the main and a cross street. I heard a rapid exchange in Russian, a short pause and the clatter of a keyboard.

'OK . . . You will be needing City Hospital Number Seventy, on Federated Avenue.'

'Anna doesn't want a public hospital. We—'

'Mr Stone, are you wanting two dead people?'

She had a point. Anna's head had lolled forward and I couldn't even tell if she was conscious. I pressed the red button, sparked up the Maps app and scrabbled to input Federated Avenue. By the time I got moving again I had half of Moscow's drivers flipping me the finger. The other half soon joined in as the Touran fish-tailed into the stream of traffic and my foot hit the floor.

4

I didn't see many films as a kid but even from half a kilometre away I reckoned City Hospital Number Seventy could have doubled for the workhouse in *Oliver Twist*.

A grime-encrusted, red-and-white barrier blocked our path. The guy in the gatehouse tried to turn us away, as Moscow hospitals do unless you arrive by prior written arrangement, ambulance or with Vladimir Putin in your passenger seat. A local politician had had a heart attack outside one a few months earlier and staggered to the main gate, but rules are rules, security said. You couldn't just wander in off the street. He turned around, collapsed over the barrier, and headed for the Great Politburo in the Sky.

I wasn't about to take no for an answer and they didn't need a grasp of English to understand my thousand-yard stare and all the cash I had on me. The barrier lifted and I raced past signs that showed a baby and red writing.

The hospital wasn't one big building. It was more like

a campus, a maze of rectangular dark-brown brick buildings for different disciplines, set in what had probably been intended to look like parkland. But the rural idyll had well and truly gone out of the window. The ground was dry-packed mud, strewn with dog-ends and takeaway wrappers. It was badly tarmacked in places, with tree roots and weeds pushing through the cracked and buckled surface.

The birth-house block was midway in. I pulled up outside the main doors and ran round to help Anna out. We were greeted by sounds of bedlam. New mothers pleaded and cried from the upper windows; the men below shouted back. Rain started to pepper the mounds of dog-ends, empty beer cans and discarded news-papers that surrounded them.

I half cradled, half carried Anna to the front of the reception queue. Three women in white coats and badly knitted cardigans sat behind the desk. Their eyes were like prison guards'. One look was enough to tell me that the only way for us to avoid extreme bodily injury was to wait in line while they bollocked the people in front of us.

Their fellow staff members buzzed back and forth at warp speed, clipboards at the ready. It reminded me of the British Army: walk around with a purposeful look and a clipboard, and everybody thinks you're doing something important. I knew plenty of lads who criss-crossed camp all day, doing absolutely nothing.

A couple of guys in doctor's uniforms – and what looked like half-sized chef's hats – pushed through a door to our right, and then reappeared some time later in biker's kit.

We finally reached the front. Receptionist Number

One clearly felt the whole thing was a massive inconvenience, but she filled in the admission forms. An orderly appeared with a wheelchair and began whisking Anna away. I made to follow, but the Gorgons at the desk had other ideas. The scariest of the three pressed a buzzer under the desk and two grey-shirted security guards materialized behind them. I got the drift. No partners allowed. No exceptions. What did I think this was? A private clinic?

5

15.50 hrs

I'd been waiting in the main reception for an hour, maybe two. I still knew nothing about what was happening to Anna and was expecting big things from the change of shift. I let the new cardigans and grey shirts settle in for a moment, then went up to the desk and asked if there was any news. Like the last lot, none of them spoke a word of English, and the look they gave me said they wouldn't have helped me even if they could.

Anna had warned me about this shit a while back, when I told her there was no point in going private. She said the Russian maternity system was a throwback to Communist days, and in no hurry to join the twenty-first century.

These 'birth-houses' were badly run and badly equipped. Up to eight women at a time gave birth in the same room while one doctor zigzagged between them. The Soviet empire had needed to repopulate after Hitler and his mates had wiped out twenty million of them. Now Russia's population had dropped another two million in the last ten years. The baby conveyor-belt needed to keep running, without people like me getting in the way.

Women in labour were treated like prisoners. Pain relief was a luxury. Mobile phones were forbidden. There were a couple of pay phones down in the lobby. If you had the coins you could make a call; if not, tough shit. Friends and family weren't allowed into the ward. Husbands or partners couldn't help their women through their contractions, and mothers couldn't even cuddle their new-borns: they were whisked away as soon as they drew breath, and not brought back until feed time.

Anna was still a heavy-duty socialist, but I'd begun to see why she'd been so keen to organize a birth contract with a private clinic.

I glanced down at my iPhone, in case Katya had returned one of my six calls. She hadn't.

I decided to join the other fathers in the rain. They sheltered under an assortment of umbrellas, carrier bags or newspapers, and smoked like Chernobyl reactors as they waited for their women to press their noses up against the glass.

Each window had a number painted on it. If you knew which room your partner was in, you could holler. If not, it could be hours before you found out what was going on – or days if the birth had gone badly and Mum didn't have the right change for the pay phone.

I finally spotted a sweat-covered Anna two storeys up. I could tell she was exhausted. She wiped the condensation from the upper pane and looked out. Then she scrawled a message in the lower pane: *Boy – sick – Katya . . .*

My first almost overpowering instinct was to turn and run back into the lobby. But I knew I wouldn't get anywhere. The message at the welcome desk was clear: if I kept fucking about, the only people I'd be seeing were the security guards, followed swiftly by the police.

I waved and broke into a run, yelling into my mobile as my call was routed to Katya's voicemail again.

There was no parking inside the hospital complex, so I'd dumped the people-carrier in a nearby side street. I turned the corner, skidding on the cobbles, to see that it was packed with vehicles – none of which was mine. The Touran had either been stolen or impounded.

I called Katya again and told her to stay put in her apartment. 'I'm on my way to you now.'

I wasn't exactly sure where the nearest Metro station was, but knew I'd find one close by. They were all over the place.

6

Novogireevo Metro station

I was on the eastern side of the city, on the outer ring road. Heading south-west meant one change.

Moscow trains took their lead from the public hospitals. They were packed and dirty, and the carriage I boarded also had its own welcoming committee – four Judge Dredd lookalikes with white helmets and black, rib-like polymer body armour sorting out a couple of pickpockets.

The far end of the thing had been cleared. Both suspects lay face down, hands cuffed behind their backs, and two of our friendly neighbourhood coppers were emptying the contents of their day-sacks onto the floor while their mates gave the bad boys a good kicking. I watched the mobile phones and wallets they'd been nicking hit the deck and reckoned their day was turning out as badly as mine.

None of the other passengers took much notice. Thieving was part of everyday life down here. In a city riven by gang wars, where private armies took out their opponents with RPGs in shopping malls, this little incident wouldn't even be worth mentioning to the family when they got home.

I gripped the rail above me with both hands as we swayed from side to side. Everyone was on guard. The cops had nailed two pickpockets, but those guys hunted in packs, using the motion of the train for cover.

The pickpockets were hauled to their feet and three of the cops pushed them out onto the platform as soon as we stopped at the next station. The fourth stayed behind to reload phones and wallets into the day-sacks, and the cash into his jacket pocket. They had a different way of handling evidence in Russia.

The bystanders mumbled away as the train moved off again, and spread the whole length of the carriage. I made my way down the aisle and leaned against the connecting door, checking the time on my iPhone every few seconds, as if it was going to get me to Katya any quicker.

7

Katya and Anna had connected six or seven years before I arrived on the scene. Katya was from Cuba. Or, rather, her parents had been. Castro had sent them to study in the Soviet Union. They had decided to stay in Moscow and got married. Her father had held down some nameless job in the Communist hierarchy and they'd had two kids; a younger brother was floating about somewhere among the second-generation Hispanics and Africans that flooded the city, but Katya didn't like to talk about him. She didn't talk about much at all, really.

I wasn't sure what she thought of me, and wasn't that fussed. All she knew was that I'd met Anna while I was working security for CNN, keeping the news crews' noses clean. I guess I must have been Anna's bit of rough.

Katya had trained as an obstetrician and bumped into Anna while she was working for an NGO in Central America. Anna was reporting on the TB epidemic in Mexico City's slums that Katya was trying to stem.

They were the same age, well educated, and both from Moscow. They spoke English in the 'World America' accent CNN loved so much, and Katya's Spanish made her the perfect interpreter.

She'd faded out of sight until just over a year ago when Anna had got an email out of the blue to say she was coming back to Moscow to work for Magee WomanCare International, the largest non-profit private provider of women's health services in the USA. They had an outreach programme, trying to improve health-care conditions for women and infants in the former Soviet Union.

Almost immediately she was headhunted by one of the new private clinics that had sprung up to cater for the biggest collection of billionaires on the planet. She worked for the Perinatal Clinic in the south-west of the city, and rented a flat nearby. No more poverty, no more rickets and malnutrition, just women too posh to push, whose only problem was working out whether to use the blue birthing pool or the green. And that was where we'd been aiming for when Hospital Number Seventy had got in the way. Now she had to show what she was really made of.

I willed the train to go faster. I drummed my fingers against the glass. I wanted Anna and my boy out of there and down to the posh place, with Katya in charge.

Katya was even harder to pin down than I was. She didn't drive, didn't use cabs, kept herself very much to herself. She didn't seem to have that many mates, and there were Masai tribesmen living in mud huts with more social networking presence. It looked like she was taking NATO's perception of its threat to global stability very seriously indeed; they ranked the top six players with the power to fuck up the planet as China, India, Facebook, the USA, Twitter and Indonesia. Facebook and Twitter were more connected to their community than any of the other four, and that made them particularly scary. What if they started to have their own ideas about how our world should be run? That was something none of the others liked to think about.

The reason I wasn't online, however, wasn't because I didn't want to be part of the new revolution. I liked not being public property. And I'd fucked up or killed plenty of enemies of the state in my time. I had lots of good reasons to stay hidden. After two years undercover in Derry with 14 Intelligence Group, identifying Provisional IRA active-service units and recruiting sources, it wasn't just my back I had to watch. I'd worked alongside Special Branch officers. If anyone managed to link my face and my CV to theirs, it would put them and their families at risk. And it wasn't just in Northern Ireland that people had long memories. My old mates in the drug cartels did too.

An old woman sitting under the no-smoking sign opposite me lit up a cigarette and gave me a glare that said: 'It wasn't like this when Khrushchev was in charge.' I started to laugh. It was the first time I'd done so all day.

8

South-west Moscow

I pressed the button for the old guy to open the door but didn't hear a buzz. Cupping my hands against the wired glass, I peered into the dimly lit foyer. The little fucker had gone AWOL again. He seemed to spend most of his time tucked away in his back room, and judging by the smell, he didn't just knock back his own vodka, he brewed it as well.

I gave the door a shove and it swung back on its hinges. Katya's fellow residents didn't want to hang around outside for longer than they had to. I walked into the lobby. Harsh white light from the overhead fluorescents was doing the concierge no favours. He was supposed to keep the public areas clean, but the swirls of dirty water where he'd lost interest in mopping up the trail of rain-sodden footprints were plain as day.

There was no lift: the management company had gone out of business before it could be installed. I headed up the stairs to the second floor. It was a boring four-storey block, built of glass and a strange yellow brick, probably a job lot from a factory demolition. These places had been thrown together in the nineties to cater for the new professionals spreading out of the city centre, with more of an eye on the developer's margin than the design awards. Any gleam had long gone, and lack of maintenance and bad workmanship had taken its toll. The New Russia was just like everywhere else: sell 'em dreams, ship 'em shit.

As I walked along the thinly carpeted corridor, my nostrils were assaulted by the stench of the flowery disinfectant Russians love to spray around their houses. Maybe it's the only way they've found to disguise the lingering aroma of boiled cabbage.

I rounded the corner and nearly got knocked off my feet by two big guys in leather jackets. They glanced back at me as I rebounded off the wall, close-mouthed, no smiles, eyes fixed on mine. I got the message: it was my fucking fault.

I raised my hands to shoulder height. '*Izvinite, izvinite . . .*' I might not know much Russian, but being able to apologize your way out of a difficult situation was useful in any language.

The door to 211 was half open. I knocked. No answer. 'Katya?'

I stepped inside, to be greeted by four bare walls and the kind of shiny, IKEA-type furniture that looked as though it had just been unwrapped. The only remotely personal touch in the whole place was a photo of her and Anna pinned to a bulletin board above her telephone. I think Sasha must have taken it in the clinic canteen. I was just visible in the background, sorting out a brew. I wasn't comfortable with it, but Anna liked it, and the two girls looked happier in it than I'd seen either of them for quite a while. Katya was in full Jennifer Lopez mode, hair scraped back in a jet-black bun.

She'd thrown her coat over a nearby chair. Beside it was a mug of coffee.

She appeared from her bedroom, looking flustered, scrambling to throw on a pair of sunglasses.

'Nick! What are you . . . ? I've only just got back.' She did her best to treat me to a welcome grin. 'I think I have an eye infection, maybe. I—'

I didn't have time to fuck around. 'Didn't you get my messages? Anna's had the baby. She's in Seventy. It's not good – the baby's sick and the place is like a *gulag*. They need your help.'

She stared at me, blank-faced, like none of this made sense. Maybe the Jackie Kennedy look was to hide a hangover.

'Hospital Seventy?' She jerked herself back to something approaching reality. 'Is Anna OK?'

'I don't know. I only saw her through an upstairs window. They won't let me go anywhere near either of them. We've got to get her out of there. You make the call – do whatever you have to do. She needs you. They both need you.'

I grabbed her coat and handed her the phone, answering-machine light still blinking. 'You need to sort an ambulance, or we pick them up. I don't want them stuck in that shit-hole.'

She tapped out some numbers and was soon waffling away in Russian as I got the rest of her brew down my neck.

She finished the call and reached for her coat. 'There's no guarantee we can move her, I'm afraid. Pre-term, there are always problems.' Her expression softened. 'I never asked: girl or boy?'

I gave her a grin. 'Boy.'

'What will you call him?'

'I was thinking Dostoevsky, but I reckon Anna prefers Tolstoy.'

9

She didn't have much to say as we headed through the old industrial zone towards Proletarskaya Metro. The sun-gigs were still firmly in place.

I led her past State Ball-bearing Plant Number One, now a memorial to the dead who'd worked there during the Great Patriotic War against the Germans. Historic-monument status hadn't stopped the factory walls decaying. Rusty steel rods stuck out of crumbling concrete, like rotten teeth. The whole area had been earmarked for redevelopment, but I guessed they were still waiting for the right oligarch to come along and make a killing.

We crossed the car park alongside what was left of the Dubrovka Theatre – just one more featureless concrete mess, but the scene of a terrorist gangfuck in 2002, when forty or fifty Chechens had taken control of an 850-strong audience and demanded the withdrawal of Russian troops from their homeland and an end to the Second Chechen War. The message from the Kremlin was, 'Dream on.' After a two-and-a-half-day siege Spetsnaz pumped a chemical agent through the ventilation system, then stormed the building. Thirty-nine of the kidnappers and at least 129 hostages were killed. The Russian authorities didn't turn a hair. While the West's stated objective would have been to rescue the hostage, theirs was: kill the terrorist.

The Metro station was a riot of shiny granite pillars, black-and-white ceramic tiles and anodized aluminium hammer-and-sickle motifs. The train was almost deserted: everybody was heading in the opposite direction at the end of the working day.

We drew a few quizzical glances from some of the older women. They were clearly trying to work out if the tall olive-skinned woman in the shades was my girl-friend or a whore. And if she was a whore, why would I want a foreign one when there were thousands of beautiful porcelain-white Russians to choose from? That was how the older generation here thought. And why was she wearing sunglasses on the Metro? To hide her identity? Or had I been giving her a good slapping?

We sat in silence, rocking with the train. Katya held her arms rigid on her thighs. I could feel the tension coming off her like nerve gas, fuck knew why. I'd leave her to deal with whatever was going on in her little world. Right now I just needed her to sort out what was going wrong in mine.

The doors opened to let a group of office workers on board. They took a sneaky look at Katya and gave me the stink-eye. I couldn't tell if they were sneering at me or simply jealous of the way she looked.

I checked the map above their heads. Two more stops to Novogireevo.

10

I cupped my hands around my mouth, as if that was going to help me be heard above the din of the other long-range conversations. 'Anna! Anna!' It was like being a little kid again, calling up from the square in my housing estate to see if a mate would come out to play.

There was no sign of movement at her window. We both hollered in unison. Then I let Katya have a go on her own: maybe a woman's voice would pierce the male chorus.

Eventually, a shadow crossed the window and Anna leaned out. The colour of her skin echoed the strange green apron she now wore, but at least she was up, she was standing, she was breathing.

I part yelled, part mimed: 'You seen the boy?'

I hoped she could lip-read, because a volley of shouts drowned me out.

Anna shook her head. 'Intensive Care . . .'

Katya gave her a wave. 'Sasha's told them you're one of our patients . . . Go and tell whoever is on your floor that your obstetrician is here. Tell them she wants to see the infant.'

Anna caught my eye and we nodded at each other. She was going to do exactly what she was told.

Katya and I started along the path towards the main entrance. 'Nick, they won't want to let Anna be with the child. And they won't let you near him either. It's the Russian way. They're paranoid about infection.'

As we walked through the large main wooden doors, I crunched a Pepsi Max carton underfoot, crushing the ice that was still inside; a stream of diluted cola spewed out. 'You've *got* to be joking. They're worried about infection – in this shit-hole?'

She gestured towards Reception. 'Bureaucracy and prejudice – a dynamite combination. This won't be plain sailing either. Private obstetricians seem to antagonize them – I'm not one of *them*.'

'So what are you telling me? I've got to go and steal the baby?'

She stopped, not sure if I was serious. 'No, no, no . . .'

A couple of nurses sauntered past, chatting and smoking, followed almost immediately by a couple of half-size chef's hats tapping a piece of paper and shouting at each other.

Katya leaned closer to me. 'I'm just telling you that the system is still stuck in the old ways. They might decide your baby isn't fit enough to be moved. And they have the final say. I can't overrule them.'

'But you're going to sort it out, yeah?'

She gave me a gleaming smile. 'Wait here and let me get on with it.' She pointed to one of the three wooden chairs that stood like islands in a sea of discarded cigarette packets and food wrappers. 'They won't allow you to come with me, and I could be an hour or so.'

She hesitated. 'And don't forget, you might have to make a contribution.'

A contribution. That was the best word for it I'd heard yet.

She got back on her mobile and I headed for the chairs. As soon as she was out of sight I turned towards the fire door.

11

I needed to do something. I wasn't sure what, but I couldn't just sit there and pick my arse.

I sheltered by the exit, out of the drizzle, and didn't have long to wait before one of the staff emerged, helmet in hand. I was through the door without him even noticing.

You could have died of smoke inhalation in the narrow corridor I found myself in. A comedy show blared from a distant TV, complete with bad canned laughter. There was a faint smell of coffee from somewhere.

Banks of lockers lined the walls on each side of me, some of them open. White coats and chef's hats in all shapes and sizes. I helped myself to one of each, not forgetting the clipboard, switched on my internal GPS and headed in what I hoped was the direction of Anna's window. The occasional nurse and doctor cast me a sidelong glance, but I carried on walking. I was in undercover-ops mode. I was a fully functioning medic; I had a reason to be there. If you can convince yourself of that, you convince those around you too. And the further you are behind the lines, the easier it becomes. No one expects the enemy to be at the heart of their world.

I pushed through yet another set of heavy wooden swing doors. Years of grey men had worn away layers of grey paint before me. The ward stank like a school canteen. There were twenty beds, maybe, ten on each side. No privacy curtains, nothing like that, they were just separated by a bedside locker. Three women whose faces I recognized were still shouting from the windows.

Anna was about halfway down on the left, huddled in an orange furry blanket.

She didn't look up as I approached. She was too busy staring at her feet. Her sweat-soaked hair was tied back at the nape of her neck. Dried blood caked her calves.

I leaned over her as two nurses walked past, leaving a cloud of cigarette smoke in their wake. 'Hello.'

Anna was too switched on to show excitement. We didn't kiss either – not that we'd done that for a while.

I looked down at her legs. She followed my gaze. 'The shower's broken. Where's Katya?'

'Downstairs, doing the paperwork. I wanted to come on ahead in case we need a Plan B.' I paused. 'What about you? You OK?'

'Nicholas, they say he's stable. But he's in the ICU. They won't let me see him because I'm not feeding him. He's too small to breastfeed.' She grabbed my arm. 'They keep saying he's fine, but . . .'

The woman in the next bed smiled conspiratorially. Anna tilted her head towards her. 'This is her third time, poor girl, so she knows where they take them. He's on the fourth floor. I've tried to go up there, but they won't let me.'

'They still got your mobile?'

'They said it was a source of contamination.'

I reached into my jeans and left her my iPhone. 'Keep it on vibrate. Soon as I know, you'll know.' I gripped her hand. 'I'll find him. We're getting you both out of here.'

She pointed at a sequence of numbers on her wristband. 'That's what he's called.'

12

I reached the fourth floor and scanned the signage. An icon of a baby and an arrow sent me down a corridor to the left of a pair of thick plastic doors that must once have been transparent.

The sound of crying drew me into a room full of plastic cots with clipboards at their feet. I could read Anna's name in Cyrillic, but didn't see anything I recognized on the first board. I checked the next one, then noticed that each baby had an ID band with a serial number on one hand and foot.

I suddenly realized these guys were all too old, and none of them was in an incubator. At least someone had given the place a splash of disinfectant. It smelt clean, even if it wasn't.

I carried on to the next ward. There wasn't much clipboard activity in here; a few nurses sitting down, reading, and another bent over an incubator. I couldn't see inside it, just the mass of tubes leading to the monitors. She turned away and I caught a glimpse of purple skin through the Perspex. Fuck, was that him?

The nurse shuffled further down the ward. Mine wasn't the only baby in Intensive Care.

A couple of guys in white coats walked past, one offering the other a cigarette. What was it with the Russians and nicotine? Somewhere along the corridor, a woman yelled in pain. The white coats didn't even look up. The lunatics really were running the asylum.

The babies were all tightly wrapped in blankets. Some had their chests exposed and plastered with ECG sensors. Every little head had been tucked into a Tubigrip beanie.

I started checking clipboards, looking for the last four numbers of Anna's sequence. It was like being back in the army.

At last I found it: 8564.

I stood at the foot of the cot, staring down at this very small bundle. A ventilating tube was taped into his mouth, a feed tube through his nose. Two ECG leads disappeared under his blanket and poked out near his chest. Machinery all around us made more pinging noises than Kraftwerk. I caught a glimpse of a blue and mottled face among the apparatus.

I stood there looking at him. My son. I didn't know what I'd been expecting – it had been so much hassle getting to this point. I knew my life had changed: this little blob in a Perspex bubble was depending on me. I just hoped we'd have the chance to get to know each other.

I cut away from all that.

There were more important things to worry about than how I felt. Right now it was all about him and Anna, and getting them out of there.

13

I headed back out into the corridor, binning the white kit on top of a shelf-load of ceramic bed-pans. Katya was still in the reception area, alongside a doctor in the full Gordon Ramsay, Russian-style.

'I've just seen Anna. You got your mobile with you?'

She nodded and pulled it out of her pocket. 'This is Dr Potznik. If all goes well, we should be able to get them back to the clinic tonight.'

The doc's swarthy features tagged him as East Russian. He looked like life in Putinworld was suiting him: he had the kind of comfortable, three-good-meals-a-day-and-plenty-of-vodka look that matched his bushy grey moustache.

'One of our ambulances is on its way here now.'

'The boy's last four digits are eight five six four. Make sure the doc picks up the right one, yeah? I'll wait here.'

I left them to it and tapped my number into Katya's mobile. It took Anna a while to answer.

'Katya?'

'No, it's me. Listen. It's all good. As long as he can be moved, you'll both be in the clinic tonight.'

'Have you seen him?'

'You bet. He's a beautiful little blue lump. He weighs two thousand and six grams, and he's forty-eight centimetres long. Is that good?'

I heard a sigh of relief. 'Good enough.'

14

Katya didn't reappear for an hour. When she did, she had my mobile in her hand. She held it out and we swapped.

'OK, we're leaving.'

'Now?'

She smiled and crooked a finger for me to follow her as she exited the main doors.

A shiny new Mercedes ambulance waited at the kerb, with red signs that said 'Perinatal Clinic' in Cyrillic and English, a driver and two nurses in crisply laundered uniforms.

'I've got a couple more things to take care of at this end. Anna's getting dressed. She says she needs her grab bag.'

I told her about our missing wagon. In our rush to get to the hospital, we'd left the bag behind.

'Then you need to go back to your apartment, pick up a nightdress, clothes, whatever else she needs.'

'She's going to stay at the clinic?'

'Of course – as long as your little boy needs to. We'll

meet you there, yes?' She gestured at the nurses and turned to walk back into the birth-house.

I grabbed her arm. 'Katya?' She recoiled for a moment, as if she expected me to hit her. 'Thank you.' I headed for the main gate.

15

Sucking in oxygen, I ran all the way from the Metro, doing my best to dodge the puddles gathering around the blocked drains. I opened the apartment door and headed straight through the living room into what the letting agent had called the spare bedroom.

My boy wasn't going to need much while he was stuck on a ventilator and being force-fed, but I decided to grab a bit of everything. I ripped open cardboard boxes and plastic bags full of romper suits, mittens, bottles, creams, and ran through a mental check-list of questions for Katya: what, where and when-type things. How long did a pre-term usually have to stay at the clinic? When would it be possible to bring him and Anna home?

I fished some Babygros and socks out of a Baby Infanti bag. It was my favourite of the maternity stores that had sprung up around Moscow for the new middle class. The idea of baby infantry always made me chuckle – it was why I'd been calling him 'little soldier'. Anna didn't get it, but it made me laugh.

I reversed out of the room with my arms full, and went to grab a Coke from the fridge. I didn't even make it to the kitchen door. A plastic bag over the head slows you down at the best of times, and this one was pulled against my nose and mouth with a huge grunt of exertion. I dropped what I was carrying and threw myself back against my attacker, but he was big enough to absorb the impact.

I tried to drop to the floor and twist myself free. The grunts behind me got harder and faster. The plastic rippled as I breathed. I brought up my hands to try to tear it away but they were immediately slapped aside.

There were at least two of them.

I tensed my stomach muscles, knowing what was coming next. A fist slammed into my solar plexus and I buckled at the knees. I tried to calm my breathing – the bag was moulded to my face, like clingfilm. My sweat was like glue. The pressure around my neck increased. My head felt as if it was about to explode.

But I knew they didn't want me dead: if they had, I would have been by now. They wanted me to collapse, to asphyxiate. They wanted me alive. So I complied. I gave myself up. I leaned forward and stopped fighting. This time they let me drop to the floor. The bag loosened; the hands controlling it shifted to my shoulders.

Before they had a chance to do anything more, I thrust up my hands and grabbed at the body above me. I felt an ear, then wet hair. I gripped the back of his head as hard as I could and raised mine, ready to take the pain. We both snarled with aggression, then he screamed as our skulls made contact and I rolled aside, pulling the bag off my head.

All I could see were bubbles of red light and star-bursts of white. All I could hear was the rasp of air in tortured lungs, his or mine, I didn't know. The pain went as my adrenalin took over.

There were two bodies. The one I'd head-butted was on his knees, trying to stem the flow of blood from his shattered nose. The other was coming in fast from my left.

Scrambling to my feet, I grabbed the TV remote from the arm of the settee. Holding it dagger-style, thumb over the top of the slim plastic sheath, I brought it down between his eyes. He staggered back but didn't fall. I got right up close, grabbed hold of the back of his neck and rammed the remote again and again into his face.

I left him to sort out his own little world of pain as his mate hauled himself off his knees. I gave him the remote treatment too, in the temple, three, maybe four times. When the plastic finally cracked I jammed it into his mouth, forcing it with both hands to the back of his throat. His eyes bulged as it cut off his oxygen supply and vomit forced its way between my fingers. His arms and legs flailed for a moment, then went limp. His mate had done the right thing, as far as I was concerned, and made a run for it.

16

I collapsed onto the settee, arms and legs outstretched, my arse hanging over the edge as I wiped his puke from my hands. The acrid smell filled the room, though maybe not as pungently as it would have done if the remote hadn't remained stuck in his throat. Only the red power button was visible between his froth-covered lips.

I didn't want to get up, but I knew I had to. I was the lucky one. Whoever was stretched out on the engineered oak by my feet wasn't moving at all.

I wasn't going to have to raise my hands in supplication and say '*Izvinite, izvinite*,' to him ever again.

As I took another couple of deep, rasping breaths, I wondered what had happened to his mate. Thank fuck he'd done a runner. I sucked in another lungful of air and dragged myself upright. I went over to the door, slammed it shut and slid home the bolts.

My body shrieked at me to go and lie down for a while, but I had too much to do. I went back to the dead one. There was nothing in his light-brown leather-jacket pockets but a pack of Marlboro Lights, a purple disposable lighter, a bundle of notes and a few coins. No wallet. No ID. He was sterile. That meant one of two things to me: that they were really switched on, or they'd been told what to do by someone who was. Going by the performance of the runner, they weren't the sharpest blades in the drawer. Which meant they'd been taking orders from elsewhere, and he'd bottled it.

This one had a black jumper, no shirt. The edge of a tattoo showed at the V-neck. I pulled it up by the waistband to take a better look. His stomach and chest were covered with ink. There were the normal tribal tats – sunrises, flags, snakes wrapped around daggers – but the blurred, badly done ones were more interesting.

He'd obviously done time and served in the military. That wasn't unusual in this part of the world, where conscription was still alive and well. His squaddie tattoo, a tank crushing a body, suggested he hadn't been much of a star when he was in, just one of the chorus line. That was why he was lying where he was instead of me. The other pix were of bears shagging women and rats with numbers above their heads, which would tell anyone in the know where he'd been imprisoned and why. There was one of the Kremlin and what looked like a goblin or a dwarf holding a wand and putting a spell on the place. I couldn't interpret them in any detail, but they were obviously the story of his life. The only chapter missing was the one explaining what he and his mate had been up to with Katya.

She hadn't just got home when I arrived. She'd had time to take her coat off, and there was warm coffee by the answerphone. Two of the messages I'd left had been played, but not the third. Eye infection? Maybe they'd hit her, or she'd been crying. Whatever, she had a fuck of a lot of explaining to do.

I sat on the floor beside the leather jacket and punched numbers into my mobile. As ever, Katya wasn't responding. I punched in another set as I headed for the bedroom.

'Have you found everything, Nicholas?'

'More than I bargained for.' I pulled T-shirts and nighties out of her top drawer, then swept her toiletries into a sports bag, like a burglar working against the clock. 'You at the clinic yet?'

'Sure. He's stable and in a unit and they're carrying out some more tests. I'm with him.'

'Katya?'

'No. She took a call. As soon as we got here she had to leave. She'll be back later.' She hesitated. 'Are you staying here as well?'

'You want me to?' A panic alarm was ringing in my head. 'I'll see you both soon.'

I felt behind the bedside cabinet for my Heckler & Koch .45 Compact. The Russians loved German kit. Maybe that was why Angela's mob had overtaken us as the third biggest arms dealers on the planet – and its third biggest exporter after China and the USA.

This thing was a snubby semi-automatic .45 close-protection weapon with an eight-round magazine. The frame was polymer the same colour as the leather jacket next door; the top-slide was black steel. It had been cheap, and easy to get hold of. Maybe the dealer had stuck it together from write-offs, like he did with the dodgy motors in his saleroom. I didn't care much. It worked, and that was all that mattered.

The Compact had a single action, once it was made

ready and the hammer was fully back, but I hit the lever on its left-hand side to release it and ensure that the trigger needed a hard squeeze, like a revolver.

With a full mag and one in the chamber I had nine rounds to kick off with, and two spare mags. If I needed any more than that I really was in the shit. I shoved it into my waistband. No need to check the safety: there wasn't one.

I picked up all the bags and took the lift down to my battered navy blue VW Golf in the basement.

17

The old guy on the desk had done his usual vanishing trick and the main door was still ajar. Rain had soaked the rough cork matting he'd laid out to protect the tiles, or what was left of them.

I took the stairs two and three at a time. Before I reached the landing, I pulled out the HK and checked the chamber, pushing back on the top-slide with the palm of my hand until I could see the glint of a .45 case in the ejection opening. Instinct made me check that the spare mags were still in the left pocket of my jeans, with the business end of the rounds facing away from my bollocks. Nothing to do with protecting the family jewels: I wanted to be able to ram it straight into the pistol grip housing, not have to twist it around or turn it upside-down.

I took a couple of deep breaths and did a final shake to get the rain off my hair and my face, and turned into the corridor.

I lay down just short of Katya's entrance, the side of my face flat against the carpet. No light spilled through the crack beneath the door. No sound, either. On my feet again, I stepped back and shoulder-barged it above the handle. The frame splintered without much complaint and I jinked right into the darkness, crouching low to present a smaller target. My HK was up at forty-five degrees, ready to react.

I kept still. I held my breath, listening for any sound above the rain pounding against the windows. The flashing red-and-blue neon sign further down the street told me it was Miller Time.

I straightened slowly, pushing the door shut, then hit the light switch. Her black raincoat was back over the arm of the dark blue settee. I quickly scanned her bedroom and shower room, half expecting to find her lying in the same condition as her mate in the leather jacket in our flat.

Her clinic pass, which hung from a red lanyard because she was always forgetting it, and her flat keys were both missing from the key-press stuck to the side of the fridge. The light was still flashing on her answering machine.

I rang her mobile and heard three rings coming from her coat pocket. The bulletin board above her landline was empty.

I tucked the HK firmly into my waistband and legged it back into the corridor – as you do when you have a vanishing woman and a missing photo to locate, a dead body to attend to, and another attacker on the loose.

The rain pummelled my head as I fumbled with the VW lock – the fob hadn't worked since way back – and jumped in. The engine started at the third time of asking and the windscreen steamed up, to match the fog in my brain.

I didn't drive off straight away. I had another phone call to make.

18

Perinatal Clinic

27 August 2011
05.54 hrs

I sat inches from Anna's bed, our heads bathed in the
glow of coloured lights on the ventilator and monitors.
My high-backed chair stank so badly of disinfectant it
was a miracle she'd managed to doze off. My boy was
asleep too – or so I assumed. There had been no movement from the Perspex box on the other side of the bed
since I'd got there. All I could see of him was a reassur-
ingly pink nose poking out from a blanket. He was still
wrapped up like a parcel, with the same Tubigrip
beanie on his head.

The only sound was the steady bleeping from the
machines and every couple of seconds the gentle hiss of
oxygen. The clinic was still in night mode and all blinds
were down. The window that divided us from the
corridor was double-glazed. I opened the venetian

blinds a touch to allow me a clear view down towards the lift and the stairs. Anybody entering this floor would have to come that way. Right now it was quiet, apart from the occasional squeak of a nurse's shoe on the polished floor.

Anna hadn't been too worried about Katya going AWOL. Everything in her private room was as it should be. The boy beside her was in good shape now, and so was she. And at last she had the chance to get her head down.

The sight of her lying there reminded me of the moment she'd told me she was pregnant, and held my head against her chest. She'd stroked my hair and whispered, 'I've got responsibilities now.'

Stomach lurching, I'd managed to grin back. 'Sounds like I have too.'

I kept the HK under my right thigh and my shoulders straight against the back of the chair. Less than thirty minutes later the light at the end of the corridor bloomed, then faded. The lift doors had opened and closed. Now I saw shadows flicker against the far wall. It looked like there were three or four of them.

I eased the weapon sideways, gripping it in my right hand and resting it between my thigh and the chair arm. My eyes were fixed on the corridor. Whoever this was, I was going to know soon. There were definitely four of them. The one in the lead was a nurse. Her shoes squeaked; the others' didn't.

Frank's men were in dark suits and ties, as if they'd been taking fashion tips from the agents in *The Matrix*. I hadn't seen Genghis and Mr Lover Man since Frank's private jet had dropped me in Egypt five months ago. They hadn't wasted any time with the 5:2 diet.

These boys were still big; it was part of their job spec.

The one I didn't recognize stood like a guardsman, eyes alert. I guessed he was ex-Spetsnaz, or at least trained by them. Mr Lover Man was a Nigerian man-mountain with nostrils like the Mont Blanc Tunnel. He always looked like he was about to inflict pain, and was probably the only black man in Moscow the right-wing gangs crossed the street to avoid. When I'd last seen him, there were blue and red beads tying off each braid of his cornrows, and a patch under his chin was pebble-dashed with shaving rash. The beads were all bright red now, and the zits had been replaced by a thin scar running up his left cheek.

The guy beside him was only fractionally shorter and had come straight from the steppes. He looked like a painting I'd seen of Genghis Khan, but with a number-one haircut and wispy goatee. He could have been a direct descendant of the great tyrant for all I knew, but I wasn't going to ask.

These two weren't big on chat, even though we had plenty to talk about. We'd flown out of Somalia together after I'd rescued Frank's son from kidnappers. But that was then. Time flies; things change.

Maybe that was why they stared at me now like we'd never set eyes on each other.

19

I slid out of Anna's room and closed the door gently behind me.

Frank's men stood like statues as I put out my hand. I got non-committal shakes back, but so what? They were there, and that was all that mattered.

I gave Mr Lover Man my keys and the penthouse address. He studied them both for a moment, then passed them to the Guardsman. I could see Anna watching us through the blinds. Her eyes followed me back into the room.

'What's happening, Nicholas?' Her voice was low. It was like the dim lighting toned everything down. 'They're not here to wet the baby's head, are they?'

I closed the door and took the HK from my waistband. Anna watched as I sat back down and slid the weapon under my thigh. I knew she wasn't happy. The oxygen machine gave a sigh. I knew exactly how it felt. 'They've come here because I asked Frank for help. We need his help. So does Katya.'

I gave her the headlines. Anna showed no reaction,

just concentrated on the details, until I got to the part about the body. She lifted a hand. 'Is he still there?'

I nodded. 'Frank's lad is sorting it out.' I hesitated. 'But we've got a bigger problem than that.'

I told her I'd been back to Katya's flat. 'Her coat was still there, but she wasn't. The picture was gone too.'

Anna's jaw muscles tightened. She got it straight away. 'That's why they came to our apartment?' Her look of concern wasn't for herself or for me. She glanced towards the incubator. 'What now?'

'You know anything? Anyone who wants to hurt her? Anything she's said or done that you think was a bit . . . unusual . . . or out of character?'

She took a deep breath and the sigh that followed was more about being pissed off with me than wondering what might have happened to Katya. 'You know what she's like. She never told me much about herself, even in Mexico.'

'She have man trouble, cash problems, drugs?'

Anna shook her head. 'No, nothing like that – and if she did, she'd never have told me. She had a boyfriend in Mexico I didn't know about until she let slip that things weren't working out. I know you've never really liked her, but you know what? Not everybody lives in your shadowy, duplicitous little world.'

She was wrong about that, actually, but now wasn't the time to tell her. I hadn't made up my mind about Katya. I just knew that she'd been lying through her teeth ever since I'd picked her up at her apartment.

'I've got to go away for a while.' I leaned over her, not sure whether I should kiss the top of her head. Not so long ago I'd have done it without thinking. I tucked the

HK under her pillow. 'It's loaded, with a full mag, and made ready.'

Anna had worked in a lot of hostile terrain and knew her way around a weapon. She knew 'loaded' meant the mag was inserted, even if it was empty. Made ready meant there was a round in the chamber. That way, there was no room for accidents.

Her eyelids flickered and she pushed herself upright. 'Does this mean I'm on guard now?'

'Not exactly.' I gestured through the blinds. 'Frank trusts them with his own kid. And I trust them too. Ninety-nine per cent . . .'

Her brow furrowed. 'The HK's for the other one per cent?'

I nodded. 'The only way I can really protect you two is to find out what's going on.'

She didn't argue. 'Where will you start?'

'Peredelkino.'

20

I kept driving west, towards a much bluer sky than the one that still hung over the city. I'd come off the M1 a while back, and the potholes were getting more treacherous. The road was lined with trees. This wasn't Navaho or Chelsea territory. The buildings I began to encounter were ancient and timber-framed. *Dacha*s three storeys high with massive overhanging roofs stood behind huge walls. These were the weekend retreats of wealthy Muscovites, first built in the time of Peter the Great. Then in the early 1930s the Soviets had decided to make it a writers' paradise and all the Russian greats had come here to do their stuff.

I saw cedar tiles cladding a steeply pitched roof and condensation billowing from modern heating ducts. I turned through an enormous set of slowly opening wooden gates.

The VW crunched across the gravel. Trees circled a playground, gardens and a swimming-pool. I carried on round to the back of the house and pulled up behind a Range Rover. In Moscow, real people's cars had white plates with black letters. The Range Rover had red ones with white numbers. Diplomatic plates. You could buy them on the black market – at least twenty-five thousand dollars, more if you threw in the blue flashing lights. They let you travel in the government-designated fast lanes and beat the Moscow jams. Lads with red plates were never stopped.

I got out and climbed the steps onto the wooden veranda. I glimpsed a face at the window before its owner turned away and disappeared.

I knew from my last visit that three doors led off the veranda: a bug screen for the summer, a triple-glazed monster with an aluminium frame, and finally the hand-carved wooden original.

I stepped into a shiny modern kitchen the size of a football pitch, all white marble and stainless steel. It couldn't have provided a more dramatic contrast to the exterior.

Frank was sitting at the white marble table with a closed laptop and a white mug in front of him. He was a small man with short brown hair brushed back and flat with a hint of grey at the temples. He looked like Dracula after a visit to the blood bank.

He obviously liked his men to look like extras in a sci-fi movie, but Frank's own fashion model was less easy to pin down. He sported red cords over dark-brown suede loafers. His shirt was also dark brown, and buttoned all the way up. He'd added a touch of Italian gigolo with a pale yellow sweater draped over his shoulders. He might have thought it was cutting edge, but it wasn't a good look for a man in his mid-forties who could have done with shedding a few pounds and buying himself some socks. What was going through his mind? As with almost everything else he got up to, it was impossible to tell.

'Coffee?' Without looking up, he pointed past me to a machine the size of a nuclear reactor. It stood beside a white marble sink large enough to dismember a body in. 'Help yourself, and sit down over here with me.'

I walked over and pressed every button in sight, hoping that something would start coming out of one of the three spouts. Then I could shove a mug underneath and look like I knew what I was doing.

He leaned forward, gaze level. 'Have you heard from them? Has anyone contacted you?'

The machine showed no sign of whirring into action. 'If they had, I wouldn't need you.'

'And how is the child?' He'd spun on a sixpence, but with no change in his tone. His English was precise, but his accent was surprisingly guttural. He sounded like Hollywood's idea of a Cold War Soviet colonel. His voice gave nothing away. The only time I had ever heard him become remotely human was when I had reunited him with his son. I hoped he could remember what it felt like.

The machine suddenly made a grinding sound.

'He's doing really well. Thanks, Frank.'

Viscous black liquid dribbled out of the middle spout. For a moment I thought I'd struck oil. I shoved a mug under it. 'How's Stefan? He settled in OK?'

I didn't look round. I wasn't too sure if it was the right thing to ask. Maybe he hadn't. Maybe his Somali kidnap experience had fucked with his young head. Seeing your mum's dead body and then having to find a place in your dad's real family was never going to be easy.

21

I spooned a couple of sugars into the pitch-black brew.

Frank's expression still wasn't giving anything away. He crossed his legs, revealing two very white and hairy calves. He shrugged. 'Things are good. My family has gone to embrace the whales.'

He motioned me to sit beside him. 'In Baja California you can reach out from your boat and touch the grey whales. Apparently they're very friendly.' He betrayed a hint of puzzlement. Frank wasn't the cuddly type. In a dog-eat-dog world, he wasn't top Rottweiler by accident.

'So you're alone?'

He devoted his considerable powers of concentration to the task of brushing a speck of something from the back of one large hairy hand with the other. His well-manicured nails glinted in the light, but not as strikingly as the half-million dollars' worth of Lang and Söhne Tourbograph. Sapphire crystals and a hand-stitched crocodile strap obviously didn't come cheap. Putin had one, and the papers were all over it. Someone had calculated that he'd have to live in a cave and go without food and drink for six years to be able to afford one on his declared income. Overnight, it had become the must-have accessory for Frank and his playgroup.

Once he'd attended to his personal grooming he waved at a small dark glass bubble in the ceiling above the sink. 'They're next door, keeping an eye on us. Don't be offended, Nick, but are you carrying a weapon? If so, just say. Don't let them see.'

I caught his drift. If I had been carrying, his guys would have shot first and not bothered to ask questions afterwards. But I was there at Frank's invitation. It would have been an insult for me to think I needed protection.

I shook my head, but Frank was already moving on. 'You have read *Dr Zhivago*, of course. Pasternak wrote it here, you know. In this village.'

I wasn't sure if he was taking the piss, but did my best to look impressed. Maybe, now that he had all the power and money a man could wish for, Frank also wanted respect. He'd bought a big slice of the great writers' heartland. Perhaps he was now aiming to knock out a novel or two and join the immortals.

When he spoke next, it was very quietly. 'To find this scum – is that all you want from me?'

'Frank, I want as much from you as I can get. Finding him is the only way I'll find Katya, the only way I'll find out what the fuck's going on here. And the only way I'll be able to keep Anna and the boy safe.'

'Everything has a cost, Nick.' Frank sighed. 'Everything.'

'I'll cross that bridge when I come to it.'

'Pasternak was a master of social realism.' He looked

110

at his watch. 'I like to think we also do our best to maintain certain . . . traditions . . .' He opened the laptop and swivelled it so we could both see the screen.

He sparked up Skype and tuned in to a webcam. I found myself looking at a naked man, plasticuffed to a chair. He was as heavily tattooed as his mate. There was a brick wall behind him, but no window. He was caught in the unforgiving glare of a mobile fluorescent lamp, the sort builders use on-site.

22

Frank didn't seem remotely interested in the drama that filled his screen. The same went for whoever was behind the camera: the hum of voices sounded as if they were discussing what to have for dinner.

'How did you find him?'

Frank brushed another imaginary speck off his trousers. 'When you look for garbage, you go to the garbage dump.'

His lads kept chatting in the background, apparently oblivious to the loud rasps of their captive fighting to get oxygen into his lungs through swollen, lacerated lips. Frank was more concerned about his thumbnail – a fleck of varnish was starting to chip away from the immaculately buffed tip.

I leaned forward so that I could study the boy on the chair more closely. Just like his dead mate, the runner was covered with ink. A blurred crucifix tattoo took pride of place across his torso; Christ's feet were nailed to his belly button and his face was covered with a tuft of blood-soaked chest hair. The only other patch of blue

I could make out beneath the red was a drawing of an iron cuff around his right ankle with a padlock resting on the top of his foot. The prison ink of choice was usually a mixture of soot and piss, injected into the skin with a sharpened guitar string attached to an electric shaver.

The runner was so ravaged and swollen I couldn't tell if his eyes were closed against the pain or so puffed up he couldn't have opened them even if he'd wanted to. His whole body was covered with bruises that were almost the same colour as his body ink. Blood dribbled from his nose, ears and mouth, and streamed down his legs from a knife cut across the top of each thigh. The damage I'd done him with the remote control paled into insignificance alongside the workout his new best friends had given him.

Frank gathered his empty mug and wandered over to the nuclear reactor. He didn't offer me a refill. He'd have figured if I wanted another brew, I'd ask him for one – or get off my arse and fetch it for myself. He might have every material thing he'd ever dreamed of, and be rocking himself to sleep every night in the cradle of Russian culture, but some things never changed. Frank was Frank. I liked that. At least you knew where you stood.

He waved his spare hand nonchalantly over his shoulder, in the direction of the screen. 'Do I recognize this vermin? Of course I don't.'

'Does he know where Katya is?'

Frank piled sugar into his mug as the nuclear reactor kicked off. 'Yes.'

'Where?'

He turned and headed back to the table with a look

I'd come to know well – as if he had another place to be. He sat down and re-engaged with the screen as he stirred his coffee. 'The two of them are peasants. They were only there to collect your . . . your Cuban woman.'

He took a sip of his brew. It looked like molten tarmac, but he seemed to like it.

'Collect for who? For what?'

'He says he doesn't know why. They were each paid five hundred dollars US by a Vasil Diminetz to make sure she went to Moldova. Half now, half on delivery.'

'Moldova? Why Moldova?'

He shrugged.

'That's it? That's all he knows?'

'Of course not. They always know more. They just don't realize it. Until they are . . . enlightened.'

'She involved with the Moldovans?'

He pursed his lips. 'We do not know yet. These things can take some time.' He tilted his head towards the wreck filling the screen. His hand went up to silence me as he listened to the slow, strange sounds emerging from a mouthful of broken teeth as the invisible interrogators fired another question at him.

I waited as Frank listened, his hand still in the shut-the-fuck-up position.

'They could not find her brother – he has become a ghost. So it seems yours is the only Moscow address in the doctor's file. They saw you in her building . . . They had already seen the photograph, so . . .'

Frank lowered his hand as the body slumped, chin resting on the top of Christ's head.

The fucking photograph. 'So, Frank? So *what*?'

He reached out a finger and poked the gel-like liquid-crystal screen, further distorting the captive's features.

'Diminetz called her and explained that if she didn't come to Moldova her friend and her husband would be killed. That's you, Nick. You and Anna.' Frank sat back in his chair. 'So she did. She went.'

'She's now in Moldova?'

'I presume so.'

'Why?'

'It could be for many reasons. Or none.'

'You know this Diminetz?'

Frank gave me his bad-smell face. 'I know none of these animals. I'm a businessman. These creatures live in the gutter. They are too stupid to see the opportunities that stare them in the face every day. Scum like Diminetz will never understand how to ... elevate himself. They spend their pitiful lives in the gutter.' Frank nodded towards the now motionless body on the screen. 'Where I found him for you.'

Somebody behind the camera shouted as Frank threw some more coffee down his neck. The prisoner didn't respond. Another shout and whatever he said then obviously wasn't the answer they were looking for.

A green fleece filled the screen for a moment as one of the interrogators moved towards him. When I could see the captive again, a pistol had been shoved into the side of his head. There was a dull thud and blood sprayed from his opposite temple. The plasticuffs securing his wrists kept him from falling off the chair. Green Fleece disappeared from view, mumbling to whoever else was behind the camera.

Frank rose to his feet. 'You have a problem, my friend. Find this woman and make her safe, or make sure these people can never find you or your family.'

My eyes locked onto his. 'Can you help me?'

There was no point in going to the police. This was Russia, and Moldova was the same but worse.

His eyes narrowed. 'These things are beneath me now.'

'What about Anna and the baby?'

His expression was still stony, but he nodded. 'I am not an animal. You need to sort this out – for your family's sake.'

'Thank you. I know Genghis and Lover Man will protect her. I've seen them in action.'

He frowned momentarily, then gave a flicker of a smile. He studied my face. 'Things have changed for you, haven't they, Nick? Responsibility. It's something men like us shouldn't be burdened with.' He gave a wry smile. 'But we are burdened, aren't we? Children . . . They are like wounds that never heal.'

PART THREE

PART THREE

1

Chisinau Airport

28 August 2011
12.26 hrs

The automatic doors opened – and it was like I hadn't just changed countries, I'd changed centuries. Moldova's main airport had been built in Brezhnev's time, and the forty years since then had taken their toll. Even the taxi drivers in their old leather jackets and baggy jeans were shabby, and the bits of cardboard they held up looked like they'd been scrawled on with lumps of coal.

Bizarrely, though, like most places this far down the food chain, its mobile-phone coverage was way better than Europe's or America's. I got straight through to Anna. 'Any luck with Lena?'

'She's been in Ukraine, but her assistant says she should be back today. I told her you're on your way, and need some help.'

The charity-shop fashion parade waved their pieces of cardboard at me. Big companies had learned long ago not to flash smart clipboards with corporate logos in places like this. Anyone with a mobile could Google the pick-up name. If the passenger was important, a few quid of ransom money would come in nicely – or business rivals would pay handsomely to find out where the competition was sending its top executives.

Once I'd got past the caveman it was time to be hassled by the guys who wanted to take me to the city in their private cars. I waved them away too.

'I'll be off air for a while. I'm binning the SIM card, OK?'

She understood.

'Anna . . .' I'd been brooding about it on the flight and couldn't let her go without asking. 'Do you know anything about Katya's problems? How she got herself into this drama?'

'People don't tell each other everything, Nicholas. You should know that very well.'

We said our frosty goodbyes and I closed down. I'd call her back after I'd seen Lena. Not just because I wanted updates on the baby, but also because Anna was going to be my ops room while I was on the move – flights, information, anything she could help with from her laptop. Affection didn't seem to be on the agenda.

I slipped my phone back into my pocket. My brown-leather bomber had seen better days too, but it was what I'd always worn for work – along with Timberlands, jeans and a sweatshirt.

It wasn't only the clothes that reminded me I was on a job. I hung the sort of brown nylon pouch around my neck that any middle-aged American tourist would have been proud of. It contained my passport, four hundred dollars in fifties and twenties, and two credit cards – my escape package. It would never leave my body unless I needed it to. It also had a safety-pin tucked into the back. Getting a SIM card out of these iPhones was a fucking nightmare.

I used to wear a watch, but my iPhone had taken over. I carried its charger in another pocket, and a wallet with more USD and one card. That was my lot. The world was full of toothpaste, socks and anything else I might need.

Moldova had slipped through the net during the post-Soviet boom years; all the high-end Western brands had given it a wide berth. Its earning potential was the same as South Sudan's, so what was the point of investing? Starbucks seemed to be the exception – well, sort of. There was a mobile coffee stall tucked into the corner of the arrivals hall. And there wasn't a queue.

I headed for the stall to its left. Scores of cheap, glittery mobile-phone cases and chargers hung like decorations on a Christmas tree. I bought two fifty-dollar Moldcell SIMs and jumped into a taxi.

The white ten-year-old Five Series Beemer stank of cigarette smoke and the minty cologne the middle-aged driver had splashed on to hide a few fragrances of his own. His hair looked like he'd greased it with what was left in the pan after that morning's fry-up. He had about four days' growth and an old jeans jacket, the collar stained dark where it touched his hair.

'Chisinau, Hotel Cosmos, mate. Hotel Cosmos? Chisinau?'

He grunted and we set off on what I remembered

from last time was about a fifteen-K drive. The road was lined each side by fields. As in most old Eastern-bloc shit-holes, the West offloaded their DDT and any other banned chemicals and pesticides there. They'd ripped the heart out of the land. Soil erosion and third-world farming methods put the final nails in their coffin. Not only was Moldova a long way from self-sufficient, it didn't have a seaport. Landlocked to the west by Romania and to the north, south and east by Ukraine, it depended on their Black Sea coastlines, and their dodgy road and rail networks. No wonder the locals had had to turn their hand to trafficking and extortion.

At least the road into the city had been given a new layer of tarmac since I was last there. It meant I could replace my Russian SIM with one of the new ones without waiting between potholes.

2

Moldova was the Silicon Valley of organized crime in Eastern Europe. And, like Microsoft and Google, the local gangsters had bucked the current recession. When the Iron Curtain was finally pulled down in 1989, it had left a vacuum for people like Frank to fill. He was one of the guys who had a talent for being in the right place at the right time. He'd made his money and got out of the game. Well, sort of. A lot of the others just wanted more and more of what was out there – and there was plenty if you knew where to look and weren't too choosy about who you fucked up. Organized crime accounted for 15 per cent of world trade: ten trillion dollars – two-thirds of the USA's GDP – and it looked like Vasil Diminetz was taking his own little slice.

I unclipped the safety-pin, fished out my Russian SIM, cracked it in half and swallowed it. Then I cancelled the call log and texts. Whatever happened, I didn't want anyone to know who and where I'd called – inside or outside Moldova.

Grey rectangular chunks of Communist-era apartment

blocks stood in ranks on either side of us. Satellite dishes scarred every balcony like blisters, and the washing that hung from their windows looked like it would go back even dirtier than it had come out.

There were a surprising number of shiny new BMWs and Mercedes weaving their way between the clapped-out trucks and tractors, but the road still wasn't exactly choked with traffic. Many of the people on the streets were pretty well turned-out, particularly the young guys. We were supposed to be in Europe's poorest country, but Moldova was the same as everywhere else in the old Soviet Union: a handful of haves and whole swathes of have-nots.

Most people here scraped by on less than three dollars a day. Away from the towns, work was scarce. In many of the rural villages, only children and grand-parents remained. More than a million people had left the country to find work – and that didn't include the ones who'd been trafficked. No wonder Starbucks had kicked off with a small stall. No one in their right mind was going to spend a day's wages on a cappuccino, no matter how nicely they wrote your name on the cup.

When the tarmac stopped and cobblestones and potholes took over, I pulled out the slip of paper Anna had given me with Lena's number. Lena had contacted CNN to try to expose the scandalous trade of human kidneys to the West. Anna had gone on to write a ground-breaking piece about every male inhabitant of a small village not far from Chisinau having the same scar on his back.

Lena's phone rang three or four times, then I got a very fast and very loud burst of Romanian in my ear. It sounded like she was having to make herself heard above a roomful of people.

'Lena, it's Nick—'

She didn't fuck around with small-talk. 'Have you brought any Russian cigarettes?'

'No one said to.'

'Oh.' She sounded crushed.

'I'm in a cab, just coming into the city. Can you meet me at the Cosmos?'

I could still hear a lot of shouting in the background. The other women in her office were making the place sound like a cattle market.

'Wait . . .' Lena yelled whatever the Moldovan was for 'Shut the fuck up' and it suddenly went quiet. 'I have to work. Do you remember where we are? Pass your cell to the driver.'

I handed it over. The steering wheel jumped around in his left hand as the tyres rumbled over the cobblestones, but he managed to keep waffling away to her without his eyes ever leaving the road.

3

The cab stopped outside a graffiti-smothered apartment block south-east of the city centre. The stretch of grass in front had long since given up the battle and was now covered with wrecked cars and plastic bags, garbage spewing through the rips.

I gave the driver a twenty-dollar bill, which seemed to make his day – maybe even his week. He sped away in case I changed my mind.

I looked up. On each landing, rusty steel reinforce-ment rods poked through the crumbling remains of the concrete Stalin had sent by the trainload from the Motherland after the Germans had flattened half of the city and an earthquake had seen off the rest. Satellite dishes covered with pigeon shit were drilled onto the outside walls, their drooping cables fed in through the nearest window. The graffiti brightened the place up a bit, not that I had a clue what it said. Moldovan looked to me like a continuous stream of lowercase Us and Ns.

I'd only been to Lena's office once before, when Anna and I had come to her for some information about people-trafficking. I was working for the Firm then, on what turned out to be my last job. There were no kisses and cuddles when I left, no engraved carriage clock or M&S gift card – and definitely no pension. They fucked me over big-time, but I hadn't expected anything else. Nine times out of ten, a pat on the back from the Firm is just the recce for a stabbing.

I started down the metal steps towards a row of heavy steel doors at basement level. There wasn't a window in sight – either these bolt-holes were bomb shelters for when the B52s flew over to give the Soviets the good news, or the brickies hadn't been arsed to put them in.

I went up to the faded blue entrance I recognized. My task last time around had been to track down the missing teenage daughter of a Moldovan missile-defence-system supremo – and Lena was a bit of an expert at locating the victims of the people-traffickers. Lily had run away with the love of her life – or so it seemed. Nobody could find her; nobody knew where she was. My job had been to get her back so the Firm could become best mates with Daddy – and implant their own technology into the kit he was building for the Russians to supply to the Iranians. Keeping Armoured-dinner-jacket and his mates on the back foot had always been high on their list of priorities.

I pressed the buzzer and it sounded like I'd sparked up a garbage-disposal grinder somewhere inside.

I got no reply so I buzzed again.

The speaker crackled. Even if the greeting had been in English, it was so loud and distorted I wouldn't have been able to understand a word of it.

'It's Nick. Nick – for Lena . . .'

All I got back was more psychotic yelling punctuated by the odd 'Lena'.

'Nick – to see Lena. *Lena!'*

The speaker went quiet. I stood and waited, but nothing happened. Maybe she thought I was selling dusters.

Finally, about a hundred bolts were thrown on the other side of the door and Miranda Hart's twin towered in front of me in flared jeans and a baggy blue jumper. She must have been north of six feet tall. Unlike her sister, she'd shaved her dark brown hair on the left of her head. The rest hung down to her right shoulder. Maybe it was on trend around here; to me it looked like the world's biggest comb-over.

She started shouting at me again. 'Lena!'

'Yes. Lena!'

I poked myself in the chest with a forefinger. 'Nick!'

She ushered me in and I stepped past her into the corridor. The steel door slammed behind me and all hundred bolts were hammered back into position. She led me past a battered red-leather sofa and a coffee-table. Nothing had changed. The walls of Lena's windowless office were still lined with archive boxes; a small desk was still strewn with files. Even the smell was the same, most of it coming from the overflowing ashtray next to the phone.

I sat on a knackered old wooden kitchen chair and waited as Miranda moved around behind me.

'*Café?*' she bellowed.

I nearly jumped out of my seat.

'*Café?*'

I turned. She had a can of instant in one hand and a

spoon in the other. I nodded like a happy chimp. 'Yes
. . . thanks . . .'

She disappeared down the corridor towards the front
door and then the buzzer went and the whole performance kicked off once more.

I heard Lena join in. The entry-phone volume was at
full blast. Miranda screamed in one direction and Lena
in the other. Then the speaker cut out and the bolts were
thrown again.

The shouting resumed as Lena entered the corridor.
Fuck me, I'd soon be trembling with shell-shock and
stinking like Lena's ashtray.

4

I stood up to greet her, but she didn't appear. I leaned into the corridor to see her – in matching black trousers and cardigan – standing just behind Miranda. The big girl threw the last bolt, turned, leaned down and they kissed. Not a polite peck or two, but full on the lips.

I waited. And I waited some more. Come on, you two, haven't you had your lunch?

They eventually managed to prise themselves apart and made their way towards me, shouting at each other as they walked. Miranda threw some shapes with her arms, in case she hadn't been heard.

Lena was all smiles. 'Nick!' She threw her arms round me and treated me to a big continental three-timer on the cheeks. I was glad I hadn't got the Miranda treatment: this girl's breath stank of cigarettes.

Miranda disappeared again as Lena moved to the other side of the desk. 'Please, Nick. Sit.'

She plonked herself on a cheap foam-padded office chair and stole a quick glance over the paperwork on her desk. 'You still searching for trafficked girls? We've got enough of them.' It was good dealing with people like Frank and Lena. They worked on the basis that I would tell them if they needed to know. For them it was all about the moment.

Her hands shot into the air and whirled around above her head, indicating the array of box files containing the details of thousands of girls who'd been kidnapped by or sold to the trafficking gangs – or who'd signed up voluntarily, thinking they were going to Turkey as cleaners or waitresses, only to have their passports removed and be forced into prostitution.

Her hands came back to land, and slammed onto the piles of paperwork on her desk, giving me the chance to admire her latest nail and hair-colour combo. Last time I'd been there, the nails had been silver and the hair short, spiky and blue. Now the nails were black and the hair was red and even shorter.

I smiled. 'Still busy, then?'

There was a mocking tone in her voice as she scanned the row upon row of files lining the office walls: 'Formerly one of the wealthiest parts of our great – but now defunct – Soviet Union, we are now officially the poorest country in Europe. We have a government with no teeth and no balls. Our judicial system is a joke. Our police are so corrupt they are worse than the gangs. The only thing we have to be proud of as a nation is that we're number one in the world for human trafficking. We're an international business success story! Young girls are still the country's biggest export. But . . . I will keep trying to get them home, wherever they are.'

Lena lit a cigarette she'd pulled from the drawer; they

seemed to be loose in there. The smoke soon filled my eyes and nostrils.

'Nick, do you know that forty per cent of Moldova's sex slaves are now kids?' The mockery was gone: she was back in serious Lena mode. 'Anna should talk to the networks about it. The big demand in the sex trade these days is for children.'

Anna obviously hadn't said anything about the baby and I wanted to leave it at that. I didn't like talking about my personal life any more than I liked having my picture taken – and look where that had got me.

She hoovered up another lungful and let the smoke roll out of her mouth. 'Soon we'll be number one at that as well. All that will be left are the old men.'

'If everybody's leaving, why all the bolts? You having problems with the gangs?'

Miranda came back into the room and the pungent smell of black instant joined the cloud of nicotine up my nose. Lena invited her to share the joke at maximum decibel level, even though she was only a couple of feet away. She pointed at me and repeated my question with a stream of Us and Ns. They both cackled. The noise nearly burst my eardrums. I bet the neighbours were glad there were no windows.

Miranda turned and shouted down at me, smiling like a lunatic and throwing a whole lot more shapes. She gave me a pat, which nearly dislocated my shoulder, and disappeared down the corridor, laughing loudly to herself. I guessed the voices in her head must have told her a follow-up joke.

Lena picked up her brew, tested it, and decided it was too hot. I didn't bother testing mine. She nodded in the direction of the corridor. 'Linda says if only that were true – because we would be more than able to handle that lot.'

It was my turn to smile to myself. I'd nearly got her name right. Well, the 'da' bit, anyway.

'We have to worry about her family. They are so pissed with her, and now with me. They blame me for her "deviancy" and have been here two or three times, trying to break in and trash the place before taking her home for . . .' her fingers curled to give me the quote marks '. . . safety.'

She waved her hands in my direction and ash cascaded off the tip of her cigarette. 'It'll pass. Anyway, Nick. What do you want? Anna didn't tell you I needed cigarettes, and said nothing to me about why you are here.'

I couldn't help laughing. She didn't need my help to smoke herself to death. 'Have you heard of a woman called Dr Katarina – or Katya – Fuentes?'

She shook her head. 'But we can start combing the files.'

'No need. She's Cuban-Russian. What about Vasil Diminetz?'

Lena's face dropped faster than it would have if Linda's family had just kicked down the door.

I picked up my brew as she stubbed out what was left of her cigarette into the overflowing ashtray.

5

'*Linda!*'

The whole room shook. Even Linda must have felt the shock waves because she rushed in seconds later. Lena screamed some more stuff at her, though the only bit I understood before Linda disappeared again was 'Diminetz'. I heard box files being ransacked as I took another sip of my brew.

Lena rested her smoking elbow on the arm of her chair. 'Diminetz is not a nice man. He used to traffic drugs, girls, guns – the normal stuff. But then he branched out.'

Linda reappeared with a box file that was so well worn it was coming apart at the spine. She started to hand it over to Lena, but the black fingernails redirected it to me. I lifted the lid to see not much at all, just some printouts in Moldovan. It meant nothing to me. There were pictures, mostly of girls, then one of a male. I held it up. 'This him?'

She nodded. 'Maybe five years ago.'

He looked like a lot of arseholes in their mid-twenties,

with a dark-brown crew-cut and uneven stubble. His first distinguishing feature was that he looked in need of some serious bulking up. His second was a tat of a dragon on the left side of his neck. It was quite a good one, not the normal prison botch-up.

She leaned over the desk and pointed at the picture. 'That was before he started his new venture. He advertised quite freely in the papers here. People lined the streets outside a store he rented. A few months later we started seeing the results. The scars . . .'

The piece Anna had written about a Moldovan village where every single male had sold a kidney flashed through my head. 'He's in the harvesting business?'

She settled back in her chair. 'He attracts them with the promise of thousands of dollars. He then makes a deal with the brokers. The middlemen could be anywhere, according to what we're piecing together from those who make it back – the US, Rio de Janeiro, Berlin. A lot of them are sent to Israel.'

The Jewish faith, she said, prohibits the donation of organs. The bodies had to be intact when they were buried.

'So they buy them instead? No hypocrisy there, then.'

'It's a marketplace, with no national boundaries. Anywhere there is money, and people who need an organ, there is an . . . opportunity and someone has to supply the goods. Diminetz will send the donor to South America, the Middle East, Europe, anywhere a broker can arrange for an operation to take place.'

'Any hospital, you mean?'

'That's the hard bit for them. Hospitals need the cash,

but it's still illegal. The brokers have to do a bit of work to co-ordinate it all. With most transplant operations, there's a window of a few hours between taking it out of one body and putting it into another. They have to get the donor and recipient in the same location. The rich one goes home with a new kidney or whatever, and the poor one comes back with bits missing and maybe just a couple of thousand dollars because the accommodation, food and flight – you name it – are deducted. Even so, still life-changing amounts of money.'

'Isn't it illegal here too? How does he get away with advertising?'

She dived back into her cigarette drawer. 'The only country where it isn't illegal, I think, is Iran. But so what? Like I said, there's no law or government here. The vice squad in this city consists of seven officers, Nick. Seven! They don't even have a vehicle. They have to catch a bus to crime scenes. That's why there are people like me.'

'So what sort of money are we talking about? How much could I get for a kidney?'

The disposable clicked but there was no flame. She gave it a couple of shakes and sparked it up this time, then wafted it across the tip of her smoke.

'He promises ten thousand US, and you'd be lucky to see half that. But if you're desperate, Nick, if you're trying to escape from poverty or debt – or this country . . .' She raised the filter to her lips. 'Diminetz will send them to wherever they need to be – to whichever broker, in whatever country. Sometimes they come back in good condition – it all depends where the operation takes place. But sometimes they don't. That's when Linda and I pick up the pieces. And sometimes they just disappear completely.'

Another toxic cloud filled the room. My eyes were watering, but Lena wasn't deterred. 'China is also a growing market. The new middle class doesn't want organs from executed prisoners any more. They want designer organs to match their designer handbags and watches. Prisoners have been on bad diets, and are probably riddled with hepatitis or HIV. They want healthy organs from healthy, strong young men and women.

'Diminetz sells the dream: clean, fit, healthy East Europeans, who have been working out in the fields, not drinking or smoking . . .' She took another long drag, then balanced the cigarette on the dog-end mountain that was toppling off the ashtray. 'They are paraded in front of the clients, like girls in a brothel. He makes sure they turn up without make-up, with short nails and no polish. If their hair is dyed he will keep them under wraps until it grows out. He wants them to look as wholesome and healthy as possible. It costs more, but the buyers don't complain.'

She swirled the remains of her coffee around a couple of times in the bottom of her mug. Her jaw clenched and I could see the anger in her face. She flicked through the pile of papers in front of her and scribbled the odd note. The end of her Bic ballpoint looked like it had been chewed by a Dobermann.

'It's all about supply and demand, of course. Their mark-up is as much as you'd expect on any designer bag – and if you want the real thing you don't buy Louis Vuitton from a Somali at a street corner. Diminetz sells them to the broker for fifty to sixty thousand dollars.

The broker sells them for a hundred and fifty to two hundred thousand, sometimes even more, depending on where the operation is taking place. Sometimes, if the girl is beautiful and her scar does not weep, she finds herself sold on as a prostitute.' She tilted back her chair, closed her eyes and massaged her temples with her fingers. For a moment I thought she was going to cry. 'So why is your friend caught up in this? You think that scum has put her up for auction?'

'I haven't got a clue. I'm just trying to cover every base.' She didn't need to know the full story, just enough to help. 'Do you know if Diminetz speaks English?'

Her eyes rolled and she burst out laughing.

6

Club Royal Park Hotel

20.32 hrs

The beaten-up Merc pulled in beside the third hotel on my circuit and I handed the cabbie a five-dollar bill. It had been a ten-minute ride so he was very happy indeed. He took off as fast as my last driver had done, before I realized my mistake.

We'd passed a whole stream of posters along the way showing a girl gripped in a huge clenched fist being exchanged for a handful of dollars. I didn't know precisely what the caption said, but it was pretty fucking obvious. I wondered if there were any other countries in the world that had to publicize the perils of people-trafficking alongside the attractions of Diet Coke and Nescafé.

Lena didn't have much solid intelligence on Diminetz, but was able to tell me he didn't have a home: he hung out in the kind of five-star hotels that had sprung up in Chisinau to suck money out of people like him. Off his tits on drink and drugs most of the time, he shagged his life away between deals. Frank was right. This lad might have a big wallet, but it hadn't lifted him out of the gutter.

Lena had listed my most likely targets and I'd already tried the Maxim Pasha and the Prezident in the centre of town. Number three was just outside, in a park called Valley of the Roses. Not that I could see any.

It was a large, two-storey, rectangular shrine to the God of White Walls and Glass. A veranda fringed the first floor like a crinoline, possibly in an attempt to give the place some kind of colonial vibe. Lights glowed; expensive cars gleamed on the gravel forecourt. An island of cash floating in a sea of corruption.

I went up a short flight of black brick steps and in through a pair of gold-sprayed, aluminium-framed doors. The riot of brass and multicoloured fabric that hit me as soon as I'd crossed the threshold was like an artist's impression of a migraine. Saddam Hussein would have felt completely at home there. Maybe he'd lent them his interior decorator; the only bit of Baghdad chic missing was a gold bust of the great man at the reception desk.

The signs were all in Moldovan with English translations, and the woman sitting behind them had scraped-back jet-black hair and drawings for eyebrows. I nodded at her as I passed, scanning the mauve chairs, swirling Oriental carpets and futuristic red lightshades. Moldovans kept their heads well below the parapet and never asked questions; it was a prerequisite of survival in this neck of the acid-rain-drenched woods. Even the shopkeepers never asked you how your day was or if they could help. They just left you to do whatever you needed to do. Old habits die hard.

It was dinnertime. Maybe Diminetz was sitting quietly with a nice bowl of boiled cabbage, but I doubted that was his style. In any event, the restaurant was the last place I'd check. I'd have to have a reason to go there – to eat or to meet – and I'd draw unwelcome attention to myself if I then walked away.

The bar and terrace were another matter. I could wander through them to my heart's content. If they were empty, I would try the gym and the swimming-pool, but something told me that Diminetz wasn't the sort to pump iron or clock up lengths. He had money to burn before it all ended in tears, and Lena had given me the impression he kept the furnace roaring.

I headed for the sliding patio doors, which were open just enough for one person to pass through. It would have made a nice spot for dinner, but now it was a smoking area. A scattering of couples chatted over a glass of something and a cigarette. Three or four women sat on their own, each with a thick layer of make-up and weapons-grade hairspray. They weren't there for the repartee. They cast an eye over me: I was alone and not about to join the natives in Marlboro Country. I had to be a foreigner and a potential punter.

For all the glitz, teak flooring and shiny chairs and tables the terrace had to offer, it had one glaring design flaw. The air-conditioning units that fed the rooms above were busy sucking up the smoke and dribbling condensation onto the deck in return, but nobody seemed to mind.

I moved back inside, past the bright red velvet

curtains and migraine-triggering wallpaper, following the sound of loud voices and laughter.

Diminetz and his entourage sat around a small cluster of low tables piled with nuts and bottles in the bar area; six of them, in leather bucket chairs. He held court with a glass of something expensive in his hand, telling some joke by the look of it; everyone was very attentive apart from the two BG in black suits who seemed much more interested in whichever stockinged thigh was nearest to them.

I perched on a stool at the far end of the bar, ordered a Coke and busied myself with a bowl of pistachios. It was easy enough to keep eyes on the group. The wall behind the optics was mirrored. Diminetz faced away from me. His hair was a bit longer than it had been in the picture and he'd put on a bit of weight. He looked like any other dickhead in his early thirties with a big gob and too much money. His girlfriend wasn't the normal pick-up for the night, though. She was in severe need of a few plates of chips. The rings around her eyes matched her frizzy dark-brown hair and her shoulder-blades stuck out from her strapless blue dress like shelf brackets. You could have fitted a wedding ring around her arms. Her look was more underfed whippet than heroin chic. She wouldn't have stood a chance against the competition on the terrace.

Diminetz dominated the room. The other customers did their best to ignore the noise as he gobbed off at a hundred miles an hour. I stole a glance at the BG. They were older, forties maybe; efficient haircut with a touch of grey at the temples. They'd seen a bit, judging by the state of their noses, but were now monstrously over-weight. This was probably the best job they'd ever had:

money, drink and women. What more could they ask for? Looking after a total dickhead just went with the turf.

Diminetz sparked up a cigar the size of a broom handle. The smoking area was clearly only for law-abiding morons. A haze of blue smoke billowed above his head and drifted round the room. The barman was unimpressed. He turned and walked to where his boss was standing. Both wore little red waistcoats, white shirts and bow-ties. The barman waffled away in an urgent whisper, but his boss just shrugged. What the fuck could they do?

7

23.56 hrs

I sat in a gilt and green velvet chair in Reception with
my latest cup of coffee, the remains of a club sandwich
and another bowl of pistachios on a table in front of me.
I flicked through the last of the pile of magazines I'd
worked hard at looking engrossed in.

I'd been there for about an hour, drinking, snacking
and paying in cash while Diminetz and his entourage
continued smoking, hollering, laughing, shouting and
drinking too much. He didn't look the gangster, organ-
trafficking kind of guy, just a dickhead. But that's the
problem with people: you can never tell. I thought I saw
the odd recreational item getting popped as well, but
maybe they kept some ready-shelled pistachios in their
pockets.

I'd had to leave the bar after an hour or so: there's
only so long you can hang around with a Diet Coke.
Staying in Reception was fine because, unless they
had a rush of blood to the head and relocated to the

terrace, they couldn't go anywhere without passing me.

The shrieks and laughs got louder as the evening wore on. My biggest problem now was boredom. I'd read every article singing Moldova's praises as a wonderful holiday destination and focus for investment.

My iPhone started to vibrate and spin on the half-nutshell I had balanced it on to pass the time. I'd texted Anna an hour ago: *Saw L. Boy OK?*

Her reply was: *Boy good.*

I deleted the message so the phone stayed sterile. She wouldn't contact me again until I contacted her – she was far too switched on. But I still needed to know how Anna and my boy were doing.

The young woman at Reception was getting ready for the long night ahead. She'd retreated to the back office, behind a frosted-glass screen. I could hear the gentle jabbering of a TV through the half-opened door. To the right of it hung two cardholders on blue lanyards. They were some distance away from the card-enabling machine behind the counter, so they had to be the admin keys.

The noise from the bar suddenly got louder. The group was on the move. As they squeaked their way across the glossy brown floor tiles, the whole entourage looked very much the worse for wear. There was a little bit of staggering as they swivelled towards the stairs, and a few giggles as they anticipated the fun and games ahead.

Diminetz was in the middle and having to bend down a little to get his hand on where the whippet's arse should have been. His two BG were having more success: they were deep in conversation with the other girls, or possibly just nibbling their ears; one's fingers brushed his girl's hip, the other was going straight for the bra straps. All this lot were interested in now was shagging. That was what I hoped, anyway.

I waited until they'd turned on the landing and headed for the second flight, then got to my feet. I followed the noise up the plush Oriental carpet.

As I reached the first floor, I raised my head slowly to see them splitting off to their rooms either side of the dimly lit corridor. Diminetz and his woman carried on all the way down to the end and turned right, out of sight. The other two had a couple of goes at getting their cards into the slots of the Onity locks and finally fell into their rooms.

I legged it down the corridor, stopping short of the turn, in case Diminetz had his hand up the whippet's skirt in his doorway or was still concentrating hard on his key card.

I eased around the corner to find that the corridor was empty. There was only one entrance, about four or five metres down, to the Presidential Suite. No surprises there, then. I shoved an ear to the door and heard muffled giggles. There would probably be a maze of different rooms in the suite, and they could be in any of them.

I pushed down gently on the handle, but of course it was locked.

I moved back towards the staircase and eventually found the cleaners' store, and three carts loaded with bedding, towels, Aveda products, pencils and pads ready for the next day. I squeezed past them and closed the door behind me. I checked the pinnies and the contents of a couple of lockers, then the carts themselves, in case a master key card had been tucked into one of the pockets. But there was nothing.

I pulled the scrap of paper from my sock and texted the number: *OK for tonight? Maybe in an hour?*

8

29 August 2011
01.15 hrs

I lay facing the door with a rolled-up bath towel as a pillow, munching on the complimentary chocolate wafers that went with the sachets of Lipton's tea. They seemed to follow me everywhere. I kept one eye in line with the gap at the bottom in case anyone passed. If Diminetz left early, I'd have to follow or intercept.

I checked the time display on my iPhone. If it didn't happen now, it never would. I got up onto my arse and took off my Timberlands, tucking them neatly under the front cart. I had no idea why, I just felt like it. Then I put the wooden doorstop that the cleaners used while moving the carts in and out alongside them.

I eased the door open a fraction, checked up and down the corridor and moved swiftly to the stairs. My socks left a few sweat marks behind me on the lobby's polished tiles as I got a bit of a stride on towards the desk, but I wasn't really bothered: they'd soon evaporate. I focused instead on what needed to happen when I got to the desk.

The brain has two orbs. One processes numbers and analyses information, the other is the creative bit, where we visualize things – and if you visualize situations, you can usually work out how to deal with them in advance. The more you visualize, the better you'll do so. It might sound like something from a tree-huggers' workshop, but it does the business.

I moved through an archway, my mind fixed on what I was going to do, when and how I was going to do it – and, more importantly still, how I was going to react if things went to rat-shit. I realized immediately there was something that might fuck it all up; I undid the steel buckle of my belt, pulled it out of my jeans, and left it on the chair I'd used earlier. The highly polished wooden top of the reception desk was the barrier between me and my target.

The TV was still jabbering in the office and I could just about make out the back of the black-haired woman's head. It was tilted to the right, as if she was asleep, or well on the way. I put my hands on the desktop, stood on the tips of my toes and pulled myself up onto my stomach. I went rigid so I could stretch further, and my fingertips brushed the cardholders hanging by their lanyards from a row of pegs. A couple more lunges and I managed to grab one.

I padded back into the hallway, retrieved my belt and headed back up the stairs.

These things are easy to do once you get yourself into the right mind-set. You don't faff around and write a 6,000-word thesis in your head. You just have to plan, visualize, then get on with it.

9

Timberlands back on, I shoved the wedge down the front of my jeans and headed for the Presidential Suite, picking up a laminated Do Not Disturb sign from one of the door handles on the way. I carried my belt in my left hand.

As I passed the two BG's rooms, I gave them both a quick ear to the door. There was no noise from the first one, and the sound of music mixed with lots of grunts and moans and cries of 'Schön! Schön!' from the next. Either they'd suddenly become fluent in German or the porn channel on the TV was getting a good seeing-to.

I turned right, transferring my wallet from my back pocket to the more secure front. I listened for a moment at Diminetz's door. I couldn't hear a thing. I slid the master-card into the lock. It gave a weak bleep and a dull green LED sparked up. Keeping the belt in my left hand, I slowly pulled down the handle. The door opened about fifteen centimetres, then stopped. Diminetz had flicked on the safety bar.

Pulling it back about five centimetres, I pushed the

end of the Do Not Disturb sign against the bar. The card was flexible but the plastic lamination kept it more or less rigid. That was exactly what I wanted. Like most hotel safety latches, this one consisted of a long steel U, hinged at the end attached to the frame, which fitted over a bulbous steel thumb on the back of the door. I now had to close the door as far as possible so the base of the U was as near as it could be to the end of the thumb, and therefore to disengaging. When the door was virtually shut, I pushed and jiggled the card until the catch popped.

I stepped carefully into the dim hallway and was immediately smothered by the stench of alcohol and cigars. The suite was designed like a large apartment. There were three doors in front of me, all open. A mirror-light had been left on in the bathroom, allowing me to make out shapes but not colours.

I stood and listened as I closed the door quietly behind me. I held my breath, tuning in to the new environment. There was no rush. They were asleep; if they weren't, they would have heard me by now, or I would have heard them. The only sound was the gentle hum of the air-con.

I put the U of the latch back over the thumb, then retrieved the wooden doorstop from my jeans. I wedged it under the door as hard as I could, about three-quarters of the way along from the hinged end. Then I sat on my arse, braced both hands on the floor behind me, and pushed it in even further with the heel of my boot. I fed the end of my belt through its buckle to make a noose and got back to my feet.

The thick-pile carpet and Oriental rugs muted my movement towards the bedroom. The smells were stronger here, and a flowery perfume joined the blend. I moved to the right as I entered the room, to avoid creating a silhouette in the doorway. I three-quarters closed the door with my shoulder, and looked across a floor strewn with clothes to a bed the size of a third-world nation. Two bodies lay back to back in the middle of it, asleep, now the deal had been done, among a mess of crumpled sheets, covers, pillows and cushions.

The larger shape on the right was wheezing gently. The closer I got, the louder it became. I wrapped my right fist around the free end of the belt, keeping the noose as big as it could be. The cabinet on his side was covered with glasses and empty bottles from the minibar. He'd drowned a cigar in one of the glasses.

I spread my left hand and eased it under his head. He murmured appreciatively. He'd be thinking he was in Never Never Land, bless him, and this was just part of the fun.

But the fun wasn't going to last long.

10

I slipped the noose over his head, stepped back and heaved the belt with both hands until it was tight around his neck. He gave a long-drawn-out groan and started to struggle, not trying to escape, just wanting to work out what was going on, and how the fuck he could breathe. By the time his brain had worked out that this was real life he was bucking and snorting like a horse.

I let go with my left hand, picked up one of the tumblers and brought it down on the side of his head a couple of times to reinforce his sense of reality.

I wrenched again with my entire body weight to try to get him off the bed. It was like trying to shift an elephant. I heard him slurp and retch as his Adam's apple went into overtime. He'd lost the ability to swallow. If he wasn't fully conscious by now, too bad. The mixture of sleep and alcohol wasn't making his reactions any sharper but as his head bounced over the edge his arms flailed to break his fall.

I kicked out as soon as he hit the carpet. I wanted to

come on like a savage, like I was out of control. I kept stamping and pulling, hammering my boots into his body. I got one between his legs and he curled up with a strangled grunt and grabbed onto his bollocks. The pain would be as horrendous in the pit of his stomach as it was between his legs.

The whippet stirred from her drunken sleep. Pulling on the belt with my right hand, I leaned over and grabbed a fistful of her mad hair with my left. I gave it a couple of twists and yanked her towards me. She cried out and brought up her hands. I didn't know what she was saying but I didn't need to. I tried to sound as gentle as possible as I pulled her towards me.

'*Sssh . . .*'

I planted a boot firmly on Diminetz's face and kept the pressure on the belt to make sure that was where his hands stayed. It's a natural instinct to fight against the thing you think is going to kill you, and in this case the thing was round his neck, stopping his body getting oxygen. I wasn't aiming for total restriction. Twenty per cent of your oxygen is needed to service your brain, and his brain was what I was there to probe.

The skin prickled on my back as the moisture broke cover. I pulled the whippet up close and treated Diminetz to another couple of kicks before slamming my boot back down on his face.

'*Sssh . . .*'

I waited for them both to calm down. They couldn't see much of me in the gloom but I hoped they'd feel at least the noise was comforting.

As Diminetz continued to fight for breath, the

whippet was flat out, belly down, head over the edge of the bed, a few centimetres from the top of my boot. I twisted her head round, bent towards her and whispered, 'You speak English?'

She tried shaking her head as she mumbled away in local but the pain got in the way.

I looked down at what I could see of her face and gave her another reassuring *sssh*. I let go of her and pulled out my iPhone. Her skeletal shoulders heaved as she, too, tried to fill her lungs.

Lena answered after three rings: 'You have him?'

'Yep. Tell this woman he's with that, if she stays calm, she won't get—'

I heard a rustle below me.

Shit!

The whippet was on her feet and sprinting for the door like I'd just fired a starting pistol. Her feet snagged in the kit they'd tossed on the floor and she stumbled, but not for long. I followed her, dragging Diminetz with me as fast as I could, but she'd made it to the main door by the time I exited the bedroom.

She pulled and jerked frantically at the handle, breaking into sobs of fear and frustration as she realized it wasn't going to open. Dragging Diminetz with me, I caught up with her. The doorstop had lived up to its name – but she didn't even seem to have noticed I'd swung the security latch back into place.

I grabbed another handful of hair and yanked her down, then turned and dragged them both back towards the bed like a psychopath in a cheap horror movie.

I tied the free end of the belt as tightly as I could to the in-pipe of the nearest radiator. If Diminetz struggled, he'd choke.

'Nick?' Lena's voice was coming from my jacket pocket.

11

Everything had calmed down. The dim light was helping; it was for me, anyway. Like the other two, I was taking big gulps of air by now, trying to get my breathing back to normal after this little bit of excitement. Sweat dripped down my back.

Diminetz was more switched on than I'd thought he'd be after seeing him in action down at the bar. He wasn't flapping: he seemed to be conserving his energy as best he could while trying to get into a comfortable position to work out what the fuck to do next. He leaned back to get the most out of the couple of millimetres' play in the belt. He wanted to get his brain working as much as I did.

'Nick? You OK? You OK?'

Lena's voice got louder as I liberated her from my pocket and put her to my ear. 'Yep. All good here.'

The whippet sat on the floor, arms hugging her knees against her chest, back against the black-leather sofa. She wasn't the slightest bit embarrassed about being naked. I guessed that was part of the job spec.

'Lena, tell this woman that everything's going to be

all right. She'll be safe as long as she does what she's told. I'm not here to hurt her.'

'Is she OK?' She sounded more concerned about the whippet's welfare than mine.

'She's more than OK. She doesn't look like one of your victims. I'm passing the mobile to her now . . .'

The iPhone disappeared under the mass of hair. I picked up one or two Moldovan mumbles. Diminetz was all ears. Saliva oozed out of his mouth and down his chin to merge with the blood streaming from where I'd whacked him with the tumbler. His chest rose and fell as he fought for air.

She handed the phone back and said something to Diminetz. I could have stopped her but maybe what she'd said would be good.

'You're right. That one is no victim.'

'This is what I want you to tell Diminetz . . .'

He raised his head at the mention of his name. I couldn't see his eyes in the gloom, but I was sure they were trying to burn into the upstart he could see towering above him.

'Tell him I'm going to ask him some questions, and that we'll both be much happier if he answers. Because if he doesn't try to make sense, I'm going to kill him.'

'You can't! That wasn't what we agreed! I can't be part of anything that—'

'Just tell him, OK? I want to scare the shit out of him. That way he'll save his own life, and he might very well save Katya's. Tell him that once I find out where she is I'll go. No one has to know the information came from him.'

Lena was still flapping. 'Nick, no killing. I will not be part of it.'

'I'm not going to do it. I just want him to think I am.'

I lowered the phone and shoved it against his ear. He answered Lena in pissed-off mode but managed to hold his temper. His head came up again and I pulled away. I couldn't see if the good-cop-bad-cop routine had worked.

I switched on the bedside light. They both blinked and the whippet buried her head between her knees so a curtain of hair fell across her face. But not Diminetz: he seized the opportunity to size me up.

He wouldn't have noticed me in the bar, but he certainly recognized me now.

I looked into his bulging eyes. 'Yeah, that's right, mate. The one in the photograph.' I didn't care if he understood or not. I just wanted to rattle him some more.

I got back on the iPhone to Lena. 'What did he say?'

12

'He said why should he tell you anything. What's to stop you killing him anyway? Why would you let him live, so he can warn people you're looking for her? Why would he do that?'

He stared at me as I listened. There wasn't a trace of fear in his eyes, just sheer pragmatism. That was impressive. Maybe Frank had been wrong: maybe Diminetz wasn't destined to remain in the gutter after all.

My eyes drilled into him. 'Tell him I'm not here to kill him. I'm here to collect Katya. If he doesn't tell me what I need to know, I'll find her eventually anyway. And I'll make sure that when I do I'll tell any fucker in this city who's in the mood to listen that he gave me the information. Tell him I guarantee he'll be fucked. He's got a good thing going at the moment, why spoil it?'

I stared at him, unblinking, throughout. He caught the tone of my voice. When I handed the phone back to him, he listened without looking up. He stared across the room instead. His lips curled into a smile as he waffled back.

'What did he say?'

'She's already out of the country. He said you should feel happy that she's gone. Otherwise you and your wife would be in even more danger than you are now.' She didn't pause for breath. 'Nick, what's happening? Anna? You never said—'

'I'll explain it all later. Did he say where she was?'

'All he knows is that they took her to the airport and put her on a flight to Frankfurt, then on to Hong Kong. They told her someone called Soapy would be waiting for her. Nick, she could be anywhere by now. Soapy could be a broker. You need to tell me what is happening. Is Anna in danger?'

I took a breath. 'That's what I'm here for, to make sure she isn't.'

'Maybe it's because she's Hispanic. Maybe they need a specific tissue match.'

'Ask him.'

Diminetz sparked up, jerking his head towards the phone. I held it against his ear again and he sounded as though he'd switched into Samaritan mode.

'Nick, he says he has the Hong Kong number on his cell.'

Diminetz muttered something to the whippet, then looked at me for permission to get her moving.

'Nick, all he wants is to get this over and done with. He will forget the whole thing if you will.'

I nodded at the whippet and watched her go over to

Diminetz's bedside cabinet. 'He says this is not only bad for business, it's very embarrassing. And he said—'

I watched her and I thought: *Shit, there's no mobile.*

I turned to dive into the hallway as the whippet spun back towards me with a pistol screaming whatever the Moldovan was for *You fucker!*

The first round kicked off and she screamed and stood, arms at full stretch, firing rapid and uncontrolled shots. The TV took a round, then the mirror above it.

There were two more shots, one of which hit the radiator.

As soon as I reached the cover of the hallway, I checked behind me. Pressurized water was spraying across the room. By the time it reached the rug it had turned a deep shade of crimson. Diminetz had taken a round in the chest and he wasn't fighting. His legs were still.

The whippet had stopped firing but she continued shrieking like a witch.

Then I heard Lena scream too.

I shoved the iPhone into my jacket pocket. The front door was being rammed hard enough from the corridor to part it from its frame but the wedge and safety latch were doing their jobs. They would keep the BG at bay for a while. I flung open the bathroom door and almost flew out of the window onto the roof of the first-floor veranda, taking time only to make sure my feet were lower than my head.

I slid off it, landing hard on the wooden deck of the terrace a couple of metres below me, closely followed by a shower of slate splinters. I lay there for a second, making sure nothing was broken, then scrambled up and stumbled into a run. I headed out into the darkness of the park with Lena still yelling in my pocket.

13

Hotel Cosmos, Negruzzi Square

03.18 hrs

I stood in the Cosmos service alley, back in a world I'd
thought I'd never inhabit again – hiding in the shadows,
shivering in the damp and cold. For one reason or
another, I seemed to have done that my whole life.

It still felt OK, it still felt comfortable – which was
strange, because it wasn't as if I needed to do this shit
for a living any more. Anna and I weren't short of cash
– not enough for a yacht, but enough to get by on;
enough to last quite a while if we were smart about it.
After that, who knew? I wasn't going to worry about
it until I had to.

When I was younger, I always thought that having a
big wad was all you needed. When I did get a couple of
serious paydays, I hadn't really known what to do with
it. A motorbike, maybe some new trainers, was as far
as it went for me. But with Anna and our son I needed

a cleverer plan, and hanging about in the dark in places like this wasn't part of it.

I'd decided to learn Russian; I'd even bought some labels to stick on everyday objects around the house so I could start getting the hang of it. We wanted our boy to be bilingual: English inside the house, Russian everywhere else. That meant the two of us could learn together – and that meant I had to be there.

That had been my plan, anyway. Now I wasn't too sure that it was Anna's.

I also wasn't sure whether I was hiding from the police or a limo full of heavyweight BG. If the whippet had stuck around, she'd keep her mouth shut: she didn't look the sort to cave in easily. But she might well have followed me out of the window. The way the BG would see it, the safety latch was across the door, their boss had been shot, and she was holding the smoking gun. Would they believe her story about a mystery intruder? They might do when they found the bits of broken slate on the terrace. I was pretty sure the BG wouldn't call the police, but who knew what they got up to in this fucked-up country?

I got out the iPhone. It was a while before Anna answered. 'It's me.' I heard the rustle of sheets and bedclothes as she sat up, and the gentle bleep of the life support doing its stuff in the background. 'Are the lads still there?'

She sighed. 'One of them is here all the time. It's the Asian guy at the moment. Don't they ever sleep?'

'I hope not. They've got a job to do. So do I.' I explained what I'd found out, and that Diminetz had been shot dead by his girlfriend, and what the next step had to be. 'Hong Kong.'

Anna was silent for a few seconds. 'Straight away?'

'I need your help. Can you book me a flight out of here ASAP – the first plane out in the morning?'

'I'll get online.'

'Wait out . . .'

A group of six or seven men in leather jackets and long coats walked past the end of the alleyway. Their heels clicked on the wet cobblestones. They weren't looking for me. By the sound of it, all they were interested in was the odd moan about life and the share of a cigarette. The night brought out all sorts of wildlife in the city.

I gave it another five seconds before getting back on the iPhone. 'As well as the flight, can you also book a hotel? A five-star. I need to look like I have cash to splash.'

She was totally awake now. 'Sure.'

'Can you find out Katya's blood type?'

I could hear the keys rattle on her laptop. 'I'll try.'

'How's the boy?'

'He's fine. He's putting on weight.' More rattling. 'OK, I've got Frankfurt at zero six oh five and . . .' The keys went into warp speed.

'I was told Katya went direct from there.'

'Correct. Direct to Hong Kong.'

'Perfect. But don't send me anything until I call you from the airport.'

'OK.'

I closed down reluctantly and deleted the log. It was good to have her at the end of the line. Not for all the PA stuff but because, well, for now at least, she was there.

14

Chisinau airport

05.37 hrs

I thrust some US dollars at the driver and stepped out of the cab, eyes peeled for police and Diminetz's BGs. I rubbed my hands together and tried to slap some warmth into my shoulder muscles. I'd binned my bomber in case the woman at Reception had talked to the police about the weirdo who'd hung around the lounge all night.

The airport was busy, but there were no groups of lads off to stag parties or families with far too many suitcases and kids draped over them trying to catch a few zeds. Moldovans didn't have the cash to burn on vacations. The crowd here was strictly business, and it looked like everyone had been to the same wheelie-case shop. And why not? It was the greatest invention on the planet, right up there with squeezable Marmite.

The locals stood out like a coach party full of sore

thumbs in their plastic shoes and shiny, badly fitting suits. If they'd brushed their hair, they needed to buy a new brush. Their shirt collars gave them away, too. The Europeans' were dry-cleaned and crisply pressed, but theirs were in shit state. I'd been able to spot bad ironing a mile off since my boy-soldier days. Pressing shirts the army way was almost our first lesson. If you started ironing a collar from the middle and worked your way towards the point, the material would gather and crinkle, and that would mean an 'extra' – a show parade at 23.00 hours, with shirt rewashed and re-pressed – for lack of attention to detail. You also had to wear your best uniform, your 'No. 2s', for the orderly officer's parade, and that meant buckles, brasses and boots had to be perfect too – or else.

The check-in queue was hardly moving. The young clerk with bed hair behind the counter seemed to have all the time in the world. Unfazed, two guys in front of me with sharp hair, good-quality suits and real leather shoes held their BlackBerrys and German passports at the ready. I wasn't sure whether they were about to invade Poland or just looking forward to another day in the Frankfurt office.

I smoothed my own hair down with my hand as we shuffled forward another couple of paces. There wasn't a woman in sight; no Chanel two-piece on its way back to Western Europe. Maybe female executives chose to leave these ex-Soviet-bloc shit-holes to their male colleagues while they jetted off to the chic places, like New York and LA. Or maybe they'd experienced the Checkpoint Charlie-style check-in arrangements once, and that had been enough.

A couple more businessmen joined the line behind

me, heads down, checking their smartphones, followed by a small group of locals: three teenage girls, accompanied by a man in his early sixties who waffled at them non-stop and kept referring to a couple of sheets of A4.

The girls' jeans and sweaters were pure street market, but as new as their identical bright green nylon suitcases. Wherever they were going, there'd be no problem finding those things on the conveyor-belt at Baggage Reclaim.

All three had short, straight brown hair. They wore no make-up, which was strange for round here, and showed no sign of excitement. In fact, they looked apprehensive. If they were going on holiday, it was to somewhere pretty grim. Judging by the brand-new, bright blue passports the old man was clutching, this was their first flight, maybe even their first time out of the country.

He was a foot shorter than everyone else in the terminal – and obviously taking his shepherding duties seriously. He wore his new denim jacket like a uniform, zipped all the way up to his jowls. His jeans were new too, and freshly creased, and – a nice touch – his trainers were the same green as the suitcases. It wasn't the too-young look of his clothes that was strange, but the jet-black hair. He carried on talking to the girls, slowly and gently, as if he was comforting them, cajoling them, making them feel that everything was going to be OK.

Bed Hair said something I didn't understand, so he mimed: No luggage?

I rolled my eyes. 'Business. Frankfurt, Moldova, one day.'

As I picked up my ticket and passport, I saw him nod at someone behind me. I turned to see a guy in a black-leather jacket legging it past the end of the queue.

I headed for the coffee stall. I spent a lot of time sipping a Nescafé instant and admiring the architecture as I watched a stream of passengers waiting at security, but I didn't see the guy in the leather jacket again. The three girls were the last to go through, glancing anxiously behind them. I followed them towards the barrier and gave them a smile of encouragement as they hesitated again; Grandpa's wave became so vigorous I thought he might take off too.

The Frankfurt flight was finally called. I left it ten minutes, then wandered towards the departure gate and studied the queue. The well-groomed Germans and the three girls were ready to board, but I didn't want to go over there. Not yet.

Another five minutes and it was thinning out. I started to move.

Then I stopped.

Bed Hair had come airside to process embarkation. Behind him there was another guy, the one in the black-leather jacket. It could have been some kind of anti-terrorist check – except that he wasn't looking at passports and boarding passes. He wasn't even looking at anyone in the queue. He was just waiting.

The flight was called again, for the last time. I had to go on. I stood behind the three girls and got out my documents.

I knew there was going to be a problem as soon as I reached Bed Hair. The guy in the leather jacket advanced along the far side of the counter, scrutinizing me and the girls, like he was weighing something up.

Bed Hair checked the girls' documents, then glanced at the guy in the leather jacket and shook his head. He waved them on and it was my turn. He checked the photo against my face. Then he flipped through two or three pages of visa stamps.

'You travel only you, yes?'

I nodded.

He still held onto the passport. Leatherman leaned over his shoulder and whispered something.

There was nothing I could do. The whispering stopped. Bed Hair gave back the passport.

I took it, and went to walk on. As I did so, Leatherman stepped in front of me and blocked my path.

'Tax,' he said.

'What?'

'Exit tax.' He held out his hand.

I got it. They weren't looking for terrorists. They were looking for passengers with foreign passports and no mates. These people were subject to a special tax. I reached into my pouch and pulled out a twenty-dollar bill. It must have been exactly the right amount because he spun on his heel and headed back to the check-in desk to start all over again.

I didn't bother waiting for change.

PART FOUR

1

30 August 2011
15.28 hrs

The German stewardess instructed me in English, then pre-recorded Cantonese to ensure my seat was in the upright position and my belt fastened as we were less than thirty minutes from landing.

At the press of a button my bed folded itself back into a very well-upholstered chair. It was a while since I'd flown business class on my own dime, but it was part of my cover story. So was staying in a five-star hotel. I had to behave like I had the kind of money it took to buy my very own cut-to-order kidney, and if Somali pirates could check out a hostage's financial status on a ten-year-old Dell powered by a diesel generator in the middle of nowhere, I was sure Diminetz's mates would be well up to speed. I had to pass their preliminary checks with enough A*s to know I wasn't just pissing them about.

The flight from Frankfurt had taken most of the night,

and the cabin staff handed out hot towels to help wipe the sleep out of our eyes. It didn't work for me: sleep was one luxury I couldn't afford right now. I was fucked: the thick wad of printouts about chronic kidney disease had taken me for ever to memorize – but I needed to convince 'Soapy' I was a serious buyer; I had to learn as much as I could about the organ-donor process, and the illness that had given me and my Hispanic partner such grief. I couldn't think of a better route to the people holding Katya; the people who'd suddenly invaded my life.

I pulled up the blind and looked out. The sky wasn't the electric blue of the tourist posters, it was dark and moody. But at least we were on time, and I could see shafts of sunlight bouncing off the South China Sea thousands of feet below, where they'd managed to pierce the handful of gaps in the cloud. Hundreds of black dots speckled the surface of the water, white wakes streaming behind them like con trails.

My first time in Hong Kong had been as a young rifleman during the illegal-immigrant drama in the 1980s. The Brits were still the controlling power, and whole families of illegal immigrants from mainland China had started jumping over the fence in search of a better life. The Cantonese-speaking locals didn't like their Mandarin neighbours breathing their oxygen, and the People's Republic of China's Communists weren't impressed that their comrades thought the grass was greener in the decadent West. Over-excited squaddies like me were sent out to stem the tide.

I'll never forget the night we arrived at Kai Tak. In those days approaching aircraft had to pull an impossibly steep turn, then fly in between the skyscrapers.

People's apartments were so close to the wingtips I could see them sitting down to bowls of chicken and rice; I could almost read the messages in their fortune cookies.

We bunked down at a camp near the airport. It was the first experience I'd had of a senior officer handing me cash. They weren't going to feed us until we were deployed north so we were given a ration allowance. It was supposed to guarantee our five-a-day but, of course, it paid for nights on the town instead, with just enough left over for a bag of something deep-fried on the way home.

Hong Kong was one of the places I'd heard about from the old and the bold, but never thought I'd see up close. New York might call itself the city that never sleeps, but Hong Kong seized the day – and the night – with a can of Red Bull up each nostril. The place never seemed to slow down, let alone stop. It teemed with neon, food stalls and mad, dense 24/7 traffic. I'd felt like I was living in the middle of a James Bond movie.

We spent two weeks at a stretch manning OPs along the border and running up and down hills to catch the IIs – illegal immigrants – when we spotted them cutting or climbing the border fence and making a run for it through the dense vegetation. I felt sorry for them: most were in shit state. The women had babies strapped to their backs with tea towels; the men had one small carrier bag containing the whole family's worldly possessions.

Their only consolation was to have been caught by us and not the Gurkhas. The IIs were shit-scared of them because the Chinese government's spin doctors had spread the rumour that if they nicked you they'd take your head off with a single swing of a *kukri*.

Of course that never happened; instead of them losing their heads we'd kiss goodbye to our rations. The Brits and the Gurkhas used to hand over their hard-earned boiled sweets and chocolate because most of the poor fuckers hadn't eaten for days.

But that was where the good news ended. We'd round them up and hand them over to the Royal Hong Kong Police, who'd hand them over to the People's Republic's Finest, and who knows what happened to them after that?

After a fortnight on the border we'd mince around Hong Kong Island for a week of sun and fun. We'd steer clear of the resort areas. A lot of IIs tried to do a runner via the South China Sea, and by the time they'd fucked up and drowned and spent a day or two floating around in the water, their corpses were bloated like puffer fish. Having a couple wash up next to your beach towel could put you right off your tofu.

I clipped on my seat belt as we cruised over the vast concrete and glass jungle. The border that I'd patrolled was still in place up in the New Territories. Since the transfer of sovereignty to the PRC in 1997, Hong Kong had become its first Special Administrative Region – which meant that it was still the high-rise land of opportunity, even by the standards of its booming mother country. This place was as awash with money as it had ever been, and as devoted to the task of making more.

2

The new airport offered a gentler approach than the old one. You no longer needed the brown trousers and bicycle clips that Kai Tak demanded, and you no longer had a ringside seat at other people's dinners. The Brits had built it outside the city, as part of the handover deal.

When the seat-belt sign was extinguished, I retrieved the small blue foldaway bag I'd bought at Frankfurt and ambled towards the door. The punters in economy were held back as us business and first-class types were fast-tracked to Baggage Reclaim and Immigration. The looks they gave us said it all – they were the same as I normally gave to the guys upfront in Gucci-land as I tried to unfold myself after eleven hours in a space the size of a small coffin.

The moment I passed through the door I collided with the damp, heavy heat and the smell of South East Asia, but as soon as we were on the walkway, the air-con took over. I followed the signs down an escalator towards an underground train. I was in a world of glass and polished concrete, and it looked like all its inhabitants were trying to board my carriage at once. It was worse than rush-hour in Tokyo.

Above the platform, an LED message board ticker-taped: *Relax! There will be another train in 2 minutes. Relax!* That was what I decided to do. I stood back and watched as two small locals in jeans and leather jackets joined the crowd. These guys weren't passengers. They'd been at the airport all day. They were wearing jackets to keep them warm from the air-con, and to conceal the pistols at their belts. The taller one came up to my chest and couldn't stop pulling down the hem of his jacket and patting the hardware underneath it. The crowd he was scanning included the three girls who'd boarded ahead of me in Moldova.

The next nice cold tram arrived exactly two minutes later and took me at warp speed to Immigration. I was issued with a 180-day visa without a second glance. This place welcomed people who were here to make or spend money. Hong Kong had one of the highest per capita incomes in the world, and the more the merrier.

The carousel at Baggage Reclaim had already swung into action. I waited for the girls to appear. They huddled together, checking their tickets and the sheets of A4 the old man must have given them. They hadn't a clue what they were doing. They clearly couldn't speak or read a word of English, let alone Cantonese.

The two security guys had followed the crowd, but they weren't interested in the girls. They probably had bigger fish to fry. As soon as three luminous green cases appeared on the conveyor-belt I left them to it, followed the herd towards Customs and passed through un-challenged. It's not like you need to smuggle anything into Hong Kong: they have more than enough of everything there already. Good stuff, bad stuff, and stuff you didn't even know existed.

3

The quiet, efficient, space-age atmosphere airside was shattered as soon as the automatic doors opened onto the arrivals hall. An excited crowd jostled with drivers for the prime positions behind a stainless-steel barrier. I scanned the cards they were holding for any sign of a Natasha, a Tanya – anything that sounded vaguely female and Eastern European.

I spotted one way down to the left that consisted of a lot of Us and Ns, held by a tanned woman in her late thirties with a little too much make-up. She was too well dressed – in beige linen trousers and a cream silk shirt – to join the scrum, but waited quietly at the end of the barrier, confident that her new arrivals would turn left and come her way. I walked past her and waited beside a mum who was too busy monstering two small boys with tear-stains down their chubby cheeks to pay me any attention. Cantonese is a fast and furious language at the best of times – even a polite 'hello' sounds like a major-league bollocking – and this little dynamo sounded like a whole herd of cats in a cage fight; the poor kids didn't stand a chance.

It was a couple of minutes before the Moldovan girls emerged through the sliding doors, eyes wide, huddled together like frightened sheep. As waves of other new arrivals washed past them, they moved slowly along the barrier, checking each taxi card for a hint of anything familiar.

Madam Beige waved and smiled, beckoning them over. Her teeth were Hollywood white. They scared the shit out of me, but the girls looked pleased. Their new guardian produced three bottles of mineral water as a little welcome, then flicked her dyed blonde hair behind her ears and kissed each of them on both cheeks. It was clear they didn't know her, but were mightily relieved to see her.

I edged closer, as if I was looking for someone, and caught an Aussie twang.

'Ladies, I need your passports.'

More Oscar-winning smiles; the overhead lighting glinted on her dental work. Mesmerized, the girls did nothing.

'Passports? *Pasaport?*'

The girls conferred and finally produced the bright blue booklets. They went straight into the Australian's handbag.

'Welcome, ladies. Welcome . . .' She treated them to so many flutterings of the hand and pats on the shoulder that even I felt pleased to see her. She started herding them towards the exit, smiling fit to bust, doing her best to ignore the slightly haunted look in their eyes.

I followed them towards short-term parking. As soon as I stepped outside, the heat swept over me, damp and heavy. I liked it, and always had. It reminded me of my first experience of being in an exotic location as a young squaddie, of fulfilling what I thought the army dream was all about.

I watched the girls take off their sweaters before climbing into a Toyota people-carrier. They'd probably put them straight back on once their new best friend got the air-con going. As the Toyota headed for the exit, I noticed that its badge was obscured by a sticker emblazoned with the PRC flag. I'd read about Japanese cars getting kicked in by the Chinese locals because of the ongoing dispute over who owned the Diaoyu Islands; maybe the PRC sticker was the riot of Beige's attempt to lessen the risk of having to bother the meerkats with an insurance claim.

I slid the camera app on my iPhone to video, turned the side of my head towards the wagon as it slowly negotiated the ticket barrier, and pretended I was making a call.

As it disappeared from view I headed back to Arrivals to stock up on Hong Kong dollars, a fistful of SIM cards and maybe a can of Fanta.

4

Blue cabs stopped on Lantau Island, the other side of the Tsing Ma Bridge. Green ones peeled off for the New Territories once they'd crossed the next bridge onto the Kowloon Peninsula. I'd selected a red one, which headed for Hong Kong Island.

One of the throwbacks to Brit rule was that, unlike mainland China, Hong Kong drove on the left, but it didn't seem to make the traffic move any quicker. We ground our way forwards in bumper-to-bumper chaos until we got within reach of the tunnel under the sea.

In any other circumstances, I'd have taken the high-speed Airport Express and got to Central in twenty-four minutes, changed to the subway for a one-stop ride to Admiralty and a short walk to the hotel. But I doubted anyone turned up on foot when they stayed at Upper House, the swanky five-star that Anna's ops room had booked me into.

I activated the SIM card and texted her.

On way to hotel Xx

It was strange leaving kisses. We never had, but it

was part of my cover story. I'd explain when I spoke to her.

I leafed through the information sheets again, as any caring partner would. I had to know everything about my loved one's condition. I needed to sound convincing enough to have travelled halfway round the world to find a way to save her.

Anna was going to be Hispanic, a racial grouping that suffered an unusually high incidence of chronic kidney disease – in the US, as many as one in eight – perhaps linked to diabetes and high blood pressure. I figured that the closer we could make the connection with Katya, the better.

The most important factors I needed to get my head around were blood matching, tissue matching and cross-matching.

Matching blood groups during transfusions had been known about for donkey's years, and was as important when transplanting kidneys as hearts. If the blood types of donor and recipient don't match, the resident anti-bodies attack the aliens and don't take any prisoners.

There also had to be a tissue match. A perfect one would only happen between twins or immediate family, but there were other acceptable levels of compatibility.

Finally, cross-matching was required to identify the presence of certain antibodies in the recipient that might cause rejection of the organ. A sample of the recipient's blood was mixed with cells from the donor. If the cells were killed, then the antibodies were present, armed and dangerous.

Convincing the fixers I could afford the operation would be the easy part; I'd have to pump in this kind of detail if I was to look the real deal.

We crept through the automated tollgate and into the tunnel, emerging soon afterwards into a sea of bright lights and huge cars. When I was here as a squaddie, I was told that Hong Kong had the highest concentration of Rolls-Royces on the planet. It looked like the only thing that had changed was the manufacturers' badges. I felt like some sort of futuristic City boy on his way to the trading floor to make a million or two.

The skyline had changed, of course, but that happened most days. Seven million inhabitants were crammed into an area three times the size of the Isle of Wight, and they had to go somewhere – and that meant somewhere vertical. All the skyscrapers looked brand new; anything more than fifty years old in this city was considered a national monument.

Hong Kong Island is one big hill, and light rain began to fall as we started to climb it. I turned in my seat for a glimpse of HMS *Tamar*, the Royal Navy shore station on the northern edge of the island – or, rather, the place it had once been. Back in the day, it was a boring, rectangular, grubby cream slab of an admin building with a weirdo high-rise supported by a triangular plinth on the roof. The base was just a glorified parking lot for warships, but had the best barber's shop in the known universe.

Samurai Sam looked old enough to have been giving out short-back-and-sides since the First Opium War in the 1800s, but he hadn't lost his touch: a few quick strokes of a cut-throat was all he needed. I guess he'd joined the Great Hairdresser in the Sky long ago – unless they'd buried him and his kit under the massive conference centre that now sat on the latest stretch of reclaimed land. If they carried on like this, they'd soon be able to swing a footbridge across to the mainland.

The street names were still refreshingly familiar. We drove along Gloucester Road and up Queensway, climbing past yet more high-rises. The Upper House was perched above a shopping and business complex in Admiralty District. It looked every bit as swanky and expensive as it sounded – very much the sort of place a man who had the cash to splash on a designer kidney would hang out. I'd taken Frank's philosophy of going to the garbage dump to look for garbage and turned it on its head.

The doorman's welcome was more Melbourne than Macau. He ushered me from the cab into an open-plan lobby that was so minimalist I felt I was cluttering up the place just by being there. I'd certainly have to up my clothing game if I was going to hang around here for any length of time. The dress code was international urban chic; everyone was dressed in neutral linens, with an extra colonial flourish of blazer and shiny shoes for the men.

The receptionist handed me my room card and asked when my bags would arrive. Her eyebrow arched a fraction when I said they wouldn't, but only for a split second.

I took the lift to the fourteenth floor and walked into a Sunday-supplement double-page spread. It was the most over-the-top suite I'd ever set eyes on, let alone stayed in. The floor-to-ceiling windows overlooked the bridge and harbour. The whole place was a shrine to bamboo, limestone, linen and giant cushions. There was a walk-in wardrobe and a bathroom big enough to sleep in, a rain shower and a giant tub complete with TV concealed behind a mirror. The blinds were remote-controlled. If I hadn't quite been in a Bond movie as a squaddie, I certainly was now.

It made me realize I'd come a long way since then. Hong Kong hadn't just been my first exotic trip: it had also been the first time I was inside an adult gaol.

Ned Kelly's Last Stand in Ashley Road on the mainland, the Kowloon Peninsula, was almost a rite of passage for squaddies. It was a small bar, all dark wood and dusty floors, with a stage for live acts that seemed to take up half the floor space. As you pushed past its Wild West-style swing doors, you really did feel you were on the set of *High Noon*. And, as in any self-respecting saloon, the night always ended with a fight.

I was there with a few mates late one Friday, trading banter with some sailors, and the banter turned into a brawl. Some of us who didn't run fast enough got lifted by the Royal Hong Kong Police, and even that felt exotic: cops with pressed khaki shorts and peaked caps.

Military prisoners were normally taken to Kowloon Police HQ, flung into the cells, and the MPs would come and collect them in the morning to be dealt with by their own units. You'd be marched double-time in front of the CO without your stable belt and beret; you were about to be charged, so had to be ritually stripped of identity and protection.

The usual defence was that the fight had started because someone had brought the battalion into disrepute. That covered a whole shitload of options: taking the piss out of the cap badge, calling the colonel a wanker, saying you'd like to shag the brigadier's daughter. If it was the navy or the RAF you were beasting – or, better still, somebody else's – you claimed that they'd taken the piss out of the British Army. That was normally enough to get away with a fine or restriction of privileges. You were given your belt and beret back and, most importantly, got to turn your offence into a badge of honour.

So off I went to the local nick with five lads from other units, sat on the cell floor in a torn and blood-stained T-shirt and waited for the MPs to arrive and take us away. But that didn't happen. Why not? It always did! When did I get awarded my badge of honour? Not this time . . .

All six of us were taken to Stanley Prison on the south side of the island, within spitting distance of our camp, given a crew-cut and orange overalls, and put in a cell with seven very pissed-off Triad members. It turned out the battalion had been called back early to the border, so by the time we were due to be collected, everybody had fucked off. That was us in the hands of the local police until they got back two weeks later.

I spent the time learning how to break rocks to make gravel, in what was known in polite circles as the Hong Kong Correctional Service facility. But at least the army brought us ration packs each day so I didn't feel totally abandoned.

I returned to the battalion as soon as my two weeks were over, to be given another short, sharp shock – and that didn't just mean the serious piss-take for failing to do a runner from Ned Kelly's. I was treated as if I'd been given a military sentence, which meant I was charged for the ration packs and for any medical care I might have needed, to the tune of forty-seven pounds a day. It didn't stop there: I also had fifteen days' pay docked. I was only earning twenty-one pounds a day, even with my overseas allowance, so it took me months to pay everything back.

It was getting dark now. Explosions of light peppered the skyline as far as the eye could see. Every building, streetlamp, boat and vehicle seemed to want to join the party. From where I was standing, it took my breath away.

It was a pity I wasn't there just to gaze out of the window.

5

I stretched out on the luxurious bed and picked up the phone, but didn't dial immediately, just rested it on my chest.

Eventually I punched in the numbers, and listened to it ring.

When she finally picked up, Anna sounded knackered.

'I'm in the hotel. A nice one – well booked! You ever been to Hong Kong?'

'Years ago, as a student.' That was what she said. What she meant was: 'I haven't had a moment's sleep in the last four days. Why did you wake me up now to ask such a fucking stupid question?'

'How's the boy? Still pink instead of blue?'

'Nicholas . . .' It sounded like she was swallowing hard. Maybe she was winding up to give me a full Cantonese-style bollocking. 'He had real problems with his breathing last night. They had to ventilate him. He's stable now, but it was touch and go . . .'

I suddenly realized I was short of breath. I'd only

ever felt that a handful of times before, but being thousands of miles away, with no control of things, seemed to make it worse. I knew I couldn't have done anything even if I had been there, but that didn't seem to make any difference. All I could manage was, 'He OK now?'

'He settled down about three hours ago.'

'Do you want me to come back?'

'No, Nicholas. No.' Her tone wasn't aggressive, just firm enough to make the point. 'The poor little thing has got even more tubes and monitors sticking out of him than before, but he's alive.' Her voice wavered. 'You can't do anything here. Find Katya.'

'The lads still there?'

'Yes.'

'Good. Then listen.' I went into sitrep mode. It was probably easier for both of us. 'I need your help with my cover. Are you OK with that? You're going to have to give up your phone number.'

'Of course. That's what these men are here for, isn't it?' She sounded a bit pissed-off that I'd even had to ask her.

'From now on, you're my Hispanic partner in Moscow and the little guy doesn't exist.'

'I understand.'

'I'm calling on the hotel phone. Your number will have been flagged for the bill, complete with Russian area code. I'll be texting and emailing you daily with concerned-partner stuff. You think I'm here on business, the energy market, oil and gas. You don't know I'm here to get you a kidney.'

I heard movement. 'OK, understood.'

'You've got my number. The kisses are what you put

when someone you love is dying of CKD. Can you send some back?'

There was a moment's silence. 'Yes.'

'Did you ping Katya's blood type?'

'O positive. Is that good?'

'Very good. I'm going to start looking straight after I clean up. Get some rest.'

'OK.'

I went to fill the limestone bath, and tapped out an email to Anna while the tap was running.

Going to meet some clients now. Will text soon. xx

Ten minutes later I climbed out of the water and shrugged on a huge fluffy bathrobe, towelled myself dry, then ruined it by putting my very smelly boxers back on.

I pictured the look Anna would have given me if she'd been watching. Maybe if I could convince her that I . . .

No, that was for later. I had to cut away now from everything except the mission.

The door to my suite closed itself behind me with a gentle *shush* and I headed for the lift.

6

My view of the sea was blocked by high-rises and the mass of traffic as I headed down towards the Admiralty area. After a while I hung a series of rights to get me into Wan Chai. Last time I was there, it was the place for a big night out. Perhaps because it was so close to HMS *Tamar*, it had also been the place for fights.

The whole stretch used to throb with neon, mostly splashing light across decaying buildings with rusty old air-conditioners. The bars advertised dancing girls and Tiger beer, neither of which were a whole lot fresher. The rats in the alleyways kept themselves busy, scampering over the bodies of drunken sailors who'd given up trying to remember the best way home.

I could see immediately that Wan Chai had lost its red-light district and gone upmarket. Shiny new shopfronts displayed Louis Vuitton bags and all that sort of gear – the genuine articles, because they were right next door to Starbucks. The rip-offs were peddled at market stalls.

The super-high buildings might look like glass,

concrete and steel space rockets, but the scaffolding they used to move the construction workers and kit around the sky was still made from bamboo tied together with string – by husband-and-wife teams, legend had it, because they could trust each other to make sure the knots were tight.

I went into a cutting-edge men's boutique and bought three pairs of jeans, three long-sleeved shirts, all white, three pairs of boxers and three pairs of socks. That was all I needed: one on, one clean, and one in the wash. Then I grabbed some toothpaste and stuff, a frothy coffee and a chocolate muffin.

My Starbucks name today was Ebenezer. I hated that 'And what's your name?' shit; it wasn't about to make my coffee taste any better. I'd amused myself one morning in Moscow by saving a page of Biblical names on my laptop and picking out the weirdest. The Russians never saw the joke, of course, and neither did the twenty-something behind the counter today. He just stood there, Sharpie in hand, waiting for me to spell it.

'Ben will do, mate.'

The rain had eased to a light spit, but it didn't make much difference to me. I was still acclimatizing, and already as damp under my sweatshirt as I was on top of it. I hovered for a moment on the kerb for a tram to rattle past. The old double-decker jobs were still going strong, two-storey advertising boards that ploughed along their tracks, oblivious to the teeming masses on foot. There wasn't a word in Cantonese for 'pedestrian crossing'.

I eventually found an Internet café on Jaffe Road. These joints are pretty much a thing of the past now, no matter where you are in the world. Most city dwellers are self-connected, and South East Asia has no shortage of free Wi-Fi. Eyes were glued to cell phones and thumbs were popping everywhere I looked.

This place was open 24/7. I paid my forty Hong Kong dollars for two hours, and cracked on. I replayed the video of the riot of Beige's people-carrier leaving the airport car park, then Googled *extra black number plate + Hong Kong* and logged onto the car registration website. The Toyota carried a mandatory cross-border plate for Guangdong Province, which meant the vehicle was registered to a foreign national or a Hong Kong Chinese, not a citizen of the PRC. So why did she have one? And how hard was it to get?

The answer seemed to be that you had to invest at least a million US dollars in China if you were based out of Hong Kong and wanted to check your investments in the PRC on a regular basis. But there were other ways. The blog sites claimed you could rent one from somebody who was already qualified, as long as you had more than three hundred thousand US dollars a year to spare. That was steep even if the Upper House room rates didn't make you blink, but I guessed it added up to no more than a couple of brokered kidneys or a lung or two in Donorland. Peanuts, if it meant she could come and go as she pleased.

Shenzhen, the nearest town across the border, was easily accessible to Hong Kong residents, but only on foot. Thirty years ago it had been a tiny fishing village. Then the PRC had decided to get busy and convert the surrounding area into their very first Special Economic Zone to kick-start their new-found enthusiasm for the capitalist ethic. It was now one of China's busiest container ports. The global supply of garden gnomes had to start their lifetime's adventure somewhere.

Hong-Kongers did shopping trips to Shenzhen the way Brits used to do booze cruises to Calais. A lot of stuff was still cheaper in the PRC, so they rode the Mass Transit Railway until the train terminated at the border, picked up a day visa at the station immigration desk, and legged it over the bridge into the world's biggest shopping mall. They'd load up their wheelie baskets and take the train home.

Google's next task was to tell me where I could give blood. I could always have gone and bought some – there was no shortage of hospital workers or clinicians in search of an extra payday – but that would take time, and I'd have had to take the blood type on trust. I'd also have had no guarantee of quality – it might have been contaminated with an STD or HIV. Katya was O positive; I was O negative. I'd read in the int that the rhesus factor didn't matter, so if I took my own, at least I'd know it was clean.

7

There were plenty of places queuing up for a pint or two of my blood: the Red Cross, every hospital and some private clinics with jazzy marketing campaigns showing happy teens giving each other high fives as they paid their weekly visit to donor clubs. But I wasn't looking for the happy-clappy approach. I needed somewhere a bit more hard-core.

I found a place on Kowloon that was open until eleven p.m. that night and hit the iPhone. The receptionist picked up before the second ring, and treated me to a ringside seat at a Cantonese cat-fight.

I interrupted her before she had a chance to get a full head of steam. 'Hello? You speak English?'

She ignored me and rattled on.

I tried again. 'Hello. Do – you – speak – English?'

She stopped, offended. 'Yes – *course* I speak English. You want appointment?'

'I need to give some of my blood for—'

'You need blood bank. You need Red Cross.'

'No, I understand. I don't need the Red Cross. I need

the blood for myself. I want to take the blood with me. I need it for an autologous donation. You understand what I mean – autologous donation?'

Silence.

I'd probably stretched her English. I'd certainly stretched my own.

'I want *my* blood. Can you do that for me?'

'*Wei.*'

'How much does it cost?'

I heard some rustling, and some fighting talk in the background.

'Seven hundred dollar.'

'Hong Kong dollars?'

'Seven hundred Hong Kong dollar.'

'All the equipment is sterile?'

'Everything sterile. When you come?'

'Tonight? Maybe in an hour?'

'OK.' The phone went down before I could even give a name.

I left the café and turned back in the direction of the hotel. It was fearsomely hot and humid; thank fuck the MTR to the peninsula would have air-con.

It had stopped raining, but the branches were still dripping. Locals with their strides rolled up dodged puddles so energetically they looked like they were playing hopscotch. I couldn't be arsed to do the same, so I just kept on going, the dickhead abroad, with my four bags of shopping and jeans soaked up to my calves.

I reached Admiralty station and put three hundred Hong Kong dollars, about forty US, on an Octopus travel card. Then I hit the Metro and headed north under the causeway at warp speed in a supercool aluminium tube. The air-con was so effective I felt like I'd just stepped into a deep freeze.

The carriage was only half full, locals mainly, but a couple of young female tourists too, backpacks dangling down their chests like baby-carriers, heads down, eyes locked on an MTR map. Everyone else was either checking their smartphones or talking into them.

As if on cue, my iPhone vibrated: Anna, replying to my email.

Have fun. Don't work too hard. xx

Moscow was only four hours behind Hong Kong. It would be mid-afternoon for her.

I'll try. How are you feeling? xx

The train kept dead level as it sped below the sea.

Not brilliant today. Miss you . . .

I felt myself break into a smile. We could still do 'normal', if only as a cover.

We stopped at the first underground station on Kowloon Peninsula, Tsim Sha Tsui. The MTR didn't surface until further into the New Territories.

Another four stops and I'd get out at Prince Edward, not that far from the centre of things. I knew it well. It was home to Police Headquarters. I hadn't bothered to venture any further on my weeks off. Go and see some ancient temple or museum? What was the point? I'd had my head up my arse for most of my life.

Some things don't change: the brown tiles at Prince Edward MTR certainly hadn't. I headed up to ground level and got mugged again by the heat.

Nothing much had changed behind the station either. My favourite food stall had treated itself to a bit of a face lift – it was more like a shop-front now, with a couple of tables, plastic chairs and a TV hanging off the wall – but at the counter it was very much business as usual. In the old days, I'd pointed and shouted at whatever had just been fried and got a plateful, most of which ended up down the front of my shirt. It was just like going to my kebab shop back home.

The specialities of the house had now been helpfully photographed for the benefit of foreigners and the illiterate – or maybe because the Chinese soap on the telly was playing at top volume and even the most switched-on customers could only communicate by sign language.

Two women were giving a lot of love and attention to a deep-fryer. The older one half turned and gave me the standard bollocking. I couldn't hear a word of it, but the lip movements said it all.

I knew exactly what I wanted: battered fish balls and curry sauce. I pointed at the picture and she turned back to the fryer. I waited, not sure if she'd taken my order or not.

'How much?'

'Fourteen dollar.' The younger one, maybe her daughter, held out her hand.

I gave her a twenty and admired the décor while I waited some more. No business enterprise in this part of the world would be complete without a lucky cat close by, right foreleg held high. This place had two: one on the counter and one on the shelf. They were battery-powered; their extended paws moved up and down as if they were saying hello. One of the very few bits of local knowledge I'd picked up when I was last there was that the cat wasn't waving. It was using its talismanic powers to beckon you in and separate you from your money.

My change appeared on the counter alongside a steaming polystyrene container. I picked them both up, helped myself to a set of wooden chopsticks from a nearby glass, and wandered back onto Nathan Road, the main thoroughfare north from the tip of the peninsula. It didn't actually reach the sea any more because of all the reclaimed land.

I went one block south and turned onto Prince Edward West. One corner of the junction was dominated by Police HQ – a sprawling complex of tower blocks, cells, vehicle compounds, old colonial buildings that were now dwarfed by everything that had been built since. Police stations here were more like small military camps: electric gates, high walls, barbed wire – they reminded me of my time in Northern Ireland.

The fish balls had cooled a little. I took a bite and started to laugh. I'd suddenly pictured myself being dragged out of the paddy-wagon after getting lifted at Ned Kelly's.

I knew where I was going. Right after the JetCo ATM there was a road that had no name. A few metres up was the Mong Kok private clinic. I got the last fish ball down my neck before I turned the corner and binned the container with the sticks.

I hit the stainless-steel intercom button and waited. Wherever you are in the world, you can get everything you need as long as you have cash in the neck pouch – and Hong Kong led the charge. I wanted a pint of my own blood, and all it had taken was one phone call and a train ride.

The woman who'd shouted at me over the phone did so again on the intercom.

'Blood donor. Seven hundred dollar. Blood donor.' I looked up at the smoked-glass bubble on the wall and gave the CCTV cam my best smile.

The door buzzed open.

8

Immediately through the door there was a bare wooden staircase, lit by a single forty-watt bulb. My boots echoed as I climbed, and the temperature dropped with each step I took towards the rumble of an air-con.

It had been framed in the lower half of the only window of the first-floor room. The pane above it was as grimy as its surroundings. All I could see through it was the occasional flash of red neon. Maybe it was Miller Time; I couldn't tell. To the right of it was a door the colour of a urine sample, to the left a receptionist behind a modern, IKEA-style desk, which looked like it belonged somewhere else. Against the wall beside her there was a highly varnished Oriental bench with dragons curling up each side. At least the light was stronger up there, and it smelt vaguely antiseptic.

The receptionist didn't look remotely interested in who'd just come up the stairs. In front of her were a phone, a little Post-it station and the laptop she was engrossed in; that was it. She was a fraction the wrong side of forty, with severely trimmed jet-black hair. She was even skinnier than Diminetz's whippet, and wore a baggy blue dress that was probably designed to be snug. She didn't move a muscle; even the Dr Scholls resting on the cross bar remained absolutely motionless.

I moved closer and realized she was busy watching the same soap as the women at the food stall.

She glanced up reluctantly. As the soundtrack swelled and her eyes returned to the screen, she held out one freakishly large hand. 'You have money? Seven hundred dollar.' Her other hand pulled open a drawer robotically and unlocked a small metal cash box. Her arms were so skinny they had veins on the outside. Maybe they used her for needle training.

'Shouldn't I be paying *after* you give me the blood?'

She wasn't impressed. She snapped the box shut and gave the kind of sigh that wouldn't have been out of place on the PRC's answer to *EastEnders*. She closed the drawer, smacked her money hand back onto the desktop, and finally managed to wrench herself away from the drama. 'You wait here.'

She opened the urine-coloured door about two inches and slipped through.

I headed for the dragon bench and sat down with my bags at my feet, like I was waiting for a bus.

She reappeared a few minutes later without saying a word, tapped away at the keyboard, and I had to listen to some old people arguing and a young couple sounding concerned all over again.

Ten minutes later the door opened. A woman emerged with a dressing on her left arm, and a pair of black eyes that had been on the receiving end of a good punch or two. She muttered to herself in hushed tones as she slipped away down the stairs. I assumed there had been a domestic and she'd wanted to stay away from the general hospital. I'd come to the right place.

The door opened again.

'Hello. I'm Kim.'

He was very old and very grey, in a shiny brown polyester suit and shirt, a tie that matched the paintwork and the kind of haircut that I'd only ever seen on Boris Johnson. His face creased into a smile that was almost bigger than he was. Everything seemed out of proportion in this place.

He held the door open, ready to usher me through. I got up, leaving my bags where they were. She could have my jeans if she wanted them; a hundred hot washes wouldn't get them to fit.

Kim beckoned me with a liver-spotted hand. 'Come, come . . .'

His surgery was straight out of a 1950s TV drama: two wooden chairs; an old varnished table laden with papers held in place by a brass Buddha, who looked every bit as cheerful as his owner; a blood-pressure cuff and monitor; a half-empty cup of tea.

Three cabinets lined one wall. A green canvas screen stood beside a well-worn PVC-covered bench spewing disintegrated foam from each corner. A paper-towel dispenser on the wall provided a much-needed layer of protection for anyone brave enough to sit on it. The window boasted the same air-con/grimy-glass combo as the one in the reception room.

'Please, please sit down.' Kim went and sat the other side of the table, smile still in place. He waited for me to settle. 'You want me to take blood, yes?'

'Yes, I want a unit.' I swivelled my left hand and pulled a not-quite-sure face. 'That's about a pint, yes?'

He nodded and beamed. 'Yes, yes. A pint. But—'

I cut in. There were things I needed to know. 'The unit would stay in good condition? I need it for three or four days, maybe longer.'

'Of course, no problem.' He waved away my concern. 'Why do you want it?'

I shoved a finger into my mouth. 'My wisdom teeth. They've got to come out. If I need a transfusion, I want to use my own, no one else's. I hate the dentist. HIV, hepatitis – they worry me.'

He nodded and agreed and clearly didn't believe a word. But what the fuck? Either he wanted my seven hundred dollars or he didn't.

He leaned forward. 'Your name, sir?'

'Harry. Harry Redknapp.'

He didn't look like a football fan.

'OK, Mr Redknapp . . .' He stood up and went over to one of the cabinets. As the door swung open, I saw a mass of giving sets. He came back with one in its sterile wrapping and a clear blood bag. These things were pre-prepared with Heparin or other anti-coagulating agents, depending on where they originated. Anti-coagulant was crucial to stop the blood decomposing. Additives like CPD (citrate phosphate dextrose) were also needed to keep the blood cells alive – which was why it was pointless drawing blood yourself: it would turn to jelly, stink like fuck within two days, and die.

I sat with my sweatshirt sleeve rolled up, arm resting on the table as he fastened the cuff. He gave it a couple of pumps to swell a vein, then snapped on a pair of clear rubber gloves, which I was sure had more to do with his protection than mine.

I didn't much care either way. We were in business.

9

The cannula slid in nice and easy. Kim bent so close to me I got quite intimate with his perfumed hair oil. It was never going to be able to control the haystack sitting on his head, but it smelt OK.

He released the pressure, slid out the needle, uncapped the cannula and taped down the plastic tube now connecting my vein to the bag. The equipment was sterile and the bag was filling. That was all I needed to know.

Kim was well pleased. 'Very good, Mr Redknapp. Seven hundred dollar very cheap, yes?'

'An absolute bargain.' I decided now was the time to take advantage of his relentless good humour. 'Kim, I need some help.'

'You all right, Mr Redknapp? You not feeling well?'

'No, no. I'm fine. But I have a friend who's very sick. He needs a new kidney. He's in America and they don't seem to be able to find a match. Do you know anyone who could help?'

His smile vanished long before I finished the

sentence. 'No, Mr Redknapp. *No*. Very bad . . . very . . . *dangerous*.' He gripped my arm. 'Tell your friend, please . . . very, very dangerous.'

I'd fucked up. He stood up, leaving the bag only about a quarter full, and headed for the door. Maybe he thought I was police, or some kind of investigative journalist.

He poked his head around the corner and gobbed off a series of instructions to the receptionist. He could have been ranting about me or asking for a weather forecast – I didn't have a clue. I looked down. The bag was a third full. I wasn't going anywhere fast.

He closed the door but didn't sit down again: he busied himself binning the wrappings instead. He didn't look like he was waiting for the heavies to arrive, but I glanced around the room for escape routes anyway. Old habits die hard. The bottom of the window was blocked by the air-con; the top by a solid pane. I eyed the Buddha. His base would fit neatly into my palm; the little fellow could head-butt someone, quickly and hard – in a Zen way, of course.

The door opened.

As Kim turned, I reached for my little brass mate. The robot appeared with a tray, a cast-iron teapot and two willow-pattern cups and saucers. She left as quickly as she'd arrived. Things were obviously hotting up on the soap front, or maybe she couldn't stand the sight of blood.

Kim poured. 'Milk, Mr Redknapp?'

I nodded, but wasn't about to drink anything unless he did too.

'Sugar?' The smile was back in place. 'Is very good. Good for your strength.'

We both ended up with milk and two sugars. I sipped the first cup of tea with condensed milk I'd had in years. By the time I'd finished it, the bag was full.

Kim started to disconnect me. He put a cotton-wool pad on the needle site, and encouraged me to press down on it. He bagged up the giving set and lobbed it into the bin with the mass of wrappers and packaging. He presented my still warm unit to me with a theatrical flourish.

'Thank you, Kim. Thank you.'

'No, thank *you*, Mr Redknapp.' He pointed at the door. 'Seven hundred dollar. Pay there, pay there.'

I pulled out my wallet and peeled off the HKD, which found their way into the money-box and back in the drawer before I could blink. As I turned to pick up my bag, the receptionist stood up, leaned towards me, and whispered, 'Kitty porn.'

I had no idea what the fuck she was talking about.

'Kitty porn? You want kitty porn?'

'Kitty porn?'

She frowned. 'You police?'

'No, I'm not police.'

'You want donor? You want donor, yes? Kitty get you donor. She know many donor. All price – man, woman, all price. Kitty got them all.'

She held up a Post-it on which she'd scrawled a whole lot of numbers.

'Kitty Porn. Four thousand dollar. Four thousand dollar.' She glanced uneasily at Kim's door.

'Four hundred American dollars, OK?' I wanted that phone number, but I didn't have four thousand Hong Kong on me.

She didn't hesitate. 'OK.'

I tucked the blood sachet into my bag and fished out a fistful of my escape package money. She was right behind me: her bonus wasn't going anywhere.

The deal was done.

'You not police? No police?'

If I was, it was a bit fucking late now, wasn't it?

'No. Not police.'

I checked the Post-it: an eight-digit number, starting with a five. That meant it was a mobile, registered on Hong Kong Island.

I legged it back down the stairs, aiming for the JetCo ATM. I was clean out of ready cash; in this place, you always needed more.

10

The Upper House

I showered this time, worked my way through all the frou-frous and big fat towels and finally stretched out on the duvet in my bathrobe and towelling slippers. I tapped out a text to Anna. *Going to bed now. Will call tomorrow. Hope you're feeling better. xx*

I dialled the number on the Post-it. It rang for what seemed like for ever. Maybe Kitty Porn had seen the number, not recognized it, and just fucked it off. Understandable – I did that myself. If it was important, they'd ring back – or try me some other way.

I expected an answering machine to kick in, but it didn't. After another fifteen seconds or so a female voice snarled at me in Cantonese. This one was extra pissed off because it was so late.

'Kitty? Kitty Porn? I was given your number.'

'What you want?' she snapped back, but at least it was in English. Sort of.

'Are you Kitty?'

'What you want?'

I kept it in slow-mo. 'I was told you could help me find a donor.'

'Donor? We not charity! Donor for what?'

It was pointless fucking about. 'I'm looking for a kidney for someone.'

'What your name?' She'd calmed down a bit.

'My name is Nick.'

'Where you?'

'I'm staying at the Upper House, on the island at—'

'I know Upper House. Tomorrow you be outside on terrace. Ten in morning. You know terrace?'

'I'll find it.'

'OK. You be there. I find. You black man? White man?'

'White. I'll be wearing a white shirt and jeans.'

A click, then silence.

I lay there, suddenly too tired to bother getting under the duvet. I couldn't even be arsed to move the iPhone off my chest or press the remote to close the blinds.

I shut my eyes.

My hair was still wet on the pillow when the iPhone vibrated. Anna's reply flashed at me.

All good here. xx

Pity the 'xx' didn't mean anything. I was getting to like them.

11

The Upper House

31 August 2011
10.17 hrs

In fact it wasn't called the Terrace, it was called the Lawn. Why wouldn't it be? It was on the sixth floor, up a ridiculously wide flight of steps lined with aromatic candles – all part of what they called 'The Guest Experience'. The hotel had been created from the top thirteen storeys of a fifty-floor 1980s tower, which put the Lawn right up there among the high-rises. I'd wondered why my room – on the thirteenth floor – gave me vertigo.

Even though the sky was as grey as the waiters' shirts, I could feel the sun on my neck and shoulders. But we were some way short of many of the buildings around us. The tops of their glass and steel towers were lost in the clouds. The ones I could look down on also had their own little gardens. With the city's noise and chaos safely below us, it was Tranquillity Central up there – and in case you hadn't got the message, the designer had gone all-out on the Zen. Pristine white stone and gravel separated stretches of lush grass; beanbags the size of UFOs sprawled around umbrellas and tables. Where the humidity had encouraged last night's rain to cling to the seats and stone pathways, it was simply vacuumed away.

The cream of the international business community had gathered there. Immaculately dressed and with freshly showered hair, they munched croissants and sipped rainbow-coloured juices or exotic blends of coffee as they scrolled their iPad Minis and tapped on their smartphones. I was the only punter on my own, and the only one looking like a tourist. I nursed my second cappuccino under an ivory-lacquered umbrella, wishing I'd bought some sun-gigs. But since the Upper House coffee cost nearly ten US dollars a throw, I thought I'd probably give the hotel shop a miss.

It was ten eighteen. In the last twenty minutes a couple of solo women had appeared at the top of the steps, but neither had given me a second glance before going to join her associates.

If Kitty or one of her sidekicks didn't turn up, I'd hit a couple of medical centres, then head out to the airport to see if I could spot the riot of beige – or anyone else waving signs for East European arrivals.

Ten nineteen. I'd give it until half past, then make a move. You can always be twenty minutes late; anything more than thirty is no accident.

I hadn't sent Anna a text or an email that morning; I didn't want to wake her. If there had been a major drama, she would have got hold of me.

Ten twenty-five, and I signalled to the waitress that I wanted to sign my bill. A woman's head emerged from the stairs. She flicked her shoulder-length black hair away from the mirrored aviators that covered half her face, and scanned the terrace. As the rest of her appeared I could see she wasn't about to go the corporate route. Her blouse and blue jeans were skin tight and she had a bright red leather bag slung over her shoulder that was big enough to sleep in.

She spotted me immediately and tottered towards my umbrella in heels that were nearly the same height as she was.

'You Nick?' She sat down without waiting for me to answer or to finish getting up to shake her hand.

'Can I get you a drink? Coffee? Iced tea?'

My new mate didn't answer me, but gave the young waitress who materialized at her shoulder both barrels in Cantonese, then sent her on her way before I could ask for anything myself.

'OK. What do you want?'

The small-talk was clearly over. She leaned forward, elbows draped over her denim-coated thighs, shoulders drooping, as if she'd already had a hard day. The handles of her bag were now locked in the crook of her arm.

The few wrinkles I could see behind her glasses matched the ones around her mouth. Her nails were perfectly manicured and polished dark red, but her hands said she'd seen worse days than this, for sure. A gold bracelet on her right wrist was meant to cover a crudely inked tattoo that might have been a fish or turtle. On the underside of her left a couple of laceration marks had aged and lightened against her darker skin.

Her clothes and handbag might have been Prada, but that girl had come from somewhere else entirely.

'Are you Kitty?'

'Yes, Kitty. Yes, yes. What you want?' She hadn't bothered with Charm School; she was on a mission.

'I need a kidney – for my partner. She could travel here, anywhere.'

She shrugged. 'How much money you got?'

I wasn't playing hard to get, but I needed her to know that I wasn't going to settle for something off the shelf. 'It depends whether you can find what I need.'

12

I sat back as the waitress returned with a tomato juice. At least, it looked like tomato juice.

Kitty delved into her bag and took out a sleek gold case and matching lighter. She flipped back the lid, sparked up a slim cigarillo and treated me to a lungful or two of noxious smoke.

I leaned forward, and so did my distorted reflection in each of her lenses. There were more fingerprints on them than at most crime scenes. 'My partner is Hispanic. She has chronic kidney disease, probably triggered by diabetes. I'm after a Hispanic kidney, from a living donor.'

'Big shopping list.' She took another drag, and when the smoke had cleared I could see that she had leaned forward too. 'How much money you got?'

I gave her my best Buddha smile. 'As much as it takes – so long as I get what I want.'

She smiled too, letting me know that her dental work didn't match her designer labels. A scrape and a polish to strip back the nicotine would have been a good place to start.

Kitty removed a small strand of tobacco from her tongue with her thumb and forefinger and flicked it aside. Then she aimed her cigarillo at me, at almost point-blank range. 'You want bespoke, you pay four hundred thousand dollar. You got that kind of money?'

I kept my gaze level. 'What's the point of money if my partner is dead?'

My reflection stayed dead centre in her gigs. I couldn't read her expression, but I knew I had her full attention.

It was at least thirty seconds before she spoke. 'How did you get my number?'

'I asked around. I have many numbers.'

She took another drag, sizing me up. I sat back, waiting to see if I'd passed the test. To help things along, I got busy with my iPhone. Fuck it, I had places to go, other people to see. She'd better get a move on if she wanted my four hundred thou.

The waitress swung by and I beckoned again for the bill. Kitty fired off another volley of Cantonese before the girl had a chance to oblige. Then she turned back to me. 'You come now.'

'Come where?'

'You get taxi. I show you.'

I shrugged apologetically at the waitress as Kitty started firing away on her mobile, hand cradling the mouthpiece, Japanese-style. I signed the bill and we made our way to the lifts.

A cab was standing at the rank, door held open by another grinning Australian. Kitty gobbed off to the driver and he set off downhill towards the causeway. I didn't have a clue where we were going, but it didn't matter. It felt like progress.

Kitty stared out of her window, with her head at enough of an angle for me to see one of her eyes for the first time. There was no light in it. She wasn't remotely interested in our surroundings. She was numb – either bored with me or bored with life.

'Where are we going?'

The eye finally moved as we passed a shoe shop. 'Not far. Aberdeen. I know the person to help you. Kitty know everyone, and this one right for you.'

13

So Kitty was the middleman for the middleman. If I was about to be dicked around, it wouldn't be her doing. And if she was lying, I'd know soon enough.

We hit the main drag and climbed an elevated section, a futuristic freeway that curved between the buildings around us, about ten storeys above ground level. I knew Aberdeen. I knew there was an exit south towards Happy Valley and on through a tunnel to the coast. Once upon a time it had probably been a happy jungle home for monkeys and lizards; now it was just a jungle – the monkeys were bouncers and the lizards owned casinos.

A giant arena loomed in front of us. I'd never been inside it, but I used to pass the floodlit track on my way back into camp, heaving with people wanting to give away their cash. The Chinese loved gambling so much they even had to invent money to do it with. They'd bet on where a fly was going to land and when it was going to take off.

There was another track up in the New Territories,

but it had also ranked alongside museums and ancient temples for me as a place I didn't want to take my wallet. Cash was for beer, paying off bar-fight fines, and saving up for a second-hand Ford Escort XR3i. What else was there?

We emerged from the two-kilometre-long tunnel under the mountains in the centre of the island into a burst of sunshine. The clouds were starting to part. The driver paid cash at the toll-booth. From here, I knew it was left towards Stanley, and straight on to Aberdeen.

Aberdeen was where you went for a night out when you couldn't afford a taxi north, or couldn't be arsed to spend for ever on a bus that took the long way round. The whole place was packed with rows and rows of very high and very dull apartment blocks – and some very Gucci ones on lush green garden plots built at weird angles overlooking the sea.

I'd never heard of *feng shui* before I'd got there, but soon discovered it dominated local architecture. Banks embraced it most enthusiastically of all. Even their most traditional concrete, glass and steel blocks would feature a strange door facing in a strange direction. It had nothing to do with fashion, and everything to do with making sure the *chi*, whatever that was, could flow into the building and bring good luck with it. It seemed to be working for Hong Kong.

We entered the sprawl of Aberdeen. Kitty got back on the phone; this time I could make out a man's voice at the other end. The taxi turned off the main drag and dropped down towards the coast. If there had ever been any beaches, they were now buried under thousands of tons of *feng shui*-oriented business enterprises and industrial-scale oil tanks.

We turned into a private drive opposite a bus terminal that deposited us beneath the Aberdeen Marina Club. It had just been built when I was last here. This was the place 007 would definitely have brought his white tuxedo for a shaken-not-stirred – but it had been out of bounds to people like me. The last thing they wanted was a bunch of squaddie dickheads baring their arses at the bar.

The Marina Club was the expats' playground within a playground, a waterside oasis for the *über*-rich in the middle of a concrete and glass desert. Swimming-pools, tennis courts, apparently even an ice rink, made it as much a social club as somewhere to park a yacht or two.

On the way into Aberdeen, jammed into a bus or a taxi, we often used to see the limos lining up to drop their well-dressed cargo for a night of boaty fun. Me and a couple of mates did try to bluff our way in one night, detouring our ride from Stanley to see if we could join the party. There was a wedding on – braziers outside and ribbons everywhere – and after a night on the town we thought it would be a piece of piss to slip past security in our Hawaiian shirts and Samurai Sam short-backs-and-sides. We hadn't even got as far as the gate before two heavies stepped out of the shadows, shaking their heads: *Don't take another step, lads, it's not worth it . . .*

Kitty didn't open her door or move to get out. 'Everything OK. Don't worry. This really nice place. Go, go – go inside!'

I got out but she stayed put and gobbed off at the driver. The heat and humidity slammed into me again as the sun found another gap in the cloud. Kitty powered down her window. 'Go inside – someone will meet you.' She shooed me away with the back of her hand.

The taxi swung round and drove off as I walked up the steps. I went through the glass doors and found myself in a vast, empty foyer, not a soul in sight. Then somebody got up from behind a huge settee and came towards me. I recognized her at once.

14

She was in a blue flowery dress that showed off her tanned arms and shoulders, sun-gigs perched on top of her head doubling as a hairband. Her white-leather bag matched her smile. She threw out her free hand to greet me and slid straight into textbook PR mode, eyes fixed on mine, voice low to draw me in. 'Hi, Nick. I'm Sophie. Sophie Derry. I'm so glad you were able to make it at such short notice. Thank you for that.'

She glided the final couple of paces and placed her cool palm in my not-so-cool one. Her expression was the perfect balance of concerned and welcoming. I'd seen it before, yesterday, at the airport. 'Kitty said you were in need of help.'

I didn't smile, didn't frown, just kept everything in neutral.

Her free hand, clear polished nails like talons, covered the two of ours that were still engaged. 'Welcome. I will do everything in my power to help you. This is a very emotional and very worrying time. I know that, Nick. I know. You're at your wit's end.

227

Seeking help for a loved one, the trauma, the distress can take its toll. But I want you to know I've helped hundreds of people like you and your partner. I can bring an end to your suffering. You've found what you've been looking for so, please, let me take some of your load.'

'Thank you.'

She finally let me have my hand back and guided me up the stairs. 'Now, Nick – may I call you Nick? Would you like some coffee?'

I nodded a yes to both questions. The first floor was yet another shrine to wood and leather. Well-dressed people sipped coffee, read papers, checked if the Hong Kong exchange was performing strongly enough for them to add to their fleet. The wall facing the marina was floor-to-ceiling glass. Hundreds of super-yachts and gin palaces were parked up cheek by jowl like limos in a short-term car park. They were hemmed in by the buildings and small industrial units surrounding the inlet, but it was clear that their owners were riding out the recession just fine. Over to the right, an elderly woman in a bathing cap was doing methodical lengths of the club pool.

Sophie saw me scanning the place. 'I know. Gorgeous, isn't it?' She put an attentive hand on my shoulder, just as she had done with the Moldovan girls.

Close up, I could see that while she kept herself in good shape, it was a struggle. She wasn't wearing a wedding ring, but the ruby on her right ring finger probably took a few hours in the gym to get the strength to lift. A gold Cartier Tank glinted on her opposite wrist – not cheap, even in Hong Kong. She smoked. I could see a pack of Benson & Hedges in her open bag. She behaved and dressed like a top executive – though her type of business didn't have cards and a boardroom.

'Have you been to Hong Kong before, Nick?'

'No. But I heard and read online that I could get what I needed here. I have to find a kidney donor. I don't care that much about the view.' It had to be said. Neither of them had come out with it, and I wanted to make sure they hadn't misunderstood me, that 'kidney' wasn't Cantonese for 'shiny new boat'.

Her hand settled on my shoulder. 'You know, I've had an idea. We could sit here and talk or, if you'd let me, I could take you out on the water. The view is stunning. You'll see Hong Kong in a totally different way. One glimpse of it and you'll want to come back with your partner afterwards, as a gift to yourselves for all you've been through.'

She could see my cogs starting to turn.

'I was going to take a couple of hours out today anyway. Then Kitty called and I thought maybe you'd like to come too. Hong Kong from the sea – a little slice of Heaven!'

She paused for a second to give me some more thinking time. It might be a stitch-up. Maybe I'd pushed a bit hard and, like Kim, she thought I was a cop or a reporter. But her dentistry was still on maximum wattage. And if I really did have four hundred K to spend, a nice boat trip was a small price to pay for my business.

'Unless you get seasick, of course. We can sit here if you prefer. Whatever you fancy, Nick.'

'You know what?' I smiled too, but didn't forget to let her see the pain behind my eyes. 'My partner loves boats.'

15

We went around to the back of the club and out onto one of the wooden pontoons. The blisteringly hot air carried the tang of the sea, the rev of an engine, the blast of a boat horn. The traffic on the main road was almost drowned by the incessant chink of the rigging. The sunlight was full-on now and Sophie's gigs had come down like the Stig's visor.

I squinted up at the vegetation hanging off the balconies of a nearby high-rise, and the massive square hole carved through the top third of the building.

She followed my gaze. 'You know about *feng shui*?'

I nodded. '*Chi* flow, something like that?'

She gave me a flash of teeth. 'Spot on. It means they can charge out the apartments at fifteen thousand dollars a square foot. The mainland Chinese are the rich ones now. People like me are the new coolie class. Those guys buy these places so they can sit and watch their babies.'

She waved in the direction of the millions of dollars bobbing up and down in front of us.

We stopped at a stainless-steel gate and she tapped the keypad. It opened with a discreet buzz. She ushered me through ahead of her. 'You're British, aren't you, Nick? Can I detect a London accent? We just adore *EastEnders* here.'

'You can. But I moved to Moscow a few years back, for work.'

'I hear Moscow is quite a place. What is it you do there?'

'Oil and gas. But I don't get out much. Admin is more my thing than fieldwork.'

'Whatever pays the bills, eh?' She stopped for a moment. 'You know what? You're now walking across a piece of British history. Right here . . .' her index fingers pointed downwards '. . . this is the original Hong Kong. You Brits came here, to this very inlet, in the seventeenth century. It was just a small fishing village. Isn't that amazing?'

I nodded – even though it wasn't as amazing as the fact that some of the opening scenes of Bruce Lee's *Enter the Dragon* had been shot here. When you're young, information like that is important.

Her nose wrinkled beneath her sun-gigs as she saw the thin film of oil coating the water around the pontoon; a hundred different shades of blue and orange, swirling in the sunlight. 'It's hard to believe, sometimes, that Hong Kong means "fragrant harbour" . . .'

She brightened again. 'Now we've got all this, just because you guys wanted to sell opium to the Chinese. A bit like you in Moscow, selling oil to the Arabs, am I right?' She didn't give me time to answer before heading on down the walkway. 'I'm so glad the Chinese didn't want to buy your opium. If you hadn't gone to war, none of this would be here.' The smile was right back in place. 'So thank you, Nick.'

She slowed.

'Here we are.' She pointed to a very shiny blue boat with a guy in white jeans and a striped T-shirt mincing around by the wheel. 'That's *my* baby . . .'

It really was. *Baby* was stencilled across the stern in gold italic lettering. But it certainly wasn't one of the smaller Sunseekers. This brand-new piece of machinery would have set her back at least 1.5 million sterling. We were a long way from *EastEnders* territory.

The Manhattan 53's roof covered the stern, shading a pair of white settees that faced each other across a slatted teak table anchored to the deck. An aluminium gangway seemed to have slid automatically from a little door in the stern. Waiting for us at the end of the pontoon were two pairs of leather deck shoes.

She started to take off her heels. 'It's what we do on boats. If not, Bruce here will get upset about the decking.'

Bruce? *Enter the Dragon?* This was becoming a bit surreal.

'Good morning, Bruce.'

He gave me a wave and a smile, then headed on board. I could see the outline of a mobile in the back pocket of his jeans. He was a little younger and shorter than Sophie. At first glance he could have passed as Chinese, but a closer look told me he was a pint-sized version of Genghis, but without the goatee. Wherever he came from, he hadn't arrived in Hong Kong as a deckhand. His short hair was expensively cut and his jeans were designer. Even the blue-and-white T-shirt looked high-end.

As I fumbled with my Timberlands, Sophie draped the neatly folded blue-and-white-striped towels over the seats so we wouldn't scald our arses. She was soon busy waffling away with Bruce and gesturing. I heard her mention Repulse Bay, which I knew was on the way to Stanley. Then, 'Bruce, go and see if we've got some shades – I don't think Nick has brought his.'

I stepped up on deck.

'Please, Nick, make yourself comfortable.'

Bruce disappeared through the door to the left of the steering wheel and down into the cabin.

I sat under the shade on one of the settees. My shirt was glued to my back. I hoped it would sort itself out once we got moving.

Bruce laid out three sets of sun-gigs on the table for me to choose from. I picked up the Ted Bakers and instantly felt better. The engine kicked off without as much as a puff of smoke and hummed gently.

Sophie swung into perfect-hostess mode. 'I never get tired of this. Now, what would you like to drink? We have beer, Coke, a very nice local lemon juice or, if you prefer, something stronger . . .'

'The local brew sounds great, thank you.'

She turned to a cabinet under the pile of towels. 'On its way. I absolutely love this stuff.'

While Bruce did things with ropes, she opened the fridge and brought out a jug of cloudy liquid with ice and slices of lemon. Condensation immediately coated its sides. She set it on the table and returned to the cabinet for glasses as we eased away from the pontoon.

Bruce was almost on tiptoe at the wheel, checking left and right for other vessels.

Sophie selected the folding chair at the head of the table, looking towards the stern, but turned it so she was sitting at forty-five degrees, knees towards me. She was making things more intimate; she knew exactly what she was doing, and she was doing it well.

She poured the juice as we worked our way past the pleasure boats and started to get in among rusty fishing smacks and a couple of old dredgers. Massive thirty-storey tower blocks lined the shore, cheek by jowl with the refineries. We carried on towards the sea, which I could begin to make out through the chicane between the two breakwaters.

16

Baby glided into the ocean. The sun came out to celebrate and bounced across the dark-green water. Bruce still had his work cut out behind the wheel. Speedboats of all shapes and sizes zipped around us, and slalomed between a string of massive cargo ships whose decks were piled high with containers. Yet more garden gnomes from Shenzhen, I guessed, en route for the world's pound-, dollar-, rouble- and euro-shops to seek their fortune.

My shirt unglued itself and Sophie's hair started to jump about as Bruce opened the throttle. I drank my lemonade and admired the lush green islands of the South China Sea. Like so many of the places I'd visited while I was in the army – and in the years since – I'd been to quite a number of them, but never actually given them a second glance. Half the time, I hadn't really wanted to. I'd needed to get there, get the job done and get out. Now there was time to soak it all in, I tried to remember if I'd ever really stopped and looked at the scenery when I was at Stanley, which was now just round the corner.

After the big build-up, Sophie seemed less interested in the view than in which direction her knees were pointing.

'So, Nick, why don't you tell me your story? The more I know, the easier it will be to find exactly what you need.'

'Well . . .' I took a breath, then trotted out the story I'd given Kitty. 'But all that's on hold, as far as she's concerned. She doesn't know I'm here to search for a donor. She doesn't want one. She thinks I'm away on business. Look, Sophie . . .' I leaned closer, so she could feel my sincerity as well as see it. 'Back home there's a four-year wait just to get on the transplant list – and she disagrees with jumping any queue, for anything. She says we'd be part of a system that's making Russia an even worse place to live in than it was during the old days.'

Sophie nodded slowly as I poured out more of my heart for her to examine.

'So then I suggested we look at some other options, maybe go to Turkey or South America to find a donor. But her answer was still no. She's frightened, I guess, not only for her own safety – the possibility of contamination – but for the donor's too. We've both done our research . . .'

I waited to see her reaction, but there wasn't one.

'Let's be clear, Sophie, I know what I want is illegal. I don't care about that – I care about Anna. Equally, I don't want some Chinese Death Row prisoner's kidney stuck into her, even if she does agree – who's to know what diseases it might carry? I know that I can get a designer kidney here, and I know that I can afford it.

'What I want is a Hispanic organ – it's partly a religious thing – from a living female donor. I want to meet the donor to know she has not been coerced, and of course I want the surgery to be the safest there is. When I go back to Moscow I want every base covered, so the only answer Anna can give me is yes. I don't care about anything else. Can you do that for me?'

Sophie was totally absorbed, as if I was revealing the secret of the universe. 'Thank you for being so candid. I can assure you, we will be able to cover every single one of your bases.' She sat back and crossed her legs. 'My husband died from CKD eight years ago. He suffered for far too long while we tried to find a donor. I understand your heartache. I understand the fear, the anger, the help-lessness. That's the reason I started my own matching service. I don't want anyone else to go through that – ever.'

I nodded.

'I have a wide selection of donors, and brand-new world-class surgical facilities. All the donors are healthy, considerate people, and well looked after. They're paid, of course, but they *care*. I think I may already have a number of possibles for Anna . . .'

She uncrossed her legs and leaned forward again. 'Are you married?'

I needed to keep the story as close to the truth as possible.

'We live together. I met her when I first moved to Moscow. She's Russian – from Cuban parents. It's not unusual there.'

'Do you have any children?'

I managed to do nothing more than shake my head. 'We're waiting until we get married. She's a good Catholic girl.'

Sophie's teeth flashed. 'How old is she?'

'Thirty-five. And she's fit – apart from the diabetes and CKD, obviously.'

She sipped some juice and wiped the corners of her mouth with a thumb and forefinger. 'A Cuban in Moscow. Why stay? I'd rather be in Havana any day, wouldn't you?'

'Warmer, for sure.'

She rose to her feet. 'I want to show you something.' She pointed to a spit of land to the port side behind us. 'You see those caves?'

The rock face was covered with greenery. Shove a lollipop stick in the mud in the tropics and it would start sprouting.

'You see? Just on the waterline?'

Turquoise water splashed in and out of five or six dark semi-circles that were clearly too symmetrical to be anything other than man-made.

'The Japanese excavated them during the war, to hide their kamikaze powerboats. They packed them with explosives and waited for you guys to come back and take the island. They protected the harbour.' Sophie moved alongside me. 'Can you imagine that? Steering a powerboat into a ship and blowing yourself to smithereens? Not my idea of a good day at the beach, I can tell you.'

I guided her back to her seat. 'Look, Sophie, I have some questions I need to ask you. I've read so much bad stuff . . .'

She picked up the jug and poured us the last of the juice. 'Of course, Nick. Whatever you need to know.'

'What sort of surgery is involved? I mean, you won't just cut her open and do it old-school?'

Sophie recoiled at the thought. 'Jesus, Nick, that's strictly for the butchers. We use only the finest surgeons available, and they go the laparoscopic route. A few very small incisions in the abdominal area, purely to insert the instruments.'

'Keyhole surgery?'

'Precisely. Keyhole surgery. A tiny camera guides the team. A minute three- to four-inch incision allows the kidney removal, then the introduction of the new organ. They close the incisions using dissolving sutures, so she won't even need a follow-up appointment. A month, six weeks down the line, you won't be able to tell it happened. We take exactly the same care of the donor.'

'How soon after the op could she come home?'

'My patients and their donors normally leave hospital one or two days after the procedure. Anna will need to go in the day before, of course. She'll feel a bit groggy when she wakes up post op, and perhaps a little bit of discomfort, but she'll always have a nurse at her bedside, closely monitoring her vital signs. If she's in any pain, we'll make sure to relieve it. I encourage my patients to get out of bed the night of the surgery. The day after, they're all up and about.'

'I don't want to rain on your parade, but what happens if something goes wrong? What if there are problems when we get back to Moscow?'

'There won't be. When you get home, Anna will need to limit her activities for a while. No lifting for about four weeks. She's going to feel tired for the first week or two. She'll probably need a nap here and there. I'll give her some very clear notes about what to expect, what to eat, how much to exercise, that sort of thing. There may be some swelling around the incision, so she should plan to wear loose, comfortable clothes for a while, but she should be able to return to work within two to three weeks.

'I'll take you both through the procedure in greater detail when we get to that point, so that you're both a hundred per cent happy.'

'What if she needs medical attention back home?'

'She shouldn't, but if she does, there are no obstacles. She'll have done nothing illegal . . .' She reached for my arm again. 'You must love her very much.'

I looked back over the stern. The madly overcrowded coastline was now a kilometre away.

17

The Stanley peninsula had taken shape over the far side of the boat. At the tip I could see Stanley Fort, a curious mixture of gracious colonial buildings, gun emplacements, bunkers and blockhouses that used to house the British garrison: gracious colonial for the head shed, blockhouses for the squaddies. Even at this distance, it looked a lot smarter than when we'd had it. The main building had been given a lick of white paint and a massive red PRC flag now hung where a smaller Union flag had done.

'I know I only got here yesterday, but that's the first sign I've seen that this place is under new management.'

'Ah, yes – the People's Liberation Army base, scene of your last stand against the Japanese.'

Bruce chose that moment to begin a sweeping clockwise circle that soon had me facing out to sea again.

Sophie raised her ruby to her mouth and coughed lightly. I knew what was coming.

'I think this might be a good moment to discuss the

financial side of things. I'd like you to understand *everything* about this journey. Is it all right to talk about this now?'

'Of course.'

She pushed her glasses up into her hair so she could rest her dark-brown eyes fully on mine. 'First, I've got to secure the perfect donor. I insist they all go through not only the run-of-the-mill health checks, but also a complete set of X-rays and' – she counted off each test with the forefinger of one hand in the palm of the other, jabbing hard each time she said 'insist' – 'I also insist on screenings for kidney function, liver function, hepatitis, heart disease, lung disease, and for any exposure to viral diseases in the past. I insist on urine testing to ensure her kidneys function normally and that the urinary tract and the blood vessels leading to the kidneys are in good shape.

'I insist on a pap smear, mammogram, colonoscopy, and all necessary medical clearance for any conditions we identify. Once that's done, and only then, I submit the results to my living-donor team, who make sure that everything is as it should be.'

She wasn't done yet. I knew that I was on the meter.

'The surgeon responsible for the procedure will meet with the donor as well as with Anna. The donor will have a complete psychological evaluation to ensure that she is mentally capable as well as physically. They deserve the best support I can give them. I'm sure Anna would approve.'

I had to agree. 'I think she'd insist on that. But I need to meet the donor before we get anywhere near that point.'

She'd seen that one coming. 'Of course. As soon as we

know for sure that we've got an acceptable candidate. I don't want you to waste your time vetting possibles.'

'You gave me the impression you'd got somebody in mind. Is that right? I've told her I'm only going to be here for four days.'

She lowered her glasses again and brought her hands together like she was in prayer. 'The choice of donor obviously depends on the outcome of Anna's tests – which may present a problem if she is unaware of your intentions . . .'

'I know you'll need to screen for matching on blood type, tissue matching and cross-matching, so I've got about four hundred mils of her blood left.' I wanted her to think she wasn't the only game in town. 'It's O pos. Three days old.'

Sophie's smile broadened. I was close to becoming teacher's pet. 'You're way ahead of me, Nick. You've obviously done your homework.'

'I've had to learn fast.'

'I'll only need a hundred and fifty.'

'I'm in your hands. So, where do we go from here?'

'Ah.' She massaged her chin, deep in thought. 'This is a slightly . . . unusual case, because the recipient is normally part of the process from the outset. Then there's the cost of identifying and testing the donor, bringing her to Hong Kong, preparing the clinic – and, of course, two procedures means two theatres. And what if Anna decides against it? I'm afraid any costs already incurred can't be recouped.'

'Let me worry about that. So – bottom line?'

'It's going to be in the region of four hundred and thirty thousand dollars US, give or take. And I'd need fifty per cent upfront to cover our initial costs.'

I held up my hands to stop her right there. 'I'll pay for the blood tests. I'll pay for the donor's tests. But only after I've met her, and seen what I'm paying for.'

She wasn't fazed. 'Of course. Whatever makes you feel comfortable. Why don't we get the ball rolling today? Anna's blood is type O, you say?'

I nodded.

'Good. As you probably know, that's very common in the Hispanic community. So ... let me have Anna's sample. I do have a woman in mind. She's lovely. If the blood tests are positive you can meet her and decide if she'd be acceptable.' I could almost hear her brain ticking over. 'Shall we say ten thousand US dollars down?'

I gave it a couple of seconds. 'Agreed. Do you want it at the same time as the blood sample?'

She was back in business mode. 'If possible. I'll have to pay the lab and the technicians immediately. I always insist on the best of the best.'

'It's going to take me a few hours. I take it we're talking cash?'

'Better for all concerned, don't you think?'

'Can you get someone to come and pick it up at six this evening? Up on the Lawn, where I met Kitty?'

'Perfect.' She was a very happy teddy. 'If there's any change to that, I'll call you. Kitty obviously has your number. And, of course, you have hers if there's a problem.'

Bruce swung wide of an oil tanker that hadn't been there when we'd headed out. Sophie stood and offered me her hand as we surged between the breakwaters and the world crowded in on me again.

I gave it a firm shake. She might be an arsehole of a trafficker, but I quite liked her.

'Just one question. If Anna doesn't know what you're up to, how did you manage to persuade her to give you a blood sample?'

I looked suitably sheepish. 'I know her doctor. He needed a holiday . . .' I paused. 'Do you mind if I ask one of my own? Why doesn't Kitty change her name? I mean, Kitty *Porn*? It sounds like a bad joke.'

I heard Bruce start to piss himself behind me.

'It's Kitty *Phong* – not Porn.'

She laughed too, and I joined in.

'It's a Cantonese problem. They find some words very hard to pronounce. Like mine – it quite often turns into Soapy.'

18

Bruce threaded the Manhattan 53 through the harbour and dropped us off at the pontoon nearest the aluminium gate. He backed up to park the boat at the same time as booking me a taxi on his cell phone. I was impressed. Who says men can't multi-task?

I'd hung onto the sun-gigs so I didn't look like I'd had my eyes gouged out in the searing sunlight. Sophie didn't seem to mind, and I figured she already owed me a party bag.

She worked her magic with the keypad beside the gate again to let us back into the clubhouse area. The old woman was still doing lengths of the swimming-pool. There was something relentless about her strokes; you certainly wouldn't have wanted her to be your mother-in-law.

Sophie escorted me back to the reception area. 'Nick, it was a pleasure to meet you.' She ramped the smilometer back up to full wattage. 'It's now my mission to make yours a complete success.'

She grabbed my hand and led me to a red taxi with

its engine running. 'Kitty will take care of everything this evening. I might be able to get the tests done before close of play. First thing tomorrow at the latest.' She trotted back up the steps.

The driver sported a crew-cut, a red check shirt and small rectangular glasses with clip-on shades that flipped up like a parcel shelf. They were at least three times as big as they needed to be.

'Upper House, yes?'

'Not yet, mate. Does the marina have a members' car park?'

'Yes. Car park.' He pointed straight ahead, then left. 'Not far.'

'Go for it.'

He was unimpressed. 'We go Upper House? Or you walk to car park. Car park not far.' He was pissed off about his fare. He pointed again. 'Just there. Twenty metre. You walk.'

I pulled out my wallet. 'This is the plan. I'll give you more than the fare to Upper House right away.' I counted out three hundred HKD. 'Now you start the clock and I'll pay you what I owe you after we're done. I need your help, mate. Woman trouble. So let's start with the car park, eh?'

He flicked down his clip-ons with the look of a man who knew a thing or two about woman trouble, and mumbled away to himself as we looped around the turning circle. I'd obviously struck a raw nerve. We passed a couple of high-end boat shops with billboards advertising gin palaces the size of apartment blocks.

'There, you see? Car park . . .' He motioned towards a ramp that led underground.

'Let's do it. I'm looking for my wife's car.'

He wasn't happy about the ticket barrier. 'No cash – only Visa.'

'Got one right here . . .' I flashed the plastic.

He drove to the entrance and grabbed a ticket. I took off my gigs and he raised his clip-ons as we rolled into a concrete bunker where vehicles with six- and seven-figure price tags sheltered from the sun. The cabbie did the circuits, and we eventually bumped into the Verso on the second floor. It was definitely the one I was after: dual plates and PRC stickers over the Toyota logo.

I let him carry on all the way back to the top level.

Tucked in the far corner there were three or four 4x4s. We could easily lose his little red runabout between them. Sophie would have to pass us on her way out, but we wouldn't be in her line of sight.

'In there, mate, on the left.'

'You pay for wait?'

'I'll pay for everything, mate. I'm that kind of guy.'

He did as he was told and turned off the engine, but not the power. He wanted to keep that meter running.

19

Ten minutes later, I gave him another twenty HKD. 'I think my wife's got a boyfriend.' I gave him my bad-smell face. 'You married, mate?'

He nodded, taking the cash.

'Kids?'

He nodded again.

I'd give it an hour. I slid down in the rear seat, my eyes on the gap between two concrete pillars. I thought about the times I'd spent like this in Northern Ireland. Sometimes waiting for most of a day or a night, hoping to be rewarded with a few seconds of exposure of a PIRA or INLA active-service unit as they loaded up for an attack, or shadowing the weak link in an ASU, building up a nice little dossier about his appetite for drugs, alcohol or choir boys – or, if push came to shove, breaking into his house and scattering around the right kind of incriminating material. Maybe we'd watch him visiting his mum who had cancer and was way down on the treatment list.

I'd Taser him, pop him in the boot and drive into the

countryside to read him his horoscope. He'd become a source, a tout, an informer, whatever he chose to call himself. In return, his bad habits would remain our little secret, or they'd be paid for, or his mother might find herself magically propelled to the top of the list for radiotherapy. It was his choice – at least, that was what we'd tell him. But as soon as he was in, there was no getting out. If everything went to rat-shit we'd simply expose him to his PIRA or INLA mates and let them deal with it.

I thought about my new best friend Sophie. I could write her backstory blindfolded; maybe that was why I liked her. Young girl; dreams of wealth; always wanted to get on. Went out with the boys who had the cars to take her places and the readies to buy her the stuff she wanted; found herself working hard for somebody else and hating it because she was making money for them instead of herself.

Maybe she'd stolen from her employers and her boyfriends; maybe she'd even been to prison. So: leave, make a fresh start; build on her personal skill-set. She must have been a really attractive girl, because she still was now, and made it work for her. Proud of where she was and the graft she'd put in to get there; clearly didn't even think of it as bending the rules. A self-made woman.

I couldn't help it, I had to admire that kind of dedication, whichever way it had taken her to the stripy towels and the boats and the ruby rings. She was a girl who'd done good, and was in no hurry to hide it. But that was as far as it went for her. She wasn't carved from the same granite as my mate in Peredelkino.

The size of Frank's watch, and the message it

broadcast to the planet had very little to do with money and everything to do with power. Frank and his kind had no time for the Sophies of this world, because all people like her craved was money, thinking it brought them some kind of protection; thinking that the close proximity of the powerful meant that their power somehow rubbed off on you. I'd spent enough time at the bottom of the food chain to see a whole lot of people make that mistake, and it always ended in tears.

Sophie's pitch had been good, without a doubt. Who cared if the thing about her husband was true? There was a load of stuff going on behind that mega-watt smile: she'd been checking me out, checking out Anna – where we both came from, the blood thing, trying to establish whether I was the genuine article. Fine. That suited me.

My phone vibrated in my jeans. It would have to wait. My eyes couldn't leave the exit route.

Another ten minutes and another twenty HKD – and a vehicle was approaching, right to left.

'OK, mate. In a minute, let's go. No lights. Nice and slow.'

It was too far away for me to tell whether Sophie was on board, but it was definitely the MPV. Its main VDMs – visual distinguishing marks – the two plates, were clear to see, even at this distance.

The brake lights glowed red in the semi-darkness as it slowed to turn the sharp left and climb up to the barrier. I passed over another twenty HKD for luck and got out my Visa. 'Stop just short of the corner, mate.'

I wound down my window and heard the Toyota ticking over at the barrier. As the metal arm started to rise, I tapped the cabbie on the shoulder. 'All right, nice and slow . . .'

The MPV's engine roared in the confined space as it took on the uphill start.

'Here we go, mate, here we go.' I thrust my Visa card into the outstretched hand in front of me. 'Double six double eight.'

I pinged the PRC sticker on the Toyota's tailgate as it emerged into the daylight and hung a left. My guy slapped the Visa card into the slot and tapped away on the keyboard. The barrier went up. 'Go left, mate.' I tapped him on the shoulder again and pointed the way I wanted him to go.

'OK, left.'

We both slid our gigs back on as we bounced out onto the tarmac. We were on a mission from God. The MPV was about two hundred in front of us. 'Close up a bit.'

He checked his meter. 'This your wife?'

'I think so. We need to get a bit closer to make sure.'

A bus exited from the terminal, making the narrow road narrower still. The MPV had to slow down.

'She not good woman?'

'I'm trying to find out, mate. But don't get too close . . .' It was feast or famine with this boy, and I didn't want to get right up the MPV's arse in case Sophie was checking her mirrors.

'She *not* good woman . . .' He was really getting into the zone.

This might have been a quaint old shanty town when they'd filmed *Enter the Dragon*, but now all I could see was lots of glass and cream rendering. We passed a stretch of development land surrounded by a high wooden hoarding, plastered with pictures of shiny buildings of the future, so you couldn't see the crap that had to be chopped down or scooped up in the present. The vegetation was already rampant enough to peek over the top of it.

'That's close enough, mate. That'll do. I've got her.' I could see her hair brushing the passenger headrest.

He continued shaking his head and tutting, getting all upset for me.

The MPV indicated and slowed, then turned right across the traffic towards a cream apartment block. A gate opened and closed, but not before I'd had time to see Bruce behind the wheel and a concrete driveway disappearing beneath the building.

My driver had gone from being quite pissed off with my wife's behaviour to being outraged about the whole situation. 'Wife not good. She no good . . .'

I motioned for him to pull over. 'Drop me off, mate. And you wait here, yeah?'

He checked his meter; it was ticking along nicely. I exited the car and tapped on his window. 'I'll be no more than ten minutes.'

I went through the pedestrian gate and up the driveway. The lawns on either side had been trimmed with nail-scissors and were fringed with palms and all that sort of landscaping stuff. I came to a *feng shui* doorway, a glass conservatory at a weird and wonderful angle. The young woman at the reception desk inside was smiling away but looking at me quizzically.

'Sophie Derry? Have I got the right place? Does she live here?'

A panel of CCTV screens blinked alongside her. Two of them showed crisp black-and-white images of the underground garage. I could see the MPV parking up. Bruce knew exactly where he was going. He wasn't cruising round looking for a spot.

The girl ran a finger down a list. 'Sophie? No Sophie . . .'

Sophie closed her door and Bruce came round to join her. A few strides from the vehicle she hit the key fob. The lights blinked as they headed for the lift.

'Sorry to bother you. I must have the wrong place. Thank you anyway.'

I could have stalled to see what floor the lift went to, but didn't want to risk it only going to the ground floor for security, as it did in our Moscow block.

My driver was steaming with rage when I got back. I thought I might have to warn Sophie and Bruce never to get into his cab.

I asked him to take me to the Upper House, but he wasn't impressed. He was still very pissed off with my wife.

I pulled out my phone as we swung back past the marina club and headed for the tunnel.

Another hard night, but now all OK. Don't worry. Call me when you can. xx

I texted back: *Will call soon as I get to hotel. Within the hour. xx*

20

The Upper House

15.38 hrs

The hotel phone only rang twice before Anna answered. She sounded tired. 'His respiration rate was really low. Too low. At one stage I thought I was going to lose him.'

I knew she was struggling to hold herself together.

'How is he now?'

'Stable. His rate is up. And he's put on a couple more grams.'

'That's good, isn't it?'

I heard her swallow. 'They say his chances are about seventy per cent. But I guess that's what you'd expect with him being so early . . .'

She was silent for a few seconds, maybe waiting for it to soak in. I didn't need that long.

'How are you?'

'The guys are still here. They're doing shifts. So I don't feel threatened. I just feel . . . helpless. I can't seem to do a thing for him, except watch and wait.'

'You want me to come back?'

'No, Nicholas. You've got to see this through. And right now Katya needs your help more than I do.'

We exchanged slightly strained small-talk for a minute or two longer, then I put down the phone. The truth was, I didn't know what the fuck to say. Me being worried about our boy at long distance wasn't going to make the situation any better for either of them. The last thing Anna needed was an extra helping of my pain – she already had enough of her own.

I fixed the alarm for a few minutes before five, but ended up thinking about going to sleep instead of actually doing it. I decided to do a couple of laps around the bath. With so much frou-frou, it was like floating in the Dead Sea. My mind was whirring. I kept thinking about what would happen if our boy didn't make it, what that would do to Anna . . . what it would do to me.

The phone vibrated.

Call me ASAP.

I jumped out of the bath.

She picked up immediately.

'Is he . . . ?'

She brushed my question aside. 'I've just had a call from someone offering me the chance to be part of a new diabetes drug trial. She asked loads of questions – if I had type one or two, that sort of thing, and would I take part.'

'Female?'

'Yes. I couldn't place the accent. And the number came up blocked. She wanted to know my history, ethnic background, that sort of thing. I told her I wasn't interested because I had my diabetes under control. She asked if I had any family members who might be interested, and if I had any problems with my kidneys. She was good, Nick.'

'She sure is. They both are. How did you leave it?'

'I told her I had CKD, so it was a thanks-but-no-thanks.'

'Perfect. I'm about to drop off the sample. I'll call you when I get back.'

I dried myself off and pulled on some clothes. I poured some fancy mineral water out of a bottle from the minibar and replaced it with a little more than 150ml of my blood. The rest of the bag went back into the fridge, and I headed outside with the bottle in my pocket. The Lawn would have to wait. I had to go to the bank to max out my cards with USD, then the Starbucks by the hotel.

And I was looking for something more than a cappuccino and a sticky bun.

21

The sun dipped below skyscraper level as I sat by the Starbucks window with my brew, eyes on the hotel turning circle. Taxi passengers were treated to the full Aussie welcome. Private cars were whisked away by valets to the underground parking area the far side of the Pacific Place Mall.

Kitty arrived three minutes before we were due to meet: same kit, white on blue, monster sun-gigs and red bag. I watched her disappear into Reception while I finished my brew, making sure nobody was shadowing her.

I stayed another five minutes, then crossed the turning circle into the air-conditioned lobby. I could hear the buzz as I walked up the white stone steps. The Lawn was heaving with HK's movers and shakers, knocking back cocktails under the darkening sky, telling each other how fantastic they'd been that day. I saw Kitty in the far corner, tucked in by the wall that stood between us and the street forty floors below, giving the full Cantonese cat-fighting routine to whoever was on the receiving end of her mobile. Her body language wasn't pretty. She paced a metre or two back and forth, then spotted me and stopped in her tracks, but carried on ranting.

I couldn't see much of her face, but I knew she wasn't impressed with me being five minutes late. In her book, the customer definitely wasn't always right. She tapped her foot as I closed in on her. 'You got money?'

'Sure. Blood as well.' I grinned. 'Thought I'd save you the trouble.'

She turned into the shadow of the wall, slid a hand into the bag and started to count the cash. I leaned back and watched the cream of HK's business community loosen its collar and let its hair down, but kept a weather eye on Kitty. She pushed the blood sample to one side. It wasn't difficult to spot where her priorities lay.

She looked up, satisfied. 'OK. Now we go.'

I caught up with her halfway to the steps. 'Where to?'

She turned and nodded in the direction of two young men at a nearby table. 'If you do not come, they will kill you.'

I believed her. They were early twenties and looked keen to prove themselves.

Kitty was still worried that I hadn't got the message. 'Come, guy. Come now or you get fucked up.'

She was almost at the steps. Her two mates never took their eyes off me. They were dull and hollow and a uniform brown; their pupils were opiate-induced pinpricks. The nearest reached between his jacket and shirt to make sure I saw his pistol grip.

I started walking.

I caught up with Kitty as she reached the bottom of

the steps. Two women joined us on our way to the lift, totally fixated on their BlackBerrys. We all kept very quiet and stood stock still, eyes front, until the door *shushed* open.

I followed the tap of Kitty's heels through Reception and out towards the car park. She didn't head for the glass lift that had taken us underground, but to the lay-by at the mall exit where shoppers stood in line surrounded by mountains of very smart bags. Cars swooped like vultures to pick them up as soon as a space fell vacant.

The Toyota waited at the head of the queue, engine purring and air-con keeping the heat and humidity at bay. Sophie's blonde hair brushed the top of the steering wheel; Bruce was now in the passenger seat. As soon as they saw us, he leaped out and opened the back door. He'd changed out of boaty kit into a smart short-sleeved shirt with a couple of pens clipped in the pocket and belted jeans. The deck shoes had been jettisoned for espadrilles.

Kitty was still doing all the talking. 'You! Get in. *Get in!*'

Sophie's happy-teddy face had slipped. I checked behind me: the two heavies were still well within firing distance. I climbed into the rear of the wagon, and Bruce punched my right leg as soon as I'd sat down. As the needle penetrated, and its contents were emptied into my thigh, I felt a golf ball growing under my skin.

I resisted at first, but knew it was useless. The auto-jet was already doing what it said on the tin: rapid heart-beat, dry mouth, vision hazy. Everything was going into slow motion. The drug had kicked in good style, depressing my central nervous system. I started to get that horrible drunk feeling. I felt myself drift away and there wasn't a fucking thing I could do about it. The urge to sleep was just too strong.

Bruce gripped my arms as I slipped down the seat. I hated it when I lost control.

PART FIVE

1

My throat was painfully dry and somebody was operating a pneumatic drill in my head. How long had I been out? No idea. I remembered the auto-jet, being dragged out of a vehicle, no more than that.

I tried to sit up, but I was too out of it.

Everything was blurred. I was curled up in a dark space, and incredibly hot. My clothes were soaked with sweat and I was fighting for air. My hands were cuffed tightly behind my back. I must have been lying on them. I arched my back to make space to work them loose, but my wrists were raw and swollen to the size of melons. I felt the agony of blood trying to pump them back to life.

I could hear the grinding of an axle and the shriek of rubber, then the whine of an automatic transmission as my head sank and my feet rose. We were moving uphill. I scrambled into a sitting position and straightened my spine. The back of my head banged against a sheet of light-gauge metal.

I was in some kind of container.

My chest heaved. I had to stay calm. There must be oxygen; otherwise I'd be dead by now. I was still breathing, so I was still winning.

I tried to wriggle my toes.

I had to keep some kind of control over what I was doing: I couldn't afford to miss a single detail. Like the fact that a stream of vehicles was overtaking us on the left.

We were driving on the right-hand side of the road.

That meant the PRC.

I had some idea of where I was; it made me feel like I wasn't completely in the shit.

There was no room to turn round. I scrunched my knees up to my chest. I had to keep still, control my breathing, control my body; I had no control of anything else.

I felt a sudden vice-like grip on the back of my calves. I stretched my legs as far as I could until my boots hit the far wall of the box, then tried to press the balls of my feet against it to alleviate the cramp. It didn't work. I had to take the pain.

I had a flashback to when I was an eight-year-old kid. I used to have cramp in my legs so badly it made me cry out. My stepdad would storm into my room and tell me they were just growing pains, so shut the fuck up and go to sleep. I remembered thinking, If this is growing, count me out.

Short, sharp breaths . . . that was all I could do . . . and try as hard as possible to tense and release every muscle; try to pump my body; try to fight this shit.

I was worried about my hands. I had no sensation whatsoever in the fingers, not even pain. I could feel nothing beyond the wrists, where the cuffs had dug so deeply into my flesh that I could feel the stickiness of blood.

We stopped.

I heard the sound of electric shutters.

The engine ticked over.

We rolled forward. The new road surface was a lot smoother, but we weren't on it for long. The vehicle slowed again, went over a bump, and all the noises became muffled. I could hear the rattle of shutters. We stopped. The engine idled for a moment, then died.

There was no waffle from whoever opened the back of whatever I was being transported in, only the incessant, high-pitched warning beep these things made when keys were still in the ignition or lights left on.

Then the top of the container opened and watery light poured in. Without warning, two pairs of hands followed. They gripped my arms and grabbed me under my armpits.

There was still no talking as they lifted me out. I gave them no resistance: my body was too busy trying to stretch itself out to relieve the pain.

2

We were inside a huge air-conditioned warehouse. I tried my best to get some idea of the layout, to start looking for a way of getting myself out of there, but my head was still hazy; details weren't being processed quickly enough.

They dragged me past two dark Merc vans and – bizarrely – a small silver people-carrier with a baby seat in the back crammed with cuddly toys. Bruce led the way. A pair of hands still gripped each of my arms. My legs were working like a new-born foal's but, fuck it, they were moving and that was good enough for me.

We were heading for a row of four white double-decker Portakabins. Sophie, now in jeans and a shirt, was halfway up a metal staircase that led to the upper storey. She was too busy on her mobile to pay any attention to the scene unfolding below.

My two handlers dragged me to the first door at ground level. They weren't fucking around. I was propelled into a bright, sterile, air-conditioned room, whiter than white, which smelt of Elastoplast. I was manhandled into a reclining chair surrounded by more grey machines than PC World. I tried to twist onto my left side to relieve some of the pain in my hands.

Bruce reappeared with a Gurkha *kukri*, which glinted in the bright fluorescent light. I suddenly made the connection: he was ex-military for sure. One of my two new best mates grabbed me by the hair, forced me to lean forwards. Bruce sliced through what turned out to be a plasticuff and they strapped each of my over-inflated wrists to the chair arms.

A third guy, in green scrubs, wheeled an ultrasound machine towards me, threw a Velcro strap around my biceps and pulled a metal trolley laden with cannulas and syringes towards us. He wiped the crook of my arm with an alcohol swab and I watched the needle plunge into a vein. My blood surged into the plastic cylinder. He removed the hardware and pressed a cotton-wool pad on the site of the needle.

He ripped my shirt open, tore my pouch off my neck and pushed me back hard into the chair. I arched the small of my back and was rewarded with a smack across the head.

He ripped the lid off a tube of KY Jelly and emptied the contents onto my abdomen. He slid a cold metal disc across the surface of my skin, working his way in small circular movements towards my heart, then up and down my sides.

The routine was absolutely silent, apart from the odd internal gurgling sound through the loudspeaker. I watched fuzzy black-and-white images flicker across the monitor. I looked at the raw and bloody wounds encircling my wrists and waggled my sausage-shaped fingers. I'd need my hands to function sooner rather than later.

They undid the straps as soon as the scan was finished, grabbed both my arms and frogmarched me out of the Portakabin. Bruce choreographed the whole performance, but only with nods. I stumbled as I tried to keep up. All I could hear was laboured breathing; all I could smell was stale nicotine on the nearest guy's breath.

I tried as best I could to remain upright. We swung left, to the next Portakabin along. This one was every bit as bright and sterile as the first, but had a lead-lined screen and control panel to the left of the door and an X-ray machine with a robotic arm in the far corner. They dragged me over to something altogether more medieval alongside it – a wooden H-shaped contraption – and spread-eagled me over it. Nylon straps were pulled tight across my arms, legs and chest.

Mr Green inserted an X-ray plate and arranged the tip of the arm a couple of inches from my chest. Everyone disappeared behind the protective screen and a low electrical hum momentarily filled the room. He emerged, inserted another plate and repositioned the arm.

All I could hear now was the squeak of this guy's trainers on the highly polished floor; Bruce and the other two just sat tight. I started to find it hard to breathe. There was no point moaning about it: no one was going to help me. Better to use the time to recover, trying to suck in what oxygen I could.

I heard a muttered exchange, then the straps were released. I tried to put in a lengthier stride or two to get my blood circulating as we headed back towards the

Toyota, but almost immediately got a toecap in the back of the knee.

We bypassed the Toyota and the two vans as Mr Green went back to his furry family in the people-carrier. We were heading towards a row of three shabby blue cabins positioned some distance away from the clean white ones, like they were the poor relations. Each had a wire-mesh-covered window and the middle one had a wooden bench beneath it. Bruce threw open the door, still gripping the *kukri*.

There was a stained rectangle of foam in the corner and the floor was littered with ripped cardboard and all sorts of grimy shit. They dropped me onto the foam and I was immediately enveloped by a cloud of construction dust.

Someone grabbed my left hand, brought out another plasticuff and fastened it to a heavy-duty metal ring bolted into the wall. I felt a short, sharp stab and looked down. Bruce had jabbed another auto-jet into my thigh.

Rapid heartbeat, dry mouth, vision beginning to go hazy.

I thought I heard the door slam.

3

I awoke in a semi-daze, my nose half blocked by the grime and dust. There was a sudden pain between my legs but I couldn't work out why. I thought I must have been dreaming. Then it was obvious I wasn't. I looked down; a clear plastic catheter was being pulled out of my cock. Seconds later, Bruce walked out with a sample bag half filled with yellow liquid. The door closed and a bolt was thrown.

I raised my legs and used my free hand to try to drag my jeans and boxers back up. I managed to tug them about halfway up my thighs, then gave up. It was like I had extra-thick gloves on: I still couldn't feel my fingers. I checked my left hand, as if a miracle might have happened, but it was still firmly attached to the ring. Looking at it closely I realized that it had probably been bolted into the wall of this shit-hole just for me. I relieved the pain a fraction by moving as close to the wall as I could then supporting my elbow to take the pressure off my cuffed wrist. Now I just needed time to sort out my head.

I had no idea how long I'd been unconscious. My brain was still semi-submerged. My vision was blurred. Everything was running at half speed. The auto-jets had probably mostly contained scopolamine, with a morphine chaser. The combo induced a state known as twilight sleep. Once used for obstetrics, it was now considered far too dangerous – except when, like the British and American intelligence services, you're not too concerned about a call from InjuryLawyers4U.

I opened my eyes again. Lying next to me was a drinks can covered with Chinese writing and pink and orange motifs, and half a dozen bite-sized cakes in a clear plastic container. The rest of the floor was littered with the remains of cardboard boxes – some intact and neatly folded, others just torn and discarded – and plastic parcel-ties of varying widths, colours and sizes.

I reached out as far as I could with my free arm, working it like a dredger as I scooped up the food and drink and dragged them across the steel floor towards me.

I tore at the cellophane cake packaging with my teeth, smearing the greasy, sugary film on the inside of it across my cheek. I had no idea when I was next going to be able to eat or drink, so I got the contents down my neck as quickly as possible, eating them straight out of the box, like a dog.

I tried and failed to open the ring-pull on the can with my index finger and ended up using my front teeth. I drank the sweet, fizzy orange all in one go, in case I didn't get the chance to pick the can up again, or dropped it when I did. Then I shoved it under the foam, away from prying eyes.

I lay down, covered with greasy crumbs. My left hand felt like it was about to explode, but I managed to close my eyes. I had no idea how long I stayed like that, drifting in and out of my twilight daze, but I began to feel better. Maybe the sugar rush was working its magic.

My hands were still swollen but my fingers started to sting, which was a good sign. I lifted the corner of the foam and fished out the can. Gripping it in my secured hand, I squeezed its sides between the thumb and forefinger of my free one until they touched in the middle. I bent top and bottom together, then apart, then together, then apart, until the thin metal cracked and I was able to tear it into separate pieces.

I gripped the base section in my secured hand and looked for the best place to start peeling the sides like an orange. I found what I wanted and started to pick and tear. My fingers slipped a couple of times, slicing themselves open on the razor-sharp alloy. But there wasn't time to worry about that: the pain was nothing compared to what they'd inflict on me if I didn't get away.

I aimed to keep peeling until I had about five millimetres of serrated blade at the base of the can. That would be enough to wound, but not so much that it would buckle when it made contact with flesh and bone.

4

Using a combination of hands and teeth, I finally sorted the bottom of the can and slid it back under the foam.

Before starting the same process with the top, I bit a chunk out of the foam to give my fingers some sort of protection. Then I ripped off strips of the metal with my teeth, slicing the inside of my bottom lip in the process. I tasted blood. I spat the next couple of pieces onto the foam, where they sat in a nest of pink saliva. Finally I had what I needed: an aluminium tool that was going to free me from this fucking plasticuff.

I heard the whirr of a roller shutter. Light and sound spilled through the mesh as a vehicle entered the compound and engine noise bounced off the Portakabin walls.

I brushed all the fragments of can under the foam, then bent and picked up the best-shaped sliver of metal with my tongue. I worked it between my gum and the inside of my cheek, in case they found the rest of my handiwork.

Trying as best I could to hold up my jeans, I managed

to lever myself onto my knees, then, painfully slowly, to my feet. I was still stooped like an ape-man because of the plasticuff, and blood and saliva dribbled from my mouth as I tried and failed to reach the window. All I could see from below it was the top floor of the white Portakabins on my far left, the roof of the Toyota and, as I continued to watch, the roof of one of the dark blue Merc vans. I couldn't see the second.

I heard doors being slid open and the welcoming, happy-to-be-here lilt of Sophie's voice. I couldn't make out what she was saying at first, but the volume steadily increased. Then I heard, 'Yes, he's in excellent condition. We should have everything co-ordinated by the start of next week. I'm confident of it. Don't worry, we take great pride in everything we do.'

I sank back down on the foam and played fucked as two heads appeared from beneath the mesh-covered window. They must have stepped up onto the bench. Sophie was on the left, all teeth and hair.

The older Chinese face beside her only came up to her ear. Slick grey hair, a side parting, collar and tie, the shoulders and lapels of what I assumed was a grey business suit. They both looked down at me like I was the runt of the litter.

'Well, this is Nick. Nick has been a very naughty boy, telling me he was a customer when he wasn't.' She turned to her new mate. 'Nonetheless, I can assure you that he is the perfect candidate.'

She turned back in my direction. Her smile was still in place, but her eyes told a different story.

She glanced down to her right as the bolt was thrown and Bruce appeared with a Velcro strap and a sterile, shrink-wrapped syringe pack.

His English was almost public schoolboy. 'Stay where you are. Stay calm and I won't harm you.'

He wrapped the Velcro round my free arm, snapped on a set of rubber gloves, then tore open the sterile pack and started to set it up. I kept my hands squeezed to hide the cuts.

Sophie continued with the sales pitch. 'The X-rays, ultrasounds and blood tests demonstrate he's in excellent health, just like I said. There's no sign of nicotine, drug or alcohol abuse.'

As the needle punctured my vein I swallowed another gob of blood and saliva to prevent them seeing the condition of my mouth. So far, he hadn't noticed the can was missing.

The moment the syringe was full, Bruce plunged it into a vial, which he then poked through the mesh. The Chinese guy checked the seal and slipped it into his top pocket.

Bruce undid the Velcro, leaving the puncture to bleed down my arm and onto the foam.

Sophie nodded for Bruce to leave. 'You've seen that the blood matches the other samples and that everything is in order. There were some residual traces of sedative, but nothing else remotely abnormal in the preliminary tests. I think you will be very, very pleased with what we have here.'

The door slammed shut and the bolt was thrown again. Both heads disappeared from the window frame, then Sophie's bobbed up once more. 'Why don't you both go to the office and I'll be with you in a minute?'

I couldn't be arsed to get a lecture from her, so I jumped in straight away. 'Where's Katya?'

'Nowhere you'd expect, Nick.'

'She still alive?'

Her eyes narrowed. 'Does Anna really have CKD?'

'Did your husband?'

She beamed. 'It seems we both like telling stories.'

I swallowed another mouthful of blood and saliva, wedging my tongue against the sliver of aluminium to make sure I didn't lose it.

She shrugged. 'But it doesn't really matter now, does it?'

I straightened my back against the wall. 'Now you're going to cut me up? Kidney, heart, liver? Make a few thousand dollars out of me.'

She gave the sort of patronizing laugh my bitch aunties did when I asked a question they thought was stupid. 'Nick, you're so last century. I've told you, we're on the cutting edge here – if you'll forgive the pun.' She tilted her head. 'Vital organs no longer have the greatest value. Do you know how much bone marrow you have in that body of yours?' I did, actually, but she didn't wait for my answer. 'Someone of your age and build will have about two point six kilos. We're going to sell that at twenty-three thousand US per gram. We won't be able to suck it all out, but that still makes you worth fifty-seven million US, even before we auction off the other goodies.'

I made sure I could still feel the aluminium against my cheek after my next swallow.

'Even your antibodies could be worth up to about seven million. And your DNA – we might get as much as nine million for that. Which brings us back to your organs: perhaps another million? So you know what, Nick? When you wake up and say you feel like a million dollars, that should really be seventy-four million. And if that doesn't give you a good enough feeling, think of all the other people you're going to make happy. I feel sorry for you, really I do – you fucked up, you got caught. But look on the bright side. You're not going to be wasted.'

'So why are you fucking about with livers and kidneys?'

She shrugged again. 'That's what we do. But, as you've seen, our new business is almost ready to roll. It's taken us three years to set up, to develop the know-how, to attract the right people, the backing. And now you're going to be the guest of honour at our grand opening!'

And her head disappeared from the frame.

5

I moved the aluminium sliver up between my front teeth with my tongue and spent about ten minutes rolling it tight.

Plasticuffs are made of polycarbon resin. They're a grown-up version of the used plastic ties that littered the floor, operated by a roller-block retention system, a little square buckle at one end that locks onto the teeth of the cuff itself and holds it in place. Normally the only way to get out of these things is by cutting them off, like Bruce had done with his *kukri*.

I manoeuvred my tightly rolled aluminium pin between the roller block and the teeth of the cuff and pushed. The pin slipped. At my second attempt I put pressure on the cuff with my secured hand to expose more of the area where the cuff went into the roller block, worked the pin back into position using my mouth and my free hand, and bit down hard. The block disengaged and the cuff started to come undone.

I widened the loop but didn't undo it totally. If they came back, I'd need to look like I was still their prisoner.

I squeezed my swollen hand out of the cuff, popped the pin back into my mouth and stood up.

I pulled up my boxers and jeans. I didn't button them or fasten the belt because that wasn't how they'd expect to find me, but at least they were over my arse and the zip held them in place.

Keeping well away from the window, I scanned what I could of the warehouse. I saw the Toyota and a left-hand-drive Merc van with PRC plates. Fuck knows where the other had gone – and, more importantly, for how long – but this was a good sign. Absent vehicles meant absent people.

I couldn't see any sign of a camera in my cabin, but these things were so small I couldn't be sure. But if there was one on the roof, looking down at the door and window, I'd soon know.

The installation was a new-build. There weren't any tyre marks on the polished concrete floor. It had the feel of a council leisure centre: white concrete blocks about two-thirds of the way up the walls, then pressed steel. The whole area was roughly the size of half a football pitch – plenty big enough to house a bunch of Portakabins.

A steel landing ran from the top of the steps that Sophie had climbed when we arrived, along the front of all four cabins. There were lights on at the top level, but I couldn't see any movement. There wasn't any down below either.

I moved to the door and started to push – first at the top third, then at the lower third, trying to work out where the bolt was. I was sure I'd heard only one being thrown. Both top and bottom gave a little, so it was probably in the middle.

I crawled beneath the window and rose to my feet to its left. The mesh was chain-link with a plastic covering, anchored by steel bars on the outside of the frame. It gave a little when pressed, but unless I suddenly found a pair of bolt-cutters under the foam, this wasn't my way out.

I pushed my head against the mesh to stretch it as far as I could. It budged just a centimetre or so, but enough for me to see the far side of the door and, most importantly, what was keeping it shut. The bolt was just over a metre away. It was a rusty old thing, about eight inches long. All I had to do now was find a way of pulling the fucking thing open.

I eased myself back down, checking above me and along the walls in case I'd missed a hatch. I hadn't. Either I was going to open the door and get out covertly, or it would be opened for me and I'd have to fight my way out. The first option was favourite, because it gave me some element of control. The second was a lottery at best – and at worst a gangfuck.

I heard the sound of footfall on the steel walkway, then voices. Maybe there was a camera after all.

I scrabbled back to the foam, making sure I could get my hand straight back into the cuff if they did come in. I checked with my tongue that the pin was still in place and started pulling down my jeans. I got them to mid-thigh, then crouched in a semi-squat with my back against the wall. I could just see the tops of the vans and movement from the top cabins. I could no longer hear the echoing footsteps. Sophie, Bruce and the Chinese suit must have reached ground level.

There was laughter as they moved towards the vehicles. I risked moving so I could see more. Two more guys in jeans and short-sleeved shirts – maybe the ones who'd done the donkeywork last night – emerged from behind the ground-level cabins. They joined the others at the van, slid the door open and powered up the roller-shutter that gave access to the compound. At first glance, they looked like two lads who enjoyed a lot of pork balls with their steamed rice. But there was something brutal in their faces and about the way they held themselves.

Sophie and Bruce shook hands with the suit. He climbed into the back of the Merc van as the two chubbies swung themselves into the cab. Sophie and Bruce stood in silence for a couple of seconds after the shutter had unwound once more, then Sophie pumped a fist in the air and did a little victory dance. She looped her arms around Bruce's neck and they kissed. I was glad the day had been a success for somebody.

6

My next task was to sort out all the discarded plastic ties with my sausage fingers and start feeding the free end of each into the roller block of the next. It didn't matter what colour or width they were, as long as the teeth engaged. By the time I'd finished, I had one continuous white, green and black daisy-chain about a metre and a half long, with a loop at the end, like one of those joke leads that are supposed to make passers-by think you're walking an invisible dog. You look a complete twat when you're holding one, but someone always smiles.

I moved back to the window to check for movement or noise. The place seemed deserted.

I pushed my head against the mesh until it ballooned.

Some of the feeling had come back into my fingers, but I still fumbled as I fed the loop of the dog lead through the left side of the fresh forehead-shaped bulge and on towards the bolt. I took a break after a while to rub the pins and needles out of my hands and realized I was totally fucking it up. My makeshift plastic lasso had dropped below the hasp, so I started pulling it back into the container with my teeth. No way was I going to let my sausage fingers drop this thing.

I gave the mesh another shove with my head, a couple of feet higher this time, and started the whole process again, about two-thirds of the way up the frame. I didn't bother to check for movement or sound out there. I needed total focus on this job, and if they'd seen me, I'd just have to deal with it the best way I could.

The loop was more or less in range of the bolt, but I had to keep twisting it to keep it flush against the outside wall. It had to catch the handle when I finally pulled it back towards me. My neck ached with the strain of forcing my head against the mesh. I was concentrating so hard I dribbled a stream of blood-flecked saliva down the front of my shirt. I had no idea where the pin had gone. For all I knew I might have swallowed it.

Half a lifetime later, my lasso fell over the bolt head like a fairground hoop around a prize. I didn't just jerk the lead and hope for the best. Slowly, slowly, I closed the loop, kept the tension, and pulled. There was a very satisfying metallic rasp as the bolt squeaked back. I kept pulling until it completely disengaged and the door drifted open.

I retrieved the two razor-sharp discs I'd managed to fashion out of the drink can from beneath the foam then slid outside. I released the loop and threw it back into my Portakabin before closing the door and resetting the bolt.

I quickly checked the other two cabins next to mine. They were full of boxes, banding and polystyrene moulds, whose former contents were, no doubt, on display in the newer cabins.

I half ran, half stumbled to the Toyota. My first instinct was to get the fuck out of there, but right now I had other priorities. I had to find out if Sophie and her mates really had chopped Katya into tiny pieces – and I wanted that photo back. Just one fucking happy-snap after all these years, and this shit had happened.

Besides, if I really was in the PRC, I didn't know how far I was from the border, or which direction to go. And without docs, I'd have to pull an II stunt to get back into Hong Kong.

The ignition keys were lying on the tray between the two front seats. I grabbed them and headed for the yellow junction box to the right of the shutter. I turned a big red handle to switch off the power. No one was getting in or out of here in a hurry.

My next target was the new white Portakabin complex.

7

As I got closer to the eight cabins I saw there was an identical row behind them, making the set-up a large rectangular block of sixteen. I moved round the corner to the right, where the driver and his mate had appeared earlier, and found a half-glazed entrance into the rear section. I stopped and listened, then gently pushed down on the handle with my wrist, a jagged drink-can disc in each hand.

The floor tiles were highly polished and there was a strong smell of antiseptic. Almost immediately I came to a set of white double doors. A corridor the far side of them opened onto a series of separate rooms. There weren't any scuffmarks on the floor, not even a finger-mark on a glass panel. There were noticeboards, but no notices. This place had just been lifted out of the box; it was a brand-new ghost town.

Behind the first door there was a small utility kitchen: an electric kettle and a microwave on a stainless-steel work-surface; a small table and four stacking chairs; a fridge-freezer; all the normal stuff. A couple of teabags with strings sat on a saucer next to two white mugs.

I opened another set of double doors wide enough to admit trolleys and gurneys. The operating theatre was as well equipped as anything I'd seen on *Grey's Anatomy*. More stainless steel gleamed in the dim light. Even the sink was spotless, not a watermark in sight.

Further down, I came to a run of four bedrooms: fresh sheets, still in their packaging, stacked on the beds; flat-screen TV on the wall; a beaker wrapped in cellophane and a bottle of mineral water on every bedside cabinet.

I had a grudging respect for Sophie's business plan. The international community was clamping down on hospitals performing illegal operations, and the kind of place where it might be tolerated was pretty scary for anyone who valued quality control. This place was state-of-the-art, providing the most sophisticated procedures in a highly sanitized environment. But it had to be stopped before it had the chance to start – especially if I was going to have a starring role in the opening ceremony.

Further on still, I found the ultrasound and X-ray facilities I'd already visited, and two labs for testing whatever they had to test. There were also two store-rooms. The first had shelf upon shelf lined with massed ranks of disinfectant and cleaning fluid, poised and combat ready. One splash mark and they'd go on the attack. The second was crammed with varying sizes of what looked like white insulated picnic hampers, but I was pretty sure they weren't designed for beer and sandwiches.

This was a central clearing-house for body parts. Maybe they were then exported to Hong Kong and the rest of the world. Or maybe the market for DNA, bone-marrow extraction and all the other bells and whistles was big enough here in the PRC for them not to have to leave the country.

I retraced my steps along the corridor, exited the way I'd come in and made my way towards the metal staircase. I reached the upper level and crept along the steel landing. The lights were still blazing in all four of the top Portakabins. The first was an office, with paperwork geometrically arranged on a shiny white desktop. I remembered Lena's workspace and felt my face creasing into a grin.

I heard movement ahead of me. Then the sound of rhythmic moaning.

I stopped short of the next window, crouched low and slowly moved my head until I could see through the bottom left-hand corner of the glass. It was a chrome and black-leather paradise in there. Sophie's jeans were down by her ankles as she gripped the back of a designer chair. Bruce was much the same. His buttocks glowed as he pumped into her from behind. By the sound of things, they were going to make this celebration last.

I ducked down and moved on past. The next two cabins were empty. Both of them, and the three behind, were bedrooms with en-suite shower rooms and all the trappings you'd hope for – even a stack of cans and food packages ready for the staff who were going to work below.

I left Bruce and Sophie to their fun and legged it back downstairs. A strong smell of car showroom came off the leather chairs and brand-new carpet tiles of what I took to be the main admin centre. All the right gear was on display, but not much happening with it – a bit like a front for the Mafia.

A spreadsheet glowed on a monitor the size of a small cinema screen. It looked like Sophie had been momentarily distracted from filling it in by the need to nip upstairs and celebrate. My name was at the top. A line of abbreviations ran down the left-hand column. They meant nothing to me at first, but the further I went, the more I understood.

The next column registered prices in *US dollars x 1,000.* I saw *Kidney x 2: 140* . . . *Liver: 130* . . . *Lung x 2: 140* . . . *Pancreas: 120* . . . *Heart: 160* . . . Further along, the date had been inserted for *Heart* and *Lung x 2*: 8 September. They were going to Hong Kong, by the look of it. My liver had *tbc* in the date column, but it seemed to be staying in the PRC.

She'd already lined up a pretty impressive range of takers for the Stone harvest. I wasn't sure how long I'd been out of it for, but I reckoned the party was due to start in about a week's time. Maybe they had more tests to do and customers to ship in from overseas, but who gave a fuck? The eighth was the big day.

There were no dates on the big-ticket items like bone marrow, which was marked up at 23 per gram. My DNA, I guessed, would be used for something like stem-cell treatment. It had been marked up at a mere six million dollars. Sophie had hoped for nine. Maybe they were doing it on special offer.

Fuck me, if the distribution was as simple as moving bits of me from one Portakabin to another or lobbing body parts into picnic hampers and jumping on a plane, this was even better than the drugs trade. The set-up costs would be enormous, but so would the returns. I couldn't help it: I had to take my hat off to these two. Becoming a panel-beater had been the limit of my ambitions back on my Bermondsey council estate, and Sophie's vision sure beat the shit out of that.

They were bound to have a back-up, but I couldn't resist deleting it. It might just put a spanner in the works.

I rifled through the drawers and fancy cabinets for some hint of Katya and my tourist pouch. A business so well run would have filed it somewhere to sell the contents on. Sophie's enterprise was even more efficient than one of those places that turned beaks, claws and arseholes into chicken nuggets. Nothing was going to waste. They'd got it all squared away. Well, until now.

I found my iPhone and passport at the bottom of a filing cabinet, with the three belonging to the girls I had seen Sophie meet and greet at the airport. I tucked all four into the pouch and looped it back around my neck. I couldn't find anything belonging to Katya.

I headed back to join the happy couple upstairs.

8

It sounded like the celebration was over.

I eased my right eye above the window ledge. They were still sharing the glow, but beginning to sort themselves out. Bruce had hitched his jeans around his thighs and Sophie was starting to pull hers up too.

It was now or never.

Checking that the discs were the right way up and gripped as firmly as possible in my fucked-up hands, I pushed my forearm down on the handle and barged open the door with my shoulder.

Bruce had his back to me, but must have seen Sophie's soft smile freeze in shock a nanosecond after hearing the crash. He spun round, scrabbling at the waistband of his jeans, trying to haul them up far enough to allow him to swing into action. I rushed him, right hand raised, focusing on his head. It didn't matter where the jagged edge of the disc made contact, as long as it did. Sophie's scream was no more than muffled background noise as I stepped into range and swung down my arm.

Bruce was still turning, in a semi-squat, hobbled by his jeans. But his left arm flew up to block my first blow and his right fist followed with a short, sharp jab into my solar plexus.

I buckled.

The air exploded out of me. I tried to gulp some back, but it wasn't happening. My lungs went rigid with shock. I stumbled backwards to get out of his reach and give myself a second or two to recover. But that wasn't happening either.

His jeans were up and he came for me, spinning on one leg with a roundhouse kick to my left arm as I brought it up to protect myself. The force of the blow smashed my forearm into my head and had the same effect as if he'd made contact direct. Fighting for breath, I fell back over Sophie's favourite leather chair and onto the floor.

I had to get up. If I stayed where I was, I could be there for ever. At least if I was on my feet I had a fighting chance.

I grabbed the chair arm and pulled myself up onto my knees, but Bruce wasn't interested in me right now. He knew he'd got me fucked. He could take care of me whenever he liked. He had his back to me again, comforting Sophie, holding her, stroking her cheek, then caressing the back of her head.

I saw a black ash and chrome cabinet by the wall to my left. A varnished wooden plinth took pride of place on it. Bruce's very smart *kukri* sat on two small steel pins that jutted from the base, above an engraved brass plaque. There was going to be no finessing this – I'd just have to hurl the thing in his direction and hope the sharp end made contact.

At least it might slow him down as I followed it in.

Bruce was still in soothing mode. He kissed her forehead.

I focused on the handle of the *kukri* as I stumbled towards it.

'*Bruce!*' Sophie's scream filled the room.

Without looking back, I gripped the handle as hard as I could. Every hint of pain disappeared from my fingers as adrenalin surged through my body.

Bruce pushed Sophie out of the way as I turned. He knew what was going to happen. He finished his own turn and catapulted himself at me. I focused on his centre mass and let the *kukri* go as if I was throwing a boomerang. I leaped up onto the leather chair and launched myself over the top of it in an attempt to give myself a bit of height and momentum. My head smashed into his; my vision went dark for a split second, then the stars burst. We both tumbled onto the carpet with me half on top of him, half not.

Somewhere above me, Sophie was still screaming. But it wasn't because of the fight. It was because the *kukri* blade was stuck in his gut and blood was pulsing out of him in synch with his short, sharp breaths.

9

I grabbed the handle and pulled, and Bruce gave a muffled gasp. The next sound I heard made me swing my head. Tears spilling down her contorted face, Sophie stood above me. She held a snub-nosed .38 in her shaking hands, its muzzle aimed at my head. It had come out of the massive handbag that now sat crumpled at her feet.

'Put it down, Sophie.' I chucked the *kukri* back towards the cabinet to show I wasn't a threat. 'It's a fucker, but I can help him now. I can keep him alive.'

I was far enough from Bruce for her to shoot me, but she wasn't going to: I could see it in her eyes. She might trade in misery and death second-hand, but she didn't have it in her to do it this way.

I heaved myself up. 'Put it down and we can both help keep him alive.'

I wasn't sure she was getting the message: her eyes were glazed. She might not have the will to shoot – the hammer wasn't even cocked – but it still had a chamber full of shiny brass-jacketed rounds either side of the barrel, and a panicky finger could accidentally squeeze one off.

'Sophie . . .'

I took a step towards her. Not so fast it confused her, but not slowly either.

'Sophie, we have to stop wasting time. He's bleeding. He needs our help.'

She took a half-step back, the weapon still clutched in her trembling hands. I had to keep moving towards her. I couldn't afford to be there all day. I had no idea where that second Merc van had gone or when it was coming back. And though the shutter would slow them down, it wouldn't do so for ever.

'Sophie, look at me, please. I'm not going to hurt you . . . Let's all get out of this alive, yeah?'

I took another step. Now I was within reach of her. I slammed the .38 with my left hand and grabbed it with my right, yanking it out of her grasp. It wasn't difficult. She didn't really want it there in the first place.

I pushed her back into the leather chair she'd been moaning against a few minutes ago and shoved the weapon into the waistband of my jeans.

Bruce was curled up in a ball of pain. Blood, dark and deoxygenated, oozed out of him. Sophie sprang out of the chair and crawled over to him. She stroked his hair, as if that was going to do any good.

I knelt beside them. 'He needs more than that.'

She lifted her head. Her eyes were swollen with fear and grief, her hair stuck to her cheeks.

'All three of us are going back to the New Territories, Sophie. I'll keep him alive until we get there. Then we find the nearest hospital.'

Her jaw hardened. 'They'll be back . . . and then—'

I yelled in her face. 'Shut the fuck up!' I needed her full attention. She was right. Those lads could be back at any moment.

'Listen. Don't worry about who's turning up, because they aren't going to save him. And if fucking about with his hair is all you can do, I'm the only one here who can keep him alive.'

I moved back to give her space to think. Bruce tried to turn over and curl up again. The front of his shirt glistened red in the fluorescent light.

'It's OK, let him. He might as well die in comfort if we're not going south.'

She touched his cheek and let out a sob.

'Sophie, he knows he needs surgery. That *kukri* went in deep enough to sever his colon and fuck knows what else. I can stop the leaking and replace the fluids, but you need to make a quick decision. We have to get started if we're going to get him safely to a hospital.'

There was still no answer from her. She was gazing down at him.

'Do you understand me? It's finished. All the shit you've got here – it's over. If you want him alive either you call an ambulance or we get the fuck out of here.'

She ignored me. Their eyes were fixed on each other. Then he gave her a nod and she slowly stood up.

'Thank fuck for that.'

She turned and headed for the door, maybe to go downstairs and fetch some trauma care. I grabbed her and shoved her back into the chair. 'Now you tell me where Katya is.'

She went grey. 'You don't understand ... They'll kill us ...'

I pointed down at the ball of pain on the floor. His breathing was shallow and sharp. He was still painting the carpet tiles crimson. I gently kicked the sole of his foot. 'Look, mate – tell her. I need to know about Katya – or we're going nowhere and we're all fucked.'

He winced, sweat pouring off his face. But he managed a nod. 'It doesn't matter, love. What can he do?'

Her face was a mixture of anger and fear as she stared at me hard. 'They've taken her to Mexico.'

'Why?'

Her head shook slowly from side to side. 'No more until he's safe.'

10

'You got any whole blood or plasma replacement down-stairs?'

'How the fuck do I know?' She glared at me, like I'd asked her for her phone number.

'Or volume fillers – you know, saline?'

'I don't *know* . . . You go and look.'

I was staying with Bruce. He was my ticket out of here. I knelt alongside him again. 'You know?'

His face was etched with pain. Blood seeped between the fingers he had pressed over the wound site. He did the goldfish trick with his lips. 'No blood . . . Ringer's and giving sets . . . in the theatres . . .'

I stood up and gripped Sophie. 'Do you hear that? The theatres. Plastic bags, maybe bottles, of clear fluid. Saline solution, Ringer's solution, whatever shit it says on the pack, get as much of it up here as you can. The giving sets – the tubes and shit that connect the bags to your arm – should be right alongside . . .'

She turned to go.

'And make sure you get the large cannulas, twenty to twenty-two gauge.'

She stopped. 'What the fuck?'

'Just gather up everything you find within reach of the fluid bags. And bandages and gauze – the wider the better.'

She turned on her heel. Her footsteps along the steel landing echoed around the building.

As I turned back to Bruce, I caught a glimpse of myself in the mirror on the far side of the room. There was a gash on the right side of my forehead where I'd made contact with him. On the left were diamond-shaped indentations from the wire mesh. I looked so ridiculous I nearly smiled.

'Mate, I'm going to have to move you. All right? I need your shirt off. You're going to have to help me.'

As I rolled him onto his back he did his best, between moans and grunts, to pull up his shirt. Blood leaked out of the five-centimetre slit in his gut, and so did a length of grey and glistening intestine.

I started to undo the buttons. It was pointless fannying about: I couldn't do anything until the shirt was off.

'You got any clean clothes here?'

He nodded.

'What battalion were you in, Bruce?'

'First . . .'

It was a fair guess he was a Gurkha, and a proud one, running around with a commemorative *kukri* on a plaque. The 1st Battalion Royal Gurkha Rifles was based in the UK. 'You've done the Iraq, Afghanistan shit?'

He gave two half-nods; they were the best his body could muster.

'I was in the Regiment, B Squadron. I was a Green Jacket before that. Did eighteen years.'

He looked up. There's always a bond between ex-squaddies, whatever the backdrop.

'Mate, I'm not interested in you two. It's Katya I'm after. All this shit . . .' I bent his elbow. 'Besides, I like you both . . .'

'You've . . . got a fucking strange . . . way of showing it . . .' His weak laugh turned into a rasping cough, which got louder with the pain of the sleeve finally leaving his arm. Little flecks of blood sprayed from his mouth.

'So?'

He clenched his jaw. 'Not yet . . . brother . . . not yet . . .'

Fair one. 'OK, Bruce, this is the plan. You're going to be in that front seat alongside her when we reach the border, just as you would normally. I'll be in the back.'

I managed to prise the sleeve off his hand. He lowered himself down onto the carpet again and lay back in a pool of his own blood.

'And if you or Sophie try anything that compromises a quick entry into the Territories . . .' I tapped the pistol grip sticking out of my jeans. 'And if I don't get what I need once we're through, no hospital. All or nothing, OK?'

I held up his chin so his eyes were locked on mine. I felt him nod.

'So keep her under control. No flapping, no fucking up.'

Bruce curled up again, exhausted, his hands cradling the pulsating eel that was still trying to escape from his stomach.

11

Sophie hurried back, arms overflowing. She'd taken me literally. Two-litre bags of Ringer's solution, three or four different-gauged giving sets, bandages, all sorts, cascaded onto the carpet tiles.

The moment she saw Bruce's exposed wound she got hysterical.

I jabbed a finger at her, making sure she gave me her total attention. 'Open the bandages.'

I looked down at Bruce. 'You start getting a vein up.'

He made a fist, pumping it as best he could.

Sophie used her teeth on the wrapping of a 4cm bandage, never taking her eyes off her lover.

I ripped away the protective plastic covering that kept the Ringer's-solution bag sterile and peeled the giving set from its shrink-wrapped tray. I picked the largest cannula, 22-gauge, and unravelled the plastic tube. I checked the Ringer's label. The solution was lactated. Good: if she'd brought plain, there wouldn't have been time to send her back. The sodium chloride, potassium chloride, calcium chloride and sodium lactate were all in the same concentrations in which they occur in body fluids. Given intravenously, this stuff rapidly restored circulating blood volume in burns and trauma victims, and during surgery. It wasn't as good as a 'massive transfusion protocol' – blood, and lots of it – but better than fuck-all.

Sophie was ready.

'Get that round his biceps – make it nice and tight. Bruce, you keep working that fist.'

She talked to him soothingly, as if that shit ever worked.

There was a clear plastic chamber a few inches from the end of the drip tube to regulate the flow of fluid. A small locking ball controlled the rate. But that wasn't what I needed today. I twisted off the cap covering the plastic spike that I'd drive into the dark blue port at the base of the Ringer's bag. There was also a white port, for injecting drugs into the solution, but that wasn't going to be needed either.

Sophie had wrapped enough bandage around Bruce's arm to cut off the circulation once and for all, let alone keep a vein up. I grabbed one of her hands and got her to hold up the bag. 'Keep it there.'

I stabbed the spike into the blue port, twisted and pushed until it was past the seal, then undid the roller so it was fully open. I unscrewed the green cap at the end with the Luer connector, and watched the liquid run through, not too fussed about air bubbles in the line. The body can take that shit. The solution splashed onto Bruce's chest before I closed down the roller ball and stopped the flow.

'Sophie, look at me.' I needed to keep her under my control: we still had a lot to do. 'All right, put the bag on the floor and start opening all the gauze and bandages. Open the lot.'

Bruce grimaced as I moved him into a better position but he knew it had to be done. I checked the veins on the underside of his right forearm. They were there somewhere, but none as pronounced as I would have liked. Maybe he'd lost too much blood, or maybe he was one of those people who had trouble giving them up.

I probed around his arm with my forefinger and middle finger and soon felt a soft spongy pipe. Keeping the tips of my two fingers on the site so as not to lose the fucker, I grabbed the cannula with my free hand and shoved it into my mouth. I bit off the protective cover of the green cannula that gloved the needle. Pulling the skin towards his wrist to expose what there was of the vein, I pushed the needle into Bruce's arm. I waited to feel the resistance of the vein wall, and the release once it had penetrated it, then stopped before it came out the other side. The clear hub at the back of the cannula flashed red as his blood started to force its way up the needle.

All I had to do now was push the cannula deeper into the vein, keeping the needle in place as a guide until the cannula was fully open. I extracted the needle and threw it across the room. I didn't want anyone getting any ideas about using it as a weapon. Blood poured from the exposed end of the cannula.

Sophie stared in horror.

I wasn't surprised. The tourniquet should have been released before I inserted the needle, and the wound should have been dressed to stop any leakage but, fuck it, I might not have been able to get a vein up if he'd lost any more body fluid. And as long as the cannula was where it needed to be, that was all that mattered.

'Sophie, open up that bandage.'

I left them to it.

Grabbing a bag of Ringer's, I scrabbled over to the *kukri*, cut away the blue port and used the liquid to clean his wound. Bruce was lying on his side, facing away from her, so she couldn't see the full extent of the damage. I squirted some more Ringer's over his arm and across his stomach to get a better look at what I was going to dress – and because I needed him looking as normal as possible at the border. I ended up emptying the bag.

I lifted Bruce carefully into a sitting position with Sophie supporting him from behind. I grabbed a fistful of gauze and covered the wound site, then wrapped the bandage around his stomach. You can't apply much pressure to a gut wound, but at least it kept everything in place. He sat there, his back against the chair, a mess of blood, Ringer's and discarded dressing wrappers, but he was as stable as I could manage once I'd twisted the giving-set line onto the cannula and fully opened the roller-ball valve.

'Sophie, go and get shirts, sweatshirts – anything big and bulky.'

She wanted to stay.

'Go.'

She gave Bruce another lingering look and turned away.

I dumped the Ringer's on the back of the chair. She hadn't brought any surgical tape, so I used a strip of bandage to secure the line and cannula to his arm to stop it getting pulled out when we moved.

He just sat there in a daze. I wasn't sure if he was taking the pain or swimming in and out of consciousness.

'Bruce, look at me.'

He did so, but his pupils were dilated, not reacting to the light.

'Mate, you know this is only volume filler, don't you? You're still going to need whole blood . . .'

He nodded.

'So no fucking about at the border, OK?'

He looked like he might have laughed, had it not hurt so much.

Sophie came back with two sweatshirts – a red Nike and a blue Lonsdale. I pulled one on and helped Bruce into the other. The IV line ran down his arm and emerged from his right cuff.

Sophie hopped from one foot to the other. 'Let's go. Come on, let's go.'

I shook my head and stared her straight in the eye. 'No, Sophie. First tell me where Katya is.'

If I'd been depending on her, I wouldn't have rated my chances of getting into the Territories. I had to know now, before we tried and failed. At least if it all went to rat-shit and I got away, I'd know where to aim for.

12

'No,' she snarled. 'He's in agony. We have to go *now*.'

She bent to help him up, but only made things worse for him.

I didn't budge. 'Where in Mexico? Who with? Who's responsible for this shit? The sooner you tell me, the sooner we get out of here.'

Bruce's breathing was getting shallower. Sophie brushed his sweat-soaked hair away from his forehead. Her head jerked up. 'For God's sake, at least let him have some painkillers . . .'

I moved back towards them. 'He's got to take the pain. Anything I give him now will affect what they can give him in hospital. So the sooner we get there, the sooner he waves the pain goodbye.'

I crouched down at their level. 'Mate, there's no time to fuck about. You really need help.'

He nodded, then slowly turned his head to her and did the same.

She took a deep breath. The palms of her hands faced the ground, like she was doing some kind of calming exercise. 'OK ... OK ... She went with them because you and your girlfriend were going to be hurt if she didn't. She did it for you.'

'With "them"? Who are they?'

She looked at me like I should know this stuff. 'The people who paid for all this.' She gestured around us.

'Who?'

She hesitated. 'We just know the guy they call El Peregrino. The Pilgrim.'

'Pilgrim? What the fuck is that about?'

'Drugs money. What else would fund something like this? HS-fucking-BC? The Pilgrim is diversifying. More cash, less risk.'

She sighed. 'Look, I don't know how he knew she was in Moscow. I don't know why he wants her in Mexico. I just know we're fucked as well, now. There are no second chances with these people. They don't do failure . . .'

She put her arms around Bruce and held his head against her chest. Strangely, she seemed a whole lot calmer now. At least she was thinking ahead instead of just flapping.

'Can we go now? Please.'

I checked her bag for any other weapons. 'You got passports and all that shit in here?'

'Always.'

'We'd better get a fucking move on then.'

I leaned down to help her lift Bruce. 'Mate, you're going to have to switch on here. Start using your legs.'

Sophie grabbed her bag, then hooked a hand under his other armpit. Between us we managed to haul him to his feet.

The three of us shuffled out of the room and along the

landing. The stairs he had to do mainly himself. I could see the pain in his every movement, but we were fresh out of choices.

As we reached the ground, we heard muffled shouts. A loud metallic clang echoed around the compound. Someone was pounding the outside of the roller-shutter.

We stopped. The shutter got thumped again.

Sophie looked at her watch. 'They're back.'

I couldn't tell if she thought it was a good or bad thing. I eased Bruce towards the MPV but she stayed where she was.

'You've got a choice, Sophie. But let me tell you right now, I'm not going quietly.'

We reached the Toyota and I levered Bruce into the front seat. 'What do you think?'

He did his goldfish trick again. His lips moved, but nothing came out. I leaned in closer to him, and this time I picked up a ragged whisper. 'We've got to disappear . . . The suit . . . he's not a . . . He's . . . Peregrino's man on the ground . . .'

Of course he was. The Pilgrim would need eyes and ears in-country. He wasn't just going to be Sophie and Bruce's fairy godfather. He'd want to grip them too.

Sophie was still frozen to the spot.

'The auto-jets, mate – where are the auto-jets?' I mimed a stabbing motion, as if that was going to help.

He grunted. 'Glass cabinet . . . Theatre . . . One . . .'

I moved back towards Sophie as the banging on the shutter got louder and angrier.

'Right, you listen in.' I pointed to the red cut-off switch on the junction box to the right of the entrance. 'See that thing? Turn it back on. Yell at them. Tell them there was a power cut. Say you have a problem, and you're trying to sort it out. Say that Bruce has had an accident in Theatre One, that you need their help. And then take them through that rear corridor, past the kitchen. You got that?'

She nodded.

'I don't care how you do it but they *must* go down that corridor.'

Her gaze was transfixed by the steel plates of the shutter rattling and rippling under the onslaught.

I took her head in my hands and turned it so my eyes could drill into hers. '*Do – you – under – stand?*'

She nodded.

'OK.'

I nipped back to the MPV and reclined Bruce's seat. 'Keep your head down, mate. We'll be leaving soon. But right now keep out of sight.'

I slammed the door and shepherded Sophie towards the shutter. 'Go, *go*. Shout. Tell them you're coming.'

I legged it to the rear Portakabins as fast as I could.

13

The chunky blue plastic cylinders lay like torpedoes in a silo, rubber-covered buttons at one end and red plastic protective caps over the needles at the other. There were six of them in a row. I needed only two.

I piled into the kitchen as Sophie went into yelling mode and the van roared into the warehouse. I closed the door but didn't engage the handle lock, then moved to the hinged side to allow myself a view through the glass panel along the corridor towards Theatre One.

I gulped in deep breaths, trying to clear my head for what was coming. Everything started to slow. Sophie was still gobbing off, her voice getting louder as she guided them into the building. I checked the revolver in my jeans, making sure the grip was pointing to the right.

The weapon would be my last resort. It would mean using rounds I might need at the border. But any threat I made with it had to be credible. So, fuck it, if there was a drama, the only option I had was to go noisy and take my chances.

I twisted off the protective caps of both auto-jets with my teeth, spat them onto the floor and waited.

The double doors swung open and three sets of foot-steps squeaked along the corridor.

The two guys came into view. Sophie was a pace or two behind them.

I let all three pass the kitchen door.

If I waited too long, I'd have a marathon run-up and give them plenty of warning. If I didn't wait long enough, I'd trip over Sophie and risk a total gangfuck.

When she was three paces past, I swung open the door and slid out into the corridor, an auto-jet in each hand, thumbs over the buttons. I barged past Sophie, shouldering her to the right, thumping her into the plasterboard. I lunged with both auto-jets and shoved them straight into the nearest available arses. My thumbs squeezed the rubber buttons like vices. Not caring if the needles stayed in or fell out, I cannoned into the chubbies, smashing them down onto the pristine floor as quickly as I could, giving them a good kicking to disorient them for the couple of seconds before the drugs took effect.

Sophie was on her knees, hands covering her face. I wasn't sure if I'd hurt her, or if she'd just had enough of this stuff for one day. I couldn't see any blood.

As the scopolamine kicked in, I searched them both. No weapons and no ID – but, then, I guess I didn't really expect them to be carrying El Peregrino Fan Club membership cards.

I pulled Sophie's hands away from her face. 'You'll live.'

I ran back to the theatre for more bandages. Grabbing armfuls of the things, I dumped them on the floor alongside the two men. 'Get these undone. We've got to tie these boys up for long enough to get over the border.'

We bound their hands behind their backs then tied their feet together. And then, arranging them on their sides, back to back, I tied their heads and necks together, grabbed Sophie's arm to help her up, and headed for the Toyota.

14

As the shutter rolled down behind us, Sophie drove through what turned out to be a brand-new high-tech business park packed with steel and smoked-glass units. The flowerbeds hadn't even been planted yet: patches of mud and weed stretched along each side of the road.

Bruce sat upright again. The Ringer's flowed down the line from a fresh bag on the dash to his right hand, which now rested on his thigh. I could see in the rear-view that the movement of the vehicle was giving him pain, but he would survive. I perched behind them on the aluminium Lacon box, surrounded by a mountain of cardboard packaging.

We bounced out of the park, between billboards proclaiming in Mandarin and English that this was the entrance to the New World. If you brought your business here, you were going to benefit from great good fortune, reasonably priced leases and future prosperity. The only thing missing was a giant waving cat.

I tapped Sophie on the shoulder. 'Where exactly are we?'

'Just east of Shenzhen. Ten, maybe fifteen, minutes away.'

That was good: the less time we had to endure in the PRC the better. 'You know the nearest hospital across the border?'

She glanced to her left as Bruce swayed from side to side. Then she nodded.

'So what's the routine on the border? What happens as you go through?'

She kept her right hand on the wheel but slid her left across the centre console towards him. He adjusted the position of the Ringer's tube so he could rest his palm on hers. 'Most of them know us. We're in and out all the time. We just show them passports and business permits, and that's it. The traffic's unbelievable, so they like to keep it moving.'

Massed ranks of Shenzhen high-rises gathered to my right, and almost immediately a mass of houses and shopfronts jostled for position on each side of the road.

I put a hand on Bruce's shoulder as we cut through the outskirts. 'Not long now, mate.'

Sophie gently squeezed his hand.

'We near?'

She let go of Bruce to hit the indicator. 'Not far. I'm pulling in here.'

She turned into a hypermarket car park, put the engine in neutral and climbed into the back.

I pulled the snub-nose from my jeans and eased myself into the Lacon box. I'd been in there once before, and I hadn't liked it then so I kept one of the two latches open a couple of centimetres with my free hand in case she had a sudden rush of blood to the head and threw the bolts.

'Sophie . . .'

'What?'

I could hear cardboard boxes being piled on top of me.

'Don't forget to hide the Ringer's. Shove it up his sweatshirt and keep the line out of sight. It's got to look completely routine – something you do every day.'

I heard her scramble back to the driver's seat, and we started to move. I tried to ignore the feeling that the sides of the Lacon were starting to press in on me.

About ten minutes passed, then: 'We're here. Keep still.'

We stopped, engine idling, moved forward a few metres and stopped again. I assumed we were in a queue for the security barrier. I imagined the border post swarming with uniformed PRC guards taking their jobs very seriously indeed.

A nearby truck's air brakes gave an explosive hiss.

There were lots of angry Chinese shouts – but, then again, maybe they were just pleased to see each other.

More movement, then we braked again. This time the waffling was right above me.

'Good morning!'

Sophie sounded like her old *über*-confident self. The guards gave her a grunt or two back.

I gripped the weapon in my right hand; my left was against the lid, ready to push it up and start firing – or do whatever I had to do to get across the border.

Things didn't sound as smooth as they should. There was some quizzing going on, and Sophie seemed to be having a bit of difficulty holding her own.

We rolled forward a few metres and the engine cut.

Ears primed, I concentrated on the tone of their exchange, trying to work out if it was time to go noisy.

Normal had gone out the window, but Sophie was doing her best to keep control. 'Go to hospital. Accident. Problem. Hospital!'

She got a bit hyper. I couldn't tell if someone was pointing a gun at her, or if it was part of her act. 'He's injured. I need to get him to Sha Tin, the hospital . . . *Sha Tin – doctor – hospital*.'

There was a rapid exchange outside the vehicle, then I heard Sophie's voice again. 'Thank you. Thank you . . .'

The engine started and we rolled.

I kept my head down until Sophie shouted the all-clear. 'You can get out now.' The relief in her voice was so strong I could almost reach out and touch it.

I pushed up the lid just enough to check we were driving on the left, then climbed out, scattering cardboard boxes. 'What happened back there?'

'It wasn't a problem. We're through now.'

I caught sight of Sophie's expression in the rear-view. She had her foot down, and the happy-teddy look was definitely a thing of the past. She pointed at Bruce's stomach.

I leaned between them to take hold of the Ringer's bag Bruce had just fished from underneath his sweatshirt. A stain the colour of treacle was spreading across it. He wasn't looking good. His face was covered with beads of sweat, even with the air-con going full blast.

I stayed where I was, Ringer's bag in my hand, my elbows resting on the console between them. 'I'll get out just before the hospital. Then that's us done—'

Sophie had both hands back on the wheel, but was now weaving between vehicles, veering dangerously close to the oncoming traffic.

'Sophie, slow down. If we crash this thing, or get pulled in, it'll fuck us up even more . . .'

She heard me but her foot didn't. We obviously didn't have much quality-conversation time left.

'How do I find this Pilgrim guy?'

'No idea. The suit was our contact. Even he uses a new cell every time.'

'So what about the money? How does that side of things work?'

'It's all done through intermediaries.'

She overtook a couple of young lads riding side by side on scooters with their girlfriends hanging on the back. They hit their tinny horns in unison and gave Sophie the finger.

'These guys know about me? Know I'm looking for her?'

She shrugged. 'Like I said, we have no direct contact. But I guess they must have the photograph.'

She glanced at Bruce. 'Nick, do you really think you're going to find her? You're living in Cloud Cuckoo Land. You should go back to Moscow, then take Anna somewhere nice, somewhere a long way away, and keep your heads down. Take what you have, and start afresh. You're just as fucked as we are.'

She brightened as she rediscovered Bruce's hand. 'But I guess it's when you're really in trouble that you remember what's important in your life.'

Bruce somehow raised her hand to his mouth and kissed it.

She flicked the wheel to get us back on the right side

of the road. Her left hand was still in Bruce's, but at least her eyes were on the road.

'What about the three girls from Moldova? The ones you picked up from the airport the other day?'

Bruce took a deep, rasping breath. 'With . . . Kitty . . . We always . . . keep the passports . . . so she won't go . . . freelance . . .'

'Well, I've got them now. Tell Kitty you're dumping the girls. Tell her they've got HIV or something, and should go and fetch their passports from the Upper House reception desk. Get them air tickets. Give them cash, whatever. Just get them home.'

Bruce let go of Sophie for a moment and rested his palm on my forearm. I think I saw him smile. Then he coughed hard, and the pain took over again.

Sophie indicated right, but stayed in the middle of the road while she waited for a gap in the traffic. 'We're here.'

The hospital was a grey concrete block, with all the outbuildings, departments and signage you could have wished for. Unless you were in a hurry to find a doctor.

'Drop me here.' I wanted to get out before she crossed the main and came within range of the CCTV cameras monitoring the hospital entry road.

Once we'd stopped, Sophie turned and flicked her hair back from her face. 'Nick, get back to Anna, then find a hiding place as far away from him as you can. Believe me, he'll want to kill you both.'

I opened the sliding door, jumped out and headed south without looking back. There was bound to be an MTR station around here somewhere.

15

The Upper House

1 September 2011
17.18 hrs

Anna sounded more frustrated and angry than I'd ever heard her.

I was lying on the bed in my second set of jeans and white shirt, towelling my hair with one hand, holding the iPhone to my ear with the other. I didn't really know what her problem was. She'd made choices. Doing the work she did – no one made her run around the world looking for trouble. And me – she'd made a choice when she'd taken me on.

I knew motherhood changed everything – it had certainly changed her – but why take it out on me? Especially when I was seven thousand Ks away, doing everything I could to protect them.

I cut away from all that emotional shit. The main thing was that the boy was stable now and doing well.

Genghis and Mr Lover Man were stagging on at the clinic; no one was going to get past them, and that was all that mattered.

'Is there anything you can think of that you haven't told me about Katya? About her work? Her love life?'

Her sheets rustled.

'She said she had a boyfriend and he was trouble. I told her that was nothing new. Work-wise, she was brilliant, really skilled and committed.' She paused. 'She's been a bit preoccupied recently, but I've no idea what that was about.'

'You know I've got to go to Mexico, don't you? I've got to settle this, once and for all.'

She sighed in a way that I'd come to know all too well. It meant I was about to get another helping of grief. And I did. 'I understand. I get it. But this really has to stop, Nicholas. I worry for you. I worry for our son. Once and for all? No. There will always be a problem like this heading our way. It's the way you are. I've changed. I've had no choice. But I don't think you ever will. We *really* need to talk about this, for our son's sake.'

'It sounds as if you've already made up your mind, so what's the point of talking?'

'Don't be like that . . .'

'Now isn't the time, Anna. Now I just need to sort this shit out. For all of us.'

She sighed again.

'I'll call you later.'

I put down the phone and headed for my Timberlands.

Ten minutes later, I stopped at the desk with the

ever-smiling receptionist and asked if the package had been picked up by the three girls. It hadn't.

The sun was dipping behind the high-rises. That was good, as far as I was concerned, because it was hot as fuck. I turned right and headed for Starbucks, making a mental note to buy another pair of sun-gigs.

I was halfway down the queue when I saw a cab pull up and the three girls climb out of the back. They were still wearing the clothes they'd left Moldova in, and each clutched a small overnight bag. Kitty got out from beside the driver and waved them towards the lobby. They obeyed like sheep as she jumped back into the cab. Seconds later, she was gone.

I picked up a sticky bun to go with my brew. When the barista asked me my name, I said the first thing that came to mind.

The girl's brow furrowed and started scribbling.

I had a munch as I waited for my cappuccino. By the time it arrived, the Moldovan crew still hadn't come out of the hotel. I went outside, in case there was a problem. As I got to the entrance, I realized what it was. They didn't speak English, so had to rely on scribbled instructions. The package was handed over, and one of the guys on the door guided them outside.

'You need a taxi?' he asked. 'Taxi to the airport?'

They nodded excitedly. 'Taxi, taxi!'

He summoned one from the rank about twenty metres away, and leaned down to the driver as the girls piled inside.

'To the airport. They've got a Lufthansa flight. You know the terminal?'

The driver nodded, pissed off that his knowledge was being questioned.

When the cab disappeared, I decided to bin the cappuccino and take off down the hill towards Admiralty. The girls would probably never know how lucky they were, and that was a pity. This time next year they might be on another flight to another place with another chance to be a dancer or a waitress, or, a year poorer, something much more desperate. But I still felt quite good about giving them a second chance. Where they came from, second chances weren't too thick on the ground.

My Aussie mates would fade from view as soon as Bruce could walk without leaking. They were either going to be multi-millionaires or convicts, but wherever they ended up, it wouldn't be Hong Kong – or anywhere else with their old identities.

I felt a little jealous of them. They had each other, they had a plan, and they knew that no one else gave a fuck about them, so why worry?

I chucked a right towards Admiralty and got another coffee. This time it had *Dino* Sharpied all over the cup.

16

Wan Chai was as hot, sticky and congested as ever. The air was heavy with carbon monoxide trapped between the high-rises. I'd only walked a few hundred metres and my shirt already had big wet patches that clung to my sides. I'd bought myself a twenty-dollar pair of gigs, not that I needed them at ground level, with hundreds of feet of vertical concrete cutting out the low sun.

I checked out the bamboo scaffold as I entered the Internet café but there were no couples scrambling across it. I bought a can of Fanta that was as ice-cold as the shop, paid cash for a chunk of airtime and settled down to Google Dino Zavagno.

I picked up two guys straight away in two different countries, both in financial services, both at the geek end of the spectrum. Neither wore his cock on his head or had been anywhere near a peroxide bottle. I also picked up a mass of LinkedIn invitations to names that were close but no cigar.

I had a go at Bernardino, his full name, on Facebook and all the social networks, but nothing was an exact match. That surprised me. He was such a fuckwit I'd thought he'd be all over the place for the ladies. On the off-chance, I searched his name on the DEA site but, of course, there was nothing.

All the same, I pinged off an email to their El Paso office, which covered New Mexico and a slice of Texas.

My name is Nick Stone. Could you please forward this message to Bernardino Zavagno?

Dino – well, it's been a few years since Costa Rica, hasn't it? Could you contact me – there's something important I'd like to talk to you about? Nick.

It was a long shot: I hadn't seen him for years. But if I did get to him, he might be able to help. If I didn't, I'd just have to go to Mexico with a name, the same as I had coming here. But first I needed to see what was out there on El Peregrino, the Pilgrim.

I hit the keys and accessed all the normal places, but it looked like Katya, Dino and I were not the only people left on the planet without a digital presence. I hit the news channels and still nothing. There were no pictures and no articles that had anything remotely to do with the Pilgrim I was after.

PART SIX

1

Dulles Airport, Virginia

4 September 2011
15.22 hrs

My two-man DEA reception committee sat granite-like in their very shiny black Ford Taurus a few metres beyond the exit from the Avis car park. Chinos and polo shirts, short-back-and-sides with expressions to match. You didn't need an eagle eye to spot them. They'd FaceTimed me as I exited the luggage hall, a hand covering the screen that would have shown Dino checking me out. And now, as if to make doubly sure they couldn't be missed, the sedan carried government plates.

I sat behind the wheel of my hired Chevy Cruze, checking the bars on my iPhone yet again in case it hadn't rung because of a weak signal. I must have been there at least fifteen minutes because I'd had to spark up the engine to blow out the mist gathering on the windows. I had a new US Sprint SIM card in my mobile. Now I just had to wait – and hope – that Dino was going to call.

It was pointless heading out of the airport: I had nowhere to go. If Dino fucked me off, I'd dump the rental and make my way to Mexico. I had to crack on, with or without his help.

Ten minutes more of the heater doing its stuff and the mobile kicked off. I grabbed the ignition key and closed down the engine. I didn't want to miss a word. I checked the screen before hitting *answer*. The number was blocked.

'Dino?'

I could hear breathing, not heavy and desperate, but like he was weighing stuff up.

'Mate, where do you want me?'

Still nothing, but I knew he was there.

'Dino, mate . . . Where do you want me?'

'One last question.' High-pitched – the same voice as twenty years ago, but sadder, more guarded.

'I'm all ears.'

'Tell me the range, man. What was the range I gave you?'

I'd made sure I remembered as much as I could about that job, but the distance between our firing position and the Wolf's lair had been etched on my brain anyway. It was the only thing that bound us.

'Four – four – seven. Metres. None of your yards shit.'

I kept it light. His emails had given me the sense that talking with him was going to be like drawing blood from a stone.

Silence again.

He had some more thinking to do, and this time I let him get on with it.

Finally: 'Sixteen eighty-seven Veld Court. Fredericksburg.'

He gave me a second to write it down, which I didn't.

'You got it?'

'I got it. On my way.'

He closed down before I could get a finger to my screen.

2

Maud had a very nice voice. She came on like a friendly shop assistant. She told me that I was seventy-three miles from my destination; my journey would take a shade over an hour and fifteen.

Maud needed to be more climate-aware. I'd heard sat-nav make plenty of promises it had failed to keep, especially when it was raining; that always slows the traffic. But for now I was following her instructions to the letter: heading east from the airport towards DC, aiming to hit the Beltway, then turn south to Fredericksburg.

I'd waved goodbye to my reception committee a few minutes ago, but they hadn't paid much attention. I checked the rear-view. They were still a couple of cars back.

It had been ten years since I last drove this route, but the airport and its surroundings still looked much the same. That time it had been summer and the place had reminded me of a high-tech business park, with everything green and manicured. Now the leaves were starting to turn red. They'd soon drop onto the grass, but would be sucked up before they had time to flatten out and go soggy.

I remembered suburbia starting about fifteen miles from the airport, mainly ribbon development either side of the Beltway: vast estates of neat wooden and brick houses, many still under construction. Now, as I made my way east towards the I-495, it began almost from the exit road and spread to the western and northern perimeters of Washington.

Swathes of exposed ground on either side of me were criss-crossed with track marks where the big plant had crawled through vast tracts of woodland, turning it into matchsticks and Dunkin' Donuts packaging. Foundations were being laid for sprawling estates of houses that each had the same footprint. Giant bill-boards invited me to share the magic of living there in fall 2012.

I turned south on the 495, through what might have been a leafy Surrey suburb if it hadn't been for the roar of eight lanes of traffic. Large detached houses lined the roads, each with a seven-seat people-carrier or a gleaming 4x4 in the drive and a basketball hoop on the car port.

After about fifteen minutes I saw the turn-off. Maud told me Dino's place was now exactly forty-nine miles away, most of it on the freeway.

Within eighteen hours of pinging off the email I'd had a reply from the DEA's El Paso office, which had nearly made me choke on my coffee. They wanted a photo-graph. I replied with a crisp 'No' and suggested they ask me a question that only Dino and I would know the answer to, a kind of proof-of-life statement.

I got one line back: *What color hair?*

The grin on my face took me straight back to Costa Rica. How the fuck could I forget that ridiculous bleach job? After three further exchanges via the El Paso office I'd finally got the call I was hoping for. The way Dino sounded, the meet wasn't going to be a social, so I wasn't expecting balloons and party poppers after all these years.

I still didn't know if he could or even would help me, and he still didn't know why I wanted to see him, but I'd decided that, whatever happened now, I was heading to Mexico tomorrow. I wanted this shit over and done with so I could get back to Moscow.

I sat in the middle lane and went with the flow. The rain had pretty much stopped, but I had my wipers on full blast to get rid of the shit being kicked up off the tarmac by the trucks.

I checked the rear-view.

Sure enough, the Taurus was still two vehicles behind, but a whole lot dirtier now than it had been when it started the day.

3

I got caught behind two massive eighteen-wheelers racing each other along the nearside lanes. Some kind of projectile arced out of one of the cabs, hit the concrete ahead of me and exploded in a burst of yellow spray.

Trucker bombs had become a national epidemic. The long-haul lads were getting a hard time for it, but I had a certain sympathy for them. They could go for a hundred miles or more without finding anywhere to park their rigs safely or legally. The average Joe could take the next exit and hit a gas station or a McDonald's whenever he felt like a piss, but the big dogs were tied up with weight and height restrictions, and the strong possibility of not being able to turn around again to get back on the freeway.

The only answer was to recycle. They'd finish off their carton of whatever kept them going, refill it and bin it out of the window. There were even piles of shit at the roadside; plastic bags full of what looked like four dog loads from the morning walk. How the fuck did they race each other and take a dump into a plastic bag at the same time?

I started to see signs for the massive US Marine Corps camp and training area at Quantico. After years of seeing it in TV crime shows, most people know Quantico as the place where impossibly good-looking baby FBI agents are trained, and all the special units are based. The DEA also had their equally massive training academy on the same patch, which was about the size of the Isle of Wight. I'd spent quite a lot of time instructing at the FBI academy whenever we'd developed a new technique – for room-clearing, covert entry or whatever – and being on the receiving end of their instruction whenever they came up with something they were happy to share. The flow of information between us had always been good.

You couldn't see it from the freeway, but Quantico looked more like a seventies university than the centre of anti-everything. Agents or students wore different colour polo shirts to ID who they were and what they were there for. Everything was squeaky clean, including the language. I swore in the dining-room once – well, I said 'shit' when I tipped over my Coke. The whole place went quiet. You'd have thought I'd slotted the cook, but maybe I'd interrupted one of the prayer gatherings they had over the lunch trays. The training area was just as bad. Bears might shit in the woods, but no one at Quantico was even allowed to piss in them. It was one hell of a training centre, but I hated the place.

I guessed the presence of the DEA academy explained why Dino was now in this part of the world. Or maybe he was big-timing it at their downtown HQ. The fact I'd been FaceTimed and treated to a Taurus escort had to mean he was something hard-core, or maybe operating super undercover.

I hadn't had the slightest indication from him about what he was doing, just a collection of one-line emails and a call that added up to: *What the fuck do you want?*

The Taurus cut past me on the inside. The two guys had their heads forward, not talking, and took the exit at speed. Surveillance over. It looked like all they wanted right now was to be first to the academy's car wash.

4

After passing most of Fredericksburg and a series of
signs for the National Military Park, Maud told me it
was time to leave the freeway.

When I'd done my junior Brecon command course as
a young infantry soldier, Fredericksburg 1862 was cited
as an example of how easily disorganized fighting can
turn into total slaughter. Nine thousand men died as the
Union tried to drive further south into the Confederacy,
and by the end of the battle the town was a burned-out
shell. This whole area had suffered more American
dead during the civil war than in two world wars, the
Korean war and the Vietnam war combined.

I drove past churches and schools that were all built
on one level with plenty of space around them. They
didn't do sidewalks here, and most of the plots weren't
fenced. The dwellings were wooden, colonial-style
single- or two-storey, some with verandas, some not.
Everything was as shiny as it would have been before
everything went tits up in 1862, but there were a whole

lot more double-door garages, basketball hoops and SUVs in evidence. Small forests of mailboxes stood alongside the road, so the posties didn't have to leave their cabs to deliver.

1687 Veld stood beside a turning circle at the end of a wooded cul-de-sac. Only the window shutters – which were the red of the Confederate flag – singled it out from its cream-painted weatherboard neighbours. They were permanently open; they wouldn't move even if you wanted them to. A black Nissan truck sat outside with a pair of sun-gigs hanging off the rear-view.

The front door opened the instant I pulled into the driveway. The shadowy figure who stood there in a black pullover and jeans didn't look much like the guy I'd spent time with in '93, and he didn't look as if he was a big noise in the DC HQ – or anywhere else – either. This version of Dino had a crew-cut, but the dyed blond was grey. He drooped at the shoulders; the air had been let out of him.

He had to turn sideways to negotiate the four stone steps that led down to the drive, like somebody had just given him a dead leg.

I climbed out of the Chevy as he passed under his hoop. It was in the same position as the others in the development, but rusty and with rotting string.

I held out a hand. 'All right, mate?'

The skin on his face had lost its lustre and elasticity. It didn't crease as he tried a smile and held out his hand in return. His shake conveyed as much commitment as his call.

'You haven't changed, Nick.'

I was about to say something similar about him, but he shook his head. 'No need to bullshit, man. Plenty's changed.' He wasn't wrong: he looked twenty years older than he should, and his teeth were worse than Kitty's.

He let go of my hand, bent down and tapped his left leg just above the knee. Only alloy or hard plastic made that sound.

I had the feeling I wasn't going to get any more of that *hombre* shit from him.

5

He did a crablike shuffle up the steps ahead of me, a performance he seemed to have well squared away. He held the door open and ushered me in. It was gloomy. Maybe he didn't like light, these days – or paying electricity bills.

'Go on through, Nick.' His high-pitched voice seemed to suit his new body better than it had the young, fit one, but it also made him sound sad and resigned. It wasn't funny any more.

The house was open plan and sparsely furnished, almost as if a bachelor pad had been planted inside a family home. The dark-wood floor was past its best, but Mr Sheen had done his stuff. There was a faint aroma of disinfectant; at least it wasn't that pungent flowery shit that filled my nose everywhere in Moscow.

Dino double-locked the front door before waving me through to the kitchen area – wall-to-wall pine with an industrial-sized two-door steel fridge in one corner. Six white mugs were lined up on a shelf, as straight as a row of guardsmen. Every surface was spotless. The sink was clean and dry, with not so much as a watermark.

The lone brown-leather sofa at the other end of the room looked like it had just been delivered by IKEA. The black leather La-Z-Boy beside it had clearly seen the lion's share of the arse time. A drinks coaster and the world's supply of remote controls had been precisely arranged on a small rectangular table by its armrest. A large flat-screen TV took pride of place, with cable, Blu-ray and Xbox wired in with similar care.

My Timberlands echoed as I headed towards the sofa.

Dino sounded so subdued as he invited me to sit that I wondered if he was on a prescription. He collapsed into the La-Z-Boy and must have pressed a button somewhere because its footrest unfolded with an electronic whine.

There was a couple of seconds' silence in the semi-darkness, broken only by a car turning out front. Dino tapped his leg once more. 'I was held hostage for thirteen months in '08 – took a round as I escaped, just above the knee. Now I got this fucker.' He tapped it again.

I didn't bother giving him sympathy. That wasn't what he needed. 'Cartel?'

'Sort of.' He nodded. 'Anyway, I'm pensioned off now, part of the agent-enrichment programme up in Quantico. They tell me I need to pass on my wealth of knowledge and experience to the next generation.'

'What about your two mates? If they'd come all the way I wouldn't have needed sat-nav.'

He didn't see the funny side of it. 'They're never far away. They kinda look after me when I need them to.' He hesitated. 'I can't stand the look in their eyes.

I'm the guy they hope they'll never become. They pity me.'

It was clear he wasn't just talking about his leg.

6

'A big part of the programme is explaining how this shit happened.' He massaged his thigh, like he was kneading dough. 'I suggest ways they can avoid getting lifted, and how they can cope with it if they do. They wheel me out on stage every two or three weeks and I do my party piece.'

If his appearance had anything to do with his time as a captive, they really must have put him through the wringer. Or maybe he was just one of those people who react badly to such things. Biology dictates destiny and all that shit.

I thought about telling him I'd been a PoW in Baghdad, and lifted a couple of times since. Maybe it would make him feel more comfortable. But maybe it wouldn't. I didn't know enough about him yet to be sure. I decided to let him do the talking.

'I'd offer you a drink, Nick, but I don't do that stuff any more. I got sodas, though.' He managed to raise a smile. 'And I went out this morning to get you some tea.'

'Not that Lipton shit – the stuff in the little yellow packets?'

He nodded. 'Sure.'

'I'll take a coffee.'

The button was pressed and the La-Z-Boy stood to attention.

I stayed put as he got up, taking in what I could of my surroundings in the gloom. This room was beyond spotless. It was sterile. There were no pictures of family, no end-of-course photos of our hero with 'DEA' emblazoned across his body armour – just a few prints of lakes on the wall in thin aluminium frames. He'd probably bought them as a job lot with the sofa. It all had the feeling of a short-term rental that had recently had a deep clean.

Lights came on at last as he made it to the kitchen area. The floor and flat-screen gleamed, and I couldn't see a single particle of airborne dust.

The only items that looked remotely like personal effects – and even then only because I knew something of his background – were two rows of books on a shelf to the left of the flat-screen. They were all drug-war related.

Dino leaned on the breakfast bar to take his weight off the prosthetic as the coffee percolator chugged away. 'Milk? Cream? Sugar?'

It was hard to tell by his tone if he was bored with me or with life in general.

'Black's fine, thanks.'

Two guardsmen were selected from the line and filled. He passed me one, positioned his own dead centre of the coaster, then stretched out the La-Z-Boy once more.

I had nowhere to put my mug so I just kept hold of it while I waited for it to cool.

Dino sparked up as soon as the chair stopped whining. 'What do you want from me, Nick? You didn't say anything in those emails of yours, and you've come all the way from Hong Kong. It must be big-time.'

'I need some of that agent-enrichment knowledge you've got tucked away in there.' I tapped my head. 'I need to find someone who's being held by a cartel in Mexico. Well, as far as I know she is. It happened a few days ago. So I thought, Who'll know the way things go down there?'

Dino nodded and took occasional sips of his brew as I started to explain the Katya situation.

'I don't have the name of the guy who's got her, but they call him Peregrino . . .'

His arm froze mid-sip. Then he slowly replaced his guardsman on the coaster. His hand gave a mild tremor – enough for a bead of coffee to roll down the outside of the mug.

'You all right, mate?'

He said nothing, just gave a couple of quick nods and took some deep breaths.

I tried a sip of my coffee. I'd thought I'd been talking long enough for it to cool, but I was wrong.

Dino had sorted himself out but left his coffee where it was. 'Nick, you've got to know something. It's worse than you thought. Peregrino . . .' he leaned towards me, as if the walls had ears '. . . that's his new name, like the artist formerly known as fucking Prince . . . He's the son of Jesús.'

'The big boy from Nazareth?'

'Jesús *Orjuela*, for fuck's sake. The Wolf. This fucker's

name is Jesús, just like his dad. He was the first and only son, remember?'

I did remember. How could I not? I remembered him staring at me through that window frame. I remembered wondering if he'd wake up at three in the morning with the same recurring nightmare.

Dino knew exactly what was going through my mind. 'Now that's kinda funny, Nick, don't you think? Poetic, almost.'

It was hard to tell if he had a smile on his face or a grimace.

7

'Why Peregrino?'

'He's supernatural, man. He's like some fucking god down there. Remember the two sisters? They're history. A vendetta killing, two thousand nine.' Dino suddenly sounded relieved to have an audience. 'The kid Jesús was at war, trying to take over the Tijuana cartel's *plaza*. The cartel paid the Zetas to fight for them, but Jesús just kicked their ass, man. So the Zetas raped and killed the girls – even posted the killings on YouTube. It happens a lot, stays on for a day or so.'

I knew about Los Zetas. Thirty-one deserters from the Mexican Army's Airborne Special Forces, originally linked to the Gulf cartel on the west coast, had pulled together one of the most powerful paramilitary groups in the region, and they'd been murdering, raping and hacking people's faces off ever since.

Back in the nineties, as the DEA targeted the air and sea routes into the US, the Mexicans had developed their old marijuana-smuggling donkey trails across the border into six-lane cocaine super-highways that became known as the *plazas*. Then Escobar and the Wolf were killed, and after years as the Colombians' drug mules, the poor relations finally started calling the shots. When their government waded in to help, it was the icing on the cake.

The Institutional Revolutionary Party, the PRI, had held power in Mexico City for seventy years. The police and the military weren't complaining: they took tens of millions in bungs, and the politicians didn't do too badly either. Bizarrely, it brought stability to the drugs trade. The PRI would smooth things over when gang warfare broke out – like Relate, but without the tea and biscuits – and even allocated access to the *plazas*.

Everything ran like clockwork – until the Mexican voters finally got fed up with being shat on and the PRI lost the 2000 election. What followed was a total gang-fuck. At least seven cartels started beating the shit out of each other, and that was just for starters. It got so bad that sometimes one half of a cartel turned on the other half.

They continued to battle with each other for control of the *plazas*, the crucial northern border cities, like Ciudad Jerez and Tijuana, and strategic ports like Acapulco – for years the holder of first prize in Mexico's annual highest-homicide-rate contest. The Zetas – and others like them – had taken the contest to a new level. The era of the pistol-, rifle- and chainsaw-toting brigand was over; these boys were heavily armed, well-trained professionals, who'd changed sides for a slice of the action until they'd decided they wanted it all.

A succession of presidents have minced around in army uniforms for the last few years, waving an angry finger on TV and promising to wage the mother of all battles against the bad guys. The military did launch the odd lightning strike, but it was never much more than a PR stunt. Like the police, they lacked the will, training, manpower and firepower to do the cartels any permanent damage.

Like the Taliban in Afghanistan, the gangs usually just waited for them to go away. But when they did stand and fight, they won – as you do when you're carrying M4 carbines with under-slung grenade launchers and all sorts of state-of-the-art weaponry smuggled south from the US, and RPG7s, machine-guns, fragmentation grenades and light tanks from Nicaragua, El Salvador and Honduras, left over from the Cold War conflicts of the eighties.

As well as distributing the lion's share of heroin from Afghanistan, Mexico itself was now also a major producer. The cartels had their fingers in every pie, and controlled more than 90 per cent of the drugs entering the US. They generated at least fifty billion US dollars a year; more revenue than almost half of the Fortune 500 companies.

Since 2006, around seventy thousand Mexican citizens had paid the price of this bonanza – decapitated and hung over motorway bridges, or left at the roadside with their entrails pouring out or their tongues ripped through their throats. No wonder the PRI were about to grab back power after twelve years in the wilderness. Better the devil you know . . .

Time alone would tell whether they'd be able to get everyone round the table like in the good old days.

8

There was no stopping Dino now. 'The Zetas used to be the big dogs. They might tell the world they still are, and the world might think so – but everyone down there knows better. They haven't been since that day in 2009. The Pilgrim is top of their shit heap.'

'His dad would have been bursting with pride.'

'He was twelve when you zapped the old man. We should have taken him out too.' Dino sighed. 'He's nearly thirty now. His birthday's coming up. November sixteen. I know how I'd like to celebrate . . .'

He took a swig and so did I, but I wouldn't be drinking any more. The coffee was as weak as the tea would have been.

'Damn right.' Dino put his mug down and gave his leg another tap. 'He owes me.'

He gazed into the middle distance for a moment. I thought he might have spotted a dust particle.

'I was lifted in Nuevo León state, about fifty Ks south of the border. You know about *los vigilantes*, Nick?'

I knew insecurity dominated the lives of Mexican 'real

351

people'. Caught between warring cartels with the law-enforcement agencies doing fuck-all to help, the locals had had to take things into their own hands. They couldn't afford to pay for organized protection, so had to police their own backyard against sex offenders, thieves and murderers. It was basically every man for himself.

'So one day a couple of kids, six, seven years old, were kidnapped from a park. We were in the wrong place at the wrong time, only been in the area for two minutes when the car was rammed – simply because it was an unknown. They dragged us out, and started fucking us up.'

Dino's eyes burned as he relived the moment. 'They went for us with lumps of concrete, Nick, iron bars . . . You name it, they fucking piled in with it. They took a shovel ten fucking times to my friend's head, man. He left three fucking kids behind . . . Fucking animals . . .'

I let him struggle with the images in his head for a while, but not so long that I lost him. I'd seen this shit before and knew tonight could end up with me not learning a thing I wanted to know. At the same time, he had to work it through so we could get to where I needed to be.

'Sounds like a fucking nightmare . . .'

'They frisked the body for cash and found his badge. Straight away some bright fuck in the crowd knew there was money to be made. Maybe they could sell me to the paramilitaries, or even to a cartel.

'It wasn't exactly music to my ears, man – but as long as they kept moving me, I was alive. And back then I thought living was all that mattered.'

He slumped back in the La-Z-Boy, his head resting on the cushion. 'They chose to sell me to Peregrino's fucking religious maniacs. Jesús de la Paz – Jesus for Peace. You get it? Fucking hilarious.' He wasn't smiling.

'So what did *they* do – sell you on?'

He shook his head, a look of infinite sadness in his eyes. 'He gave me to his fucking mother as a present.' His face contorted. 'Locked me up like a fucking animal in a cage. Over a year, man, a fucking year. She treated the fucking dogs better. She'd bring me out, parade me around, no clothes or some fucking fancy dress, beaten, on a chain, all kinds of shit. To their friends, to other cartels – their very own DEA gimp, ha-fucking-ha. Kicked about, used as an ashtray, a fucking footstool.' He had to stop: he'd run out of breath.

I leaned in. 'They didn't try to trade you back to the DEA?'

'For what? I had more value to her as a toy, a fucking curiosity for her amusement. I pretended I was Italian-American and didn't understand Spanish. I expected to be interrogated for information, but the fucks are so arrogant they couldn't give a shit what a low-life grunt would know that could possibly help them. Why the fuck should she care? They're untouchable down there. Neither of those fucks even saw me as a fucking human being.'

He drifted off into his own tortured world.

'That fucking bitch ... Liseth ... Remember her, Nick? Yeah, Liseth ... We thought she might need some protection without the Wolf around, didn't we?'

His eyes darted towards me.

'The trophy wife?' I grinned at him. 'I can remember you wanting to fuck her ...' It wasn't saying much. He'd wanted to fuck anything in a skirt back then.

'We got that shit completely wrong. She's a praying

mantis, man. You remember we were told that Jesús used to read the classics? You believe it, that fat fuck reading Voltaire? You remember, Nick?'

I could only nod: nothing was going to stop him now. 'I learned all about that bitch, lying there in my cage, playing the dumb-ass. She was the one that got the Wolf into all the politics and philosophy shit. She was the one that made him think everybody needed encouragement – got him to believe he was the defender of civil liberties – leaving herself plenty of space to fuck everybody over.

'And now that fuck of a son is one dangerous, fucked-up individual – and, have no doubt, Jesús de la Paz is one dangerous, fucked-up organization. But believe me, man, Peregrino is just the poster-boy for all that shit. The bitch runs the show.'

He hit the La-Z-Boy button and hauled himself to his feet. 'I had thirteen fucking months of her in my face. She has that boy of hers on a tighter lead than her dogs. He makes no move without her say-so.'

He started limping up and down the room. I didn't know if it was anger or cramp. 'For her, the Wolf was really just a pussy. That, in her mind, was why the cartels got fucked over. But she's taking care of business, man. She might have started off as some street kid with a great ass, but she used it, man – she used it to get places. She used it to get an education and a position in life. But that doesn't make her any less of a dangerous motherfucker.'

He stopped pacing and stared at the floor, mumbling away to himself. His breathing was quicker and shallower by the moment.

'If you hadn't done the job for her, she'd have either

killed her old man herself or got him to fuck Escobar up the ass and take control. Like I said, man, she's a praying mantis. But you're the one who needs to do the praying.'

9

'You know where they are?'

'Right there in Narcopulco.'

'Narco-who?'

'It's what they're calling Acapulco, these days. They live outside of town.'

'Is that where they kept you?'

He nodded, eyes still rooted to the floor.

I let him try to process the pictures bouncing around in his head. They would have been there ever since Liseth and her crew had worked their magic on him.

He headed back to the La-Z-Boy a lot more slowly this time, and didn't bother activating the footrest before collapsing into the chair. 'These fucks, they've got to be stopped, Nick. It's not just Mexico that's fucked, man, but us up here as well. We got a war going on that's bigger than Iraq and Afghanistan put together, right on our fucking stoop. It's banging on the front door, man, and it's only going to get worse. We ain't seen nothing yet.'

He lost interest in the floor and lifted his head. He

looked sadder than ever. 'The fucking drugs, man. They're ripping the heart out of this country.' His eyes wobbled like they were on springs. 'Robbing people of their . . . family . . . friends . . . self-respect . . .'

He slumped back in the black leather and ran his hand over the little hair he had left. 'You know what? Before I got lifted, I was really going places. Things were going good for me. But look at me now, a fucking exhibit at an academy freak show . . .'

His eyes burned.

He leaned forward and cradled his face in his hands. He looked like he was crying.

'Nick, I'm kind of wiped out. It's been a long day for me. I'm going to hit the sack, OK?' He raised his head once more. 'You're in the guest room.' He pointed to the far end of the house, across the hallway and past the front door. 'You need anything, go get it. There's a bathroom, all that kinda thing.'

I stood up as he limped away. 'Thanks, Dino. Maybe you can help me with the stuff I need to know in the morning, yeah?'

He headed for the stairs, not looking back. 'Sure, sure. No problem. Later.'

I binned the brew in the spotless sink and scouted around for the teabags. There wasn't a kettle. I switched on one of the infra-red hob rings and quarter-filled a saucepan from the tap, then threw three of the Lipton's bags into a fresh mug. I rinsed my old one, gave it a wipe, and replaced it carefully in the parade line. If it was a millimetre out, it might push him over the edge. I'd seen it happen.

I opened the fridge door to find not very much. Two half-empty packs of cold cuts, four cans of Mountain

Dew, a plastic carton of 2 per cent milk, and that was it.

The interior light gave me a glimpse of something on the nearby wall – pencil marks charting two kids' heights as they grew up. James and Jacob were obviously growing fast. The last recorded score for James was on his ninth birthday, and for Jacob, the smaller one, on his seventh, six months ago.

I went to the bottom of the stairs. 'Dino – you want anything from the shop, mate? I've got to go and get a toothbrush, that kind of shit.'

'No . . . no . . . I'm good . . .' The bout of coughing that followed said otherwise. 'Take my key. It's on the table in the hall. Lock up tight on the way out.'

I got back from the mall about an hour later with washing and shaving kit and some clothes, the normal urban-armour stuff: cheap jeans, dark blue wash-and-weep shirts, underwear and socks. I'd also treated myself to a foot-long Philly cheese Subway and a party-size bottle of Coke.

I heard Dino bumping around upstairs, but not for long. I fell asleep, fucked over by jet-lag.

10

I was woken by a cry in the night.

It was followed seconds later by a desperate-sounding sob.

I swung my legs over the edge of the bed and sat there for a moment, rubbing my face back to life. Then I stood up and reached for the light switch. I couldn't find it, so felt for the door handle instead, stumbled out into the hallway and had better luck there.

I went up the stairs and put my ear to Dino's bedroom door. I heard another muffled sob, then muttering, garbled words and numbers. Not much of it made sense until he started to scream.

'No! Please . . . No! No! Don't . . . please . . . don't, please! Liseth . . . please, tell him, no!'

I stood there as the screams subsided.

This time I heard the numbers more clearly: *'8 – 1 – 8 – 2 – 8 – 3 . . .'*

Then the sobs took over once more.

I turned the handle and went inside. It was dark, but

in the glow from downstairs I could see him kneeling on the floor next to his bed, swatting invisible insects from his face.

I put a hand on his shoulder.

'Mate, it's OK . . . Dino, it's OK. Just a dream, that's all.'

He opened his eyes. He wrapped an arm around my leg, pulling me towards him.

'It's OK, you're at home. It's safe.'

He seemed to come to his senses, released his grip and crawled back onto the bed. But I could see enough to know he was absolutely distraught.

There was a half-empty glass of water on the bedside cabinet. I passed it to him. 'Here, have some of this.'

He took it from me and raised it to his lips. Then he cleared his throat, looking embarrassed. 'Thanks, man. Thank you.'

'You taking medication, mate? Anything I can get you? More water?'

He shook his head, like he was trying to clear the demons that had sparked this outburst. 'How long have you been here?'

'Couple of minutes. You only just woke me.'

'I was having a nightmare? I can't even remember what it was about.' He tugged his soaking wet sweatshirt away from his skin as I got to my feet.

'It happens. You OK now?'

He took a deep breath. 'Sure. Thanks.'

'I'll see you in the morning.'

'Yeah . . . OK, man . . . Thanks for the drink.'

I retreated to the landing and closed his door behind me. I understood the pain in his head. And it made me feel mightily relieved that I wasn't one of those poor fuckers who couldn't process the trauma, then cut away from it.

11

My body kept telling me I still needed sleep, but I fought not to close my eyes again.

I tapped my iPhone: 01.18.

I didn't want to lie there and think too much about Dino's pain. It wasn't going to help him, and it certainly wasn't going to help me. I decided to go walkabout to keep my head busy.

I made my way into the living room and flicked on the light. Everything was as sterile as we'd left it. Dino hadn't sneaked back down and emptied a bottle of Jack Daniel's. The kitchen, too, was spotlessly clean. I noticed a door off to the left and opened it, as you do when you're being nosy. It was an office.

Dino's PC stood on a desk in the corner. The pinboard behind it was covered with printouts and newspaper cuttings. When I moved closer, I could see some were in Spanish, some in English. The headlines I could understand spoke of Mexican gang shootings and murders. I couldn't read the Spanish captions but the pictures were mostly of decapitated bodies sprawled in dusty streets.

To the left of it was a corkboard with a montage of photographs: the usual mishmash of family snaps, some black-and-white, some colour, all showing a life that Dino had once had. Wedding pix, with Dino centre stage – a Dino I recognized a whole lot better than the one upstairs. The bride was blonde and good-looking, a touch of Angelina Jolie about her. Then the two boys, at all the different stages: big ears; no teeth; birthday parties; school teams.

I sat down at the desk. Tired copies of *Time* and *Newsweek* were strewn across it; glossy Spanish titles I didn't recognize; a pile of DEA Classified reports.

I ran my eye along the shelves to my right. A selection of hardbacks, paperbacks, carefully folded maps. The well-worn spines covered everything from natural history to geography, and quite a lot of American and Mexican political history. But most seemed to be stern-looking textbooks and reports on drug-related matters.

Two worn paperbacks and a thick black file had been stacked against each other. The books were by Frank Kitson. *Gangs and Counter-gangs* and *Low Intensity Operations: Subversion, Insurgency and Peacekeeping*. The file contained a detailed briefing document by Bernardino Zavagno: *Kitson Doctrine and the Mexican Cartels*.

I thumbed through it. Back in the day, I'd thought Dino couldn't even write his own name. This thing had really got to him.

I'd never served with Frank Kitson, but when I joined the Green Jackets he was already a legend. He came to see the battalion at Tidworth when I was a very young corporal, and it was like a royal visit. The whole battalion was put to area-cleaning the camp. Even the

363

guardroom got a quick lick of paint, just because Kitson would be driving past it.

We sat spellbound in the cookhouse as he told us about fighting the Mau-Mau uprising in Kenya in the late fifties, where he'd won a Military Cross, then in the jungle during the Malayan Emergency, where he'd won another. While I'd been busy bunking primary school, he'd been a brigade commander in Belfast at the time of Bloody Sunday.

Despite his reputation, Kitson's ideas weren't all about blood and guts, and I could see why Dino would have backed him against the cartels. He understood there had to be an end-game once you'd ripped the enemy apart. To get to that point, the masses engaged in the insurgency had to be lured away from the leadership with the promise of concessions – which would only kick in when life returned to normal. The sooner that happened, the sooner the sun would come out. And the moment a concession could be given, you gave it. You didn't risk allegations of bad faith, of fucking the masses over.

Dominating the battle space reinforced the message: 'Get out of the way, you'll be fine. Get *in* the way and we're going to fuck you.' No more force than necessary should be employed to maintain the allegiance of the masses – but no mercy either, if anyone didn't play the game.

Bribery, coercion, lies, assassinations, bombs – you'd use whatever it took to find the top dogs and wipe them out. Their replacements would also have to be destroyed, time after time, until only the mentally deficient would want to risk sticking their heads above the parapet.

The justice system needed to move swiftly to cement the legitimacy of their military commanders' actions, and confirm them as a mechanism of government.

And the powers-that-be had to embrace as many prominent members of the masses as possible, as well as any surviving leaders who'd seen the light – at least for now. Bring them all inside the tent, pissing out; make them part of policy – that was Kitson's way ahead.

His doctrine was the mother of all hearts-and-minds operations, but it wasn't about giving them seeds to grow corn or polio vaccinations: that was soft power, and came later, once you'd gripped them by the bollocks and shown them who was boss – and invited them to become part of the solution.

Whatever, Dino Zavagno was obviously a fan, and the State Department wasn't. The inside page of his report had been rubber-stamped: *Received and Returned*. Another slap in the face for fucked-up Dino.

To twist the knife, three words had been scrawled across the inked box: *No action advised*.

12

5 September 2011

05.19 hrs

I tried to get my head down this time, but knew it wasn't going to happen.

I hauled myself up and made for the bathroom. I pulled back the immaculate shower screen, took off my kit and dropped it on the tiled floor, but left the plasters on the two cannula sites in my right arm. I stepped into the cubicle and lifted my hands to inspect the wounds on my wrists. My shirt sleeves had kept them so well covered I might have forgotten about them if they hadn't been so incredibly sore. The plasticuff welts were lumpy and livid, and a good inch wide. The bruising on my right thigh had come on nicely and my ribs burned even when I reached out to turn on the tap.

I lathered myself with the mall's flowery gel and rubbed their best shampoo into my hair. Towelling myself dry, I wandered back to my room, put on my nice new jeans and blue shirt, and went across the hall for the first Lipton's of the day.

The back porch had a raised wooden deck big enough for a bench and table, with a nylon windbreak to protect them from the neighbours' prying eyes. I sat sipping my brew as the first glimmers of dawn broke over the horizon. It had taken three teabags to bring it up to full monkey strength.

A light or two flickered in the windows of many of the houses nearby as their inhabitants ran around like lunatics trying to get to work on time or deliver the kids to school. The local bird population was starting to get vocal in the woods about fifty metres back from the house, competing with the distant rumble of the freeway. The shadowy remains of a swing and a slide stood out on the unkempt grass.

In my head, I started to run through the questions I wanted Dino to answer. I'd start with the basics. Was the target overlooked? What were the main access routes? Where were the garages, parking spaces and outbuildings? What were the dimensions and layouts of key rooms? Where was the power supply? Which doors were secured? Bolts or lever locks? Did they make a noise when they opened? Did I need to take in some oil to stop them creaking?

Were there any covered approach routes? Major obstacles? Was the surrounding ground ploughed, rocky, boggy? What about security fences, proximity lights? He'd already told me about the dogs, but were there any other animals? Horses, maybe? Geese? Those little bastards could wake the dead. The list went on – and that was even before I moved on to manpower and weapons.

In a perfect world, I'd take time to find out the target's routine. But this world was far from perfect. I was running out of time and, although I still had no idea what the fuck Katya was up to, I guessed she was as well.

13

The kitchen door swung open and I heard footsteps making their way towards me. When Dino appeared around the edge of the screen and saw me, he froze like a deer in a set of oncoming headlights.

The titanium tubing and the hydraulics that made up his new knee glinted below a midnight-blue towelling bathrobe. He swayed slightly, as if he wanted to back away but I'd nailed his real foot and the false one to the deck. The crimson scar tissue and brutal toothmarks around his remaining calf showed that dogs weren't always Man's Best Friend.

Even in this light I could see that his expression had nothing to do with being startled by my unexpected presence – and everything to do with what I'd caught him holding. He'd been dropping blue-white crystals from a clear plastic zip-up into a glass pipe shaped like a test-tube, with an air-vented table-tennis ball on its end. Judging by the dark-brown stains and scorch-marks that covered it, Dino was already way past the experimental stage. He stared at me for another second or two, began to shake his head slowly from side to side, then turned back into the house.

The crystals explained the weight loss and fuck-all in the fridge, the loss of appetite, bad skin and 'meth-mouth' teeth. The attempt to self-medicate the trauma away was often a symptom of his condition, but it never worked.

I gave him five to sort himself out, then got up and went inside.

I followed the sound of sobbing to the La-Z-Boy. He leaned forward, his head almost touching his man-made knee. His pipe, bag and disposable lighter were squashed between his hand and his face.

I sat down on the sofa. 'It's OK, mate. No one has to know.'

'No – *not* OK, Nick. *Not OK.*'

I could just about make out the words trying to fight their way past his hand and the jumble of meth gear.

'I can't keep it together any more. I'm wasted, man.' His head rocked back and forth between sobs. 'A wasted fuck . . .'

The best thing was to let him get it all out.

'Mate, I'm sure you're not the first DEA guy to suffer like this. Your people must have programmes that can help.'

His face remained buried among the paraphernalia. 'It's too late, Nick. I fucked up. It's all gone – kids, wife. I'm just a wasted fuck.'

At last, with a superhuman effort, he managed to collect himself. He laid his gear carefully on the table and wiped his face with the heels of both hands. 'It isn't the meth, Nick. That just gets me through the day. It's the pain I can't handle. The failure. Seeing those assholes, right up close, every time I close my eyes, you know?'

I didn't, but I nodded anyway.

'Since I got back from Mexico . . . my head got fucked up big-time. I couldn't sleep – still can't. I keep going over everything that happened – all the things that fucker and his bitch of a mother did to me. Over and over. It's like my fucking head can't turn the page, man.

'I know she'd be insane to come for me here, but that don't stop the attacks, man. That don't stop the paranoia. That don't stop me locking myself in this fucking house, sometimes for weeks, thinking – *knowing* – they're out there, on the fucking drive, waiting for me. I've lost count the number of times I've called for back-up. Then I have to deal with the fucking pity, you hear what I'm saying?'

His face twisted as he did everything he could to fight back the confusion and the shame. Every breath he took rasped like sandpaper.

'The truth is, that bitch doesn't need to take me back, Nick. She's already inside my head . . .'

He knew as well as I did that, no matter how untouchable she was down there, they wouldn't come up here and fuck about on DC's doorstep. If they did, there wouldn't just be a two-man DEA welcoming committee, there'd be a Combat Aviation Brigade complete with Blackhawks and Apaches coming their way to 'assist' the Mexican government to rid themselves of Public Enemy Number One.

'Mate, you know you've got PTSD, don't you? The meth – it's just a part of it. Didn't the Agency fix you up with counselling or whatever when you got back?'

He glared at me. 'They offered it, but I didn't need that shit.'

I moved in closer and gripped him by the arm. 'You do, mate, *you do.*'

14

I'd seen it far too many times. PTSD was the silent killer. It could invade every fibre of your being. It wasn't just the flashbacks and the anger. Guys like Dino couldn't even communicate with loved ones, let alone accept their love and help. They pushed them away. The self-medication only increased the pain as they spiralled out of control.

He went quiet, rubbing his temples with his thumbs.

'Dino, I know this shit is real. It's fucked up some of my mates big-time. But you can pull yourself out of it. I've seen it happen.'

I'd also seen strong men destroyed because they didn't understand that PTSD has nothing to do with machismo: it's a normal reaction to an abnormal event. Some people suffer; others don't.

He was still looking down at the floor, apparently mesmerized by the shiny little puddles of tears gathering around his feet. I was no expert, but the white mugs on parade, the lack of dust, the spotless sink, the absence of hairy soap in the shower was his way of trying to impose some order on his nightmare of a life.

'Dino, mate . . .' I waited for him to raise his glazed, watery eyes to mine. 'The flashbacks are only your brain trying to process the shit that happened to you. The nightmares, the paranoia: they just mean your brain's filing system is a little fucked up, that's all. You're not pitiful. You're not bad. You're not a wasted fuck. You're not useless. There's just a little bit of wiring that needs sorting between your left and right hemispheres, so you can put that stuff in its proper place and get your life back. It can be sorted. You hear what *I*'m saying?'

I hoped he did. The three or four lads I'd served with who hadn't got help when they should have had ended up killing themselves. Dino had been humiliated, badly injured, then shuffled sideways when he'd got back to work. His solo gigs for the new DEA intakes weren't going to save him; his Kitson theory wasn't either. All the ingredients were there for a very sad final chapter to the Dino Zavagno story.

'Nick, I'm so sorry for letting you see this. It's pathetic.'

'It's part of the life we lead, mate. But there's a way back. Think of your wife. And James and Jacob . . .'

He fought back another flood of tears. 'It ever happen to you?'

I gave him a gentle smile. 'I'm one of the lucky ones. I've always been too thick to understand what the fuck is going on around me. I don't notice much, so I have nothing to process. If I did, I'd probably be in worse shape than you. Thankfully, I've got fuck-all wiring to repair.'

'You got kids, Nick?'

I'd always batted any personal questions to one side: where I came from, you didn't wear your heart on your sleeve. But for some reason I heard myself explaining the situation with Anna and our boy.

'Poor little fucker hasn't a clue who or what I am, and his mother seems to want to keep it that way.'

He was looking more confused than he probably did when he was hoovering up that shit on the table.

I rapped a set of knuckles on my head and got a dull, empty sound. 'See? There's nothing inside. This is me for life, mate, doing this shit.'

He sat back and laughed, and at last I saw a brief flash of the old Dino. 'Man, I might not be all there but I reckon I got a better handle on my shit than you have on yours. You're just as fucked up.'

I suddenly felt uncomfortable with the spotlight turned on me. Maybe that was because he'd veered pretty close to the truth. On the doorstep he'd told me I hadn't changed. That wasn't right in a whole lot of ways, but it was Anna's mantra, and I couldn't deny that both of them had a point.

We sat for a while longer, until car doors began closing and engines started up, ready for another day of normality.

'Nick, mind if I . . . ?' His gaze drifted back to the table. 'I've got to . . . You know what I'm saying?'

'Mate, knock yourself out. Whatever gets you through the day. But you will go and get some help, yeah? You need this shit like a hole in the head.'

He leaned over and picked up his paraphernalia. 'Sure.'

We sat there in silence as he finished loading the crystals, held a lighter beneath the cup and inhaled. A stream of white smoke seeped from his mouth and nostrils and his whole body relaxed.

I realized where the slight smell of disinfectant had come from.

15

Energized by the hit, Dino was in full-on answering mode. That suited me just fine. I wanted as much out of him as he could give me before he slid back down and the paranoia and confusion took over again.

It sounded like the journey from the Costa Rica shack to the luxury *estancia* north-east of Narcopulco had been an eventful one for Liseth and her children.

'She even had the fat fuck's body driven north from CR for burial, man. Then kept digging him up and taking him with her every time she moved from one fucking pot of opulence to another.'

'I didn't have her down as sentimental.'

Dino snorted. 'She didn't keep him as some kind of beacon of hope, man, that's for sure. The bitch has a different agenda. She don't think like normal people. She wanted the kids to be reminded twenty-four/seven that their old man lost an empire, and none of them must ever be as weak as he was.' Dino went quiet for a moment as he placed the pipe gently back on the table. 'She buried him at the *casa* ... in a one-fucking-third scale replica of the Lincoln Memorial – can you believe it, one-third? How the fuck is Peregrino going to miss that shit when he opens his curtains every morning?

'You ever seen the real one? Nice piece of stonework, just up the road. The only thing missing is a statue of the Wolf looking thoughtful. He's lying in a crypt.'

'With my Mauser rounds still in him, you reckon?'

Dino threw his head back and laughed a bit too heartily – it wasn't that funny.

'Yeah, man, weak is definitely something her son is not – not on her watch. Even the name of the *casa* – Casa fucking Esperanza – has a different meaning for her.'

'Not "hope"?'

He rolled his eyes. 'That's just the crap Jesus for Fucking Peace feeds the people. The version Liseth prefers means "desire" and "expectation".'

I needed to drag him back to specifics. 'And the Casa of Desire is about eighteen Ks north-east of Acapulco?'

'Correct. Near a shit-kickers' town, El Veintiuno. Or, at least, that's the nearest point where mere mortals dare to breathe the same fucking oxygen. The ranch is another ten Ks from anything and anyone, man, surrounded by mountains and scrubland.'

'Roads?'

Dino shook his head. 'The only way for wheels, in and out, is private and patrolled. No vehicle can make it over that terrain cross-country, man. Rocks, boulders, gulches – impenetrable. They got a fucking helicopter up there – escape tunnel, all kinds of shit. Just like the old days.'

I had another question lined up but Dino was off on one.

'That bitch has bigger plans for the boy than she ever dreamed of for his pop.'

His face glowed with the wonder of the thing. I was beginning to get the impression that a part of him admired 'that bitch'. Part of me did too.

'The Wolf always had grab bags, man, even in that shack. She headed north with close on thirty-two million – pocket change for her, but she knew the big sharks in the pool up north wanted it, and they were going to take it the first chance they got.

'The bitch was smart enough to know she needed a new Big Swinging Dick to protect her and her family – but it wasn't easy. She told me and the dogs that whoever she attached herself to had to be smart enough to stay at the top of the greasy pole – with her help, of course.'

'She found someone?'

'Sure she did. Husband number two was a big-time gang leader in Acapulco. And it was just peachy to start with. The kids were safe, the PRI were still in power, and everyone was making money. But then the cracks started to show. She came round to thinking that he also suffered from limited horizons.'

He adjusted himself in his chair and closely examined the pipe, debating another hit.

'She formed a plan early on to get rid of him and have Jesús Junior take over, but had to wait until the boy was older – ready to rule the roost. Her game plan was royally fucked for a year or two when the PRI lost their grip and the gangs went to war. But Liseth knew there would be a power vacuum at some point. They kept killing each other, she kept waiting – and then she saw her opportunity.'

'To kill off number two?'

'You got it.' This time he pointed at me instead of heading for the pipe. 'He didn't find his way into the firing line as quickly as she'd have liked. Rumour has it, she instructed Peregrino to give her husband both barrels, point blank in the fucking face. Rumour? I fucking know it for fact, man. She told us. We were her pets, but we were also her sounding board.'

'We?'

'The German Shepherds – three of the fuckers – and me. They were pampered, even shampooed and blow-dried every other day, man. Unlike me. But she also had their claws ripped out so they didn't make any noise on her marble floors.

'We were the only living things to hear her deepest thoughts. She'd tell us how weak her husbands were, how proud she was of her fucking son, you name it. She didn't ask for our opinions, of course. Just our devotion. I figured it was best to act as confused as the dogs were – and to leave her with the impression all I wanted to know was when I'd be fed.

'Anyway, she told us that sweet little Jesús left him with half a head, tied to a chair in the middle of a fucking roundabout on the Costera, to put commuters off their breakfast tacos.'

16

'The bitch saw the future.'

The way Dino was studying the pipe you'd have thought he was valuing it for *Antiques Roadshow*. 'She knew the gangs would eventually choose sides and amalgamate into full-blown cartels ... and she also knew that would keep escalating the war. The bigger the cartels got, the more power they'd want. She'd seen all that shit in Colombia.

'That was when she set her little boy on the path towards becoming a paramilitary leader. She knew there was more chance of surviving the war and winning the peace if they had no allegiance to any one of the new cartels. She did her deals behind closed doors – and Jesús followed her instructions to the letter. He became El Peregrino, like some fucking Mexican version of Allah's favourite prophet. There are no pictures of the fuck. They knew Facebook wasn't the answer, man. Just the name, and the awe they've created around it, is enough for now. But he's fucking worshipped by those who toed the line.'

'And those who didn't?'

'Those who didn't, he fucked up the ass.' He put down the pipe and massaged his cheeks with his hands, like he was rubbing shaving oil into a beard. His voice dropped; he was in memory mode once more. 'Sometimes she took pictures of me on her cell to send as invitations to her Come-and-Poke-Fun-at-the-DEA-Gimp dinner parties. She dressed me up like a fucking jester, a clown, even a fucking orang-utan one time. Sometimes they'd talk about making me jump out of El Peregrino's birthday cake ... or killing me right there ... Shit ...' His right hand moved to the back of his head, as if it was going to help him sort out his mental filing cabinet.

I didn't want him to play with his thoughts: I wanted him focused. 'What else did the She Wolf talk about?'

He came right back on track. 'The bitch used to tell her dogs and me how she'd guided her *protégé* through the war – decided who to fight for, who to destroy – and what she thought of the government and the evolving cartels. They were weak, in her book – and, like I said, she despises weakness more than anything. As far as she's concerned the weak deserve to be exploited.'

Dino's jaw clenched. 'That fucker Peregrino – you gotta watch him, man. He's his mother's son. If there wasn't the right toy in his cereal box to complete his collection, he'd want the grocery store manager killed.

'Yeah, sounds funny, doesn't it?' His smile was bleak, and slid swiftly from his face. 'Until you find out it's true. It really happened, when he was just fucking fourteen. A fraction older than my boys are now ...'

I could see him wandering off again. 'So she's got him in pole position?'

'Getting there. They even have their own cell-phone network. Jesus for Peace has telecoms towers like you wouldn't believe – their very own fucking national encrypted communications system. That's pole position and then some, man.' He arched his neck and pushed his head back against the leather.

I sat back too, thinking about the investment cost, innovation and infrastructure required to build a system like that. Then I remembered my iPhone's performance in DC: just a few miles from the centre of the world's most powerful capital city, and only one bar of signal. 'SIM cards and organ harvesting . . . It's one hell of a portfolio . . .'

Dino closely scrutinized the ceiling. 'They've got a whole heap of other businesses too, man. They've got coal mines, oil off the Gulf coast, all kinds of shit.' His eye line returned briefly to Planet Earth. 'But it's just the beginning. This boy is going all the way, unless someone stops him. Liseth is set on him following in the footsteps of his Uncle Pablo. We're talking the fucking presidency, man, Mexico's answer to Barack Hussein Obama.'

Surreal, but it made sense to me. El Peregrino and his mum might have been Colombian once, but what the fuck did that matter? Peru had had a Japanese immigrant's son as its president for ten corrupt and very violent years. And, as Dino said, Escobar had nearly made it to the top job in Colombia without much more of a skill set than knowing an opportunity when he saw one and not worrying too much about who he bludgeoned to death on the way. Liseth, on the other hand, had it all, and she knew it.

'It may take another ten years, Nick, but it's gonna

fucking happen. That bitch might be one fucking crazy dog-whispering psycho, but she has a blueprint. She read Kitson, man. Two of his books, over and fucking over.'

'*Gangs and Counter-gangs* and *Low Intensity Operations?*'

I couldn't tell if he was surprised that I knew them.

'I'll never forget them, man – the covers had the first English words I'd seen for one fuck of a long time . . .' He rubbed his stump to liven it up a little, and levered himself off the La-Z-Boy.

'Peregrino is organizing all *los vigilantes*. He's forming a countrywide community police network that's funded and trained by Jesus for Peace. In maybe seven or eight years, he'll not only be the bringer of health, education and clean water to the masses, he'll be the patron saint of protection from the cartels, gangsters, even the fucking sex offenders.

'He'll have the masses totally onside, because he'll provide them with everything the government are fucking up. That's when his fucking supernatural presence will get a face. By then he'll be the government in everything but name. Election will be nothing more than a formality. That bitch will have him running everything down there, man – everything. Then we'll see how far their tentacles can really reach.'

He stopped pacing and looked down at me. 'You think that's crazy?'

'Sane as you and me, mate.'

He nodded. Irony had never been his strong suit.

'Fucking right, man. I told you, Nick, she thinks differently – I know her. Everything she's dreamed of has worked out for her. That's why I wrote a paper on how to squeeze those drug fucks out of existence. We need to keep a very close eye on people like her. Kitson knew it. I know it. And you clearly know that Kitson shit, but the State Department? They got no balls to take action, man.'

Dino's eyes drilled into me. 'Let me tell you why I really want those cunts dead.'

17

'He was playing polo against a team from Tijuana. Fuck knows why anybody bothered turning up. Peregrino's team always won. That was the rule.'

Dino resumed the position on the La-Z-Boy. He wasn't looking at me any more: he was staring at the ceiling again, like it was a cinema screen.

'So this one day Liseth stops the game and calls Peregrino over. We're with her, on our leashes, sitting at her feet. She says Morales, one of Peregrino's players, has been disloyal. She don't say how and she don't say why. And Peregrino? He asks her jack.

'The fat fuck steers his pony back onto the lawn, goes up to this guy and swings a mallet straight into his head. Morales has one of those polo helmets on, complete with face guard, but he still goes down like a sack of shit. Even when he hits the ground, Peregrino ain't finished with him. He leans out of his saddle and rips the fucking helmet off this guy. By now he's begging, screaming at him to stop, but no way. The fat fuck swings that mallet again, and again, and again . . .

Jesus Christ, man, you ever seen what one of those things can do to a guy's head? Imagine taking a sledge-hammer to a watermelon. Blood everywhere. Brains and shit all over the grass.'

His eyes were still fixed on the scene playing out on the imaginary screen above him. I wasn't too sure I was needed there.

'Without even blinking, Peregrino removes a fleck from his jodhpurs and restarts the game. They play to the end. The body gets trampled to fuck. When it's all over, Liseth's gofers gather around it like flies. They dump it in a wheelbarrow, then about ten of them give the grass a good spray – would you believe, with bottles of fucking mineral water?'

He pushed himself upright again.

'I was numb, man. Totally – fucking – *numb*. It was like nothing had happened. I felt no emotion at all. I was just unbelievably glad it wasn't me. And I made a cold, clear promise to myself. The first chance I got not to be on the business end of that mallet, I was going to take it. You know what I'm saying.'

It wasn't a question.

'But later, when I got back to what I used to think of as the real world – maybe a couple of months out of hospital – that whole experience hit me like a fucking express train. *Whoosh*. Slammed straight into me, man. I couldn't clear it from my head – and then it started kicking up all the other kinds of bad shit in there.

'There's one nightmare I keep having, man. This fucking nightmare, I'm running through the scrub, trying to escape El Peregrino. He's in his fancy fucking polo gear, riding his fancy fucking horse. Calling for me, like he's looking for a lost dog.

'He finds me and he's hitting me over the head with his mallet. I ain't got no fucking helmet. I really go down. And he's dismounting to fuck me up, and I'm, like, begging, covering my head. Then the bitch is there with him, high above me on her horse. She's screaming down at me: "No one runs away from me! *No one!*" She's screaming it, like, over and over. Then she's telling her fucking psycho of a son to make it slow, man, make it painful.

'Peregrino don't need to be told twice. He whirls the mallet around his head and hammers it down – but now it's not me lying there any more. I'm close by, watching my partner's head being split open like a grapefruit by *los* fucking *vigilantes*.

'I start reliving that shit again. What's left of him gets showered with fucking mineral water. But it doesn't clean the grass, just spreads the mess. It's a total mess. *I'm* a fucking mess.'

'Mate, you're not, you're—'

'Yeah? So how come sometimes I'm even afraid to look up in case that fat fuck is there, ready to play polo with my head? How come I feel like I'm surrounded by a million people, all taking my breath away? Why does my heart beat so fast, Nick? Why do I get so scared when someone gets too close to me? It's like a tornado, crushing and tearing up everything in its path.'

He turned towards me again, eyes wild.

'I'm scared of the world, and scared of everyone in it. Every fucking day is a struggle. Every one. I want it to stop.'

'But you escaped, yeah? That bit's over. Done.'

'Really? You think so? Look at me . . . That day – that day at the polo – I knew it was now or never. They were going to kill me for sure, one way or another.

'A couple of nights later, the kennel girl leaves my cage open like she sometimes does while she goes to fill up my water bowl. That's all I need. That's it. I'm out of there. I take her down, tie her up, gag her, run. Man, do I fucking run . . .'

His face crumples.

'One of those fucking dogs comes after me . . .'

'I know, mate. I saw the scars.'

'Those scars, I can handle.' There were tears in his eyes. 'It's the others . . .'

He went silent for a while, then gave another heart-wrenching sob. 'I thought the dogs were my *friends*, man. We shared everything. We even had to listen to Liseth's psycho shit together.'

'What happened?'

'I guess I should have grabbed a knife or something, on my way out of there . . .'

I knew what was coming.

'One of the Shepherds. I have to kill it with my bare hands. Push the poor fucker's eyes out first. Then I run . . .'

He sighed.

'Almost made it, too. Almost all the way across the polo lawn to the scrub. Eight hundred, man. I'm maybe twenty metres from cover when some fucker spots me and gives me a burst with an MG4. You know what I'm saying, you know the weapon . . .'

Of course I did: a Heckler & Koch 5.56 belt-fed machine-gun. I gave him a nod.

'So I make it into the scrub but they keep hosing the area down and I take a round.' He tapped his knee in case I needed the hollow reminder. 'Can you believe that, man? The fucker wasn't even aiming.

'I manage to drag myself further into the under-growth. It's real dense, so I just keep crawling. Three fucking days crawling through it, until I find myself near El Veintiuno. By then I know the leg is history but, fuck it, I'm alive. So I steal a truck and get myself to Acapulco, using my good leg, until I crash into a police convoy near the coast.

'That's where the Feds are, man – where the tourists hang out. Not the local guys, they'd have handed me right back. The Feds make some calls, the DEA have me medevaced north, and here I am.'

Dino shook his head. His eyes never left the ceiling.

'Except that I left a big part of myself behind. I can't close my eyes without seeing their faces. I check windows, doors, every fucking lock and bolt, every step of the way. I've no fucking patience with anyone. I can't sit still for more than five minutes unless I'm plugged into the Xbox. Shitloads of Xbox, just to keep a grip on . . . something . . .

'I get disoriented . . . displaced . . . One day I lost it on the freeway . . . forgot who I was, forgot how to drive. It was like I'd completely lost my mind. For a few weeks I managed to keep it together on the outside, then got to the point where I almost couldn't leave the house. There was no safe place in the world for me.

'I was an easy-going guy. You knew me, man, back in the day. I was married, good kids. But when I came home, everything went haywire. I was on edge, and I mean seriously. Short temper, short fuse. The smallest thing could set me off. I'd blow up if my wife was five minutes late. Out in the field, five minutes late can get you killed! She never really understood. She said she did, but I could see the fucking pity in her eyes too . . .

'I started in on our boys. I was constantly on their case. I was so trapped inside my own fucking head I couldn't feel their pain. I had no idea what was going on around me.

'I was still fighting a war I didn't understand against an enemy I couldn't kill.'

His gaze finally drifted back in my direction and he lay there staring into my eyes, looking to me for answers I couldn't give.

18

South Union Street, Alexandria, Virginia

15.33 hrs

Ye olde towne north of the Beltway consisted of a labyrinth of brick buildings that must have been thrown together at quirky angles by a nineteenth-century *feng-shui* enthusiast. Most of them were now boutiques peddling high-end visitor tat or lace cushions and scented candles. A twenty-first-century Starbucks rubbed shoulders with them, doing its best to blend in. I sat inside it with a brew in a paper cup; I wasn't sure if Dino would want to stay or go somewhere more private.

I was doing a little research on my iPhone when I spotted his truck through the rain-stained windows, heading for the marina car park on the Potomac less than a hundred metres away.

I'd suggested we met closer to the airport after he'd checked out the Academy databases. I needed to travel down to Narcopulco and get on with it.

Dino appeared with a bottle of mineral water in one hand and a plastic cup in the other. He looked a whole lot better than he had this morning, but still ragged. He sat down and straightened out his prosthetic beneath the table.

I put my iPhone down so he couldn't see the screen. 'Any luck?'

He leaned towards me as a couple of teenagers in sweats, rain-soaked and clinging, made their way past us to a window seat. The light had come back into his eyes. 'A female Hispanic, mid-thirties, has been at the house.' He tapped an index finger on the table-top in case I hadn't tuned in to the significance of his announcement. 'I don't know if she's still there, but for sure she's not a whore. The hookers come in busloads, for the parties, but leave the next morning. El Peregrino is a possessive fucker – that's the way Liseth has raised him. So if she's there, he ain't going to let her out of his sight. The fucker takes what he wants – and hangs on to it.'

I watched him swallow a mouthful, waiting for the inevitable.

'I can *help*, Nick. I know that place inside out. I know how to get to the fucker – and to that bitch. Take me with you.'

'Mate, you know you'd just be a pain in the arse. You've got half a fucking steel factory hanging off your leg, so you're not exactly going to be climbing walls and jumping fences, are you?'

His tone was urgent again, but low: 'I could give you real-time shit on the ground. It could save your ass, man, and hers. I know these people. I know that fucking *casa* like the back of my hand.'

I shook my head. 'Three problems. First, you walk like you're a crab on stilts. Second, what if you're recognized? That would put all three of us in the shit. And, third, you've got a problem that needs some attention . . .' I reached across and tapped his head. 'We don't want to make it any worse than it is already, do we? Flashbacks and all that shit messing with the inside of your head once you're back down there. The two of them would be in spitting distance. Don't you think that would fuck you up a bit?'

'I can handle it, man. I gotta grip this shit, you know that. Maybe if I come down with you, maybe if—'

I held up a hand. 'I do need your help. Real-time int? Yes, please.' I pointed at the phone on the table. 'I need you on one of these things, twenty-four/seven. I need you every step of the way. But let's keep Mission Control up here, mate, where you can stay out of trouble, not down south.'

I was about to sit back when he gripped my shoulder and his eyes bored into mine. Energized became desperate again. 'We fucked up. We should have drilled that bitch in 'ninety-three.'

'That wasn't the task, was it? No one knew then.'

'It's not just about us, Nick. Liseth is pushing that fucking son of hers to the top. You know what that means? It means a narco state on my fucking doorstep. Our kids are gonna suffer, man. And not just our kids. Their kids too. We gotta stop 'em.'

We both knew the future leadership of Mexico wasn't the only reason he wanted them dead.

'Mate, it won't stop the nightmares, the paranoia, the meth – or get your family back. Nor will going in-country and exposing yourself to all the physical triggers. For what? So you can try to face your fears, tackle the demons? You really want to take that risk? A couple of dead bodies and a tray of tacos is gonna do fuck-all for you, mate. You need time, care and therapy to turn the page. I don't know much, but I know about this shit.'

I watched him sip water with a shaking hand and stare out of the window.

After a few moments he turned back to me. 'You've got to kill them, Nick. You've got to kill them both.'

19

I picked up my mobile and moved my chair round to his side of the table. As I did so, I caught a glimpse of the two teenagers sitting opposite each other, thumbing their smartphones in silence by the window.

I leaned closer to his shoulder. 'Listen, mate. I've been lifted myself a couple of times, and I was a PoW in the Gulf. I know what it's like. I know about the pain.'

I rolled up my right sleeve to show him the pattern of dog-bite puncture marks that decorated my arm. 'I've even had some of that shit. I may not know much . . .' I got half a smile out of him as I knuckled my head . . . 'but I've learned something from it all.' I let the cuff fall back to my wrist. 'I bet when you were captured there was nothing you could do about preventing the physical pain. Am I right? They could do whatever they wanted to do to you and you could do fuck-all about it . . .'

He nodded. I could see his mind ticking over and some of those images coming back into his head.

'That's right, mate. Even the leg.' Through his jeans, I

tapped the composite where it cupped the stump. 'There was fuck-all you could do about it. You got fucked over, and you had no control.'

He nodded again.

'But you aren't *living* the pain any more. That's all in the past. Nobody's taking a mallet to your head. No one's spraying rounds into you. No one's burning, biting or doing whatever the fuck they did to you. That's no longer happening.' I tapped my temple again. 'It's just this fucking thing refusing to let go, that's all. Just your head. The physical shit has gone, mate. *They* have gone. Liseth and the Pilgrim can't hurt you any more. You can only hurt yourself now, and the people close to you. The people who love you, the people you love.'

I tapped my iPhone screen and passed it over.

Dino took it. His eyes bounced between the read-out and me as the last drop of rain dribbled down the side of his face. I'd been Googling therapists.

'Mate, no one needs to know about this apart from you. Contact one of these fuckers. There's thousands of them.'

Dino handed me back the mobile with a look of sadness. 'Those thousands cost thousands, Nick.'

I thrust the screen at him, held it no more than an inch from his nose. 'Bollocks. I counted six of these fuckers in Alexandria alone. They won't be the overpriced wankers who see you twice a week and then tell you your mum fucked up your potty training. I bet there were shed-loads of people – civilians, military, who cares? – who needed help after the nine/eleven hit on the Pentagon. They wouldn't have wanted anyone to know they had problems, but I bet they decided it was money well spent.'

I put the mobile back on the table, screen up. 'So here's the deal. You promise to get help. I'll go and lift Katya, and try to find out what the fuck this is all about.'

He steepled his fingers in front of his nose and took a couple of deep breaths. Then he nodded and pointed to the phone. 'I'll be on one of those things, twenty-four/seven. I'll be there for you, man. Every step of the way.'

I picked up my brew and stood. 'We need to sort out comms, that sort of shit, but I'll do that as soon as I get a flight. And I'm going to need a whole lot more detail about the *casa*. I'll call you when I'm on the road, OK?'

He nodded like a lunatic. Then his face clouded again. 'I think it's her, Nick. I think Katya is there. But there's something you should know . . .'

He grasped the neck of his bottle like he was going to strangle the fucker.

'She seems to have the freedom of the place. We've only got partial imagery, but she may not be a prisoner.'

I put a hand on his shoulder. 'I don't know what's going on with her, mate, and to be honest, I'm not sure I care. But Anna and our boy are under threat, and Katya's the one with the answers.'

I paused. 'Last night, when you were back there, you mumbled a whole bunch of numbers. Were you trying to remember something? A code maybe?'

He went very still.

'Like I said, man, they've got their own escape route. The tunnel goes from inside the house – from inside the kitchen – to the hangar where they keep the chopper. Steel door both ends. Only Liseth and Peregrino know the access code. They don't even trust the guy in charge of security with it.'

'Just in case he helps himself to their grab bags.'

He nodded. 'The money must be in there somewhere. Miguel had to turn his back each time she tapped the numbers into the keypad. But she didn't worry about us dogs – as long as we stayed on our leashes and didn't shit on her floor.'

I had one last question before I hit the road. 'What would have happened if I hadn't remembered the range?'

He put his water bottle carefully on the table. 'We wouldn't be here, man.' Then he noticed the name scribbled on my cup and smiled a real big one, the kind of smile I hadn't seen on his face since he was all cock and no brain a couple of lifetimes ago.

'Perry?'

I smiled right back. 'The lad even got the short version wrong. You sure our kids' futures are worth saving?'

PART SEVEN

1

Acapulco, Mexico

6 September 2011
14.25 hrs

It was only a short twenty-dollar ride into Acapulco, fixed in advance, but it seemed to take hours to make distance between each of the bright blue traffic signs counting down the kilometres from General Juan N. Álvarez International Airport to El Centro.

My head was roasting in the back seat. The rip-off sun-gigs I'd bought on the way to Dino's slithered from side to side as I tried to escape the rays the curved rear window focused on my neck. It was a really dry heat here, not at all like Hong Kong, but the back of my sweat-soaked shirt was already clinging to the worn-out PVC of the twenty-year-old cab upholstery.

Power and telephone lines hung low and lazily from their poles, feeding the houses and the megastores each side of the dual carriageway. I could have been in any one of the Moscow suburbs Anna was so fond of – had it not been for the sunshine and the Spanish road signs, and the fact that I was surrounded by Nissans, American Ford pick-ups the size of troop carriers, and more VW Beetles than you could shake a stick at.

Volkswagen had been spewing them off the local production lines for years, and white V-Bugs with blue wheel arches were Acapulco's taxi of choice. The one I was melting in had a modification that hadn't been factory-fitted: the windshield was coated with a layer of greasy dead-bug juice that made it almost impossible to see the road ahead. The driver had been trying to dislodge it ever since he'd picked me up from the terminal rank, but without screen-wash to back them up, the wipers had simply spread the problem more evenly.

Acapulco was one of Mexico's oldest and best-known beach resorts. It had really come into its own in the fifties as a getaway for the Hollywood élite. Clark Gable and Elizabeth Taylor were almost considered residents, and Frank Sinatra was so taken with the place he couldn't stop crooning all that 'Come Fly With Me' shit. Then Elvis invited us to share the *Fun in Acapulco* in 1963, and John Wayne bought every hotel he could lay his hands on and imported palm trees for the tourists to sit under.

The funny thing was, Elvis never actually came here: all of his scenes were shot in Hollywood. But that didn't seem to matter. Big chunks of America wanted to come down Mexico way and have a touch of the good life, and Acapulco boomed. Within thirty years the place was no longer a hideaway for the rich and famous, and started to look more like Benidorm.

And thanks to its location, sandwiched between the world's biggest drug producers in the south and its biggest consumers in the north, it had long since sold its visitors – and its inhabitants – a different kind of dream. These days Narcopulco was more famous for what happened in the shadows than the sunshine.

Travelling to Acapulco is extremely dangerous [the online travel sites warned me], *and is strongly discouraged as the city has been taken over by violent drug cartels. The Mexican government has little control over large parts of the city; Acapulco is effectively a war zone. Bear in mind that by travelling in Acapulco you are putting yourself at serious risk of being robbed, raped, kidnapped or murdered (foreigners are normally beheaded when killed). Law enforcement officers and local authorities collude with criminals and will not help in case of trouble. Needless to say threats are unpredictable and the situation is volatile.*

A few holidaymakers still made the trip to the beach, but they were locals and mostly from Mexico City, about four hours inland along a motorway that hadn't been there ten years ago. The nation's capital was a nightmare too, so maybe death on an expensively hired sun-lounger was more fun than it was in your own backyard.

I moved my head again. On the opposite carriageway, three police technicals with machine-guns mounted on their rear flatbeds were barging through the traffic. The only difference between these pick-ups and the Taliban's was the word POLICIA stencilled across their dark blue or black paintwork, and the fact that the guys manning the weapons were in black or combat fatigues, their faces covered with black balaclavas instead of *shemags*. It must have been as dangerous for Dino to crash into these fuckers as it was being banged up at the *casa*.

John Wayne's palm trees were still there in force, but they now lined the meridian between the dual-carriageways. The bottom third of their trunks was whitewashed, bouncing the sunlight in all directions.

The future of Acapulco's tourist industry didn't look nearly as bright and shiny. Every hotel had a vacancy sign – and that just applied to the ones that were open. Many of them hadn't even been finished. Their builders had given up a long time ago. Multi-storey chunks of concrete littered the place, stained by the elements, with hardly a crane breaking the skyline above them.

The tourist shops selling designer goods their visitors could buy much more cheaply at home had given up the ghost as well. Every third or fourth store-front was boarded up. Even from this distance I could see unopened mail piled up on the other side of their grimy glass doors.

The traffic ground to a complete halt and the driver gave a groan of frustration. Even if my Spanish had been up to it, I was too knackered to ask questions.

I'd had an eight-hour stopover after the flight from DC to Phoenix, during which I'd read all I could about Acapulco – after downloading it from the world's most expensive Internet connection in the Sky Harbor terminal. I'd called Dino to fill in the gaps, then memorized all the routes from the city towards the *casa*. It had been covered by cloud on Google Maps. That's par for the course with government locations, so it looked like either Peregrino already had the right connections in high places or he had put a gun to a few heads.

The more I stored inside mine, the less I had to carry about with me and the lower my chances were of being compromised. I'd ditched the downloads as soon as I'd read them, then hit the airport shops for a couple of odds and sods I thought I'd need for the job. They were safely stored in the bag on the seat beside me.

The one thing I couldn't quite ditch was the white noise still bouncing around inside my head.

They've taken her to Mexico . . .

I'd understood Sophie's words, the bruises on Katya's face and the signs that she'd left her Moscow apartment in one fuck of a hurry to mean the Pilgrim had taken Katya against her will.

But now I had the DEA's interpretation.

She seems to have the freedom of the place . . . Dino had warned me. *She may not be a prisoner . . .*

All I knew for sure was that they couldn't both be right.

2

A rash of technicals started to appear on my side of the carriageway too, not barging their way through the traffic but parked up at the roadside, blue lights blinking rather weakly in the blinding light.

Hooded operators manned the weapons; black-clad figures in Kevlar helmets with M4 assault rifles dangling off their body armour ran around getting sweaty. They were channelling three lanes of traffic into one, the fast lane on the left, and I soon saw why. Two bodies lay at the side of the road, as if they were car-crash casualties. But there hadn't been an accident. There was no wreckage. I was pretty certain they'd been pushed off the graffiti-covered pedestrian walkway above us.

One of the bodies was in his mid-sixties, peppered with gunshot wounds in the chest and abdomen. It was hard to tell the age of the other because it was headless but, judging by the stonewashed jeans and on-trend Nikes, he'd been younger. Blood congealed in big pools around them.

A small crowd had gathered on the walkway, but most of the locals carried on moving, chatting into their mobiles or tucking into their snacks. A couple of guys in suits, sun-gigs and cowboy hats, with badges hanging from their necks, looked down at the bodies. Even their clouds of cigarette smoke couldn't conceal their boredom.

The traffic began moving again and we carried on towards what I knew was going to be Costera Miguel Alemán, a six-lane thoroughfare that hugged the curve of the bay. The locals just called it the Costera. We were heading for the Zona Dorada, the Golden Zone, home of the best nightlife and beaches. Or that was what the Hotel El Tropicano website had told me.

> *Surrounded by beautiful tropical gardens, right in the center of the Acapulco Dorado* [it boasted], *a pretty property of two floors is elevated throughout the day.* [Fuck knew what that meant.] *It counts with two colorful restaurants open throughout the day, as well as with a piano bar of amused atmosphere and warm service.* [All in all, apparently] *Hotel El Tropicano is an excellent option for one familiar vacation, very near of the beach and the main entretainment centers of the bay. Their comfortable facilities and beautiful gardens will offer you tranquillity to spends unforgettable days. Our personnel is highly qualified to make your vacations an unforgettable ones. Came with your family and enjoy this paradise.*

I didn't think Anna and our son would be rushing to join me there anytime soon.

Both sides of the Costera were lined with apartments, bars and hotels, infested with lunatics trying to jump the traffic to reach the beach a block away. Every intersection offered a glimpse of sea and sand.

We hit a roundabout and the driver diced with death as he tried to accelerate through a gap. I looked at the closely cropped oval mound at its centre, fringed with palm trees, and wondered if this was where Liseth's husband number two had given his last public appearance. Or what was left of him – it sounded as if most of his head had been splattered across a wall somewhere else.

The driver muttered something and pointed. We'd arrived. El Tropicano could have been the Spanish for 'faded glory'. Its whitewashed walls and arches were straight out of a spaghetti western. A swarm of V-Bugs buzzed alongside it, ready to sting anybody who ventured out.

I expected us to drive through the main arch but the driver obviously thought he'd done his job in getting me that far. He stopped with the rest of his mates and shouted something about the traffic behind us, leaving me to fight my way out through the front passenger door. I dropped him his twenty USD, and was immediately approached by three guys in bleached polo shirts.

'What you need, Señor? Women?'

'No.'

'OK. Boys?'

'No.'

'Drugs? Good bars? I got cocaine, I got heroin. I can get—'

'No.'

'OK, cool. Tickets for the water park? Bungee jump? You want city tour?'

I kept walking until I reached the cool of the

hacienda-style, terracotta-tiled and ceiling-fanned reception area. What I really wanted from the local guys – a weapon – a white boy couldn't ask for. It would raise awareness, and that was the last thing I needed. The only friendly force on this job was Dino.

I got hold of him on the mobile. 'Mate, I'm here. Give me a couple of hours to re-SIM and sort my shit out, and I'll call back.'

'Affirmative.'

Dino hadn't been one for pleasantries these last few days, but now there was an extra edge of urgency to his voice.

He'd sounded like he was running the Space Shuttle control room ever since I'd landed in Phoenix. That could have been down to me helping him get what he wanted out of this shit, but I reckoned there was a bit more to it than that. Despite all he'd been through, he was loving life back in the saddle. I knew that feeling well.

'Never forget why it's called Narcopulco, Nick. Too close to the US and too far from God . . .'

'I won't make that mistake, mate. Talk soon.'

He'd been saying it since Phoenix, but I still had no idea what he was talking about. It didn't much matter: he'd be sure to bore me to death with it one day.

3

My first-floor room was pretty much an extension of the lobby, with the same terracotta floor tiles, and air-conditioning that worked – thank fuck. The hotel was designed as a quadrangle, with all the rooms over-looking a blob-shaped swimming-pool surrounded by clumps of grass and bushes. The window on the other side gave me a view of the Walmart up the road.

I switched on the old box-like TV and left the screen to de-fuzz while I took a shower.

I took my life-support pouch from around my neck and hooked it onto the towel rail. I thought about having a shave but, fuck it, I was going to be in shit state again soon enough. In any case, the *Fistful of Dollars* look wouldn't do me any harm where I was going.

I felt a bit more awake as I got dressed, even though I was climbing back into the clothes I'd just taken off. I was keeping the new set folded so I'd look freshly laundered and unsuspicious on the journey home.

The TV news treated me to a parade of recent killings: corpses hanging from bridges, shot to bits in cars or just lying in the street. The picture still wasn't crisp enough for me to be able to tell if they'd been the two I'd seen on the way in. From the tone of the anchor's voice, it was just business as usual. No wonder my hotel was as empty as the one in *The Shining*.

I counted out my pesos. Taking commissions and the shit tourist exchange rate into account, it worked out at about twelve to the dollar. I still had plenty of the things in my neck pouch.

It always felt good, this part of the process – getting my shit sorted before an operation. It was like a runner going to the start line and putting his toes in the blocks. I tipped the Sky Harbor bag upside-down and my Phoenix purchases fell onto the bed.

First out was a dark-brown CamelBak hydration pack, a three-litre plastic bladder with a suction tube fitted inside a day sack with extra storage pockets. I'd dumped its fancy packaging at the airport, along with the almost impregnable fused plastic blister-pack that protected the x12 telephoto lens that clipped onto my iPhone.

I'd also bought a set of ear-bud headphones with a mic, twenty-four AA batteries and two emergency charger cases to keep my mobile topped up. If I needed more power than that, I'd have been on the ground far too long and fucked up.

I sorted the gear into the pouches on the CamelBak's padded waist belt and laid out my washing kit in the bathroom as a normal guest would – if there was any such thing as 'normal' in Narcopulco.

On my way out I discovered a Mexican family setting up shop around the pool. Maybe they hadn't read the same travel warnings. Dad was busy puffing up his daughter's massive yellow water-wings as Mum nagged him to go *más rápido*. Their little boy already had his in place and was about to launch himself off the side like an over-inflated miniature zeppelin. None of them had held back on the tortillas.

Back out on the main drag, the blanket of exhaust fumes was so thick and the air temperature so fierce I could hardly breathe. Black-clad technicals with their black-clad crews patrolled back and forth along the Costera. The rear gunners exchanged crisp salutes whenever they passed each other, to give the few remaining tourists the impression all was good. I hoped their shooting was as sharp if I got caught up in the middle of one of their gangfucks while moving about the town.

I turned left along a road lined with such a haphazard array of buildings I wondered whether the Moscow planning regulators had done a bit of Latin American moonlighting.

I tapped Dino's number into my iPhone.

'You set, Nick?'

'Yep. You sure that's still the best way in?'

He took a deep breath because we'd already gone through this ten times.

'Nick, are you stuck on stupid? A white boy in a car going where you're going? Come *on*, man. Do like the DEA. Get the bus. It isn't far. If anyone hassles you, play the dumb-gringo card – you should find that easy enough. But you know what? There'll be no hassle, man. Call me when you get there.'

'The Autopista bus, yeah?'

'You got it. *Not* the Autopista del Sol bus. That takes the freeway. You fuck up, man, next stop is Mexico City.'

'Got it.'

'And for fuck's sake, remember the buses are privatized. They paint them any shit colour they want. Look for the sign on the front.'

'Got it.'

'OK.' He didn't sound convinced. 'You call when you get there.'

'Got it.'

'You still got the access code in that stupid gringo head of yours?'

I felt myself break into a grin. 'Got it.' I wasn't going to rattle off the numbers to confirm it. He might be the only ally I had right now, but a little suffering would do him good.

I deleted the call log and closed down on my way into Walmart. It was going to be a long night, and fuck knew how long a day tomorrow would turn out to be.

The plan to get on target was very simple: to catch the Autopista bus from General Juan N. Álvarez International. The Autopista was the old road to Mexico City, taking in places like Cuernavaca and Chilpancingo en route. The Autopista del Sol was the ten-year-old Federal Highway that cut the journey to the capital to about four hours and had turned the old Autopista into a back alley. I was going to jump off about eighteen Ks out of town, at what Dino called the shit-kickers' dump. He should know, he said. He'd been born in one. I told him he hadn't seen Bermondsey.

I'd know if I'd overshot at El Veintiuno if I saw signs for Kilómetro Treinta, which was twenty-eight Ks out of town. That would mean I'd have even more tabbing to do to get where I needed to be.

I returned to the hotel with a freezer bag full of

mineral water, a four-pack of Monster and enough SIM cards to last Mr Average a lifetime.

Telmex seemed to be Walmart SIM card of choice. No wonder its owner, Carlos Slim, was the richest man in the world. Last time I looked he had $74 billion in his hip pocket – and that didn't include his share of my fistful of pesos. He and Bill Gates battled to top the *Forbes* list each year, and 2011 was Carlos's turn; Bill only had $60 billion to his name right now.

The only reason I knew this was because the Moscow press were obsessed with it. They didn't like a Russian not being in the game. Putin was pissed off about it, and I mean personally. Maybe he was thinking of throwing his hat into the ring.

4

I took a V-Bug back to the airport. The entire bus queue – even three old women in their nineties – had to go through metal detectors and have their bags X-rayed. I wondered what the security guys would make of the fact that I was carrying enough batteries to power a small town and SIM cards to replace after every call. It was a strange collection of gear, but none of them batted an eyelid. They were only going through the motions. We finally boarded the bus at 18.20.

I peeled back the ring-pull on my first Monster as we rolled back through Acapulco, heading north-east out of the city. It wouldn't be long till last light. I safety-pinned the iPhone and changed the SIM, broke the old one in two, and swallowed the bits with a couple of slugs of whatever that stuff was made of. It tasted strong enough to dissolve everything in its path before my gastric juices had had a chance to kick in.

As the caffeine surged around my system, I sat back in air-conditioned comfort and pretended to doze. My head rocked rhythmically against the window, and it wasn't long before I'd left a nice greasy forehead stain on the glass.

It was a guilty relief not to have to contact Anna now that Dino had taken over my ops room. We'd talked while I was waiting in the Sky Harbor, and agreed on radio silence until this shit was over. I had to focus. Besides, the baby was out of the danger zone; he'd even put on a little more weight. The break would give her some time to think about how she really felt, so maybe we could sort out our bad stuff when I got back. No drama.

My ticket had cost me just over a hundred pesos, which seemed like money well spent. The wagon was like an American school bus, except that it was a sickly blue instead of yellow, and much more comfortable. Blue LED lighting tubes beneath its skirting gave the impression that it just glided on its way. From what I could see, the thing was packed with recently arrived international travellers or old women laden with onions and carrots.

Three minutes away from the main and we'd left the tourist hotspots behind. It was blindingly clear that there were two Acapulcos: the police-patrolled area straddling the Costera, and everywhere else. Sandbagged positions now stood at intersections, maybe for *los vigilantes*, but none was manned. The only whiff of authority came from the endless banners and billboards bigging up Jesús de la Paz. There were no posters of the man himself: it was too early for that. They wouldn't spark up the election campaign until he looked a bit older and more statesmanlike. For now, he had to remain a supernatural presence.

We hit the old main drag out of the city, which

paralleled the newer, elevated Federal Highway, and were soon in the boondocks. Scores of flat, wiggly-tin roofs and dust-covered vehicles clustered either side of us. Rabid-looking dogs charged out from between them and chased after us.

We passed a few more sandbagged fortifications, thick-set men sitting outside shops and cafés with shot-guns, old carbine rifles and the odd automatic assault rifle across their knees. Like the police, their identities were hidden behind woollen balaclavas or KKK-style hoods. These boys felt as enthusiastic as I did about having their pictures taken, but I'd have been dis-appointed if there wasn't the odd Zapata moustache hiding in there somewhere.

I checked my iPhone. At this speed we'd be out of town and hitting the shit-kickers' dump in less than twenty minutes. It didn't look like *los vigilantes* were going to stop and search the bus. As long as you stayed on the main and didn't invade their turf, I guessed it was all right with them.

Now that I'd finished the Monster I took a warm swig of Walmart's finest spring water, before my teeth dissolved. Then I settled back into my seat again and studied the tin roofs and graffiti-coated concrete blocks. As darkness fell, pinpricks of light flickered in the high ground on the other side of the city.

The tarmac soon became as worn-out and potholed as the encroaching scrubland on either side of it. The Autopista del Sol glowed white and red in the distance, but there wasn't even a streetlight on the old road out here.

The locals had obviously done a bit of DIY on the main power lines running down to the coast: cables dangled from it at intervals, like spaghetti, allowing stalls and shacks every few hundred metres or so to keep trying to sell watermelons, apples and very old T-shirts that were still desperate for us to *Go Loco In Acapulco*.

It must have been tough enough for these poor fuckers to scrape a living when this was the main drag, but now life itself seemed to be slipping out of reach.

5

The driver shouted something, and a passenger near me muttered, 'Veintiuno.' The bus carried on lurching left and right to avoid the craters but that didn't stop the three old girls in pinafore dresses leaping out of their seats to sort out their bags in the overhead racks.

We careered to a halt with a hiss of air brakes and I peered out. I was expecting a village, but it didn't look like El Veintiuno was anything more than a few pools of light gathered a bit closer together than the ones along the track.

The old girls said their goodbyes to just about everybody on board as a couple of equally ancient guys tap-danced up the steps, swerved past them and took their place. It made the security checks at the start of the journey a bit of a farce, but there was probably a piece of paper in a government office somewhere that hadn't really been thought through.

I hung back, checking both sides of the road. A couple of cigarette ends glowed in the semi-darkness and the bus headlights swept across dozens of Jesús de la Paz posters that had been slapped onto a breeze-block wall. These ones showed a group of smiling children with nice white teeth. I guessed the message was: *Sign up with Jesus and share the magic of His dental plan.* Maybe it was the local HQ.

A couple of lads sat outside it with shotguns on their laps, swigging from beer bottles and generally keeping an eye on things. Every time a car passed, they craned their necks to see inside. As far as I could make out, all they were protecting was a few tin huts selling apples and watermelons and a jumble of power lines looped between them.

As the last of the old girls exited, I got up. Bathed in the LED glow, they skirted the front bumper on their way to a rusty pick-up that looked like it belonged in a transport museum.

Keeping the bus between us, I cut away from the *vigilantes* camped out beside the main and melted into the darkness. The scrub was two or three metres high in places and I was soon in cover. The air felt warm, and I hoped it wasn't just because I'd stepped out of an air-conditioned cocoon. It was going to be a long night, and the temperature could plummet on the hillside.

I waited until I was a good thirty metres away before I powered up my phone. I got down on my knees and leaned forward to hide the glow.

'You took your fucking time, man.' Dino was still in fighting form.

'I'm at the shit-kickers' dump. Just checking – in about a K, there's a road that cuts in from the main, then continues towards the high ground, yeah?'

'Sure. And that strip of tarmac is in better condition than the I-fucking-95 up here. Follow it for about ten Ks

422

and you'll hit the *casa*. They've got cameras every five hundred metres or so, and it's crawling with patrol vehicles. The main gate is manned as well.'

'I'll call you when I get there. Or when I'm in the shit. Whichever comes first.'

It took a couple of seconds to sink in.

'Remember, the east side of the *casa* – the higher ground, man – the hangar and the tunnel.'

'Got it.'

'And the code.'

'Got it.'

I switched the phone to silent and closed down. I knew he would be flapping now, and it made me smile.

6

It was easy enough at first to stay parallel to the road, just by keeping away from the patches of light that punctured the darkness. I could picture the people inside those shacks, huddling around tired TV sets, wishing they were drug lords so they could buy all the shit they saw in the ads.

I kept as close to the road as I could, even when the odd car trundled by, picking my feet up and putting them down with extra care so I didn't kick any of the empty beer bottles, cans or plastic bags hurled from their windows – or not-so-empty ones thrown from trucks.

It didn't take long to hit the newer stretch of tarmac heading away to my right, into the deeper shadow of the mountains – or, rather, the two-metre-high steel mesh fence protecting it. As I turned and moved back towards the junction with the old highway I began to hear waffle and laughter. The thick scrub blocked my view but not the sound. They weren't leaving me or coming towards me: they were static. I'd found the gatehouse.

I checked nothing was going to fall from the CamelBak at a critical moment; that my neck pouch was nice and secure; and moved forward on hands and knees. I went four or five metres, one ear cocked towards the sound source, then stopped and listened. There was a lot of hilarity going on the other side of the scrub.

On the next bound I caught a whiff of cigarette smoke. Still on my belly, I lifted myself up on the tips of my Timberlands and my elbows. Inched forward, stopped and listened again. My hand touched a plastic carrier bag. I moved it slowly and deliberately aside before moving on.

I could make out a pole on each side of the gates supporting a huge, curved, ranch-style sign. I guessed it announced the presence of the Casa Esperanza to passers-by, but didn't promise a warm welcome.

I crawled forward another couple of metres. Now I had clear line of sight of the gatehouse window. I could make out four heads and two glowing cigarettes. There might be others, but if there were, I couldn't see or hear them.

The place might have been mistaken for the lodge to a secluded and ultra-private stately home, had it not been for the black technical parked alongside with a belt-fed machine-gun on the back. The HK MG4 was so well balanced that even a ten-year-old could have fired 200 rounds of link from the hip in one burst, and this one would be equally lethal at night. Its roof-mounted power beam would pump several million candlepower into the scrub when called upon.

I'd seen all that I needed to, but stayed absolutely still for a couple of minutes longer. Movement, even the slightest scuff or clink, was what compromised you. It was human nature to move away from something faster than you'd arrived – and that was when you fucked up.

So the routine was: stop; take a breath; freeze for a couple of minutes; reverse a foot or two. I stayed on elbows and toes. I didn't turn, just inched backwards.

Once I'd gone six metres, I waited, got up on my hands and knees, turned and crept, Komodo dragon-style, another ten or twelve. Only then did I rise to my feet and walk back to where I'd first encountered the steel mesh.

Once there, I moved back and paralleled it, keeping to the scrub. Whenever I lost sight of it, I angled back in. I had to keep checking. For all I knew, the fence might veer off to the left; I didn't want suddenly to discover I was a kilometre out.

I did that two or three times before spotting the first of the CCTV cameras. This was no Mickey Mouse gizmo gaffer-taped to a tree. It was mounted on the kind of fifteen-metre-high steel post that you'd see beside any European motorway.

I carried on uphill, following the liquorice strip as it carved its way through the bush. Only nine kilometres to go. I grabbed the CamelBak tube and gave the mouthpiece a quick suck. The water was warm and tasted of plastic after its hours in the bladder, but you know what? It was more than OK. I really loved doing this shit.

7

7 September 2011
02.07 hrs

The night sky was crystal clear and peppered with stars.

The range to target from where I was concealed inside the scrub-line was about eight hundred metres. Gentle slopes surrounded the plateau, so although there was a ridge behind me, I wasn't actually on what Dino had described as high ground. He'd made it sound like I'd be looking down on the *casa* at forty-five degrees, but a head full of crystal meth doesn't do much for your powers of recall. He had got two things right, though: the Pilgrim's country seat was set in acres of immaculately cut grass, and it was floodlit.

The irrigation system was kicking off big-time. Jets of spray from a network of pipes buried under the green stuff glittered in the lights that swept across the front of the *casa*. I couldn't see from this angle, but Dino had said it was the same set-up at the rear.

The lighting was clearly designed to show off the

place rather than catch intruders. Its ambient glow had guided me in from more than three Ks away, and made everything in the immediate vicinity of the sprawling hacienda – the terracotta-roofed outbuildings and garages, the fleet of chunky 4x4s – shimmer like a Sunday-supplement spread for an exclusive country hotel. I'd been expecting major-league bling, but what I saw was fit for a discerning movie star – or a president in the making.

There were horses somewhere; I couldn't see or hear them, but a white-fenced dressage arena stood this side of the tree-lined drive, and sections of the surrounding field had been corralled.

The She Wolf's answer to the Lincoln Memorial lay in the dead ground at the rear of the *casa*. The hangar and helipad stood about two hundred metres away to my half-right. A wind-sock hung lifeless nearby, beside a path that curved through the grass towards the light show.

I retreated behind the ridge, shrugged off the CamelBak and grabbed the last can of Monster. I wasn't too sure what flavour it was – but I was after a caffeine high, not a taste sensation. I knew that the military in Afghanistan had restricted young squaddies to no more than three cans of the stuff a day because armoured-vehicle drivers were getting hyper at the wheel. But after so much travelling and so little sleep, that was the effect I was aiming for. I eased back the ring-pull and it gave a gentle hiss.

Between swigs I fished out the telescopic lens and mini-tripod and used them to transform my iPhone into a night viewing aid. Then I unrolled the freezer bag and bit a hole through its base, big enough to accommodate the lens but small enough to conceal the light from the screen, and poked the tripod legs through its side.

I finished the last of the Monster, carefully squashed the can and tucked it into the CamelBak. I didn't really have to take it with me – this wasn't a long-term hide I might need to return to – but old habits die hard.

I scrunched together the open end of the freezer bag and scrambled back to the edge of the scrub. I pressed the tripod into the ground until it was stable, then powered up the phone and got a full signal immediately – of course.

I inserted the ear-plugs, stuck my head and left hand into the bag and tapped the screen to wake it up again. Making sure the lens was still poking through its hole, I adjusted the focus with my right.

I closed my right eye before sparking up the camera app; I wanted to keep some night vision for when I moved in on the target.

8

Eyes take a long time to adjust to the darkness. The cones inside them – which enable you to see in the daytime, giving colour and perception – are no good at night. The rods at the edge of your irises take over. Because of the convex shape of the eyeball, they're angled at forty-five degrees, so if you look straight at something at night you don't really see it: it's a blur. You have to look above it or around it; that lines up the rods and gives you a clearer picture.

It takes forty minutes or so for them to become fully effective, but you start to see better after five. What you see when you have a light-affected eye, and what you see those five minutes later, are two very different things. Even small amounts of light can wreck your night vision, and the process has to start all over again. That's why I closed the eye that I aimed with – my 'master eye' – and monitored the iPhone screen with the other.

I twisted the lens and the hangar came into sharper focus through the crystalline haze thrown up by the sprinklers. A dark vertical shadow told me that the doors were a metre or so ajar. Dino had said there was always a helicopter docked inside; he just didn't know what kind it was.

I took a series of pictures and pressed *send*.

I kept checking the target, gently moving the camera left and right. At this distance it didn't take long to scan the place for signs of life – a light that had just been switched on, maybe, or a shadow across a window. The more I knew about what lay ahead of me, the better.

My plan was to leg it to the chopper and access the house via the escape tunnel – then get out the same way, with Katya in tow. If I couldn't get into the tunnel, I'd activate Plan B: another six hundred metres across the open ground to the house, and get on with it. Plan C? I didn't have a Plan C.

I watched the last of the images being uploaded and waited for the ring tone in my ear. When it came I hit the screen and let Dino do the talking.

'It's looking good, Nick. Nothing has changed. There's a signal in the basement, so I'll be with you all of the way. If she's there, we're going to find her. Eight one eight two eight three – you got that?'

'Got it.'

As I prepared to close down, Dino's tone changed. 'Hey . . . Nick?'

'What?'

'It's kinda like what we did all those years ago, know what I'm saying? Wish I was there with you, man.'

'You'd be just as fucking useless.'

Each time he laughed, he sounded ever so slightly more like the Dino I used to know.

9

I stayed where I was for another ten minutes, right eye still firmly shut, squinting at the image of the hangar, then the house with my left. Tuning in for the insertion, I went through the what-ifs. What if I was spotted halfway across the open ground? What if the hangar doors weren't really ajar – that what I thought was a gap was just a shadow? Once I had given myself a few answers, I picked up the freezer bag and scrambled three or four metres below the ridge to sort myself out.

My first task was to delete the call log and replace the SIM card. The old one went down my throat and joined the others in the litre or so of Monster seething in my gut. I shovelled the phone rechargers into one of my jeans pockets and slid the cash – both pesos and USD – into the other. I transferred my cards and passport from my neck pouch to the CamelBak, along with the tripod and the folded bag, then looked around for a place to cache them.

Two large boulders close together would be hard to miss, even if I was running fast. I scraped a hole in the dirt and buried the CamelBak between them. All I needed to do now was work out which direction to leg it if the shit hit the fan.

I returned to the ridge to take a fix on the hangar. It was roughly to my half-left; on the way out, I'd reverse the angle and head for the scrub-line. If I was in a flap with an HK spitting 5.56 and a pack of dogs behind me, I wanted to hit the CamelBak first time.

I double-checked the cache site to fix the boulder combo in my head, then went right, towards the rear of the *casa*, for sixty metres behind the ridgeline and left again until I got to the edge of the scrub. I wanted to break cover some distance from where I'd hidden the CamelBak: if I was seen or caught, I didn't want them rerunning the CCTV footage and zeroing in on my real start point.

I lay there another couple of minutes, made sure that everything in my pockets was secure, and tucked the iPhone, with earphones attached, into the neck pouch.

Then, fuck it.

I launched myself to my feet and started running.

10

There's no clever way of crossing open ground apart from putting one foot in front of the other as fast as you possibly can. And that was all I could do now, apart from keeping the hangar as much as I could between me and the target.

It wasn't long before the sprinklers were giving me the good news. My shirt and jeans got wetter and wetter as I legged it past the dressage arena. When I hit the grey concrete helipad I slowed to a walk, eyes on the hangar entrance, hands checking my pocket and pouch. If anything had fallen out I'd have to go back.

I reached the steel sliding doors and swivelled so that my back was against the right side of the gap between them. I held my breath. All I could hear was the hiss of the water being forced out of the irrigation pipes. As I listened, I scanned my escape route back to the CamelBak. Once I'd made sure I had it fixed, I dropped to the ground and poked my head into the darkness of the hangar.

Small pools of light spilled from various bits of

machinery but there was no sound; no TV, no snoring or talking. If I'd missed anything I was about to find out.

I slipped through the gap and jinked immediately to the right. It was second nature, making entry into a building. I couldn't see why people got nervous or anticipated a drama the other side – or were sometimes just plain scared. It seemed very simple to me: the less you flapped about what might be on the other side, the quicker you were going to get in there and find out. If there was a drama to deal with, the sooner you gripped it, the better.

The building was empty, apart from the chopper and its support kit. I scanned the silhouette of rotor blades, nose and tail-plane and breathed in the distinctive aroma – not the oily-rag-in-a-workshop smell, more hint-of-avgas-spilled-in-a-clinic. These places are always immaculate, every tool and component precisely where it should be.

I pulled the iPhone from the pouch, powered up the torch beam app and swept it around the large open space in search of the tunnel door. It wasn't hard to find, between two chest-high multi-drawer toolboxes.

The keys bleeped as I punched in the digits. The 818283 code was designed to be used in a panic, in darkness or in smoke: start at the centre of the bottom row of keys then hit the top three in sequence, alternating with the 8.

The steel-plated door opened with the gentle electronic whine of a hotel safe. The other side of it was solid wood, with a metal bar like you'd find on a fire exit. I wheeled one of the toolboxes across to keep it ajar and ran through its drawers for some heavy-duty pliers. Then I headed to the chopper.

As I got closer I could see it was a Bell 430; it said so on the fuselage. Any president worth his salt would want to be seen climbing aboard one of these four-rotor monsters and settling into one of its six leather seats.

I slid my hand behind the instrument console, grabbed a fistful of wires and chopped at them in a frenzy. If I was running around in the scrub at first light because it had been a total fuck-up, I didn't want this thing hovering overhead, loaded with lads gripping HK machine-guns.

I severed seven or eight cables. That had to be enough to keep the fucker grounded; I didn't want to be here playing aircraft vandal all night. I still had to get in, find Katya, and maybe do a favour or two for Dino.

He'd told me the location of Peregrino's and Liseth's apartments within the *casa*, and where they put their guests. But what if Katya wasn't in any of those places? I needed to crack on before everybody started tucking into their cornflakes and Peregrino wanted to kill someone because he hadn't got a free toy.

11

The tunnel had been constructed from sewage pipes, with a steel walkway running along the floor. I closed the door behind me and heard the lock whine back into position. I didn't want anyone popping into the hangar and thinking they might help themselves to a Christmas bonus.

I pushed the bar to check the exit mechanism and the door whined open again. I closed it once more and set off along the walkway. I took my time to keep the noise down, but the sound of my footsteps still echoed in the space ahead of me.

I caught sight of a chamber, three or four metres up to my right, as I moved through the gloom. I sparked up the iPhone beam and pinged a row of large black nylon sail-bags. Liseth didn't sound like running away was her thing, but planning ahead obviously was.

I unzipped the nearest. It was filled with banded bundles of hundred-dollar bills. I grabbed it by the handles and lifted. Whatever the denomination, a US dollar bill weighs a fraction under a gram, so ten thousand hundred-dollar bills hits the scales at about ten kilos. This thing felt like it weighed thirty. I'd learned shit like that over the years.

So – three million dollars a bag, give or take, multiplied by twelve. She had it all worked out: three bags per spare seat on the aircraft, at ninety kilos a throw and in manageable weights, quick to load. All very nice, but not much use to me right now. I'd been hoping to find a weapon, not win the lottery. I moved back into the tunnel proper.

It took me ten minutes to reach the far end. I took a breath and repeated my listening drills. This time I put my ear to the door. I couldn't hear anything, so gently pushed the bar. The lock mechanism whirred. I was immediately engulfed by cooking smells.

I craned my neck and found myself looking through a concrete archway into a kitchen that Claridge's would have envied. Dino had told me there were two – a party kitchen, and an everyday set-up on the other side of the house. Everything I could see, from the worktops and cookers to the rows of utensils and hanging pots and pans, was shiny stainless steel.

In one of the rooms beyond it, Dino had lived with the dogs. But I was heading elsewhere.

The door clicked shut behind me and I went left, up the bare concrete service stairs that led to the banqueting suite and main reception room. The floors were marble, and the centrepiece of the *casa* was a *Scarface* staircase that curved left to Liseth's chambers and right to Peregrino's apartments, two floors above me.

A corridor the width of a four-lane highway led from the top landing to the guest suites at the back of the house. That was where I was hoping to find Katya.

I reached a door one flight up and went into stopping and listening mode. Silence. I turned the handle as slowly as I possibly could and pushed.

It didn't give an inch.

I tried again.

Shit, I was going to have to take another route. I didn't want to go through the admin rooms and risk sparking up the dogs, so I decided to retrace my steps into the belly of the *casa* and call Dino.

Before I had a chance to return to stainless-steel heaven, the lights came on.

I was fucked – I knew it instantly. I had nowhere to go, other than into the fists of four heavies who'd appeared through the kitchen archway.

The guy in front brought up a bright yellow Taser handgun. I saw the electronic initiation and heard the sigh of compressed nitrogen as the two barbs shot towards me, their wires trailing like kite tails.

One hit my shoulder and one hit my arm and I couldn't do anything except take the pain. I was slammed against the wall with the G force of a Tornado and dropped like a sack of shit.

Apart from 50,000 volts, the only thing that went through my mind was the idea that I should try to curl up and protect my head as I tumbled down the stairs like a second-rate stuntman.

12

The current bounced around my body for far too long as the guy kept his finger on the trigger. I couldn't do anything but try my best to ride out the muscle convulsions and get ready for what came next. Toecaps piled into my body, punctuated by angry shouts. I curled up and waited for them to drag me to wherever. They'd used the Taser instead of lethal rounds, so they didn't want me dead straight away.

My heart thumped like a bass drum. It felt like every single one of my organs had been given a massive kicking. The pain sparked up again when they grabbed me by my arms and dragged my arse across the floor, my Timberlands scraping along behind me, my head back, the world upside-down.

They pulled me under the archway and into the kitchen, then ripped the Taser barbs from my body. One of them had buried itself in my skin; the other was firmly implanted in my shirt.

I needed to feel I still had a little control, even if I didn't: I tried to make sure I knew where I was the whole time, where I was about to end up and who I was against. The two older guys sported thick moustaches and, as always seemed to be the case with Arab and Latin American lip hair, every word they spoke sounded like a command.

The five of us barrelled through a pair of large double doors to a chorus of dog barks bouncing off the bare concrete walls and ceiling. As we pushed through another set, the growls and snarls got a whole lot louder. Then I could smell them, their animal scent blended, bizarrely, with the salon aroma of hairspray and shampoo. I was dragged past three long-haired German Shepherds in floor-to-ceiling cages, their slavering jaws pressed against the steel mesh. I wondered which had replaced the dog that had tried to hang onto Dino.

They swung me onto the floor of the first empty cage and one of the moustaches grunted an order. My Timberlands were wrenched off and stashed in a black bin-liner. A boot pressed down hard on my neck and my shirt, neck pouch, belt, jeans and boxers followed.

The cage door was locked and four pairs of eyes looked in at me. They weren't glaring or laughing or taking the piss. It was much worse than that. They obviously pitied me.

The three dogs were still going berserk. The head of the nearest one smacked against the mesh and its saliva splashed onto my chest. I scrabbled towards a sheepskin-lined dog-bed in the furthest corner. Leaning against the back wall, I scanned the row of cages. We all had one.

The air-con down here was severe. I grabbed the sheepskin and pulled it round me for warmth. The four gave me one last glance before heading for the door, one of the younger ones clutching the bin-liner. They turned off the lights as they left.

The dogs started to lose interest in me. It wasn't long before all I heard was the gentle padding of paws on concrete as they went back to their beds.

I felt my way slowly to the door of my cage and took in as much as I could of my immediate surroundings: a solid concrete wall along the rear; another to my right; to my left, three steel cages and three German Shepherds.

I felt around the key well and tested the fastening: a lever lock. The square steel mesh was wide enough for me to poke all four fingers through, stopping at the web, so the cage felt more like a police station drunk tank than a kennel. I climbed high enough to confirm that it was secured to the ceiling. Could I maybe bend it or prise it loose? Of course I couldn't.

I guessed the dogs would only be bolted in, not locked, so grabbed the fence between me and the first Shepherd and gave it a good shake, hoping I could somehow dislodge the bolt and wriggle through. He went ballistic and his mates joined in. I pulled and pushed against the mesh, but nothing gave.

I hunkered down in the bed and wondered if it was where Dino had spent thirteen months of his life. I listened to the whirr of the air-con and the dogs barking occasionally in the darkness for no better reason than that they were dogs. I hadn't seen much of the room as I'd been dragged in, but the echoes told me it was probably as big as the kitchen.

The dogs eventually got bored. When they finally shut up I started to hear the drip of a tap. I sat with my legs crossed and the sheepskin wrapped more tightly around me. All I could do now was wait, and think about the slickness of the lift. There had been no panic, no shouts or screams, no rounds sprayed at an unexpected intruder.

They'd been waiting.

13

The fluorescent lights flickered on again an hour or so later and three women trooped in, dressed in the traditional flower-patterned pinnies. I stayed where I was, curled up but watching. They kept their eyes to the ground as they headed for the cages alongside mine. The dogs were very pleased to see them – up on all clawless fours, barking away, wagging their tails.

The whole of one cupboard was stacked with litre bottles of mineral water to replenish their heavy ceramic drinking bowls. I watched as the women filled three stainless-steel dishes with dried food, but not as eagerly as the German Shepherds did. They worked quickly, putting bowls and dishes in front of each of the cage doors and then throwing the bolts. Never once did they catch my eye.

The dogs didn't either. They went for their dinner as if they hadn't eaten for days – as dogs do.

I stood up, wrapped the sheepskin around me sarong style, and shuffled to the front of my pen. '*Agua? Agua, por favor?*' I pointed at the shelves. If they didn't help me, I didn't know when I'd get fed or watered. '*Agua? Agua?*' I rattled the mesh to catch their attention. '*Por favor?*'

It wasn't only about getting liquid down me. The bottles weren't going to fit through the mesh, so maybe they had a key. If that was the case, I'd follow Dino's example and make the quickest exit possible. I'd plunge back along the tunnel and take my chances at the other end.

The women still didn't look at me, but at least they mumbled to each other and seemed to be nodding in my general direction. A decision was made. The youngest one selected a bottle. She unscrewed the top as she came over, waffling to me conspiratorially and raising a finger to her lips.

'*No habla . . .*'

I nodded.

I forced a couple of fingers through on each side to help support the neck as she pushed it through the mesh and sucked in two or three serious mouthfuls as the other women came past, a dog each on a lead, and disappeared around the other side of the wall.

I carried on forcing as much water down my throat as I could. When I stopped to take a breath, what was left splashed around as the bottle was able to recover its original shape. She tilted it back as if to give me time to breathe, but then started to retreat, an anxious look on her face and the bottle only half empty.

'*Gracias, Señora. Gracias . . .*' For all I knew I might be seeing her on a daily basis, so I wanted to stay in her good books.

'*De nada.*' She didn't look back.

She put the bottle down to one side, ducked into the

cage furthest away from me and escorted the third dog to join the rest.

I could hear water spraying round the corner, and the odd canine murmur of approval. A sweet citrus smell wafted my way. It sounded like the dogs were being treated to a shampoo and some loving. The women were obviously devoted to their work: there was no more waffling.

I sat back on my bed as the dogs were blow-dried.

It must have been at least an hour before they returned, clawless paws making hardly a sound on the floor. They now looked twice the size, their glossy coats fluffed up, like early eighties porn stars' hair.

They went back into the cages, the bolts slid into place and bowls and dishes were removed once more. Buckets and mops swung into action and the whole place soon reeked of disinfectant. They worked in silence, still avoiding even the slightest eye contact; it was as if I simply didn't exist. They left as soon as they'd finished and turned off the lights. The dogs skulked back to their beds.

I still had no idea of what time it was.

There was nothing I could do but try to sleep, which wasn't too hard. I was fucked, and in any case, I'd always grabbed some kip if I got the chance, no matter what was going on. 'Whenever there's a lull in battle, get your head down. You never know when you'll be given another chance.' It had been drummed into me as a sixteen-year-old soldier, and I'd stuck with it ever since.

14

Fuck knows how long I'd been lying there before the dogs started whining and mumbling again. Seconds later, all three sprang up and went berserk.

The door burst open, and above the racket I began to make out the sound of a woman singing.

The fluorescent lights flickered on.

I stayed curled up, one eye half-open.

I recognized the singer at once, even after all these years.

The body in front of her was blindfolded with a red silk scarf; she had a guiding hand on either side of him. If this was Peregrino, he was well on his way to emulating his dad's waistline.

She didn't acknowledge me: she was too busy congratulating herself on his early birthday surprise. They were both in riding boots, light-brown jodhpurs and matching brown-and-white-striped polo shirts – collars up, of course. The dog walker who'd given me the drink followed behind them, struggling to carry the kind of gilded chair that Louis XV would have been pleased to give some arse time.

Still serenading him and ignoring me, Liseth guided Peregrino all the way to my cage. Whatever the song was, the dogs seemed to like it. They had calmed right down and gazed at her adoringly as she treated each of them in turn to some quality eye contact.

Peregrino liked it too. His smile widened beneath the silk. It was a surreal moment: I felt like I'd been invited to one of those makeover shows where the good-looking presenter is about to reveal to the minging home-owner how they've just redecorated his living room.

Liseth hadn't aged a bit since I'd last seen her. Her hair was still jet black and centre-parted, and now reached past her shoulders. Jesús Junior was a lot taller, and needed to hold back on the *fritadas* if he wanted to look remotely presidential.

Liseth still didn't acknowledge me; it was like my cage was empty. The dog woman positioned the chair to the right of them, put a crisp white envelope carefully on the seat and left as quickly as she could. Whatever was about to happen, she wanted out of here.

I thought I heard a couple of 'Peregrinos' in the tune.

The dogs gave a little yelp as Liseth came to the end of her song; she wagged a finger at them and gently admonished them in Spanish. Then she turned and raised her hands to the knot in the blindfold. She whispered something in Peregrino's ear, then whisked away the silk with a theatrical flourish and a beaming smile, proudly presenting him with the curled-up mess at the back of the cage.

He might have been twenty years older, but I was

always going to remember those eyes and the way they had stared at me, unblinking, like stone. He recognized me too: from the contortion of his face it was clear I'd featured in his three a.m. nightmares.

His eyes burned into mine with a mixture of anger and hatred. '*Papa ... Costa Rica ... matado ...*' The words came out in a low growl as he moved towards my cage.

I watched him every step of the way and got myself into gear for when he stepped inside to kill me.

15

I stayed motionless on the bed. Unless he pulled a weapon and shot me through the mesh, he was going to have to open the gate.

Peregrino stopped and draped his fingers through the steel. He stared at me without blinking as the scene played out in his head: his dad bleeding to death under the pick-up as the rain pounded down on the tin roof of the shack . . . me running with the weapon that had dropped him still in the shoulder, to make sure I'd finished the job . . .

His mother moved half a step behind him, gently murmuring to him, but Peregrino's eyes, dark and life-less, never left me.

At length he turned, kissed her cheek and made to leave. Liseth stopped him; she seemed to be reminding him that his work was not yet done.

He pulled a smartphone from his jodhpurs and took a couple of snaps of me curled up in my basket.

Liseth wasn't happy with my pose – she looked at me

for the first time and motioned with her palm. 'Sit up! Sit up!'

I wasn't happy either, but I stayed precisely where I was. Maybe she'd get someone to open the cage and come in and teach me a lesson. But Peregrino checked his screen and was happy with what he saw. With another kiss on his mother's cheek – and one last searing glare at me – he left us.

Liseth reached for the envelope and sat down, slowly crossing her legs. She sent soothing sounds to her three babies to her half-right. The one to her half-left, she ignored.

She flicked her hair back and finally gave me her full attention. 'My son, he's grown into a fine young man, don't you think?' Her gaze was as steadfast as his. 'Do you think he looks like his father? But maybe you cannot remember. After all, you only saw him through a rifle sight . . .'

Her eyes pierced mine, searching for a reaction. A waft of perfume, heavy and cloying, made its way to the back of the cage.

I kept quiet. Maybe she'd open up and let the dogs in. If that gate opened, I'd take my chances.

She paused for a couple of seconds.

'My English is very good, Nick, isn't it? I've been taking lessons every day for over two years now. I've had to – English is the political language of the world.'

I stayed quiet. I didn't think she was really looking for an answer. Her entire demeanour belonged to someone confident in command, happier on transmit than receive.

'Nick, you have nothing to fear from me. In fact, I have you – partly – to thank for our good fortune. But

451

you are my gift to El Peregrino. What he chooses to do with you is entirely up to him.'

One of the dogs barked its agreement, its nose pressed up against the mesh. She uncrossed her legs, slid a finger into the envelope, and leaned towards me.

'Of course you'd like me to tell you how we found you. I think I owe you that.'

She smiled, but I didn't join in.

She extracted a photograph and held it up triumphantly: a blown-up version of the Anna and Katya snap, with me in the background making a brew.

16

She let the photo drop to the floor, and showed me another. 'He has this one in his bedroom. Don't they look wonderful together? She is also a gift to us . . .'

They were both a few years younger. Katya looked radiant, and he wasn't so fat. She was in her doctor's kit, standing outside a hospital – I could see a Red Cross and a bunch of important-looking signs in Spanish. There were lots of smiles and the sun was shining. Katya had gathered up her hair in a big messy bun.

Liseth turned the photo to take another appreciative look at it herself. 'He always wanted her. Always. But she . . . she needed time to come to her senses . . .' She smiled. 'An awareness of destiny can be a heavy cross to bear.'

She turned back to her darlings.

I pulled myself up. 'You found me because of a picture?'

'Destiny again.' She said it to the dogs and they seemed to enjoy the joke. She took the applause for a moment, then fanned them quiet with the picture of

Katya and Peregrino. She waited for them to settle before turning back to me. 'The strange thing is, I wasn't even looking for you.'

She stood up and took a step closer to me. 'I had no idea you were going to be returning to our lives until I saw this photograph of you and your lovely lady. Anna . . . such a beautiful name . . .'

I pictured her and the baby in the safety of the clinic under Frank's protection; at least something was OK.

'Our young business partners in China – a scheme you have only delayed, by the way – seemed to think you were on some kind of rescue mission. They explained about the photograph – and the moment I saw the scan of it, I realized the Fates had presented us with a gift my Peregrino could not be denied.

'Then we simply had to wait as you made the journey to the Casa Esperanza. And now here you are.'

She took a third photograph from the envelope. 'I had this taken for you. I suspected you might be asking after them.'

She held the glossy ten-by-eight against the mesh, and it didn't leave much to the imagination: two naked, mutilated bodies; razor-thin slices all over their bruised and battered torsos; hair matted with blood. Sophie's arms were bent at angles they shouldn't have been. Bruce's intestines had been reintroduced to the daylight. They'd taken a long time to 'explain'.

She sighed regretfully. 'We cannot tolerate inefficiency, you know that. Tolerance would make my Peregrino look weak. And as you are about to find out, weakness leads to defeat.'

As if to demonstrate that she was already tiring of me, she turned back towards the door. 'Miguel! *Miguel!*'

It burst open and two guys almost leaped into the room. The older, moustachioed one acknowledged Liseth. His younger, smooth-faced sidekick didn't even dare look at her: he kept his eyes fixed firmly on the bin-liner he'd brought with him.

Liseth pulled a lever-lock key from her jodhpurs, handed it to Miguel, then strode from the room.

Fuck knew what was going to happen next, but the dogs seemed to think it was show time.

17

The two heavies both had Tasers and big pistols in polymer holsters tugging at their belts; the leather sagged between the hoops where the weapons were attached.

The younger gun pulled my shirt and jeans out of the bin-liner. I kept an eye on it in case the mobile was still there in the pouch, but I couldn't see anything.

Miguel fetched nylon-webbing leads and harnesses from one of the white cupboards and the dogs began to hyperventilate. Then he went into each cage in turn to rig them up, taking a lot of care not to mess with their coiffures.

Once they were fully kitted out, he motioned for me to go to the back of my pen, then unlocked the gate and threw in my clothes, minus the boots. They both stood and watched as I got dressed. I wasn't fast enough for Miguel's liking.

'Rápido, rápido . . .'

The Shepherds were right with him: they barked their heads off, raring to go.

As I fastened my belt, the young gun handed his weapons to Miguel and joined me in the cage. He harnessed me up like my furry friends, which didn't worry me at all. It meant I was getting out of there. It meant I had options.

Young Gun went to grab the other dogs and was soon standing there with two leads in his left hand and one in his right.

Miguel beckoned me to join them. *'Vamos, vamos . . .'*

I looked around as he handed over my lead, but no way was I going to be able to make a break for it right then. I didn't care. I was no longer under lock and key. Every step I took from now on was a bonus.

Miguel kept behind us with the weapons as my three new best mates and I were led into a long, wide, bare corridor. The *casa's* skeleton was constructed from reinforced concrete and, like any office block, they hadn't bothered primping the below-stairs bits.

I could see admin rooms through arches each side of me, like a series of large, cube-shaped caves. There were washing-machines and dryers in one, sheets and pillows in another. Then a steam pressing room, where the staff suddenly got extra busy with the folding, not wanting eye-to-eye. The next cave along was stacked with dining chairs.

Wide concrete steps led to a set of large double doors that opened onto the first floor of the living quarters, which was where the luxury began. The main staircase towered above us as we headed down to the front of the *casa*.

My bare feet left sweat marks for a second or two on the white marble floor as the dogs pulled on their leads and Young Gun struggled to keep them in check. The

457

furniture was classic French; gilded Louis XV seemed to be all the rage with the drug baron who enjoyed the finer things in life. I hoped Katya was impressed.

While we waited inside the main entrance, I studied the portraits hung on either side of it. You could hardly miss them: they were the size of West End cinema screens. A young woman smiled down on us from each of them. They were both the spitting image of their mother, right down to their hairstyle and the way they sat with their hands on their laps.

Miguel pulled open the doors and light poured into the hallway. Our handler led us down a few steps and onto a forecourt the size of a football pitch, where the sun bounced off three glossy black Escalade SUVs with darkened glass and sparkling alloys, as pristine as if they'd just taken a short break from the showroom.

I squinted across to the grass, where Liseth was talking intently into her cell phone. Massive oval sun-gigs almost covered her face, and a baseball cap took care of the rest.

She turned and closed it down as we approached. Judging by what I could see of her smile, she was very happy indeed to be reunited with her three babies after all of fifteen minutes, but she couldn't have been as happy as I was that the gravel beneath the soles of my feet was more like pea shale than that flint chip stuff that can really fuck you up. She took all four leads from Young Gun, seemingly unaware that one of the harnesses wasn't attached to something furry and freshly coiffed.

The two guys stayed behind us as we headed off across the turf. We'd gone maybe a dozen steps before she stopped and finally turned to acknowledge me.

'Get down.'

I clearly hadn't obeyed quickly enough, as a foot was rammed into me from behind, knocking me into a very pissed-off German Shepherd. It barked and snarled and I covered my face against the bite I thought was coming. My sleeve rode up my arm as I got up off my arse, revealing the puncture wounds that I'd shared with Dino.

She didn't miss a thing. 'It seems that dogs don't love you as much as I love them.'

One of the Escalades sparked up as she set off again, and followed us round from the front of the house. I stayed on all fours, trying my best to keep up, but the dogs weren't impressed. Maybe Liseth was right. She waffled away to them in Spanish, telling them not to be so naughty. The Escalade's engine remained a low growl immediately behind us.

The dog nearest me slowed, did a couple of tight circles, then hunched up, spread its hind legs and quivered. Liseth stared at the horizon as it coiled a big one onto the grass. Young Gun jumped out of the 4x4 with a plastic bag over one hand and a bottle of the *casa*'s finest mineral water in the other. He obviously got all the best jobs.

He gloved up the pile and poured the water over the grass. Liseth glanced down and inspected his efforts then headed off once more as if nothing had happened.

There was nothing but mountainous scrub between the extensive manicured lawns and the far horizon. A cell-net tower, presumably one of their own, punctured the skyline. The sun wasn't that high and the distant view didn't yet ripple in the heat haze, but it had been up long enough to dry the grass. I guessed it was mid-morning.

Liseth spoke to me again as she strode on; at least, I assumed it was to me, because she didn't look down. 'I used to have someone just like you.'

'Where is he now?'

She ignored me as I scampered to keep up, one ear on the engine note of the ever-watchful Escalade behind us.

As we approached the rear of the house I could hear shouts, and the rapid thud of hoofs. We rounded the corner and I could see Dino was right: it was almost an exact replica of the front, with balconies and acres of terracotta tiles and stone.

I caught movement on one of the second-floor balconies. She had her back to me, but I knew exactly who it was. Katya turned, leaned forward, both hands on the balustrade, and looked straight at me. At this distance, her expression was impossible to read.

Liseth didn't miss a beat. 'She loves it here. You should be more concerned about yourself. You're the one on a leash.'

18

Fat bastards on polo ponies charged up and down a rich green velvet pitch under a cloudless blue sky. A fleet of horse trucks and SUVs with trailers was parked to one side, bodies running about between them, preparing fresh mounts.

Peregrino spotted his mother as she headed towards a parasol the size of the O2 centre about thirty metres back from the touchline. He broke from the game long enough to come over and scowl at me from his saddle.

Liseth led me and my fellow dogs into the shade as he returned to the fray. Yet another of her favourite chairs stood alongside a highly polished mahogany table carrying a jug of ice-packed orange juice on a silver tray. There were only two glasses and I guessed one of them wasn't for me.

What really grabbed my attention as we settled beside her feet was the memorial off to our right. It was about twenty metres by ten, and ten metres high. From the edge of a reflecting pool, gleaming white steps led up to the shrine, flanked by two buttresses, each crowned with a one-metre-tall tripod carved from pink marble.

I remembered visiting Lincoln's version on my first ever visit to Washington and seeing the words 'I Have a Dream' engraved near the spot where Martin Luther King had stood in 1963. I wondered if there was a similar quotation by the Wolf on this one. After all, he too was a great visionary, reformer and defender of human rights.

The real memorial featured on the back of the US five-dollar bill, with the great man's portrait on the front. It was probably only a matter of time before Liseth had her son immortalized on peso notes.

She saw me staring at her own little piece of Washington, DC. 'That is where you placed Jesús. He lies there, at rest.'

I hoped the fucker was burning in Hell, but now wasn't the time to mention it.

The Escalade stopped a little way back, its engine noise barely a murmur as it ticked over just enough to keep the air-con going.

She poured some juice into a glass that almost instantly frosted with condensation. She wrapped a linen napkin around it but didn't raise it to her lips: she was far too engrossed in the performance of the *casa* team's star player.

She looked down at me. 'My son is an excellent horseman, no?'

I nodded eagerly. 'Best I've ever seen.'

'And he's so much happier now that Katya has returned to us. I think this, too, is improving his game.'

She turned back to watch the apple of her eye, apparently failing to recognize that he looked like an over-stuffed *chorizo* on four legs. 'He will need a wife soon.'

She took a sip from her glass, returned it to the tray and leaned down to her other three dogs. 'She will be very happy. She already understands that there are causes greater than the individual, that we must all embrace our destiny. Truly we must, mustn't we?' The dogs didn't respond immediately, so she repeated, but louder: '*Mustn't we?*'

They barked their agreement, and licked their lips. If they thought their destiny was sharing some of that juice, I reckoned they were about to be disappointed.

She turned back to me. 'You see, my Shepherds are extremely intelligent. They are fluent in English, just like me.'

I was straight in there. 'They probably speak it better than I do.'

Something passing for a smile began to take shape behind her sun-gigs but a mobile kicked off and the moment was broken. She rose to her feet and pulled a golden iPhone from her bag. Diamonds glittered round the edge of the screen. Russian oligarchs paid over four hundred thousand US for those pieces of designer lunacy, and I'd read about a Chinese guy snapping one up for more than ten million. It looked like the Mexicans had developed a similar weakness.

She tilted it to shade the screen, flicked *answer*, and started talking. With one hand holding her mobile to her ear and the other jabbing the air, she was clearly giving someone somewhere a hard time. She wasn't angry, she wasn't shouting, but her machine-gun delivery spelt bollocking in any language. I wondered if she'd ever considered learning Cantonese.

She sprang up and strode towards the reflection pool. The Escalade crept forward as she moved out of earshot.

While Liseth gripped whoever was unfortunate enough to have reached out to her on the phone, I watched Peregrino canter across to the trucks. He stopped there for a while, then began to move back in our direction, leading a spare pony by the reins.

Young Gun took this as his cue to lead the Shepherds away and load them into the back of the Escalade. He made it clear Dog Number Four should stay where he was. The whole performance suddenly seemed like it had been carefully rehearsed.

I glanced back towards the house, but couldn't see Katya. At least I knew she was within reach.

The game had come to a halt and the players were congregating beside the trucks on the far side of the pitch. The ponies were taking a drinks break around a couple of mobile troughs.

Liseth closed down her iPhone as Peregrino reached us. He sat astride his pony, his eyes channelling hate towards an imaginary target somewhere between my eyes. This boy had plans for me.

Liseth reached for the second set of reins and Peregrino kept hold of his mother's mount until she had climbed into the saddle. She fed her feet into the stirrups and steered the beast over to me.

'Now we're going to have some fun.'

Peregrino sat sucking his teeth as she pointed in the

direction of the scrub to my left, about four hundred metres away.

'OK, now's your chance. Go!'

I didn't need any second bidding.

19

The leash snaked behind me as I sprinted for the scrub-line. My ears strained for the thunder of hoofs but the only sounds I heard were whoops of delight from over by the trucks. They'd done this before.

The game was on.

My lungs were already bursting with the bushes still fifty ahead. My legs were pumping as fast as they could, but if my mind was in fifth gear, they felt like they were stuck in third.

Fuck it, I was going as fast as I could. Swinging my arms hard to push my body forward, bare feet pounding on the manicured grass, I finally hit the scrub. My feet were lacerated by stones like knife blades and needle-pointed thorn. I turned and collapsed in a cloud of dust, gulping in oxygen, liquid with sweat.

I watched as the last of the players mounted their ponies. The others were drifting towards Liseth and Peregrino at a gentle trot. All of them wore big leather shin and knee protectors. And they all wielded their mallets, ready for some fun. Fuck that. They wouldn't have any fun with me. I didn't mind featuring in Peregrino's nightmares. I wasn't after a starring role in one of Dino's.

The pack broke into a canter towards me. I pushed deeper into the scrub, keeping low so they couldn't see their prey.

I needed to make distance. If I got away, I'd hide up and come back for Katya tonight. As for Liseth and Peregrino, fuck 'em: Dino was definitely going to get his wish.

Throat burning, I started running, ducking and side-stepping as best I could to avoid the thorns. They cut into the flesh of my arms and I lifted my hands to protect my face. Old growth sliced into my feet as I pushed on.

Behind me, I began to hear the rumble of hoofs on the turf. It was pointless trying to be clever about what I was doing. Zigzagging or any of that sort of shit wasn't going to help me make distance. I'd just be more knackered when they caught me. These guys had speed and mobility, and they had all day. What I needed was a way of levelling the odds. If not, I was history.

The whoops were joined by shouts and hollers as they entered the scrub. They'd have to spread the pack because of the terrain. Maybe there was a prize for whoever found me. I didn't care: I kept going, looking for somewhere to hide and wait.

A couple of the shouters were closing in behind me, to the right, getting louder with every passing second. I could hear a cell phone kicking off somewhere.

I kept low but fast, not daring to lose ground. My head was burning. Sweat dripped off my forehead and stung my eyes. Dust caked my face.

Within minutes, I came to a dried-up watercourse, not much more than a dip in the ground, a metre deep and the same wide. I dived into it, pushed my back against the wall, trying to control my breathing so I could hear. The sun glared into my face. I hugged the side of the bank to give myself an extra centimetre of cover, as if that was going to make the slightest difference.

I heard the two horses first. Then their riders: they were chatting, swapping jokes. Having a great day out.

One of their cell phones gave a blast of its 'Crazy In Love' ring tone. The other rider sang a couple of bars, treating us all to his best Beyoncé impression, and they both laughed. Those lads must have been the dog's bollocks on the karaoke circuit.

I heard more shouts in the distance. One of the ponies snorted. I hugged the dirt wall and bided my time. I wanted one target, not two.

The mobile closed down but the Beyoncé impression was still hitting its stride. I didn't give a fuck: the ponies were moving on.

A minute or so later I could hear another giving a whinny of protest. I couldn't blame it: one minute you're mincing around the polo field, the next you're being forced through a fucking great thorn bush. It was no longer a good day out.

I poked my head above the bank and saw what I needed. I didn't waste any time thinking. I leaped up and charged at the fucker side on. The pony sensed my presence before the rider did, and swung violently away from me. I grabbed the mallet in the rider's right hand and gave it a yank. The strap round his wrist brought his arm with it. A shriek of alarm fought its way through the steel face cage beneath his peaked helmet. This wasn't what he'd had in mind at all.

The pony went crazy and kept trying to pull away from me. His rider slipped sideways in the saddle. I wrenched his mallet more fiercely to take him down, but his right foot was stuck fast in the stirrup.

The pony twisted and the rider crashed backwards into the dust. I kicked at whatever I could connect with in the centre of what I could see of him and tried to grab the reins as the pony enveloped us in a cloud of dust. The fucking thing kept turning away from me so I decided to bin it, snatched the mallet away from the rider's wrist and swung it down onto his chest.

He screamed and buckled up as he took the pain. I spun around, finally managed to get hold of the swinging reins and separated his foot from the stirrup.

The pony reared as I scrabbled frantically aboard. Sitting up in the saddle, feet finding the stirrups, I kicked my heels and turned the reins like I'd seen on TV.

It worked. It was happening. But it wasn't pretty. The guy I'd left in the dirt would soon be on his mobile. I kicked again. The pony got the message. I gripped the reins and felt my arse bounce up and down completely out of synch with the animal. But it was moving in the direction I wanted, and that was all that mattered.

20

The yelling behind me became more urgent and I caught glimpses of horseflesh and brown-leather shin- and knee-protectors through the bush to my right. I pulled the reins to my left and kicked the pony's flanks. He moved away from the action, but I immediately saw more brown leather and movement ahead. I turned him again to try to head between the two posses.

I heard another chorus of ring tones and clocked what was happening. They were herding me. Well, they could herd me all they wanted. I'd just keep going.

I steered the pony down into the shallow gulch, but the others were already closing in on the high ground either side. The shouts and mobile rings became more frenzied by the second.

The next thing I knew, a body was scrambling down the bank ahead of me, a player with a peaked black helmet and a steel face guard – the full Darth Vader. But instead of a light sabre, this boy had a mallet.

It was too late for any kind of evasive action. I didn't know how to get this thing into reverse and the pony wouldn't climb the bank. I dug it in the ribs with my heels. As we got within range, he swung the mallet like a samurai and thumped it hard into the pony's chest. The wounded beast bucked and reared. A split second later, I was lying in the dust.

Fuck it, I wasn't about to hang around. I scrambled up the bank, but my assailant was well ahead of the game. He might have been built like Mr Blobby, but he moved like Usain Bolt. He swung his mallet again, struck me on the shin and took me down. For a second or two it felt like I'd been speared by a red-hot poker, but then my leg just went numb from knee to ankle. I couldn't feel it as I started to crawl.

I looked up as his shadow fell across me. We had quite an audience now, bellowing and cheering from the higher ground, leaning forward on their saddles, enjoying the view, but my number-one fan wasn't playing to the crowd: this was strictly personal.

The mallet came down again and this time it landed at the top of my right arse cheek. Six inches higher and it would have fucked my kidney; I'd have been pissing blood for the duration. As I tried to get up, Peregrino's eyes glinted behind the face guard.

The eyes told me he was going to finish me off right there – but I wasn't going quietly: I was going to take him with me. I managed to haul myself onto my hands and knees as he stepped forward.

All I could do was make this quick. If I could get my teeth within reach of his throat I'd rip the fucking thing out: he'd be as dead as I would be moments later.

A pony was being steered down the cut behind him. 'Peregrino?'

A woman's voice.

'*Por qué?*'

Liseth's tone was inquisitive rather than accusing. She was trying to make sense of this. The other players went silent as she approached, kept their mounts steady. None of them knew which way she was going to jump, any more than I did.

'*Que pasa?*'

She smiled down at her son from the saddle, talked to him earnestly for a moment, then cajoled him.

Finally Peregrino burst out laughing, then turned and shouted to his companions. '*Vamos a celebrar!*'

I didn't speak much Spanish, but I knew enough to understand 'Let's party!'

Everybody else certainly liked the idea, but Peregrino's happy face had disappeared by the time he turned back to me. He bent down and stretched out his hand towards me. He squeezed my cheeks like a jolly, drunken uncle at first, then his grip became more pincer-like – and those eyes told me this wasn't the end of the story, not by a long chalk.

He held on long enough to leave me in no doubt that it was his party, not mine, and by the time he walked back up the cut to his pony, Liseth had gone.

At a nod of his head another player led a pony down to me. He shouted and pointed: he wanted me back in the saddle. It took me two or three attempts to swing myself up – each met with raucous laughter and mocking applause – before he could lead me out of the cut. A barrage of excited chat was fired off in all directions as they steered me back towards the *casa*.

As we broke out of the scrub, I saw Miguel standing beside the Escalade. As the players stopped and waffled, he grabbed the leash, still hanging down my back, and dragged me out of the saddle. I landed in a heap at his feet.

Peregrino and Liseth watched from the house as he manhandled me into the vehicle. Young Gun held the rear door open as Miguel shoved me in with the dogs. I guess she hadn't wanted them to go out in that nasty scrubland and end up looking like me.

The back of the Escalade was caged off from the driver's cab, so no way was I going to get to the two of them as we drove back. I moved towards the nearest side door instead, and after making a meal of checking every inch of my body for injuries, grabbed the handle to swing myself out. It was child-locked. I caught sight of Miguel's expression in the rear-view. I was starting to understand how Dino felt about other people's pity.

The dogs made themselves comfortable around me. I didn't even glance at them; I didn't want them to think I posed any threat. They might have smelt of summer meadows and looked like Dolly Parton, but German Shepherds are German Shepherds. I'd already seen that it didn't take much to set them off.

As the SUV rolled round to the front of the house I couldn't help but admire Liseth – just a bit. Yes, she was totally fucked in the head and might have me killed for not nodding quickly enough every time she said something; and, yes, she was responsible for who knew how many dead bodies lying in streets or hanging from bridges around the country, but a little bit of me thought the same way it did about Sophie: not bad for a street kid.

A street kid who was determined to make a president out of that psycho kid of hers.

21

It had been hours since they'd thrown me back in the cage. My throat was bone dry and I still had grit in my mouth. Hunger grabbed at me in waves, but that was OK – it wasn't the first time I'd gone for long stretches without food. It was the lack of water that worried me. Getting out of this shit was going to take some serious effort, and I didn't want to go down with dehydration in the process.

The lights had been kept on, and now and again the dogs gave a fitful whine. My feet throbbed; the mallet blows made every move painful.

At least they'd left me fully dressed, which made the air-con less of a nightmare. I looked around for something I could use as a weapon. My belt was the only thing that came close. I took it off and stuck it down the back of my jeans. The other good news was that the bin-liner had been dumped by the lockers. I could see a Timberland heel poking out of it, but no sign of my iPhone or other gear.

The dogs went mad again. They jumped up and ran

to the front of their cages, barking like crazy. Liseth appeared and gently calmed them on her way to the chair, greeting them each by name. She'd changed out of her riding kit into killer evening wear. She was now in a loud red dress that brushed her knees, with a matching silk cardigan and heels. Her hair had been ironed extra straight, and shone in the fluorescent light. In one hand she carried a clutch bag – loud red, of course – and in the other a red hardback book without its dust jacket. A white-gold Cartier Tank gleamed on her wrist.

She'd changed her perfume too. The scent of orange groves wafted towards me as I got up and moved to the door of my cage. I followed the Shepherds' example and pressed my nose against the mesh. I wanted to get a good look at that watch – and some water down my neck.

She settled into the chair and rested the book on her lap.

Maybe gratitude would press the right buttons. 'Thank you for saving my life out there.'

Her only reaction was a faint smile.

Maybe flattery would work. 'I always knew you were a woman of vision . . .'

Her left eyebrow seemed to rise fractionally, but I might have imagined it.

'What's the book?' The cardigan probably meant she was expecting to be there for a while, so I guessed I'd find out sooner or later.

'I think you will find it interesting. Our friends in China said you are British?'

I nodded, trying not to think about the mess they'd made of Sophie and Bruce.

'It's about Elizabeth Tudor. Have you seen the film?'

'I don't get to the pictures much.'

'Sadly, neither do I. But I was fortunate enough to see this one. It tells the story of how her lover, Lord Dudley, plotted against her. But instead of having him executed with the rest of the conspirators, she kept him at court – to remind her how close she was to danger.'

She looked over and smiled at the dogs. 'It's not true, of course. But the lesson remains. We must keep our enemies close.'

The dogs whined their approval.

'There were many plots to kill your queen – yet in the end her enemies knelt to her will. She became the most feared monarch in Europe. She has much to teach us, even today.'

She held up the book and, more importantly, the face of the watch. It was nearly half past seven.

'Lessons not only in leadership, but also in life . . .'

She replaced it in her lap and brought the dogs back into the conversation.

'But, first, we must discuss tomorrow's party. Nick will have something special to wear.'

Her knowing smile was met with an approving bark or two, and I suddenly realized what this morning's pictures were all about. Their secure network must have been buzzing with excitement as the invitations went out: there was a new gimp in town, and – better still – he was a white boy.

'Now . . .' the dogs and I were all ears '. . . we have a number of important guests coming to the house, so we need to decide how they will help Peregrino. I am already concerned about Cesar Ramos. He is too ambitious. We cannot trust him. Peregrino knows this. He will do what he has to do with him.'

She finally turned to me, her eyes no longer reflecting the light. 'Just as he will with the man who killed his father.'

Her tone had the dogs up on tiptoe. It was clearly the reaction she was looking for. None of them seemed to notice that the doors that led into the kitchen area were moving, ever so slightly.

I kept my head low so she couldn't follow my gaze, but then the dogs went ballistic.

For a split second Katya seemed surprised to find she had company, but she recovered just as fast.

'*Madre!*'

'Katya, my dear, how wonderful of you to join us.'

All smiles, Katya kissed Liseth on both cheeks. 'I've been looking for you everywhere, *Madre*. I need your advice . . .'

Liseth's attention was drawn to a stain on Katya's blouse.

Katya nodded sadly. 'Jesús has been showing me the ponies. He thinks one of them burst a vessel during the match. Or after it . . .' She gave me a significant look. 'But they're lovely creatures, aren't they? So strong – so like your son.' She beamed at her mother-in-law-to-be. 'I always say to him, "If you were a pony, my darling, you would be a grey – a noble and dignified leader. Me, I'm a dark horse . . ."'

She seemed careful to avoid my eye now. I did my best to keep my expression neutral, but hung on her every word.

'So, *Madre*, may I ask you something? When Jesús makes his entrance tomorrow night, I will be at his side.

But this creature . . .' her eyes flicked momentarily in my direction '. . . how can we be sure that this creature will know his place?'

Liseth smiled indulgently. 'I think he knows already, my dear. He learned a very important lesson this afternoon.'

'I have a gift for Jesús, Madre. I'd like to present it to him when he announces our marriage. May I show it to you?'

Liseth looked pleased but bemused. 'What is the gift, my dear?'

'Oh, *Madre* – that is a surprise. Shut your eyes for a moment, and open them when I tell you . . .'

Liseth sat stock still, and joined in the game.

Katya leaned into the cupboard and took down one of the heavy ceramic water bowls. Then she tiptoed behind Liseth's chair and raised it high above her head.

22

Liseth was quick.

Her eyes snapped open and her street girl's hands whipped into the air, grabbing Katya's wrists as they fell, using her attacker's own momentum to swing her down and sideways. Katya cannoned into my cage and the bowl crashed to the floor and shattered.

Liseth sprang to her feet and swung a huge round-house punch into Katya's face. I thought she was going to follow up with another, but she skipped back out of range.

Katya's back moulded itself against the steel mesh. I moved my head as close as I could to hers.

Liseth confronted her. She wasn't flapping: her voice was in control. 'You stupid, stupid bitch . . .'

Then she looked more closely at the stain on Katya's blouse. Her face clouded. 'Where is my son?'

Katya said nothing, stayed where she was.

Liseth repeated her question. Her tone was suddenly harsh, almost mechanical. '*Where – is – Peregrino?*'

Katya still didn't answer.

Liseth had had enough. She headed back to the chair and reached for her clutch bag.

I made the most of her distraction, and muttered in Katya's ear, 'Get her against the mesh.'

She didn't react. I banged the cage door then prodded her head through the wire with my fingers.

'Katya, *move*!'

At last she came to her senses and stumbled to her feet. She lunged forward with a shriek so loud it echoed off the walls.

Before she'd even reached Liseth I'd slid my belt out from the back of my jeans and wrapped the buckle end around my right hand.

Katya didn't know what the fuck she was doing. But the street kid did. She took a stride forward and head-butted her, a cool, calm, collected attack.

I slammed my hand against the door frame. 'Katya! Get her over here! Get her to me!'

She was reeling, but finally understood what she had to do. She ran clumsily at Liseth again, threw her arms round the older woman's waist in a crude rugby tackle.

Liseth's fists pounded into Katya's kidneys.

'Keep her going, get her to me! Katya, keep going!'

The dogs were beside themselves, foaming at the mouth.

Liseth had the skill and the instincts of the ghetto, but Katya had height and strength. She kept pushing and managed to slam Liseth's back against the front of my cage.

'Keep her there. Push! *Push!*'

I rammed my fingers as far as I could through the mesh and grabbed as much as I could of her shiny black hair and twisted it around my hand.

Liseth lashed out again at Katya, realized her head was trapped, that her only way out of this was to pull so hard she ripped off her scalp, and began to shout for Miguel. But the sound was as constricted as she was. The mesh rattled as her arms and legs flailed, but Katya's weight kept her pinned.

She tried to jerk her head left and right, but only succeeded in exposing her throat.

I fed the end of the belt through the mesh; Katya looped it around Liseth's neck and back towards me. I scrabbled for it with my left hand while somehow still managing to hang onto the fistful of hair with my right. Sweat now streaked Liseth's cheeks and my fingers slid across her skin.

She understood exactly what was happening. Her head jerked again and again to try to get out of reach. I gripped the leather tongue and worked it further into my hand. The moment I could close around it properly I yanked it back through the mesh. Now, finally, I had maximum pressure across her throat. Liseth thrashed about like she was plugged into the mains. I leaned back and pulled even harder.

The dogs were in a frenzy, yelping and hurling themselves against their cages.

Katya stepped away. A second or two later there was a dull thud and blood spattered across my face. Liseth's head lolled to one side as Katya prepared to hammer it again with a big lump of heavy bowl.

I yelled at her. *'No! Stop! Don't do it!'*

Too late: the bowl crushed the side of Liseth's skull and blood sprayed across the wall.

If the belt hadn't killed her, she was definitely dead now.

I loosened my grip and the body slumped to the floor. But Katya kept right on going. Twice more the bowl smashed down.

'Stop, for fuck's sake! The blood! *Stop!'*

At last, Katya was still.

She stood over Liseth's body, surveying the damage at our feet, and allowed the bowl to slip from her hands. Her yellow blouse was soaked with sweat. The intricate lacework of her bra imprinted itself on the silk as she took short, juddering breaths. Fuck knew what she was going to do next; I needed her to keep switched on.

I yelled above the din of the dogs and banged my fists against the wire. 'Liseth's bag! *Check the bag!'*

My words finally seemed to register. She turned, almost like an automaton.

'Open the bag ... That's good ... The key ...' I rattled the cage door. 'See if she's got a key.'

Drained, she bent down and did as I said. The key appeared, as if by magic. Her hand was shaking so badly I wondered whether she'd be able to introduce it to the lock.

23

'Take your time ... Turn it ... No hurry ... It's all good ...'

I was talking bollocks, obviously, but I needed to soothe her; there was a wild look in her eyes, and I was still on the wrong side of the wire.

I heard the tumblers rotate in the lock and pushed open the gate. I had to push hard to shift Liseth's corpse. Eyes on the door, I slid out of the cage and threaded my belt back through my jeans.

Katya stood trembling in front of me. I couldn't blame her. She'd have seen a few dead bodies in her line of work, but none that she'd just battered to a pulp.

I put a hand on her shoulder and looked into her eyes. 'You kill him?'

'I ... I'm not sure ... I played along, Nick ... but I couldn't take it any more ... He ...'

I gripped both of her shoulders, keeping eye-to-eye, wanting to make sure she knew what she now had to do.

'Later. We have to hide the body. And we've got to get

rid of that blood if we're going to get out of here, OK? The cleaning stuff is just around that corner, the other side of the wall.'

I hoped that anyone looking for Liseth would think she'd taken me off on one of her mad dog walkies or something – anything, really, apart from being the victim of a blood-stained drama in front of an empty cage. I needed to buy some time, buy some doubt – and buy it as quickly as possible. This wasn't over yet.

I emptied everything out of the bin-liner. It was all there except the phone, which was probably hanging out of the back of a pair of Mexican jeans by now. I shoved my stuff back in my pockets and pulled on my Timberlands.

I grabbed a bottle of water from the cabinet and got as much of it down my shirt as my throat. I retrieved Liseth's cell from her clutch bag. It was on, coded up, ready to go. I wasn't surprised. What kind of lunatic was going to risk nicking this fucker?

Katya reappeared with a bucket, mop and dog towels and set to, swabbing up the mess. I tugged the empty bin-liner over what was left of Liseth's head and tied it under her chin.

Once I'd made sure that she wasn't going to leave a nice red trail between there and the tunnel, I pushed in my earphones and called Dino on Liseth's tab.

'Where the fuck have you been, man?'

'I've got Katya.'

'Those fucking dogs, man, shut them the fuck up! She OK?'

'A bit fucked up, but she's breathing.'

She'd finished putting the bits of water bowl and blood-soaked towels into a laundry bag and headed around the corner to replace the mop and cleaning shit.

I put the cell in my shirt pocket and grabbed Liseth's limp wrists, ready to drag her on her arse. I left the key in the lock and started pulling as Katya reappeared and picked up the bag.

I gave her a smile of encouragement. 'Good thinking. We'll take that with us. Bring her handbag too. And as many water bottles as you can carry.'

She did what she needed to and followed. One of Liseth's shoes fell off, so she picked it up, then went ahead to push open the door into stainless-steel heaven.

'Dino, stay with me. We're going into the tunnel. We'll talk then. If there's no signal, I'll come back to you when I'm out.'

We made it through the party kitchen and under the archway to the tunnel entrance. Liseth's arms hit the floor as I tapped the keypad. The door whined open. I pulled Katya into the darkness, then bent down and pulled Liseth in too. Her other shoe slipped off and Katya whisked it across the threshold as the door clicked shut.

She threw the shoes ahead of us and they echoed on the steel walkway. I heard her struggle to regain some sort of normal breathing pattern. I pulled the cell out of my pocket to give us some light.

'Dino – you got me?'

'Fucking A. They both dead?'

'Liseth is for sure. Not sure about Peregrino.'

'Not sure ain't good enough, man.'

'Yep, I know. Wait . . .'

I fumbled for a water bottle and untwisted the top with my teeth. I got some liquid down me, then shone the cell light at Katya. 'Where did you leave him?'

'In the tack room. That's where he tried to—'

'Dino – you get that? Where's the tactical room? Like an ops room, command room, maybe?'

Katya cut in: 'No – the *tack* room. Where they keep the horse tack.'

How was I to know? There weren't too many polo games in my world. I wished there had been: I might have got away.

'Nick, the party, he was going to—'

'Later, Katya. Dino, the tack room, can you get me there?'

'No problem. But you gotta go now, man.'

I gripped Katya's arm and made sure I had her full attention.

'The only three people who know how to get past that keypad are me, Peregrino and the guy on the end of the phone. So get ready for a problem if I fuck up and he isn't dead.

'I'm going to knock four times before hitting the buttons. If you hear that lock unwinding without it, start running down the tunnel and hit the exit bar at the far end. You'll find yourself in a helicopter hangar. Get straight out of there. Run like fuck across the grass and into the scrub. After that, you're on your own. Got it?'

It was pointless telling her about the CamelBak. It would slow her down big-time trying to find it in the dark.

She didn't acknowledge.

'You got that? Do you understand that?'

'Yes.'

'Good. Have you got a watch?'

'Yes.'

'Can you see it in the dark?'

'No.'

'You're going to have to count then. If I'm not back within an hour, go for it. Above all, make distance. And as soon as you've got the chance, ring Anna. That's all I can do for you.'

24

I got the rest of the water down me, then took a deep breath to get my head in gear.

'Dino?'

He was firing on all cylinders. 'Yep!'

'I'm ready.'

'OK – out of the tunnel, turn left, go up the stairs, exactly the same as before, man.'

'Wait. I'm going to put you on FaceTime. Take the call.'

His face uploaded onto the screen, real close and ugly. I dug out my neck pouch and slid the gold iPhone into it so the camera lens was exposed but the screen remained hidden. Instead of getting my face on his screen, he'd be seeing what I was seeing.

'Nothing, I got *nada* . . .'

'I haven't gone anywhere yet. Wait out.'

I hit the bar and light seeped into the tunnel.

Dino swung back into sat-nav mode. If I ever got out of this shit I'd take him on a date with Maud. 'OK, go up the stairs into the banqueting hall, then head right.

It's going to be a motherfucker – you have to get to the other side of the house.'

The hall doors were ajar. I lifted the pouch away from my neck, eased it through the gap, and moved it around.

'Looks clear to me, man. Make entry and go right. I repeat, go right.'

I turned the phone towards me, nodded and put it back in the pouch. I pushed the doors open enough to slip through. I found myself in a large rectangular room with a long, highly polished table down the middle that could have seated thirty or forty people.

Several of the huge oil paintings on the walls were of Peregrino's sisters, but pride of place, at the far end of the room, went to one of him, looking much slimmer and more presidential, standing beside the Mexican flag. Every dinner guest would be under his shadow.

I headed right, as Dino had instructed. I hoped the damaged bits of my body would soon warm up; my feet just had to take the pain.

'You've got a drinks-before-dinner kind of place the other side of this room. Be careful, man, it's one big fuck-off foyer that leads into the hallway. It's really open out there . . .'

I shoved my finger against the left earphone to make sure it stayed in and threw the other round the back of my neck. At least I had half my hearing.

I opened the next door far enough to poke through the iPhone, right at the bottom, and moved it left and right, up and down to show Dino as much of the area as I could.

'Wait . . . wait . . . There's movement. Stay where

you are. Wait . . . OK, it's just house staff. But wait . . .'

I could hear Dino breathing heavily, living the moment as if he were right beside me. 'OK. Move, but be careful. That main door can be opened anytime, and there's always somebody outside. Cross the hallway as if you belong. And don't forget the landings.'

Dino was getting excited. The man with the mallet was about to check out of his nightmares.

I shoved the phone back into my neck pouch so Dino could have a ringside seat at whatever happened next. My Timberlands squeaked gently on the marble as I made my way past plush leather chairs, oriental rugs and massive flower arrangements on every table. As far as I was concerned, the hallway was just an open expanse that I had to cross.

The bottom of the staircase came into view, then the door I'd come out of earlier, and the main entrance. The front door was wide open.

Dino sparked up in my ear. 'Any problems, you go to the right of the stairs. There's a door there that takes you down to the cages.'

I gave him a quick thumbs-up. There wasn't a clever way of getting past the hallway. I had no choice but to keep walking. Not especially fast or slow, just one foot in front of the other.

My eyes swivelled as I passed a window. Two technicals were parked among the SUVs in the floodlit area at the front of the *casa*. A number of bodies milled around them, talking in low tones and swigging from cans as what looked like the domestic staff climbed into the back of one of the Escalades.

I lifted the mic to keep my voice low. 'Where the fuck is everyone?'

'She doesn't like too many people about. She trusts nobody, except maybe the dogs. The staff come, play, eat, whatever, and then go. Even the gardeners are shipped in and out. Only Miguel stays permanently.'

A few more steps and I was past the staircase.

'You see that turning to the right of the stairs, in the far right-hand corner?'

Thumb up.

'Go there. That's it. We got it, man. Keep going.' He was taking every step with me. 'That's it. Keep going.'

I moved out at an angle so I could see down the corridor. Light grey carpet all the way from the threshold, not the concrete slabs of the basement.

'That's good, man. It's all clear.'

I could see that for myself.

'Follow the corridor. Stairs on the left take us down.'

I pulled up the mic. 'You sure? The horses underground?'

'Fuck, no, just the tack room. She didn't like all that shit on display. And she hated having too many places people might hide.'

25

The body lay face up in the middle of the tack-room floor. Even from the doorway I could see that one side of his head was a mass of contusions and puncture wounds. There were a couple in his cheek the exact shape of the steel-pronged tool that lay in his right hand. It looked like a hoof pick I'd seen the Lone Ranger use one Saturday morning when I was glued to the TV as a kid. I guessed she must have left the thing sticking into him when she ran and the last thing he did before he died was pull it out. There were other wounds in his shoulder, some in his chest. He was wearing an open-neck shirt and the damage was clear to see. She'd really gone to town.

I left the door open and stepped into the room. Dino was still banging on in my ear that I had a body to confirm, but I wanted that hoof pick. It had some blood-soaked wire mesh at one end and a steel pin the opposite side that wasn't long enough to do much damage to any organs, but would do until I found something better.

A row of waist-high worktops lined the room, probably where they polished saddles and did other horsy stuff after a game. They were covered with bits of leather and all sorts; I checked them out, in case I came across a better weapon.

When I drew level with Peregrino I gave him a nudge with the toe of my Timberland.

It wasn't good enough for Dino. 'Check his breath, man, or his pulse.'

I knelt alongside him as best I could without getting my jeans soaked with the red stuff, and breathed in a blend of cologne and blood.

I moved two fingers towards the site of his carotid pulse and reached across him for the hoof pick. Bad mistake. His eyes snapped open and his left hand shot up and clutched my throat like a vice. His saliva sprayed my face as he rammed his thumb into my Adam's apple and tried to push it out through the back of my neck.

I struggled to get my hands around his throat too, but he tensed his neck muscles and breathed between his teeth. His right hand, still gripping the hoof pick, soon joined the party. He was trying to crush the life out of me.

My head swelled to bursting point. I was going to black out. I writhed and kicked and flailed. I knew it wasn't working, but there was nothing else I could do. I fought to fill my lungs with oxygen. My Adam's apple felt like it was about to choke me.

'Miguel!'

The shout was feeble, but it was a shout.

I tried to suck in air but my Adam's apple was still glued to the back of my throat. I wrapped myself around Peregrino, hanging on to him like a drowning man, trying to get his arms down and the weapon neutral.

The hoof pick clattered to the floor and I slithered on top of him. I fought for breath. He screamed, more with anger than pain, as he squirmed beneath me. The hoof pick was just over a metre away. My brain shrank. That weapon became my whole world.

I fell sideways, arm outstretched, but Peregrino managed to slow me down, grunting with the effort, trying to beat me to it. My hand was no more than six inches from the hoof pick. I could feel his fingers scrabbling at me. He rolled towards me, and suddenly I couldn't breathe. I couldn't suck in any air.

I touched it with my right hand; tried to turn the thing round. He climbed on top of me, crushing the air from my lungs, forcing the weapon down between me and the tiles. Eighteen, maybe nineteen stone of him pressed down on me. My ribcage started to collapse. I kicked and bucked to try to dislodge him, but it was like being trapped under a grizzly.

I pushed up with my arse, trying to make space below me, trying to spin the weapon round, stripping the skin off my knuckles. If I didn't get some air into my lungs soon, I was going down. Starbursts of light flickered across my retinas; my head was about to explode.

I managed to get the weapon in my hand, but his weight was still pressing down on me too heavily to move it. I twisted left and right, jerking up and down, trying to free my hand.

His hands shifted from my throat to my arms. I rolled onto my right side and jabbed the hoof pick into his wrist. He shrieked and recoiled, clutching the wound. I could see bone and blood as I lay there trying to breathe. The only sound louder than my rasping attempts to regain my breath was a yell from the end of the corridor.

I had to act. I sat up, bringing my head level with the worktop. My fuzzy vision locked onto a large glass bottle, shaped like a two-litre moulded-plastic milk container, complete with handle. It looked like it held some kind of brown liquid. Whatever it was, most of the label was taken up with a big yellow flame warning graphic.

'Miguel!'

Peregrino was a couple of metres to one side of me and the bottle was one metre to the other. I squinted at the heavy glass canister and, taking a deep breath, I launched myself off the floor.

Muffled shouts came from halfway down the corridor. That didn't matter: the bottle did. Jabbing out my arm like I was throwing a punch, I slipped my fingers around its neck, gripped hard and swung round. Focusing on his head, I took three paces towards him, brandishing my fistful of bottle like a bludgeon. I closed in, my eyes fixed on his face, and swung the bottle downwards, making contact above his cheek-bone. His skin folded over below his eye, then split open. He gave a scream that echoed round the room.

His scream was answered by a shout from the corridor.

I lashed out again. The heavy glass hammered twice against his skull, both times with such force that my arm jarred as it made contact. I jumped onto his chest and continued to rain blows on the top of his head.

Somewhere in the back of my mind I knew I'd lost it, but I didn't care.

Three times there was a crunching, cracking sound as glass hit bone and tooth. Not even a top-of-the-range Jesus for Peace dental plan was going to save his day.

The glass shattered. Liquid erupted from inside, filling the room with a stink like ammonia and menthol.

I raised my hand, ready to hammer him again, but stopped myself. I'd done enough. Thick, almost brown blood oozed from his head wounds. His stare was empty, eyes wide open, pupils fully dilated.

I glanced down and read the label. It was horse liniment, *altamente inflamable*, and his clothes were soaking it up like blotting paper.

He was choking now. Wheezing, gurgling noises tumbled from his nose and mouth. His hair soaked up the spilled contents of the bottle.

I knew I couldn't just lie there watching him; I knew I had to get up.

Miguel hurtled into the room, drawing down his bright yellow weapon. He wasn't about to fuck up and shoot his boss.

I heard the electronic initiation, the nitrogen kicking off the barbs, and all I could do was drop behind Peregrino and use him as my shield.

26

The barbs crackled like a bonfire as they made contact, but I felt no pain.

Peregrino juddered, and then there was a vivid flash, yellow and orange like an oil-rig flare, as the liniment combusted and he burst into flames.

His screams echoed up and down the corridor as his body sizzled and my lungs filled with the acrid, gagging stench of burning flesh and hair.

Within seconds he was a human torch, his hands and cheeks melting, the skin bubbling and flaking away. His eyes pierced through what was left of his charred features like those of a demon from Hell.

I rolled away from him, my hands against my face for protection, but I was too late. My shirtsleeve and the side of my jeans ignited. Peregrino's arms and legs were bouncing around the floor like a puppet dancing a horizontal reel. He squealed like a pig, his blistered hands outstretched as he called for his mama and the fire peeled back his lips in a hideous grin.

Miguel pulled a fire blanket off the wall; I knew it

wasn't for me. I kept low as he barrelled into the room, then jumped up and scrambled round the corner, swatting frantically at my clothes to kill the flames.

I finally got the better of them, but smoke still billowed around me as I ran. I kept on going, my hand on the pouch to stop it bouncing into my face. I passed more expanses of bare concrete left and right – more admin cubes like on the other side of the house.

I turned left by the tack room and reached the steps. I threw myself up them three at a time, still pursued by ear-splitting screams.

Swivelling right, I pounded down the carpeted corridor towards the hallway. As my boots hit the marble, the hired help poured into the *casa* from the technicals, hollering, weapons up, confused.

I ran across the hallway shouting, '*Fuego! Fuego! Fuego!*' I motioned behind me. 'El Peregrino! *Fuego! Fuego!*'

They headed the way I'd pointed and I lunged for the door under the stairs, but as soon as I came level with the front entrance and saw the vehicles gleaming in the floodlights, I had a change of plan.

Miguel would know where the tunnel started and where it ended. He'd also know that only Liseth and Peregrino had the combination – so if he couldn't find Liseth, where was she going to be, and where was she going to emerge? It would only be a matter of time before he went to the hangar – and he might get there before we did.

I took the nearest technical. The keys were in the ignition.

It was pointless trying to sabotage the others. There were too many of the fuckers: it would take too long.

I flicked it into drive and headed for the road to the hangar, not wanting to leave sign on the grass; they'd have to work that one out for themselves. Behind me, the HK spun on its firing post, a box of 5.56 link sliding around on the flatbed beneath it.

I kept one eye glued to the rear-view; there was no follow-up yet. I guessed they were flapping about Peregrino, and running around looking for Liseth. Miguel would save me for afters.

I braked to a halt, with the tailgate protruding far enough from the corner of the hangar to give me an arc of fire. I climbed onto it, checked back to the house, and brought the MG4's cocking lever down into its horizontal position. The handle was loose on its way back and forward; the working parts were already to the rear, cocked for when I squeezed the trigger.

There was still no threat emerging from the flood-lit house. And nothing outside looked any different from last night.

I pushed the cocking lever back into its upright position then jumped off and made for the inside of the hangar, hoping like fuck that Katya was this end of the tunnel – and fearing that she might have lost count and already legged it into the scrub.

27

I knocked four times. The whirring of the lock was a whole lot quieter than my breathing.

'*Katya!*'

I propped the door open with the tool-box and moved inside.

'Katya, it's Nick! Hurry up – come to me. On me! *On me!*'

My shouts echoed down the tunnel. There was nothing in there to absorb them. In the darkness, I skimmed a hand along the concrete and was soon pushing against thin air. I turned into the money cave.

'*Katya!*'

I could hear her reply, but I couldn't understand it. 'Move to this end! Move to the hangar end! Hurry. Move!'

I heard her again, this time a bit louder.

'Come on! On me! On me!'

As I swung one of the thirty-kilo bags onto my back, a strap over each shoulder, I heard the steel walkway taking a pounding.

'Nick?'

She appeared out of the gloom and I pointed her at the nearest two bags. 'Take these fuckers.'

'They're at the kitchen door, Nick.'

I picked up a fourth and fifth bag, one in each hand, and led her back the way I'd come.

It had been a while since I'd hefted a ninety-kilo load, but this was a whole lot more worthwhile than a Bergen full of rocks. Leaning forward, I half shuffled, half ran towards the technical, with Katya not too far behind me. As I reached the wagon the irrigation system went apeshit and started treating the ranch to its nightly downpour. I dumped the bags on the flatbed and hauled myself up to man the gun.

Katya emerged from the hangar.

'Fucking – hurry – up!'

Yelling at her wasn't going to win me a Tree-hugger of the Year Award, but I wanted her close – really, really close.

Vehicles were now kicking off at the front of the house, their headlamp beams bouncing all over the sky. I checked the link, making sure there weren't any obvious kinks, but kept eyes on the movements of Miguel's crew. Where the fuck were they going?

The first of Katya's bags joined mine, then the second.

'You drive.' I turned and pointed back towards the rear of the *casa*, well past where I'd broken cover last night.

'I want you to drive straight there, OK? But only when I say.'

She nodded, but I didn't want to leave anything to chance. 'You see where I mean?'

'Got it.'

'Don't move until I bang on the roof of the cab, OK?'

'OK.'

She jumped in behind the wheel and fired up the windscreen wipers against the sprinkler spray as two of Miguel's wagons surged our way along the concrete.

I gave them a couple of hundred metres, making sure the butt was in my right shoulder, left hand gripping it nice and tight, right hand on the pistol grip. I rested the pad of my forefinger on the trigger, ready to take up first pressure. As the lead wagon drew nearer, I closed my left eye and adjusted the weapon until the foresight rested just above its headlights.

When they were about four hundred metres away I started hosing them down with rapid five-shot bursts, controlling the rate of fire rather than just going for it. Each time I squeezed the trigger, the working parts pushed rounds from the feed tray into the chamber, then sucked the empty cases out again. They bounced off my Timberlands as the disintegrating link rattled across the flatbed.

The wagons kept moving towards us; I kept up the five-round routine in return. White tracer pinged off their engine blocks and spun wildly into the air like miniature Catherine wheels until their propellant burned out. They veered off across the grass after the third or fourth burst, once they'd worked out what was going on and their windscreens were paying the price. Then they split up.

I fired at what I could see through the sprinkler haze, at where I thought their drivers might be. One stopped. Fuel must have been leaking from a ruptured tank. The tracer ignited it. The whole area was suddenly a riot of yellow and orange.

The other technical carried on coming, returning fire manically from the rear. I kept my finger on the trigger until there was nothing but a *clunk* from the working parts as they went forwards but had no more rounds to push into the chamber. I spun round and pounded on the cab roof. 'Go, go, go!'

She put her foot down and drove off like a maniac – far too fast, slewing, skidding, almost losing it in the water haze. I dropped to my knees to stop myself falling out and banged on the window. 'Left! Further left!'

We careered past the rear of the *casa*, then the Lincoln Memorial, which was about to welcome a couple of extra guests.

I checked behind me and couldn't see any follow-up. We were nearly at the edge of the scrub. 'Slower! Keep control! Slow down! Stop. *Stop here!*'

She braked to a halt. I vaulted off the flatbed and grabbed my three bags. She jumped out of the cab and followed suit; she didn't ask why, or what was inside them.

Checking continuously behind me, I helped her thread each arm through the handles of the first, then threw the second over the top so that they looked like a sagging T. I did the same with mine, but with two on top. It was the only way to carry a big load; the higher on your shoulder, the less effort required.

'OK, stay close. If you get lost, don't shout. I'll find you. Got that? But keep close and there'll be no drama.'

There were still no headlights approaching through the spray, but there would be. I headed into the scrub. We had eight, maybe nine, hours of darkness ahead.

I wanted to get in nice and deep, then double back for the CamelBak.

28

I headed half-right from the vehicle and plunged about a hundred metres through the foliage before I stopped to listen. Then I bounced up and down on the balls of my feet, trying to adjust the weight on my back.

It was just like the old days: a Bergen as big as a removal van, straps cutting into my shoulders, leaning forward to relieve the weight because it was too much hassle getting the fucking thing off and back on.

Katya bumped into me. Her breath came in ragged snorts.

'Lean forward. Put your hands on your thighs. Let them take the weight.'

'How far, Nick?'

'Later.'

She stood there, trying to control her breath.

I couldn't hear any sign of pursuit, so I grabbed the earphones and moved closer to Katya. I pulled the iPhone out of the pouch and shielded it with my hand. Dino's face filled the screen.

I lifted the mic to my mouth. 'You hear me?'

'Fucking A, I'm still here. But I can't see shit, man. You both OK?'

'Both good. We've got you. We can see you.'

He burst into a smile, the first real one I'd seen from him in two decades. 'Is he dead?'

'Didn't you see what happened?'

He nodded. 'Kind of. But is he dead?'

'Mate, if he's not, he's Superman.'

Dino's smile evaporated. 'You don't *know* he's dead?'

'I wasn't going to go back in there and check his pulse, was I? He was on his last legs even before he blew up. But enough of this shit. I'm going to bin this phone now – you bin your SIM, too. I'll call you at home as soon as possible and you can work out how the fuck to get us out of here.'

The smile returned. 'No *problema*. I'm already on it – see?'

He swept the camera around the room he was sitting in. He wasn't at home. No dark wood, just lots of cheap yellow pine. Dino zoomed through a glass sliding door to the neon-splashed Costera, where the Acapulco party people were gearing themselves up for a night out on the dancing juice.

Dino reappeared centre-screen. 'I listened to you, man. I really did. I get it. I get that those two fucks only existed in my head. I'm here for you.'

I didn't know whether to laugh or cry.

'Here's the deal, man. I'll be on the western outskirts of El Veintiuno – the Acapulco side – about an hour after first light. Copy?'

'Got it.'

'I'll be in a white Chevrolet van. You're going to have

to move ass and find me. I'm not getting out of that fucking van.'

'Yep, got it. Bin your SIM now, mate.'

I erased the call log. It wouldn't stop them if they checked the cell system, but it would slow them down a little.

I shoved the earphones into the pouch and threw my SIM card into the undergrowth.

I could hear vehicles closing in on our abandoned technical as I led Katya towards the CamelBak.

A long burst of 5.56 raked the scrub about a hundred metres behind us. They were hoping to drop us now and maybe pick us up in the morning.

The rounds cracked as they went supersonic, then thudded into the dust ahead and to the side of us as they hosed down the whole area, until all I could hear was an almost rhythmic *crack thump, crack thump, crack thump* as they opened up big-time.

'Keep going, Katya. Stay close!'

It was only effective fire when one of us went down. The trick was to get out of the arc, not stay static in it.

They slammed into the thorn bushes, still slightly ahead and to my left. 'Stay with me!'

We had cover from view but not from fire; dead ground would give us both.

'We've got to keep moving!'

The next thing I heard was a strangulated scream behind me. Half gasp, half howl of pain.

Another burst ripped through the scrub and the rounds gave a high-pitched whine as they ricocheted off the rocks.

The fire became increasingly relentless as I moved back towards the screams, keeping as low as possible.

'Where the fuck *are* you?'

'Here . . . here. I'm sorry . . .' She groaned. 'I thought I'd been hit. It must have been rock splinters.'

'Get up and keep close, like I told you. They aren't firing at us. They're firing blind. You'll know if you're hit.'

She might have nodded, then realized I couldn't see her, because it was a while before I got an answer.

'I'm good.'

'Pick up that bag and stay close.'

29

Several million candle-power lit up the darkness around us. Miguel's lads loosed off a couple of bursts along it. I felt a thump as a round rammed into the ground far too close to us. The spotlight blazed left and right, searching for targets, creating shadows as it passed through the scrub.

'Katya, *move your arse.*'

We'd reached dead ground but it had taken far too long to get there. You have to move at the speed of the slowest; that's just how it is if you want to keep together, and she wasn't used to carrying a load.

Katya shuffled up alongside me and I gave her thirty seconds before we moved on. The good news was that the pain in my arse from the polo mallet had now melted away. Also, with the stars out, and a quarter-moon, it was easier to see. I felt good about that, even though it meant it was easier for them, too, to see us if they got close enough.

I still led the way, breaking the trail, then stopping but no longer turning to allow Katya to catch up. When

I heard her move up behind me I'd go on a few more steps.

It took me a while to grasp that she was lagging further and further behind. I'd been so determined to make distance that I hadn't noticed how much she was slowing down.

There was still a good chance she might lose me in the dark and I didn't want to have to run around calling for her. I pulled my belt from my jeans, made one end into a noose and pulled it tight round her wrist. I gripped the other end along with the bag handle cutting into my shoulder.

I stood still, knees bent, waiting to regain my breath. I could see Katya's face in the ambient light. She was in a bad way: her hair was sticking up all over the place; she was covered with dust and blood.

'Katya, look at me.' I needed her to be in no doubt about what I expected of her. When people flap, they nod and agree to everything without really under-standing what's being said. 'We've *got* to stay together.' I looked into her eyes for a sign of acknowledgement. 'Don't worry, it's not far.'

That wasn't true but, fuck it, there's a time and a place . . .

I set off again, lengthening my stride, tugging on the belt, trying to keep upright on the slippery ground as I urged her on. Her gasps and cries told me that her bare flesh was getting zapped left and right by the thorn bushes. I knew she was suffering, but all I could do was grip her and plunge on. At least I knew she was breathing.

I tripped and went down, letting go of the belt so I didn't take her with me. My two loose top bags fell into the dirt. My knees hit rock and felt like they were on fire, but I stayed where I was, screwing up my face as I waited for it to die down. There was nothing more I could do. I just hoped I hadn't smashed a kneecap. My chest heaved as I tried to catch my breath.

'Nick?'

I grabbed her hand. 'Give me a minute.'

I shrugged the straps off my shoulders and let the third bag fall. It was as if I was floating on air.

Katya dropped her bags next to me as another burst of fire kicked off on the higher ground. Her brain was probably telling her to get moving, but her body was begging her to stay where she was. This time her body was going to win.

'I've got to get my backpack. It's a bit further uphill. You stay here with the bags. Don't move, don't make any noise. I'll be ten minutes max. If there's a drama, you'll hear it. And you'll know if you have to get moving without me. Take what you can carry and try to get to Dino.' I explained the pick-up details to her. 'If you don't make it to the road on time, you're on your own.'

I didn't wait for an answer because I didn't need one. I turned towards the *casa* and headed uphill. My throat was parched; fuck knew what Katya's was like.

30

I crawled to the edge of the scrub on my stomach. There was still plenty of commotion in the distance; screaming and hollering punctuated by automatic fire. Somebody – maybe Miguel – was having a ballistic fit.

The technical was still burning, about five hundred metres away by the *casa*. To my right, about four hundred along the scrub-line, at the point where we had entered it, there was another of the fuckers, its power beam jerking left and right across the vegetation. The gunner reacted to the shadows with another long burst.

Fuck 'em. I was here to work out where I was in relation to my passport. No way was I leaving that in a hole in the ground. I wanted to get back to Moscow ASAP. I didn't want to spend days at the consulate trying to get a replacement using some bullshit 'I've been mugged' story.

I checked my position in relation to the hangar and knew I had to move twenty metres left before going back into the scrub.

I could see headlights approaching the *casa* – a line of

vehicles coming up the tarmac road, red and blue flashes glimmering through the irrigation haze. I wasn't that worried about them right now. *Vigilantes*, local police – I didn't give a shit who they were. In the dark they'd do no more than contain the area or mince around in the scrub shooting at each other. Concealment was my best weapon.

At first light, however, it would be a different story.

31

We covered seven hard Ks, stopping every hundred or so paces and resting without taking the bags off, then every hour for ten minutes with them all at our feet. Katya didn't complain. She must have guessed what they contained.

I crested a rise and moved downhill with her coughing and panting behind me. Her lungs were heaving. If I was feeling bad, she must have been in all kinds of shit.

My CamelBak was safely in the bag on my shoulders now that we had shared what was left in the reservoir. Maybe I was too busy congratulating myself on getting that bit right, because my boot landed awkwardly on a rock and I tumbled. I knew not to resist: it would cause me even more injury and we still had a long way to go. Katya fought to break free and save herself, but it was too late. She and her bags came down on top of me.

She tried to wriggle out of her straps as I just lay there, her hair in my face, unable to do anything until she'd sorted herself.

'My ankle, Nick . . .'

As soon as she'd managed to roll off me I slid the straps off my shoulders and crawled over to her.

'Which one?'

'Left. I felt it go.'

I could see the shape of her calf in the moonlight and ran my fingers gently over the injury.

'Where does it hurt most? Over the horizontal anterior talofibular ligament?' You don't often get the chance to ask a girl that sort of shit. I hoped for a yes. It would indicate less damage than a tear in the major calcaneofibular ligament. Even a mild sprain might also involve other bones and ligaments, but I didn't have an X-ray unit immediately to hand. Not that it made much difference: no matter what condition they were in, she still needed to get one foot in front of the other.

'It's definitely the horizontal anterior talofibular.'

'So it could be worse.'

She didn't ask me why I assumed my medical knowledge trumped hers.

I pulled off my shirt and ripped away the sleeves. I strapped up her ankle as tightly as I possibly could. It would loosen as she walked, but any support was better than none.

'I'm afraid you've still got to move on it. Not far, though – maybe three Ks.'

She stood, pushing down on my shoulder as she tried to put some weight on it. 'Give me a minute.'

I could see the glimmer of first light beyond the horizon. 'Time's up.'

I shouldered my first bag again and piled on the other two. She struggled to lift even one. I picked up her two, then had second thoughts. I hoisted one onto my right shoulder and left the other in the dust. We wouldn't have a dog's chance of finding it again, but maybe a deserving local would stumble across a nice Christmas bonus.

She didn't say anything; she didn't need to.

'And I'll still move faster than you.'

She started to laugh, but I was too busy gulping in oxygen to join her as I waddled towards the dawn.

32

We kept going for about forty minutes. I had to stop every twenty paces or so to catch my breath and ease the pain in my back, thighs and arms.

Katya had started to shiver uncontrollably. Her hair was wet with sweat and flat against her head. Her blouse was drenched. Dried blood ringed her nostrils; blood was also seeping from cuts on her legs where they weren't already smothered in dirt and leaf litter. But she was still with me and we were nearly there.

'I . . . I've had it, Nick . . .' She faltered. 'Everything's spinning . . . Please . . . We have to stop . . .'

'No time. We have to keep going. You understand that, don't you? We're fucked if we don't.'

The only reaction I got from her was a low moan.

'Katya, look at me!' I cupped her chin in my hand. 'We *must* go on. We don't have any choice. You must help me, OK?' I tried to get eye-to-eye. 'There's nothing more I can do to help you here. You've got to dig deep . . .'

We moved on, painfully slowly.

'Not far now . . .'

Her shoulders jerked as she fought to contain the sobs. She was slipping beyond exhaustion. 'We're going to be . . . OK . . . aren't we?'

I nodded. 'It's a fucker. But it's not going to kill us.' It was my hundredth lie of the night.

She didn't reply. She had almost no strength left now. Neither did I, but we had to crack on.

Dino was so close now I could almost smell the disinfectant.

33

El Veintiuno

8 September 2011

The sun was trying its hardest to break cover from the high ground and join the clear sky above us. We'd been lying in the shit and the dust for less than an hour. Half the landscape was stuck to our sweat-soaked clothes, but when you're fucked and static your head tells you you're in a five-star spa.

My feet throbbed. Two big fuck-off blisters had joined the party: one felt like it covered the whole of my left heel; the other was swilling around on the ball of my right foot. I hadn't bothered checking out the damage; I didn't want to take my boots off again because I didn't want the pain of putting them back on. The right one had burst; the left hadn't joined it yet, but I knew it would – the grit that had found its way into my boots during the night would see to that.

They weren't as bad as Katya's ankle, though. It looked like an over-inflated football. Her lips were also swollen and badly split, but I knew she'd have accepted any amount of pain if it meant getting a drink. We were both gagging for water.

We lay several metres back from the road, still in the cover of the scrub. I could see what I needed of the tarmac, past the piles of discarded and sun-faded bottles and cans. A couple of crows did their stuff in the distance.

I'd got to check out the bottom half of a rusty pick-up heading towards the coast; otherwise there had been no movement, no sound in the last hour, apart from Katya still trying to catch her breath.

I pulled her wrist towards me to check her watch again. It was 07.28. She looked like she'd be prepared to lie there for ever.

'Nick . . .'

She went silent again, for so long that I had to re-assure myself that she was still breathing. Her dust-caked face made her look like a heavily made-up punch dummy.

'How . . . did you find me?'

'It doesn't matter, does it? I did, and we're here.' I gave her a smile and got my eyes back on the road. 'So it's all good.'

'You didn't trust me, did you?'

'That was my mistake. I didn't know what the fuck you were up to, right from that moment in your flat.'

She rested her hand on my wrist. 'I don't blame you. I should have said . . . something . . . I didn't know you could . . . help.'

'This sort of shit is all I'm really good for.'

'I saw you ... I saw you ... with *her* ... outside, yesterday. She told me ... to watch from the house. She knew you were coming ... She even showed me ... where they were going to keep you ...'

She gently rubbed my arm.

'He was going to kill you ... but Liseth stopped him. She wanted ... to deal with you at the party ... To encourage the others ... He told me ... he was going to slit your throat on the grass ... and pull your tongue through it ... Then he was going to shoot you.'

I put a hand on hers to comfort her but kept my eyes on the road.

'Listen, thanks for what you did back there. You did good ...'

It didn't have the effect I was hoping for: she started to well up.

'He – he raped me, Nick ... over and over. He had to be in control ... He wanted me in a harness ... down there ... I couldn't ... wouldn't ... do it. I lashed out ... with the first thing I could lay my hands on ... I wasn't even thinking ... what I was doing ... what I was going to do next ... I just wanted him *dead* ... Then all I could think of was getting to you ... And when I saw Liseth ... I just wanted to kill her too.'

'We're safe now.' I squeezed her hand. 'Dino will be here soon.'

She tried to make herself more comfortable, resting her head against one of the dust-laden bags.

'What's going to happen ... to all this?'

'I'll explain when we're in the wagon. You'll like Dino. He's a bit of a miserable fucker, but you'll like him. Let's do this later – in the wagon.'

She fell silent.

521

I kept my eyes, ears and head totally focused on the road.

'I'm so sorry . . . you and Anna . . . getting dragged into this . . . But they couldn't find Roman . . .'

'Your brother?' I turned back to her.

She nodded, and the tears welled up again. There were going to be a lot more of them once we were in the wagon. Relief can do that after a drama.

My eyes swivelled back to the road.

This really wasn't the time for a sob-fest and a big in-depth chat, but she was clearly in the mood. 'Where is he? You tucked him away?'

'I don't know . . . I didn't want to . . . in case they made me tell them . . . He has . . . a wife, a family . . . I told him . . . leave Russia . . . go . . . anywhere.'

'Any idea where he is?'

She sniffed. 'Maybe Cuba . . .' She fell silent again.

A wagon swung by. I saw the bottom half of a blue-cabbed truck dragging a trailer-load of logs, coming from the direction of Acapulco and heading for Mexico City.

Katya didn't speak again until some time after the truck had gone. 'How's the baby, Nick?'

I glanced at the tears carving grooves in the dirt on her cheeks. 'Last I heard, he's doing great. Gaining weight, looking good.'

She tried to smile but her lips wouldn't obey. 'Have you chosen a name for him yet?'

'Not yet. But I'm pretty sure we won't be calling him Jesús.'

34

Another vehicle approached from the Acapulco side, more slowly than anything else that had come our way. I watched the bottom half of a clean white van crawl past, then kick up a little dust cloud as it veered off the tarmac.

I got to my knees, waited for it to stop.

Katya looked at me as if I had all the answers.

'Wait here.'

I wasn't sure why I said that. It wasn't as if she had other plans for the morning.

I got to my feet and hobbled away, like a ninety-year-old. My blisters wept and my leg muscles screamed with every step. I dragged myself slowly towards the road, keeping low, at the edge of the scrub. A white Chevrolet was parked up, about thirty metres along the road, engine running. But just because it was white, static and on time didn't mean Dino was inside it.

I moved back into the scrub and paralleled the verge towards the sound of the gently idling engine. Eventually I got level with the cab.

Dino wasn't looking a hundred per cent happy; perhaps he was reliving the last time he was in that neck of the woods. As soon as he spotted me, I heard the clunk of the central locking. He thumbed vigorously over his shoulder, signalling me to get into the back, but I went for the passenger door instead.

A waft of the familiar disinfectant smell greeted me as I opened it. I wasn't worried, as long as he could still function. Besides, it was strangely reassuring.

'In the back, man – out of sight – in the back!'

He checked his mirrors frantically. 'Where the fuck is she, man?'

'Go back thirty.'

'She OK?'

'Not in showroom condition, but she'll scrub up fine. Go back down the road and throw those doors open.' I gave him a big smile. 'Cheer up, mate – you're going to like this next bit a lot.'

I moved back into the scrub and headed towards Katya, my CamelBak and the moneybags as Dino swung a 180 on the tarmac and headed for his new pick-up point.

EPILOGUE

1

Perinatal Clinic, Moscow

14 September 2011
05.28 hrs

The lift opened and its bright light elbowed its way into the gloom of Anna's floor.

The blinds were closed on the internal windows at the far end of the corridor. I started towards them, a bulging bin-liner in each hand. I didn't exactly have a spring in my step, but my limp had improved since the burst blisters had warmed up under their dressings. I was glad to be back, though, even if my face looked like it never wanted to go out in public again.

The weather was colder, though maybe that was because I was only hours away from sweating it out in the scrub. I wondered what the temperature was going to be like with Anna today. Not surprisingly, she hadn't been too happy about having a dead body in the flat and never wanted to return to it. She'd spelt that out to me when I'd phoned from Mexico. Fair one: it was why I'd gone and collected everything a mother and baby could need from the box room. She was going to have to stay at the clinic until the boy was OK enough to leave.

There was no sign of Mr Lover Man or Genghis. Frank had called them off once Dino had picked us up and I'd told him the heat was off. I didn't know what Miguel would get up to next, but he hadn't struck me as a lad with global ambitions. For that matter, he wasn't even too clever with a Taser.

I'd called Frank from Baja California. Dino had driven us straight there from El Veintiuno. The cartels had no presence up in the north-west. There was nothing for them to fight over, apart from sand and tourists hooked on whale-spotting – and that was what had got me thinking about Frank.

I tapped gently and opened the door. The only light came from the glow of the machinery; the only sounds the gentle bleeps of the baby monitors. The room was warm and it smelt of sleep, just as it should.

I left the bags on the highly polished tiles and walked over to the incubator. A much healthier-looking baby gazed back at me. There were still tubes everywhere and sensors all over his chest and abdomen, but he seemed a bit bigger and stronger. The beanie had come off. He didn't have much hair, but his skin was pink.

Anna stirred behind me and the sheets rustled. Instinct had told her someone was near her child and she needed to check it out.

'Nicholas?'

2

I gave her a subdued 'Hello', partly because she'd only just woken up, partly because the darkness of the room and gentle bleeping noises somehow dictated it.

I leaned over and brushed a strand or two of hair away from her face so I could kiss her. She smelt the same as the room.

She sighed and rubbed her eyes, then reached over and picked up the small plastic clock on the bedside cabinet.

'I know, I know, I'm sorry ... But I thought, Why hang about in the flat? I've missed you guys.' I thumbed behind me. 'And I brought the stuff.'

The sheets rustled again as she sorted herself out, adjusting the pillow so she could sit up.

'He's looking good, isn't he?'

She gave a gentle smile. 'He's doing really well. I see a difference in him every day. We might be able to leave in a couple of weeks if he keeps it up.'

I sat on the side of the bed, wincing a bit as the mallet wound on my shin reminded me of unhappier days.

She looked quizzical, then cupped my face in her hands and kissed me softly on the forehead. She dropped her hands again and I slipped mine around hers.

Anna nodded at the iPhone sitting in a charger on the bedside cabinet. 'Katya called last night while you were in the air. She says to tell you Dino sits at the back window twenty-four/seven, whatever that means.'

I grinned as I pictured him there. It wasn't as if he could run the thirty metres to stop anyone digging it up. 'Good to hear he's looking after our money!'

I traced my thumbs across the back of her hands. 'It's all OK now, Anna. The drama's over. We're safe.'

The baby monitors gave another bleep or two and the smile faded from her eyes. I felt her withdraw from me again. 'Really, Nicholas? You really think everything is good? That we are safe? Really? You know there will always be somebody from your past. Someone somewhere who wants to hurt you. I knew this from the start. I knew what you were. I knew what I was getting into. But that was OK. I wanted *you*. But that was then, Nicholas . . . Now we have someone else to think about.'

'Let's give it a little time, yeah? Let things settle down. Get us sorted with a house at least.'

She studied my face. 'Time isn't the problem, though, is it?'

She wasn't leaking any tears. It was too serious for that.

She stared into my eyes with steely determination. 'Nicholas, please listen. You may think of these things as "dramas". You may tell yourself that. But in the real world they are *dangers*. We cannot have our child waiting for *danger* to come his way.

'I don't think you pick fights, Nicholas. But they sure pick you. Don't you get that? You were the kid who always got into fights at school and didn't know why. How do I know that? I know it because trouble always finds you. Nothing's going to change that – it's the way you are.'

She grabbed hold of my wrists, brought my hands up to her face and kissed them. 'Nothing will change, you know that. Look at the state of you . . .'

I pulled away enough to have eye-to-eye. 'But we've got to give it a go, haven't we?'

She sighed. 'I *know* you, Nicholas. And I know that whatever you did while you were away you enjoyed it. So it's not just about the danger coming *your* way. It's about the people around you. They're *scared*. *I*'m scared – for our child, even for myself, now.

'It's not that you don't see danger, I know that. But you do see it differently. You look at it as a challenge – a game, even. You're wired that way. That's who you are – and we can't have that near our child, no matter how much I care for you.'

She looked across to check the baby. It was pointless arguing; I knew I'd lose. After all, we both knew she was right.

She exhaled slowly and I could feel the warmth of her breath on my hands.

'Let's talk about all that later. Let's get both you guys out of here, into a new house – a new start.'

Her smile returned – but it was her bleak smile, not her happy one. 'Go house-hunting, Nicholas, and then come back this afternoon when the baby's awake and we'll start thinking of a name. I know you love that little man. I know you'll make a wonderful father ... but ... it's more complicated than that ...'

She let go of my hands.

I stood up and kissed her forehead. 'At least we can agree on one thing: no happy snaps, eh?'

I finally got what I was after: a real smile.

'You need anything else from the flat? I'm going to get myself sorted first.'

'If you see any good places, do a video.'

I went over to the incubator and had one last long look at our son. I couldn't touch him yet, but I hoped there'd still be time enough for that. 'Mate, see you later.'

And then I nodded and walked out.

3

It took the best part of an hour to get anywhere near the apartment in the morning rush. I had one more set of lights to go before I was having a shit-shave-shower and then heading out to the real-estate people. I'd get back to Anna in the afternoon, and this evening I'd clean up the flat for the rental guys to check it out for the handover. Frank's guys had removed the body, but hadn't done anything about the damage – or the pool of dried vomit the brown-leather jackets had left as a souvenir.

The cash came to twelve million dollars in hundred-dollar bills, nicely banded up in $100,000 bundles, which made the maths easy. Owning big chunks of cash was all well and good, but getting it into the real world wasn't straightforward. It wasn't like you could turn up at the Halifax and open an account with a holdall full of greenbacks. So once Dino, Katya and I were holed up in a holiday shack overlooking a picture-postcard bay on the Pacific coast, we buried the bags about thirty metres from the window and I'd made the call to Peredelkino.

Frank was his usual unflappable self as he offered to ease the cash into the real world for only twenty-five cents in the dollar. At that rate he was doing us a favour, he said, and who were we to argue? So Frank, great humanitarian that he was, took on the problem, and was going to take a three-million-dollar cut. It wouldn't exactly be a life-changer for him. That sort of money wouldn't cover much more than his annual mineral-water bill. But for the price Frank was going to throw in getting the passport-and-visa-less Katya out of Mexico at the same time as the cash. Frank would spit Katya out in Moscow, where she could sort herself out, then he'd launder the money through property and artwork companies, or whatever. It was going to take a couple of months before we got our thirds, but I knew he wouldn't let us down.

We talked about what we were going to do with our share while we were trying to sort out a flight to get me home – as you do.

Dino's paranoia was back, but at least it meant he kept his eyes glued on the cash. And Katya was now on his case, making sure he didn't fuck himself up.

I'd kept my promise; now it was his turn. He wanted his family back, and a normal life. I had no idea whether that was going to happen – but he was going to have three million dollars with which to give it his best shot, and that had to be good enough.

As soon as Frank had worked his magic, Katya was going to go and look for her brother. How long that would take, and where it would lead her, none of us knew.

I'd wiped the slate clean with Frank, and not just on the currency exchange. The Narcopulco locals were already singing new folk songs about the death of Peregrino, and Frank was going to fill the vacuum, like he had when the Iron Curtain was pulled down. Right place, right time – it was his special talent. The cartels could kick the shit out of each other as much as they liked, as far as he was concerned, but there was still work to be done.

The cash would come in handy for Anna and me, but it wasn't going towards a yacht in the Bahamas.

4

The final set of lights seemed to keep turning red every thirty seconds, but I finally covered the remaining two hundred metres and turned down the ramp into our basement car park.

I was going to miss this place. I was going to miss the views over the Moskva River and Borodinsky Bridge. I was even going to miss the world's most miserable front-desk jockeys.

There had been a brand-new government-issue concierge sitting there this morning, with the TV on full blast, smoking something that smelt like boiling tarmac. It was good to know the factory that made these old men was still going strong. The production line turned out only one model: guys who hated everything and everyone in creation.

I wound down my window and thrust my battered face towards the camera so Comrade Misery-guts upstairs could check my registration against the vehicle log and lift the shutter. It would have been easier to install a card-entry system, of course, but that would have meant fewer jobs for the boys. A lot of that old Communist stuff died hard.

My parking space was in the first row, directly opposite the entrance. The shutter clanked and groaned as it started its slow descent behind me while I climbed out and put the key in the lock; the fob needed a new battery.

A movement caught my eye. I looked across the bonnet to see two massive hulks emerge from the shadows, storming my way. There was drama in their stride. They might have been collecting for the Mormons, but I wasn't going to stick around long enough to find out.

I turned and shot back up the slope to the shutter, dived through the gap that was still left beneath it and took a couple of rolls on the far side.

I glanced back into the car park as I picked myself up. The two guys were piling towards me, dressed in black leather and looking very pissed off. Forties, maybe; efficient haircuts, a touch of grey at the temples. They'd seen a bit, judging by the state of their noses, but were now monstrously overweight. Either Diminetz's guys had come all the way from Moldova for tea and cakes, or Anna was the most prophetic person on the planet.

I started running as fast as I could towards the shelter of the rush-hour Metro.

My feet didn't feel a thing.

FIND OUT ABOUT
ANDY
McNAB'S
BOOKS FOR 2014

FOR VALOUR

ANDY McNAB

When a young trooper is shot in the head at the Regiment's renowned Killing House at the SAS's base in Hereford, Nick Stone is perfectly qualified to investigate the mysterious circumstances.

But less than forty-eight hours later, a second death catapults him back into the firing line – into the telescopic sights of an unknown assassin bent on protecting a secret that could strike at the heart of the establishment that Stone has, in his maverick fashion, spent most of his life fighting to protect.

And now that the clock is ticking, Stone hurtles from the solitude of a remote Welsh confessional to Glencoe – whose shadows still whisper of murder and betrayal – and on to southern Spain, in an increasingly desperate quest to uncover the truth about a chain of events that began in the darkness of an Afghan hillside, and left a young man haunted by the never-ending screams of a friend the Taliban skinned alive.

Nick Stone's most heart-stopping adventure yet will force the reader to recognize the thinness of the line that separates sacrifice from suicide, to share the nightmares that walk hand in hand with heroism – and to count the real cost of actions taken in the name of loyalty.

THE GOOD PSYCHOPATH'S

GUIDE TO SUCCESS

DR KEVIN DUTTON & ANDY McNAB DCM MM

What is a good psychopath? And how can thinking like one help you to be the best that you can be?

Dr Kevin Dutton has spent a lifetime studying **psychopaths**. He first met SAS hero Andy McNab during a research project. What he found surprised him. McNab is a diagnosed psychopath but he is a **GOOD** PSYCHOPATH. Unlike a **BAD** PSYCHOPATH, he is able to dial up or down qualities such as ruthlessness, fearlessness, **decisiveness**, conscience and empathy to get the very **best** out of himself – and others – in a wide range of situations.

DR **KEVIN DUTTON** and
ANDY McNAB
DCM MM

THE
GOOD
PSYCHOPATH'S
GUIDE TO
SUCCESS
How to use your
inner psychopath
to get the most out of life

Using the **unique** combination of Andy McNab's wild and various experiences and Dr Kevin Dutton's expertise, together they explore the ways in which a good psychopath thinks **differently** – and what that could mean for you. What do you really **want** from life, and how can you **develop** and use qualities such as charm, coolness under pressure, self-confidence and courage to get it? *The Good Psychopath's Guide to Success* gives you an entertaining and thought-provoking road-map to **self-fulfilment**, both in your personal life and your career.

THE NEW PATROL

ANDY McNAB

Liam Scott is back in Afghanistan, this time with 4 Rifles. No longer the new guy, it's his chance to prove himself and take the lead. But the warzone has changed dramatically, and so have the rules.

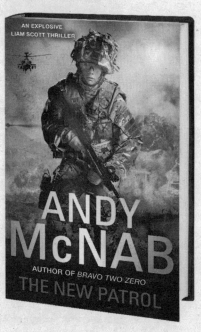

Working alongside the Afghan National Army, Liam and his new patrol face daily attacks from Taliban insurgents. But the real threat seems to be coming from within his unit.

It looks like there's a traitor in their midst.

The second explosive Liam Scott thriller